War in the Wilderness

Other books by Adam Lofthouse

Path of Nemesis:
The Centurion's Son
Shield of the Rising Sun

Oathbreaker

PATH OF NEMESIS BOOK I

WAR
IN THE
WILDERNESS

ADAM LOFTHOUSE

LUME BOOKS

LUME BOOKS

First published in 2020 by Lume Books
30 Great Guildford Street,
Borough, SE1 0HS

ISBN 978-1-83901-270-9

Typeset using Atomik ePublisher from Easypress Technologies

www.lumebooks.co.uk

About the Author

Adam Lofthouse has for many years held a passion for the ancient world. As a teenager he picked up Gates of Rome by Conn Iggulden, and has been obsessed with all things Rome ever since. After ten years of immersing himself in stories of the Roman world, he decided to have a go at writing one for himself. The Centurion's Son is the first novel in the series, with a third in the planning. He lives in Kent with his wife and three sons.

For Jack
Daddy's little soldier

Prologue

It was quiet in the bathhouse, a relief – if only temporary – from the hustle and bustle of the nocturnal streets outside. Just the gentle swirling of the water, the odd soft splash as he twitched and jerked in pleasure.

His shoulders tensed as he felt his anticipated relief coming, ever closer. He moaned out loud, a slave – unseen in the darkened corners – scuttled off light-stepped so as not to be seen disturbing his peace.

It was getting closer now, building to a beautiful and blinding crescendo. *Jupiter, Best and Greatest! Father of the gods, surely even you have never felt such joy!*

He sighed in pleasure as he eventually gave into the orgasm. Writhing hands fixed on the shoulders of the squirming prostitute struggling beneath the water. He didn't let her up, so consumed in the moment of his joy. *An orgasm fit for Bassus himself.* He sank lower into the waters warmth, revelling in its soothing touch on his skin.

He sat there a while longer; the struggles of the woman beneath the water becoming more urgent, desperate. She had bet him she could get him to climax before she drowned. Arrogant she had been, dismissive of his ability to hold his seed in his loins. *Guess she was right after all,* he chuckled as he looked upon her writhing form, shaded under the murky water.

He gazed upon her bare back, buttocks upturned as she frantically kicked out with her legs. *And what a lovely arse it is.* He was lost in the moment, all thought of letting her up banished to the back of his mind.

1

'Good evening senator.' The voice was a whisper, it slithered through the mist-strewn room like a snake through tall grass.

The man jumped, shamed by the fear he knew etched his face. The prostitute seized the moment when his grip slackened, and surged up to the surface. Her breath came in grunts, the only sound within the bath house walls. She spat a lungful of water on his face.

'Oh, it's you,' remarked the man, trying to sound calmer than he was. He shrugged off the still gagging prostitute, paused a heartbeat to take in her large, round, heaving breasts. *Gods, there's a sight worth living for.*

He rose from the water, penis still erect, not that he cared. His body was big, belly rotund, he had let himself run to fat, despite the recent years spent campaigning in the east.

'Why are you here? Surely a risk for you to be in Rome at times such as this? I would have thought you'd want to be in the north, where the … action is.' He smiled as he spoke the last words. It was a sickly smile, evil. It did not reach his eyes.

'I was, I will be again soon. You have not been replying to my letters, I thought it wise to come and meet you in person, see how our … plans … are developing.' Again, the voice was a whisper. The intruder was hooded, his face masked in shadow. The hint of a greying beard showed on his chin. His cloak was the deepest green, and as he stepped forwards, he limped heavily on his left leg.

'We can talk if you wish, but not here. One thing you must learn about Rome, my friend: there is always someone listening, someone watching.' The fat-bellied man thrust his eyes in the direction of the east wall. There was a mosaic, bright and glorious, covering the full length of the chamber. It showed Jupiter, in all his glory, awarding his son Mars with a fine ivory-handled sword.

The hooded man took the scene in, disdain plain on his face. 'You think the gods are spying on us, Cassius? I'd wager they have better things to be doing than observing two old friends converse in a bath house.' The whisper became a rasp, a mocking tone that made clear his feelings.

'Look again, my friend. Look at Jupiter, best and greatest, father of the gods. Look into his eyes and tell me they do not see us now.' Cassius spoke in a whisper, shallower than the one of his hooded companion.

2

Once more, the limping man looked upon the great mosaic, his eyes burned into those of Jupiter. His body stiffened when they blinked.

'Get my point?' Cassius laughed. 'Come to my house. We can dine together and talk with a little more privacy.' Still naked, Cassius walked over to a bench where he wrapped himself in a towel. 'I trust you know where it is?' he said.

The cloaked man looked uncomfortable, his posture still stiff. 'Of course I know.' His voice a rake through the steam. 'I will see you there within the hour.'

The prostitute stood still until the men had left, trying to control her shivering. She didn't know whether to shout at the senator for not paying her, or run and pray to Juno that she was still alive to be annoyed.

Gaius Avidius Cassius lounged back on the couch, his fat belly finally satisfied as he and his companion polished off their eighth course – roasted duck, it had gone down a treat, especially when accompanied with a vintage Falerian.

They dined in the senator's winter dining room, small, but lavishly furnished. The floor was solid marble, their two couches and low dining table placed in the centre of the room, atop a circular Persian rug. Underfloor heating warmed the chamber; you could feel the heat rising from the warm water that ran from the giant cistern into the pipes through the rug. On the coldest nights it would cause the air to steam, and the delightful feeling of heat rising and winning its war against the winter was usually enough to send Cassius to sleep. But not tonight.

He studied his guest, who drank slowly from his cup. Cassius noticed he had kept his wine heavily watered, and guessed it must take effect on his body quicker, given his age. 'So how are you, Alexander? I notice your limp is getting worse, such a long journey must have been hard for you.' He hadn't meant his tone to sound mocking, and worried that it did so.

'I have not journeyed from the north to discuss my health, *senator*. I have come to discuss our plans, and make sure you are keeping to your side of the bargain.' Alexander's voice sounded almost human, such was the venom in his tone.

3

'I am of course. Everything is moving forward as it should be. The senators we had previously discussed are onboard, you won't have any problems in Rome.' Again, Cassius thought he sounded mocking, arrogant; he decided he didn't care. *Who is this man to come to my house and speak to me with such insolence? Gods! I am a senator of Rome.*

'Good. That's good. But more importantly, what of the army? Will they side with me when the time comes?'

Ahh, now we come to it. Cassius pursed his lips in a smile. 'Of course. You have Gaius Avidius Cassius on your side! My star is burning brighter than it ever has before. When I am back in Syria, I will proclaim you Augustus to the eastern legions. The rest will soon follow suit.' He sounded arrogant again, only this time he meant it.

Alexander creased his brow, concern was etched across his face. 'My point exactly, senator. You are Gaius Avidius Cassius. Not all men see you as the victorious general who quashed the Parthians. Some see you as the sacker of Seleucia, the man who brought the plague.' It had been Cassius who had ordered the sacking of the former capital of Armenia – despite them opening their gates to the legion without resistance. The dreaded plague that had stalked the bedraggled soldiers home had begun there with the Second Adiutrix Legion.

'Do not worry about my reputation, my friend. I am newly made governor of Syria; my legates are loyal to me, you will have no trouble mustering soldiers if the need arises.' A twinge of doubt crept into Cassius. *Would they march against another Roman army for him? For Alexander?* He pushed the dark thoughts away. *One step at a time.* 'What about the other governors in the east, I have had little contact with any. Is Rutilianus aware of your plans? Does he intend to support? The old bugger is your son-in-law after all!' Alexander had secured his daughter's hand in marriage to the ageing Publius Mummius Sisenna Rutilianus some years before. Cassius had heard him joke before that he must be the only man in the empire with a son-in-law older than he was.

'Yes, he will of course support. Although I hear tidings from that part of the land that my daughter has not exactly been a dutiful wife.' Cassius tried to hide his grin; he had spent more than one night locked between Corvinia's thighs. She was a beauty and he took a heartbeat to picture her form in his head and startled when his hazy eyes met those of the Paphlagonian soothsayer. 'Something amuses you, senator?' Cassius winced at the rasp; the voice had no texture, it just tore right through him.

'Nothing, my friend, just thinking. You say she has not been dutiful? This is the first I've heard,' Cassius said, trying hard to sound innocent. He hoped he pulled it off. He didn't.

'Do you know, Cassius, how many spies I have working for me across the empire and beyond?' Cassius gulped. 'Did you really not think that your rutting with my daughter would go unnoticed? How about your private audiences with Faustina? Wife of our *beloved* Augustus. Hmm?' That voice was pure spite now, it could have been the snake god Glycon spitting accusations as him.

Cassius sought the right words; he was silent a long while.

'Relax, senator, if I was going to kill you, you would already be dead. But to repay me for keeping your small indiscretions a secret, you might do me a favour when you return to the east?' Alexander said, his turn to look smug now.

'Yes. Of course,' Cassius managed to stutter out.

'There is a man in the employ of my son-in-law, Lucian of Samosata, he is called. He is becoming a problem, perhaps too much of a problem.' Cassius nodded, all too aware of the direction their conversation was taking. 'You will recall of course, that at the time of my daughter's engagement to Rutilianus, he attempted quite publicly to dissuade the senator from entering the engagement.'

'Yes, and if I remember correctly you tried to have him executed – quite publicly.' Again, Cassius gulped. Sometimes, so blinded he was by his own ambition, he forgot the dangerous game he had committed himself to, and the lethal players that played it.

'Well, yes. It is lucky that Governor Avitus in Bithynia is such a close friend, he managed to sweep it away quickly.' Cassius noticed Alexander's voice was becoming more human the more he spoke. The whisper had more gravel, substance. He wondered if the wine helped the old man.

'Yes, quite. Anyway, tell me of the north, what goes up there? It is all very hushed in the Senate, as if Aurelius does not want us to know the extent of the situation.'

He was encouraged by the small smile that tugged the corners of Alexander's mouth. His dry grey eyes seemed to moisten as they lit up slightly in the brazier's glow. 'It goes well, Balomar was the perfect choice for a protagonist. You know of course his army made it all the way to Aquileia in the summer.' Cassius nodded. 'If it wasn't for lack of provisions he could have carried on south. Although he made a rash and regrettable decision outside those walls.' Alexander stopped, thoughts deep in the previous summer.

'What?' Concern was etched in Cassius' tone. *Don't tell me it's over. Have I backed the wrong horse?*

'He beheaded the king of the Quadi, Areogaesus was his name. I presume you've heard of him?' Cassius nodded. The Quadi were the second largest tribe on the north banks of the great Danube, and vital to the German alliance. 'They had some sort of disagreement. Balomar thought the man was going behind his back, stirring trouble with the lesser chieftains. He cut the man's head clean off his body. In fairness he probably did the right thing; if Areogaesus had succeeded then the alliance would have fallen apart, the man didn't possess the strength of personality to hold the tribes together.' Alexander sounded downcast, as if he didn't truly believe the words he spoke.

'And what of next spring? Will the tribes reform under Balomar's banner?' Cassius leant forward; it was crucial to their plans that Aurelius was kept fixed in the north, his focus solely on the rebellious barbarians.

'I'm not certain. We had another little snag with a runaway slave from Balomar's retinue. A girl taken from Pannonia in the initial raid last winter; one of my men took a fancy to her, ended up costing me one of my best warriors. She escaped and fled north, I sent my man with some of Balomar's to find and capture her, but to my knowledge they haven't yet returned.'

'What does she know? Enough to incriminate you?' *Me! Does she know about me?*

'I've no idea, but not much I'd guess. But as I'm sure you can understand it was a risk I was not willing to take.'

'Of course. So will the tribes reform without the Quadi's numbers?' Cassius was urgent now, he had to know.

'I believe so. Balomar is touring the tribes over the winter, speaking to each chieftain in turn. I think the general concern will be that the Quadi go full circle and let the legions cross the river into their lands. It will give Aurelius the perfect base to launch a war on their own turf. But I have taken steps to secure an alliance between the Marcomanni and the Naristae.' Again, the easterner offered Cassius one of his sickly smiles.

'What have you done?' Cassius felt uncomfortable now, wanting the man out of his home.

'When the king visits the lands of the Iazyges, their chieftain will suggest the marriage to the eldest daughter of the Naristaes' chief; he will accept I'm sure. I thought it better the idea came from one of the tribes, I feel he tires of my interfering his side of the river'

'Why the marriage?'

'Because he needs the men of the Naristae, and the two tribes have never been friendly. And if he wants to continue his war, he needs men. And if he wants to live, he must continue. Rome will forgive the lesser chiefs, the sheep in Balomar's flock, but they won't forgive the shepherd.'

PART I

WINTER'S FURY

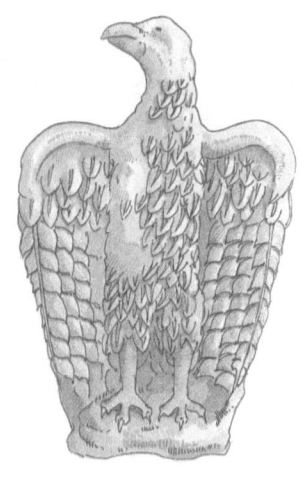

December AD 168–March AD 169

I

December AD 168 – Germania

'Is he there? Just think brother, the greatest threat to the empire, sitting within those walls.' Albinus sounded wistful, awe-stricken. Fullo looked upon his friend. Two weeks out travelling at the winter's mercy and already he was a different person – distant, determined. Where had the cowardly boy he had grown up with gone? That boy was dead, swept up in an urn with his father's ashes.

'Who knows. I'll tell you one thing, I ain't going in there to find out!' Fullo rubbed his scars as he spoke, livid white lines that ran like sword cuts across his brow. He pulled off his helmet, adjusted the position of his felt and leather liner underneath. 'We should get going, brother, find somewhere to camp out of sight, before we lose the last of the light.'

They stood upon a small ridge, looking south onto the walls of Goridorgis, home to Balomar, king of the Marcomanni. The walls were huge; tall beams of wood nailed together, it completely encircled the small hill the king's hall sat upon. The gates were imposing, thick iron bars running vertically across. Three of them, it would be tough to break, even with a thousand men and the sturdiest battering ram.

'The place looks deserted: no warriors on the ramparts, no fires. Where are they all?' Albinus hadn't moved, nor reacted to Fullo's suggestion. He watched the town intently. A light snow drifted from the low hanging clouds, floating down onto the frost-bitten ground, though mercifully it didn't lay.

11

Fullo watched as his friend reached up his right hand to stroke the forming scar on his cheek. He had been badly wounded in the summer's fighting. First, he had popped his shoulder out of joint, then taken a savage spear thrust to the face as he stood his ground against Balomar's ravaging army. The remainder of his teeth had been visible through the side of his face the rest of the day. It hadn't stopped him fighting. *Where has that cowardly child gone?* Again, the thought crossed Fullo's mind. He wondered if Silus was proud of his son, watching on from the heavens. He was sure he was.

Of course, it wasn't until after their legion had been cut to pieces they found out it was Balomar for certain, though it had been easy to guess. It had been him who had feigned friendship and obedience when called upon by Bassus, governor of Pannonia. Him who had signed the peace treaty between the tribes and the empire. He had broken it within the month. His armies had fallen upon the empire like rain in a river, swamping it, filling it to breaking point. It had nearly caused its dams to burst.

'Just doesn't seem right,' Abinus said. Fullo paused. He had already turned to walk away, iron-nailed boots crunching through the frosty undergrowth. 'Our enemy is right there, and we're just walking away.' Fullo sighed and turned back, again the crunch as his feet retraced their steps.

'Why are we here Albinus?' he said

'I know I'm just say—'

'Why are we here?' Fullo repeated with more force. Albinus sighed, his shoulders slumped as he did.

'For her.' His words were mumbled, apologetic, the words of a truant student who had been caught and brought back to his tutor.

'For her, brother. For your fiancée. And you would jeopardise our rescuing her on some suicidal mission into the home of the most powerful king in Germania? What do you think is the best that could happen? We knock on those bloody great gates and he invites us to winter round his hearth?' Albinus opened his mouth, trying to get a word in edgeways, but couldn't.

'It has been a year since she was taken, pretty much to the day! And now we are finally on the way to rescue her, finally on the verge of bringing her back home, and all you can think about is storming the biggest town this side of the Danube! Jupiter's piss, Albinus, but there's something not right with you!'

Fullo turned and trudged off, the hot steam of his breath left drifting on the icy air. 'Fullo, wait!' Albinus jogged to catch his friend, his cloak trailing behind him in the light winter's breeze. 'I'm sorry brother. It's just frustrating. That man – he motioned back to the fortress – is probably responsible for killing our fathers, and your mother! Are you telling me you don't want revenge?'

Fullo stopped again, eyes down. 'Course I do. But we ain't gonna get our revenge trying to kill the man in his bed. Our best chance is with the legion, with Taurus.' Taurus was the First Spear Centurion of the Fourteenth Legion which the two young men were enrolled in – the legion their fathers had served in. It had been nearly a year since they signed up, grief and rage burning through their veins. They had grown in that time, changed by combat, hardened by defeat.

They walked together in silence, going deeper into the forest's gloom. It wasn't long before they heard the cackle of voices, saw the dull brown cloaks through the white snow and the black shadow of the trees.

'Ahh, we were just deciding whether to send out a search party!' Bucco strode from the group of huddled cloaks, right arm resting lightly on the hilt of his gladius. He wore just a knee-length tunic under his old segmented cuirass, a design of armour long since retired by the legions. But so should Bucco be. He hadn't taken the offer of warm leather boots before they'd left Carnuntum, home to their beloved Fourteenth. He preferred the familiarity of his old worn sandals. Fullo looked upon his blue-tinged toes and marvelled the man hadn't fallen foul to the ice burn. He'd seen it in veterans before: stumps where toes or fingers once grew, turned blue then black in the winter's murk; sometimes they just fell off. Bucco moved closer, his sandals a softer crunch on the frozen snow. He seemed imperious to the conditions with bare arms and legs, no fur line round the leather cap under his helmet; he appeared to be as comfortable as a camel in the desert's sun.

'Ain't you cold?' said Fullo, as he looked down slightly embarrassed at the layers he'd coated himself in. Only Bucco had journeyed north in the tunics worn by the legionaries. The rest were dressed as Germani: knee-high leather boots, with long woollen socks underneath; baggy trousers under

13

short tunics; thick layers of wolf and bear wrapped round their mail; dull brown cloaks fastened securely overhead. Their helmets too were indistinctive, just solid pots of iron, no cheek or neck guards; no elaborate cross pieces decorated the tops, but what Fullo missed most was the gap for his ears. Though they were nice and snug under his fur lined cap, he couldn't hear a thing when the metal was placed over them.

'Don't be a pussy all your life, Fullo!' Bucco sneered and Fullo felt his cheeks burn red. He opened his mouth to reply, but it seemed the cold had taken his usually quick wits.

'Leave the lad alone,' barked Calvus. The Briton limped towards Fullo, a sword thrust wound to his left calf in the summer's fighting still not fully healed. 'I seem to remember you shivering your way through your winter watches when you were younger. 'Avin said that, you did have a bit less padding to keep you warm through the cold nights.' He threw Fullo a wink as he limped alongside him. 'Av a good look did ya? Anything to report?'

Fullo supressed a grin as he watched Bucco hold his belly in with tight-gripped hands. 'Nothing much, brother. Place looks deserted, no smoke, no signs of movement.' He stamped his feet as he spoke, winced as the bliss numbness quickly resorting back to glaring pain.

'Well that fucker's there all right! Sitting pretty with some whore on his lap, resting his sword arm for the spring. Well let him have his rest, that's what I say. Let his ale slow his wits and fatten his belly, he'll be easier to gut come spring.' Habitus spat from beneath his silver beard, which looked whiter than ever now it was dotted in snow. The Syrian claimed to have served more than his compulsory twenty-six years' service, and despite only being two weeks away from Carnuntum, he was desperate to be back. 'Are we gonna get going or what? All this journeying west just to take a look at some shithole barbarian town! Thought we was meant to be going north?' He scoffed a sarcastic laugh, kicking frozen debris across the forest floor.

'Relax, big brother! There will be no discharge ceremony until the spring, you will be back in plenty of time to stand at attention for hours and listen as your name isn't called out!' The group laughed at Longus' joke. The young Italian had befriended Habitus soon after enrolling in the Fourteenth, and the two had been poking fun at each other ever since.

14

'Piss off, puppy! I know none of you bastards believe me, but I'm well overdue my honesta missio, and don't even get me started on the bonus that comes with it!' Soldiers who survived long enough to see out there twenty-five or twenty-six years' service – depending on what year they joined, as the papers and bonuses were only given out every other year – were awarded with a cash bonus amounting up to twelve years' salary, a tidy sum to go and purchase some land with.

'Stupid clerks, eh, brother! Dunno how they get away with it!' Rullus was pissing up a nearby tree; Fullo could see the back of his head nodding in laughter as he shook himself off. Rullus was technically the ranking man out of the group, being the standard bearer for the legion's First Cohort. He'd brought with him the wolf head pelt he wore over his helmet, saying there was no better protection from the cold. He wasn't so complimentary about it in the summer.

'Where's Libo?' Albinus piped up, changing the subject, a frown upon his face. Fullo smiled to see his small button nose scrunched up in concern, the one childish trait his friend hadn't lost in the last year.

'Went north looking for a good spot to make camp. He's African ain't he! Said his balls were starting to freeze off standing around in this cold,' said Rullus, imitating an overburdened man, lugging two heavy boulders around in front of his knees. 'Imagine if those bad boys freeze off and hit the ground, the land will shake!' Laughter erupted, Fullo was pleased to notice that even Albinus joined in; his friend didn't smile enough these days.

'Well, Habitus is right, we have lost time diverting west. We need to get back on track. What way do you think is best, Bucco?' Fullo watched Albinus as he spoke. He sounded more like his father every day, his words barked, everything a challenge. He would be an officer before long, of that there was no doubt. His eyes met Fullo's and he recoiled at the ice that laid in the stare: bare, like naked iron.

'A day's walk east and then follow the road north, will take us to the River Oder. Follow that all the way north, and it will lead us to Rugnum. Simple! Though when we get there …' Bucco let the tension hang in the air. It rose like the tide, Fullo could feel it.

None were fully aware of what they were walking into. Albinus had received a letter earlier in the winter; it was addressed from Licina. The letter said she was in Rugnum, having fled from Balomar, who had been keeping her as a slave. Albinus had tried to sneak out of Carnuntum on his own, ride through the winter to meet his love and bring her home. Taurus, though, had caught him in the act, and took the opportunity to give the younger man some life lessons.

He had found Fullo and the others first, and told them to be ready to leave before the end of the day. The centurion was willing to let Albinus go and see if his lost love really was hiding in the north of Germania, but he didn't want him going alone.

'I never did thank you all.' Albinus looked at his boots, hand rubbing his scarred cheek. 'For coming with me. I know you didn't have to, and it's really touching that you chose to accompany me.' Fullo thought the words sounded forced, like he didn't want to say them, but thought he should.

'No way we were gonna let you do this on your own, lad. Was there, boys?' Bucco had promised Silus he would protect his son for the rest of his life, and he'd always kept his promises to his beloved centurion. He had been furious with Albinus when he had discovered the centurion's son had tried to go alone. A chorus of 'aye' rippled through the men as one by one they agreed.

'You know it could be a trap? This could be a journey we don't return from. If any of you don't want to come, you're free to go. You all know that right?' *Ahh, so he's still trying to get rid of us.* Fullo smiled at his friend.

'Brother, there's no way we are letting you do this on your own. We are here precisely because it could be a trap! Together, remember?' Fullo reached an arm out, grabbed hold of Albinus' shoulder. Albinus nodded, grasping his friend's arm.

'It's not a trap, brother. I've told you. I know it's her, I can feel it.' He spoke with such conviction, Fullo almost believed him.

'Yes, yes and she comes to you in your dreams blah blah blah.' She *had* appeared to him when he had passed out, just as the barbarian horde were screaming their barritus and preparing to charge the Roman line. It hadn't been the best of times to lose consciousness. 'So let's find Libo, get bedded down for the night and get moving north shall we? Must be Saturnalia soon

16

right? Means we only got weeks until we need to be back at Carnuntum, and a lot of ground to cover.' Saturnalia was the festival of celebration of the god Saturn, held in the latter part of December, and known to be one of the best celebrations on the Roman calendar.

'Another bloody party we're missing! Typical!' Nothing pleased Habitus.

There was a rustle in the branches, the crunch of footsteps in the shadows. All seven men turned, hands on sword hilts. 'What the fuck you lot staring at?' A man darker than night stalked from the winter's gloom, a great black bear pelt running from atop his head to down past his knees. 'Found a place, we going or what?' His voice was so deep the ground rumbled when he spoke, a flash of white as he grinned in Fullo's direction.

'Thought you'd got lost Libo! Heard a loud thud earlier, weren't your balls falling off was it?' Then there was a loud thud as Libo struck Longus round the side of the head.

The wind howled, screamed as it pierced through Calvus's ears. He staggered back, squinting through the snowstorm, the only thing he could make out the hulking back of Libo in front.

He reached up with gloved hands and pulled his fur cap further down his head, so it ran atop his slit eyes. *Christ on the cross, let me live through this.* He had still not confessed to his friends his defection to the latest cult to come out of the east. After all, they were still killing Christians in arenas up and down the provinces. In fact, just earlier today Bucco again moaned that the battle they had lost the previous summer in Pannonia had cost him the chance to see some Christians fight the Camel-Leopards that had been shipped in from Africa.

Calvus remembered watching them being dragged from the ship that had sailed them down the Danube. A dark yellow, with great brown spots. They were huge, their legs alone longer than a standing man. And that was before you got to their necks: stout as mini tree trunks, they arched their way towards the heavens, ending in a small head, buck teeth that chewed noisily on the leaves from tall trees.

He shuddered at the thought of meeting his end at the sharp end of their teeth, or under a gangly leg with a hoof crushing his bones to dust.

Jesu protect me, watch over me. He hoped the nailed god was listening. Again the wind howled, a great rush directly into his face. He staggered back, feet slipping on the thick snow, Bucco's hands firm on his back stopping him falling any further.

'Are you okay, brother?' Bucco screamed, but to Calvus it was just a whisper.

'Yes, brother, gratitude.' He leant forward, hands nearly touching the snow, he thought it the best way to stop him rolling down the hill.

He daren't look to his right. They were scaling the side of what he thought a mountain, but in reality was probably only a steep incline at best. They were on a small path, that would have been clean stone if it wasn't covered in thick snow. To his left was a cliff face, the jagged edges giving them good grip for their hands; to his right was nothing but raging snow and freezing air.

He concentrated on his feet, just taking one step at a time. *Left, right. Left, right.* Just like he was on parade. *For the first time in my life, I wish I fucking was.* The wound in his left calf burned, he grimaced and tried to ignore it. Winters were bad in Briton, but never had he seen anything like this.

It had been more than fifteen years since he had last seen his homeland. Fifteen years since he had fled on the first ship he could find out of Londinium, huddled in the ship's hold, hoping the captain wouldn't come and inspect his cargo until they were out into the open sea.

He grabbed the cliff face, left hand desperately trying to grasp a decent purchase as again the gods rained their ice-ridden venom into his face. He felt Bucco's hand on the small of his back, holding him steady, and thought how good it was to be surrounded by friends – Especially given their current predicament.

Calvus had never had friends, not really. He'd spent his whole life in the backstreets of Londinium, robbing and fighting the days away, doing what he could to earn his coin. One night his luck had come in, stumbling across a drunken merchant on his way back from the local brothel. He'd herd the chink of his purse long before he'd seen the man. It had been a heartbeat's work to slit the man's throat and relieve him of the leather purse.

Scurrying off to the shadows, his eyes had glistened with silver as pure as the clearest moon when he had seen the denarii inside. There must have been more than a hundred of the silver coins within, enough to set him and his woman up in a nice home outside the cities walls and keep them fed and clothed for some time.

But, the gods take no pity on thieves and murderers; they lift them up just to revel in their downfall. Calvus had been seen. A rival from the streets, he'd confronted him one night in his local tavern, demanded half the coin or he would go and tell the centurion in charge of the city garrison. It was a death sentence, and Calvus knew it.

For the thousandth time as he stumbled up the icy path, his breath coming in rasps and his torso numb, he wished he had not been so drunk when the man challenged him. Wished he'd had the foresight to share the coin, to live in peace with his wife and daughter. *God above I hope they still live. Let Meredith have grown to be healthy and strong.* But he had been drunk, angry and reckless. He'd whipped out his knife in plain sight of his fellow drinkers, and spilt the man's blood all over the bar.

Been nothing left for it then, he'd legged it. Didn't even have time to give his woman the rest of the coin. 'Aife.' He made himself speak her name, he shouted it at the heavens. *Jesu help me, but I have lived the life of a fool.*

'What the fuck did you say?' Libo turned back, impervious to the weather; there was a man born to survive.

'Nothing, brother! Just screaming at the gods! A bit of Jupiter's warmth would do us some good here!' He hoped it sounded more convincing to Libo than it did to him. He had never told his mess-mates the sorry story of his past. *More secrets.*

'We're in the wild lands now, brother, our gods don't live here.' He didn't shout, his low grumble seemed to echo off the cliff face.

Mine does brother. He lives everywhere.

On they went, up and up until they were level with the black clouds. The air became thinner, harder to suck in. Calvus had his right hand on Libo's back, his left on the cliff. He panted, quick, shallow breaths. He cursed as the shaft of his short axe knocked into his right knee with every step forwards, and determined to re-position it on his belt before they set off the next day. The storm didn't slacken, just their pace. Bucco had told them it would take days off their journey if they cut through the mountains rather than go around them, and it had seemed a grand idea at the time. Grand ideas always do.

Calvus continued to trudge through the thickening snow, carefully planting his feet in the yellow holes left by Libo. His left hand brushed along the cliff, ready to grab a hold if he felt his feet slip. He was conscious that if he fell backwards, the rest of the group would tumble down the small path like dominos behind him. Despite himself, he smiled at the thought.

For half a heartbeat he let his concentration slip. He planted his right foot on the ground, and waited for the painful impact of his axe shaft hitting his knee as he straightened his leg. It never came. His foot missed the gap made by Libo, and instead plunged into two feet of white powder. He never found the security of the stone below, he just felt his whole body surge backwards, carried by the wind.

He grabbed the cliff face desperately looking for a grip, anything, to help right himself. A searing pain starting at his fingers and shooting up his arm caused him to scream, and he barely noticed Bucco and the others heave him back into a standing position. The storm seemed to stop for a time, so did time itself. He stood there in that blissful moment when you know you have injured yourself badly, but the first wave of pain has vanished and second not yet begun. It was like a spear to the guts when it did.

'Aaaaaaahhhhh!' His scream was high-pitched, a wail at the falling heavens. His fingers were stuck fast in a small crack in the cliff, and he could tell by the angle of his hand they were broken. Libo turned in a flash, grabbed Calvus' arm and pulled with all his strength. The Briton didn't move, just screamed louder. 'Stop, brother! Leave it, Christ have mercy on my soul!'

Bucco was behind him, head in the crevice of his neck as he inspected the stricken hand. 'Your fingers have snapped, Calvus, the gods only know how you got them in there in the first place!' His voice was gentle, soothing. He always had been a good man to be around in a crisis.

The path was only wide enough for one man to walk along, and Calvus could dimly hear the others screaming at Bucco, asking what was going on. Calvus arched his head back, used his right hand to throw off his felt cap. It flew from his grip, lost in the raging torrent of the four winds.

The cold shocked him as it swept over his bald head, the pain suddenly intense behind his eyes. 'Calvus! Calvus! Listen to me. brother, if you can't pull your hand out, then we are going to have to think of another solution,' said Bucco. Again his voice not raised, compassion in his tone.

Calvus nodded. He sucked in two deep breaths, and mumbled a swift prayer to the Christ god, then yanked with all he had. Left leg raised so his iron-nailed boot was pushing on the cliff, he leaned his body back into the snow-filled abyss and shrieked in agony as he pulled. Nothing happened. He tried again, and again.

He lowered his left boot back to the ground, leant on the cliff and sighed. 'Oh, Aife, what I wouldn't give to be back with you now.' His right hand found the shaft of his axe; he lifted it from the furs that covered his torso and grasped it just below the head. The iron gleamed in the dim winter light.

Libo leaned in. 'Brother, you sure about this?' Calvus nodded. 'Do you want me to—'

'No Libo. Some things a man must do himself.' He waved the axe to signal Libo to step back, repeating the gesture to Bucco.

Again, time seemed to stop. The wind ceased to howl, the snow stopped stinging his eyes. The pain in his hand lessened, hopeful, he had one last go at pulling it free. He thought of the first story he had heard of the Lord Jesu. How he had been crucified by the Romans in the great city of Jerusalem. It had taken an age for him to die, or so the story went. But when he had finally breathed his last, his body taken down and encased in his tomb, he had risen from the dead, walked from his final resting place and found his devoted disciples. If you believed in the one true god, you would live forever.

The story gave Calvus comfort as he raised his small axe, single-headed, the blade sharpened to perfection. He had always preferred the axe over the sword: it was handier in a shield wall, a perfect weapon for hacking down an enemy's shield so your neighbour could spit them in the belly. Or, you know, hacking off your fingers.

With one great cut, he swept the axe down and watched in horror as it tore through glove, skin and bone. It went clean through with one strike. A great spray of dark blood misted the white-hazed air. Calvus screamed. His world went black.

21

II

December AD 168 – Across the Northern Sea, Gotland

The land was silent, sleeping. No wind roared through her ears, no ferocious snowstorm barrelled down to sting her pale skin. The clear sky was a pastel blue, the weak winter sun a pale yellow disc. Not for the first time, she wondered if it seemed bigger the further north she travelled. And if she was indeed closer to it, why it failed to warm her bones.

Julius had told her it was because the sun god Apollo didn't want to waste his warmth on lands so far from the beloved empire, but all he ever seemed to talk of these days was the mighty Rome and her beloved gods.

Licina sat atop a small ridge, protected from the snow underneath by a great skin of wolf, gifted to her shortly after her arrival. She marvelled as she gazed onto her surroundings: a land of pure white, as far as the eye could see. She had heard stories of great deserts to the east, where men said you could walk for days and see nothing but the golden yellow of the scorching sand. She hadn't truly believed them, until she'd arrived at Gotland.

Her new friends said that there were lakes hidden under the white blanket, frozen solid and waiting for the spring sun to thaw away their winter coat. This was nothing new to her. She remembered her father once taking an axe to a frozen lake just south of the Danube; he had sweated through his tunic despite the cold to forge a small round hole, into which he'd thrown in his line and waited patiently for a fish to bite. 'Won't the fish be frozen,

22

father? Surely they can't swim through the ice?' Her father had laughed aloud for an age, she smiled at the memory.

Memories of her past came easier to her now. She didn't know if it was the journey to the north that had brought them back, or just the new pain that had caused her mind to forget the old, but she could remember everything. For a long time after the dreaded plague had beaten first her mother then her father, she had struggled to remember any details of them – their faces, voices, the happy times they had shared. It was only after she had been kidnapped by a man named Cocconas, in the employ of Alexander of Abonoteichos, that she had begun to remember details of her parents.

Since her arrival, she had found herself falling in love with them all over again; the sound of her mother's voice as she sung her to sleep at night, her father's gruff laugh and rough Latin as he chased her round the farm they had shared with hundreds of other veterans and their families. *And Albinus.*

Her memories of her parents had come at a price: memories of him. Licina could remember his hair, dark brown specked with sparks of blond, it had always brought to mind the colour of sand when Neptune was pulling the tide back to sea. His eyes were a crystal blue – ice, like the shards hanging off the bare pine trees around her; his small button nose, that would scrunch up when he was angry or deep in thought; a taut mouth with thin dry lips. She could remember all this, but couldn't put them together to make his face.

About this time a year ago, they had become engaged. Albinus had finally made peace with his formidable father, an imposing former First Spear Centurion of the Fourteenth Gemina, and he had been overcome with joy when his son had told him of the engagement. Licina herself had spent the months leading up to the engagement trapped within herself, overcome with grief at the loss of both her parents. Albinus had released her from her self-imprisonment.

The short time that followed had been the happiest of her life. They would spend their days hand in hand and the nights entwined in each other's bodies. For a long time after she had been taken during the winter raid on their home, she had thought her love dead at the hands of the rampaging Germani. Hope had kept her going throughout the long months of slavery in the home of Balomar, king of the Marcomanni. Hope that Albinus was alive and would one day break down the great wooden gates at Goridorgis and storm the king's hall and whisk her away. But in her heart, she had always known it to be folly.

That had been until she had escaped with the help of Julius Decanus, another Roman who had been a captive at Goridorgis along with his sister, although she had since proved her loyalty lay with the barbarian king rather than her own flesh and blood. Aelinia had turned against Rome, had used her position as the king's bedwarmer to seduce him into war with the empire, talked him into an alliance with Alexander of Abonoteichos – an eastern soothsayer who had grown in power and influence through marrying his daughter to a Roman senator, prophesying the birth of a new god, and the using the senator to spread propaganda around the empire like wildfire. And now it seemed he thought to don himself in purple.

Licina had discovered the plot too late. Thinking her friends in Pannonia dead, she had fled north at the first opportunity, hoping for a clean break from her blood-filled past. But it had followed her and Julius north, stalked her the way a lion sneaks up on a gazelle, pouncing when is least expected.

Julius and she had been running from men sent by Balomar and Alexander, who were worried Licina would find someone sympathetic towards the empire and tell them her tale. Desperate, and with Licina struggling with a twisted ankle, they had taken refuge in a barn, hiding deep within the hay.

Thanks to the help of the barn's owner, they had remained undetected. The man had even offered his own son's services in helping them reach the northern banks of Germania. The son was called Alaric. He, it turned out, was the man who had delivered Julius and his sister to Goridorgis in chains, after taking them from Gaul, where they had been holed up in an inn, Julius recovering from a nasty sword wound in his left side he had taken in the arena.

Julius had practically soiled himself as soon as he saw the man: tall, imposing, thick-bearded and one-eyed, he looked every inch the rogue. He had been recovering from a wound to the shoulder himself, but he hadn't said how he'd got it, until they reached the slate grey waters in the north. Turns out he had been a long-time enemy of Silus, father of Albinus, and it had been him who had sold Silus and his friends the cartload of amber

Silus had used to keep his colony fed throughout the famine that had ruled Pannonia in the last year; whilst Julius and his sister Aelinia had watched the trade take place from within a metal cage.

Alaric had said that it had been him who had led the raid on Licina's home the previous winter; him who had slain Silus in combat; and him who would complete his revenge by murdering the centurion's son. Alaric had known who Licina was, she had no idea how. But he had bought the loyalty of a Roman merchant, whom her beloved Albinus had entrusted with a letter, and asked to deliver to her if he found her in the towns and villages of Germania whilst he was about his business. He had found Alaric first.

Thrown onto a ship, condemned to a journey across the salt spray, the last thing Alaric had done was throw her the papyrus covered in Albinus' neat handwriting. The letter had made her heart hurt.

He was alive – a soldier of all things, serving under his father's old eagle just like the old man had always wanted, just like Albinus said he would never do. It seemed his father's death and his betrothed's capture had changed Albinus.

Alaric's last words to Licina had been that he had sent a reply to Albinus, telling him she was in a nearby fort, and asking him to come to her rescue with all haste. For all she knew her love was already dead, nothing more than rotting flesh lying in a frozen hole in the mud. She had tried to force him from her mind; the sea was unpassable in winter, and there was nothing she could do to save him.

She had always dreamed of running north, and on those days she would sit at the banks of the great River Danube and marvel at the mysterious mountains on the northern horizon. Well, she had made her bed, now she had to lie in it. Or Julius' bed to be precise.

It had been on their journey north she had eventually given in and opened her legs for the ex-gladiator. He had been like a lost puppy around her since he had first laid eyes on her, and his eagerness for her body had not lessened since she had first let him have it. His appetite was insatiable, he seemed to long for her every second of the day. She knew it was the only thing keeping him going in these strange distant lands.

Sitting atop the ridge, gazing listlessly at the white world around her,

25

she watched as he approached, head held low, as it always seemed to be these days. His left hand still grabbed his side as he walked, the old wound still not fully healed, the scar tissue was horrific, hard and scaly to touch. It was hard to lie to him and say it was barely noticeable, the mere sight of it sent shivers up her spine. His face was now knotted with new scars, earned from the beating he had been given by Alaric and his cronies. His nose was flat and bent to the right, missing teeth showing between his dark red lips. Dark eyes bore a pained expression always, even when they were making love.

He forced a smile as he closed on her. His hands and forearms covered in matt black, the smell of smoke drifted off him – he had spent the morning hard at work with hammer and anvil, wielding some old iron into a blade. It was the way he spent his days since their arrival.

'May I sit?' Julius said, his voice quiet, nervous. He was always wary of disturbing her alone time.

Licina too forced a smile. 'Of course, I have been boring myself with my thoughts.' The lie came easy; the lies always came easy these days.

'How has your day been?' As always the question felt forced. They would attempt a civil and dull conversation, before ending in an argument about what they should be doing with their lives, where they should be going.

'Okay. I helped Heide to muck out the animals barns this morning. The other women have gone into the forest to pray and practise with their weapons. Heide thinks I should join them.' Licina knew it would provoke him, and waited in what was almost glee for his obvious retort.

'Weapon practice? Praying? You know what goddesses they worship? What they demand from their followers? It's sickening! I don't understand these people. Why would you want your woman to fight with you in the shield wall? Shieldmaidens they call themselves, well there's no way I'd want a woman protecting me when the sparks fly and shield hits shield! Give me a Roman legionary any day!'

A moment's silence. Licina tried to keep her voice calm, neutral. 'I think they have the right to do as they please. There is no emperor telling them what to do, no senator to lord over them and tell them how they should be leading their lives. And anyway, how many battles have you fought in?

26

No, not in the arena, proper battles, shield walls as you call it. What makes you think a woman couldn't do just as well as a man?'

She watched the rage build within him. 'A woman? In a battle? It's not right! What self-respecting man would take the life of a woman, on or off the battlefield!' Julius scoffed, spittle flew from his mouth.

'It is what they believe. I actually think there is something beautiful in it, heroic. The women are strong, I dare say they could put you on your behind in the circle!' The circle was a sphere of shields. The tribe's warriors would stand shield to shield round a patch of land, split into two teams, and would each take a turn at facing a warrior from the opposing team in a battle to first blood. The team with the most wins at the end was victorious, and held the bragging rights until the next circle was held.

'Yeah well that's not going to happen! No way I'd practise with these animals. We've only been here a few weeks, already it feels like a lifetime.' He looked down onto the snow and sat down slowly next to Licina. 'Have you thought any more about what you plan to do?'

Licina sighed. They always seemed to have the same conversations. 'I've told you. I'm not going anywhere. I'm happy here, and the Heruli are nice people. They have shown us nothing but kindness, and I intend on repaying it.' The Heruli were the tribe that inhabited the lands they knew as Gotland. Their home was harsh, the summers short and the crops sparse, whilst the winters were brutal, claiming the lives of many greybeards and children every year.

'By learning the way of the spear? Devoting yourself to Urd and these three spinners they talk incessantly about?' Urd was the goddess of fate. Her two sisters were Verdandi and Skuld, who were the goddesses of the present and future respectively. They were the chosen deities of Heide and her fellow shieldmaidens. The men worshipped Wotan and Donar above all others, but were always quick to pay their respects to the three spinners who wove their fate in the thread.

'I may choose to learn the ways of war. I may just learn to weave wool and help with the chores around the village. I will help anyway I can, but it will be my choice, not yours.' Licina said with finality.

'You do not wish to go back across the sea, to Germania, to …?' Julius trailed off, he couldn't speak the name out loud.

'No. Albinus is my past. I long thought him dead, I think it was better when I did. And for all I know he may well be! Alaric said a big battle was fought in Pannonia, remember? Most of the Fourteenth wiped out, he probably died with them.' Her voice quivered as she choked back hot tears.

'But you don't want to know? If it was me—'

'Why do you want me to go back so much? What if Albinus is alive and I do find him? You think I'm still going to fuck you? Are you so desperate to be away from this place you would see me scamper to another man?'

Her outburst hurt him. Licina could see it in his dark eyes. 'I spoke to Wulfric yesterday, the man who captained the ship that brought us here. You may not remember as Alaric had beaten you to a pulp and I had to nurse you through the entire journey. But in case you do, he's taking a ship and going back to the place he picked us up from for the year's first trading next week. If you're so desperate to go, then see him and book yourself passage on his ship.'

Licina didn't wait for Julius to answer. Throwing her wolf skin over her shoulders, she set off at pace back for the village, eager to be away from him.

A week later and Licina found herself standing on a shingle beach, watching the preparations of Wulfric and his crew, who sought to manhandle their goods onto the ship. The sea though, had other plans. White-topped waves hurled onto the shingle, ferocious and wild, they were Neptune's army, sent to destroy those who would seek to travel his salt-sprayed road.

'Rán is unhappy it seems.' Licina jumped at Heide's softly spoken comment. She had crept up on her, not for the first time. Licina wondered how she managed to stalk through the snow without it crunching under her feet.

'I thought it the sea belonged to Aegir? The jötunn? No?' Licina kept her voice level. She knew that some people among the Heruli had taken her curious questioning of their gods to be belittling.

Heide laughed. Licina thought it the purest laugh she had ever heard. 'Well done, my friend, it indeed does. Rán is the goddess of the sea. Aegir is her husband, and he is indeed a jötunn, or giant in your tongue.' Licina's

28

mastery of the German language had got stronger since her arrival in the lands of the Heruli. But she had been shocked to find most of the people had some mastery of Latin, even though the legions had never ventured this far north. 'It is said she bore her husband nine daughters, I forget who they are. Something to do with the waves I think?'

Licina smiled at her friend's expression. It seemed as though she was trying to remember the name of some old crush or a boy she kissed when still a girl, not the names of the daughters of a goddess and her jötunn husband. Licina continued to stare at the shieldmaiden. She had a tuft of bright blonde hair, gleaming blue eyes that brought memories of Albinus, a slim nose and small mouth with full, red lips. She was beautiful. Her body was that of a warrior: broad-shouldered, muscled arms, small-breasted and thick-waisted, Licina thought her as formidable as any man she had met.

'So, the giant in not a god? He just married one?'

'Correct. His father was Fornjótr, who was once the king of these lands. He himself had two brothers, Logi and Kári – fire and wind.' Her voice was awe-stricken. Not for the first time Licina felt impressed and humbled by this people's devotion to their gods – so more pious than the people within the empire. 'He was once made a fool of by Donar himself you know. They say no one was safe to travel by sea for over a year afterwards, such was his rage.'

Her interest piqued, Licina pressed for details. 'Tell me.'

'Donar wanted Aegir to brew ale for the gods, for a feast in Wotan's hall. Wotan and his family were new to these lands then, not the power they are today. Aegir had no interest in brewing ale for these new gods. He was a jötunn, and the son of a king after all. So, he told Donar he had no cauldron to brew the ale, and sent him on his way.

'Not one to take no for an answer, Donar stalked the frozen caverns of the far north to find a cauldron big enough. He sneaked into the lair of Hymir, a frost giant that dwelled in a mountain cave. In he crept, his boots a soft pad on the black ice.'

Licina found she was holding her breath, caught in the spell of Heide's story of gods and giants.

'He found the cauldron, but it was so big that when he hoisted its great weight onto his broad shoulders, its handles reaching down to his ankles.

29

He was creeping out, when his boot slipped on the ice. Donar fell onto his back, the cauldron thrown up into the air. His mail made such a clatter when he hit the ice that Hymir woke from his slumber and charged in anger when he saw Donar trying to steal away his cauldron. Jumping to his feet, Donar grabbed Mjollnir – his great war hammer – from his belt and beat the frost giant to death.

'He then journeyed back south and threw the cauldron through the front door of Aegir's underwater hall. Humbled and humiliated, the giant had no excuse to ignore Donar's request, and therefore brewed the ale for Wotan's feast.' Heide finished her tale with a flurry, her eyes bright with the glory of the gods.

'That is quite a story. Our gods have tales that are less impressive, I fear I would send you to sleep with the story of Romulus and Remus.' Licina spoke sadly, strangely ashamed of the gods of her homeland, though she couldn't put her finger on why.

'The twins raised by the wolves? The founders of the city of Rome? That is not a boring story, Licina. I have heard it from three different merchants, each time the tale was woven with more bravado. I was transfixed.'

Licina blushed, again wondering why she had such strong emotions about the deities of her homeland. After all, they had sat by and let a tidal wave of misery engulf her.

'But that is not the end of the tale.' Licina's head shot up, eager eyes meeting Heide's fierce grin. 'Aegir delivered the cauldron of ale to Wotan's hall, as ordered. Accompanying him was his faithful servant Fimafeng. Inside the hall the gods were already deep in their cups, and the fire god Loki was growing bored. Ever the trickster, the lord of mischief, he regaled his fellow revellers in the tale of Aegir's misery as the giant stumbled through the crowded hall with the vast cauldron on his back. When he had set it down, Loki confronted him, his bravery inflamed by the ale. He bared his knives and challenged the giant to a fight. Aegir was tired, bone-weary, and in no condition to meet the challenge.'

Licina was practically foaming at the mouth, hanging off every word. She had leaned forward so her face was just a hand's width from Heide's, so close that passers-by would be forgiven for thinking them lovers.

'Fimafeng saw his master's wariness, and knew he had to spare him from further embarrassment. He stood between his master and the lord of the flames, and told Loki in no uncertain terms to find another victim to torment. Enraged, Loki launched at him with a short blade in each hand. A master in their art, he danced around the untrained servant, the blades punching through flesh and bone so fast that Fimafeng collapsed in a puddle of his own blood before he even knew he was dead.

'A silence descended in the great Wotan's hall, the feasters not knowing whether to cheer or bow their heads in shame. After a time, Wotan himself rose from his throne. He ordered Loki to be banished from his presence, imprisoned in the darkest of cells, where he would await the end of days – Ragnarok – so sick he was of Loki and his tricks and schemes.'

Licina breathed out slowly, unaware that she had been holding it in. 'What a tale! And you believe this to be true?' Again, she hoped her tone lacked a mocking edge.

'Do you believe that twin boys were raised by a pack of wolves and then went on to found the city that would eventually engulf most of the known world?' Heide did not try to hide the mocking tone in *her* voice.

Licina threw her head up and laughed. 'You have me there. Do I believe? No, that particular tale I don't think I do. I think there could be hints of truth, but these stories tend to become … exaggerated over time.' She laughed again, gazing into Heide's eyes. *I could stay here forever with you and be happy.* A curious feeling.

'What? You're thinking something, say it.' Heide stared back into Licina's eyes, seeing the thoughtful glare.

'I was thinking that I could stay with the Heruli forever. That you make me feel welcome, happy. I've not been truly happy in a long time.' Licina's eyes dropped to her boots, a wave of sadness washed over her face.

'You've never told anyone your own story, I have a feeling it may be a saga worthy of any of our gods. You've seen things, bad things. Fire and blood is in your past. I can see it, feel it oozing off you. Those eyes have seen friends and family put to the sword, your nose has smelt the smoke that consumed the world as you knew it. But you persevered, put your troubles behind you and journeyed north, until you ended up at our shores.' Heide spoke as if in a trance.

'How ... how do you know all that?' Licina stared at her friend in shock, tongue almost hanging from her gaping mouth.

'The Norns show me. But they have not yet revealed your future.' Heide snapped her eyes open, as if waking from a daze.

'The Norns? Who are the Norns?' She thought she already knew the answer, but asked the obvious question anyway.

'Come with me and my sisters to the grove, we leave at dawn tomorrow. When we get there, all will be revealed.' And with that she turned and walked away, her booted feet silent over the thick white snow.

Licina watched her go, aware she had an important decision to make. She lusted after Heide, not necessarily for her body, but for her company. She hero-worshipped her, longed to spend her days in her company. *Is that what is holding me here?*

Licina turned away and gazed back out over the slate grey waters. The ship still swayed in the shallows, the waves rocked and rolled and the crew struggled up the gangplank with heavy barrels of fish oil the captain was hoping to turn to coin once he docked in Germania.

She spotted Julius making his way towards her, his boots and trousers wet to his knees from helping the crew with their load. He looked angry, sullen, his eyes moist with confused emotion as he drew up in front of her. Licina stared into those dark eyes. This man had risked it all to save her from his twisted sister, escaped from slavery and journeyed the length of Germania to see her safe. He had been her lover, the rock she had relied on to get her through the darkest days. She wondered why she felt so completely devoid of emotion to see him go. Licina forced a smile, racking her mind for the right words.

III

Bucco deflected the spear point away with the flat of his gladius, then swung the point around and swiped the edge cleanly through his adversary's throat. The next man leapt over his dying comrade, a double-headed axe grasped in both hands. His snarled teeth were a flash of white in the dim light of the fire, the axe blade glimmered in the flames glow as he raised it above his head to send it crashing down into Bucco's. Bucco was just sending his final prayers to Jupiter when a white fletched arrow appeared in the axe man's throat. He gurgled in shock, and slumped down to his knees.

'You're welcome, brother!' Bucco turned to his rear to see the dark outline of Habitus in the shadows, staying out of the fire's light to stalk his prey with his deadly short bow.

Bucco lurched back to his front and took in the battle's din, sheathing his sword and grabbing up the axe as he did. Not an hour ago the eight men had been bedding down for the night, bellies full of wild rabbit and their bones warmed by the fire. Bucco was just giving into the urge to sleep when Longus had raised the alarm. It had been chaos since then.

With a heavy sigh, he moved forward, ignoring the sharp stitch in his side. *Not as young as I used to be.* The grey specks on his mostly bald head were the truth of that. His growing waist was another; keeping the weight off became harder the older you got. As he moved, scouring the ground in

33

the flickering light for an enemy, he thought how he would have revelled in the excitement of a night fight twenty years ago. Now, he just felt tired.

There was a blur to his left, the silver flash of a blade reflected in his eyes. Instinct took over. He hunched down beneath the cleave of the sword and brought the point of the axe shaft up and jabbed it in his assailant's stomach. The German doubled over in agony, the wind driven from his lungs. Not hesitating, Bucco raised the axe and cleaved it into the top of the man's skull; it split like a watermelon. He looked up, warm blood and brain matter dripping down his face, scanning the mêlée for one of his brothers, a comrade to fight beside.

Albinus was hunched behind a pillaged German shield, desperately fending off two attackers. Bucco screamed a raging war cry and leapt into the fray, nearly taking the head clean off the nearest man to Albinus. He fell in to his friend's left as the younger man felled his other assailant with a thrust to the groin. The German dropped to the shadows without a sound.

'Bucco, what in Jupiter's name is going on?!' Albinus sounded calm, resilient. So different from the boy who had joined the legions last year.

'Mithras knows, little brother! We must be treading on someone's toes! Just keep killing!' With that Bucco stalked off, keeping the fire on his right.

Another shape leapt from the trees gloom, and another arrow flew into the assailant's eye socket. *Habitus is one good shot.* Bucco took another man in the chest with the axe, and wrenched the blade clear of the bone and mail. Rullus appeared at his side, his face and beard a matt of gore; he looked horrific in the half light. 'Still alive, brother?' He sounded like he was enjoying himself.

'Just about, brother! Where are the others?'

'No idea! The lads can all handle themselves, though I'm worried about Calvus. Can you fight with half a hand when your body and mind are full of fever?' Calvus had deteriorated rapidly since they had carried him off the mountain pass. His wound was swollen and foul with puss; he screamed as he sweat, lost in a fever.

'We need to group together, fight as a unit, we've more chance that way.' Two more mailed men approached at a crouch. Greybeards, they had the look of veterans who knew their way around the spears they grasped.

The first one lunged for Rullus, the thrust good and true, the point aimed straight for his groin. But Rullus was the signifer of the First Cohort of the Fourteenth Legion, and therefore was used to fighting without a shield. He grabbed the shaft of the spear just below its leaf-shaped point; stepping to the side, he yanked the shaft towards him and the German on the other end staggered forwards and fell onto the point of Rullus' sword.

Bucco sensed the opportunity as the other German looked at his comrade dying in horror, and leapt forwards, swinging the axe true and sending it crushing through helmet and skull. 'Well, come on then, signifer, let's hear your best parade ground voice!'

Rullus breathed in deep and bellowed as loud as he could: 'FIRST COHORT TO ME. TO ME FIRST COHORT.' The other six men rallied to the call in heartbeats, years of training taking over instinct.

Libo was first, his skin blacker than the moonless sky, the whites of his eyes wild in the firelight. 'What the fuck?!' There really wasn't much else to say. Longus was behind him, his blade wetted a dark red. There was a rip on the left hip of his mail shirt, the small iron chains broken by a blade. 'It's okay, I'm not hurt.' He was panting, leaning forwards as if winded.

Bucco glanced behind and saw the others had all formed to his rear. They had made a small circle, with a pale Calvus in the middle. 'Calvus, brother, you still with us?'

The Briton looked at Bucco, red-rimmed eyes glazed. He said nothing, just stared. 'Gods above, protect Calvus, don't let any of the bastards through! Who's got a shield?' Fullo, Habitus and Albinus all shouted 'Aye', and Bucco got them to spread round the circle, so at least three sides had a shield on to help protect their comrades.

There was a pause in the battle. The eight Roman's panted and sweated in silence as they waited for the inevitable onslaught. Shadows moved in the darkness, mail glistened in the fires glow. Bucco heard hoofbeats, felt the ground vibrate as he saw the torch wielding horsemen canter into view. A man barked an order in German, the harsh sound almost hurting Bucco's ears. The horses stopped. Silence ruled the night for a time. Bucco had the feeling he and his comrades were being considered, their threat weighed in the German commander's mind.

'What do we do?' Fullo was panting, and a shallow cut ran from his right hand up to his elbow, blood trickling out.

'Hold. What happened to your arm?' Bucco asked, trying to keep his tone relaxed – he thought it might help the younger man's nerves. Nothing like a break in a fight to provoke dark thoughts that consumed your mind and could cause a self-fulfilling prophecy.

'Took a blade right under my hand guard. Stings like a bitch.' Fullo's voice quivered, the first sign that the nerves were starting to take toll.

'That's why I kept my old gladius – better blade, and a better hilt to boot.' Bucco hadn't taken the offer of re-equipping himself when he had signed back up for the legions. He still wore the old-style segmented cuirass – iron plates held together with leather and copper buckles that offered better protection, especially to direct impact from a sword blow. But it was susceptible to break in or out of battle, a pain to repair, and the effect of the copper on the iron plates would cause it to rust at the slightest hint of moisture in the air. He also still used an old-style gladius, forged on the western banks of the Rhine. It had a bone-handled hilt with a thick, octagonal hand guard and the blade was waisted, heavier in the middle, the blade four fingers wide at the base, it curved like a river, in then out before coming back to a point. The newer swords were hilted with maple wood, their hands guards thinner and rounder, with a slimmer blade straight as an arrow, ending neatly in a triangular point.

'Just keep calm, lad, it will hurt more now as you got a shit-load of adrenalin wearing off. And I have a feeling you're gonna need a second wave.' He scanned the lines of waiting Germani. More still were coming into the small opening in the woods the group had chosen as their campsite. It had seemed perfect, the ground flat, a wide open circular space that was easy to patrol and gave enough space for the eight men to fan out if they had to fight. Although, they hadn't bargained on having to fight so many.

There must have been over a hundred warriors massed around the eight Romans, to Bucco's reckoning anyway. They still stood in silence, huddled in a small circle, awaiting the barbarians to charge in and finish them off. Instead of a massed charge, one man kicked his horse forward and approached the group.

'Roman?' he asked in mongrel Latin. Bucco tried to get a good look at the man, but his face was hidden under the shadow of a thick wolf skin. The teeth had been left in the animal when it had been skinned, and lined the top of the German's face, shining off-white in the fire's glow.

'We are. We didn't come here looking for trouble. We … we don't even know where we are exactly.' Bucco spoke in rough German; he had some understanding of the harsh barbarian tongue, having spent much of his life with the Fourteenth patrolling and fighting north of the Danube.

'Ha!' The German's laugh held no mercy. He turned to share his amusement with his waiting men, who joined in dutifully. He spoke this time in his native tongue. 'You are in the Hercynian Forest, in the lands of the Cogni. I am Haribert, son of Hrodger, chief of the Cogni. You are trespassing on my lands.'

There was a moment of silence. 'What'd he say?' Habitus broke the quiet.

'It seems we are in the Black Forest. I had not thought we'd travelled so far east.' Bucco was concerned. His plan had been to travel north whilst bearing slightly east, keeping them in a sort of no-man's-land, between the borders of the local tribes. It appeared he had got his bearings wrong. *Damn mountainous country.*

He switched back to German to address the chieftain. 'My apologies, Chief Haribert. We had no idea we had travelled so far to the east. As I said before, we did not come here seeking a fight, I am sorry for the blood that has been spilt.' The old soldier rallied his mind. *Think. What would Silus have done?* He was conscious that although he and the Romans had not started the fight in the darkness, they had spilt a lot of German blood. Haribert would not want it to go unpunished.

Again, there was a moment's silence, just the flickering of the fire to Bucco's rear, his racing heartbeat drumming in his ears. Haribert dismounted, signalling for the nearest of his warriors to grab the reins and steer his horse away. He walked slowly towards the Romans, head bowed, fingers playing with a dark bushy beard. 'I did not order this attack on you and your men.' He spoke in Latin, meeting the gaze of each of the Romans. Bucco thought his eyes seemed friendly, they were dark like his beard, big and open. He thought the chief looked an honest man, at least he hoped

37

he was. 'The warrior who commanded the scouting party that found you was young, eager to prove himself. He thought to earn his spear fame this night.' Bucco saw genuine sadness in those big dark eyes.

'I am sorry, Chief Haribert. We had no warning of an attack, no chance to speak and state our business. It was straight to blade work. I would be happy to speak to your young commander though, our mere presence here was the cause for his … excitement after all.' *Please don't kill us all.*

'He's dead I'm afraid. He was always very fond of that axe.' He motioned to the weapon in Bucco's hand. 'How many dead do you have?'

Bollocks. Now he knew he and his friends were dead men. 'None.' He spoke with pride. Pride that eight legionaries had held off more than three times their number. He would be proud in a few moments' time when this chief unleashed the hundreds of men at his back to slaughter them; he would hold his ground in defiance with his brothers either side.

'None?' Haribert looked inquisitively at the seven men behind Bucco. 'What in Donar's name are eight Romans doing in the Hercynian Forest with no shields and little armour? You *are* aware the tribes are at war with the empire?' The Cogni chief looked genuinely amused, a wry smile spreading from his mouth to his eyes.

'We are yes.' Bucco tried to keep his growing annoyance from his tone. 'As I said, we aren't here looking for trouble, neither are we here on business of the empire. We're going north, on a personal mission.'

Haribert still looked amused. He could contain himself no longer and threw his head back and roared with laughter. 'By Wotan, I've heard of people doing some stupid things before, but you Romans …' he stopped and pointed in hilarity at the confused legionaries, '… might just be the stupidest people I've ever met!' He turned back to his men and repeated what Bucco had told him in German. Bucco understood enough of what was being said to realise when he was having the piss taken out of him.

'Bucco what in Jupiter's name is going on? If we're not going to fight these curs then we need to get Calvus over by the fire, he's freezing.' Longus had hold of the Briton, who was shivering visibly in the blistering night air.

For the first time since the fighting started Bucco realised he was cold himself. His quivering hands were blue and his nose streamed. 'Longus,

Libo, take him to the fire for Mars's sake, look at the state of him. The rest of you stay with me, I'm still not sure how this is gonna pan out.' He looked to the remaining legionaries. Albinus held a fierce glare as he looked upon the warriors awaiting the order to tear them to shreds; His ice blue eyes were colder than the winter air, and Bucco thought how much he was coming to resemble his father. Then Haribert spoke again.

'Your man there, is he unwell?'

'He has a fever, Chief Haribert. We passed through the mountains to the south of here. There was an accident. His hand got stuck on the cliff face on one of the passes. There was a winter gale battering us from all sides. We were freezing; we had to get off the pass or we would have all been dead men. Calvus here knew that, so he chopped his own fingers off to escape. But the wound has turned bad, his hand is full of puss and the fever has a firm grip of his mind.'

Haribert stood in shocked silence. 'So, let me make sure I have all the facts here. Eight Romans ventured north into the wilds of Germania in the depths of winter. Alone, no support, they thought to travel through miles and miles of enemy territory. And one of them cut his own fingers off to ensure he and his comrades made it off a treacherous mountain pass. Oh, and by the way, I have crossed those mountains many times, and I can tell you they are dangerous in the summer, let alone winter! And after all that, they fought a band of hardened warriors numbering three times their own, and fought them off without taking a single casualty?' Bucco nodded, but spoken out loud he thought how stupid their quest sounded. 'All for some personal business in the north?' Again, Bucco nodded. 'Well if you men aren't the hardest, bravest soldiers I've ever met, then I'm old One Eye himself! What do you say to a hot meal and a skin full of ale?'

The fortress of Budorgis was alive with excitement. Longus tried to guess how far into the night they were, but it was hard to tell without the standard sandglass or water clock to judge the passing of time. Somewhere between the second or third watched he reckoned.

The gates were in poor condition, even in the darkness that was clear. The wood smelt of rot and decay, and Longus guessed if he had seen the gates in daylight he would have seen dark and soft posts, not cared for in the harsh, cold climate. He looked up as he passed underneath them; there was a hole on the battlement, a clear sign that the tribe had let the defences of their capital run to disarray.

Haribert's hall was in better condition. The timber used here was fresh, the smell of chopped wood reminding the soldier as it always did of autumn. His father was a farmer, who owned good land just a day's ride from Rome itself. He would take Longus deep into the woods when the sun's heat began to cool, there they would fell as many trees as they could, and take the fresh logs back home and hoist them up on ready-made stilts in a barn, where they would air out and avoid the winter's dew. In essence, the smell brought back memories of a happier time. Not for the first time since joining the army, he began to feel pangs of homesickness.

They were ushered onto a raised dais at the far end of the hall, given seats on the chief's high table, shown honour by their host. Looking down the hall once he was seated, Longus took a deep breath to dispel the whirling fear in his belly as he gazed upon row after row of angry-looking tribesmen, their faces flickering against the dancing flames of the hall's great hearth.

'I get the feeling we ain't exactly the most welcome guests.' Rullus muttered as he sat beside Longus. Concern was etched on his face under his great red bushy beard. Longus nodded his agreement. He reached out for one of the ale-filled jugs that littered the table, and poured himself a drink until his cup was brimming full. He necked the thick liquid in one, grimacing as he swallowed it. 'Jupiter's cock! What *is* this stuff?!'

Rullus cackled a laugh. 'Don't make it like they do back home! Best get used to it, brother, none of our new mates are gonna be bringing you any sweet Falerian up here.' Rullus copied Longus and necked his cup in one go, immediately refilling it.

'I'd happily take a jug of Posca right now, and you know how much I hate the stuff!' Posca was a cheap way of getting drunk quick. Sour wine, vinegar, a splash of water and some herbs, it was a staple of every soldier's daily diet.

'I'd take a jug of Posca any day! You're still fairly new to the army, once you've got as many years under your belt as me, it'll be the sweetest thing to ever pass your lips!' Rullus was once again refilling his cup, the second already working its way down to his bladder.

'Aye, well I've got a *long* time before I catch up to you, big man.' He threw a wink at his signifer, poured himself another cup and sipped it, grimaced again.

Rullus was just about to respond to his retort when Haribert entered the hall and a hush fell over the gathered warriors. He walked quickly through the throng to the high table, his gaze neither moving left or right. The hearth's smoke billowed around him, shrouding his face in fog. To Longus, it seemed he was all too aware of the ill-feeling of his warriors, he looked as though he wanted to be past them as quickly as he could.

The Cogni chief smiled as he climbed the small flight of stairs to the dais. He and Bucco clasped hands and he sat down next to the veteran. 'Since when did that old fart become our leader? Should be you over there Rullus, you're the senior man here.' Longus nudged him as he spoke, Rullus swatted his arm away.

'Don't be stupid, boy! Bucco has seen more action then me, served for longer than me, and has a great deal more experience dealing with the tribes than me. Let him get on with it. There's more chance of him getting us out of here alive than me!' He burped as he finished speaking, Longus thinking that may have confirmed his point.

'But you're from the tribes, right? That's got to count for something?'

'Yes and no. My mother was German, my father from Pannonia. Although I can't really remember either of them, or what tribe she was from.'

Longus paused, a wry grin spreading slowly across his face. 'You do look a bit like Balomar – not related to him, are you? Maybe that's why you decided to grow that lice-catcher!' That was the name the men in the contubernium had decided to give Rullus' beard, which was a fairly new addition.

'Oh, it's Balomar now is it? Funny that, it was bloody Taurus the other week!' Taurus was the First Spear Centurion of the Fourteenth Legion, and therefore the commander of the First Cohort, of which the eight men were enrolled in. He was also a barrel of a man with a giant red beard, Longus and the others thought growing a beard was Rullus' way of trying to acquire a promotion.

'Well come to think of it all, three of you do look a bit alike ...' Longus paused, mischief glimmered in his eyes, '... maybe Balomar is your brother, same father, different mother, that's what I reckon. And Taurus ...' he snorted as he spoke, unable to stifle a laugh. Rullus made ready to upend the jug of beer over his head, '... Taurus, is your cousin. Son of your father's brother. And this war we're all balls deep in, is just some family argument that's got way out of hand!' He snorted another laugh, very happy with his own hilarity.

'Longus, you really are the very essence of the word cunt.' Rullus' retort caused Albinus and Full to spray beer all over the table as they snorted a laugh. Longus had the nerve to look offended for a moment, then shrugged it off. 'Harsh, but possibly true,' he admitted.

A period of silence descended over the Romans. Each man sat and gazed into his beer cup. Longus thought how the men's camaraderie made it easy to forget that they were deep in enemy territory, and that only hours ago they had been engaged in a bitter struggle against the very people who now hosted them.

'How's Calvus?' This was directed to Habitus, who had just made his way through the snarling throng of warriors to take his seat. He'd seen the Briton to what passed in these parts as a hospital – a mud hut, with a crippled old lady who stunk of stale ale and incense.

'Sweating, shivering, talking a load of old bollocks. The healer they have apparently has some skill, she thinks Calvus will be fine. She's drawn the puss from the wound, I helped the old girl bathe him. Hey, did any of you boys know he was a Christian?' Longus and the others all shook their heads with confusion and surprise. Longus was shocked: worshipping the nailed god was a crime punishable by death. Calvus himself should know; many times the eight men had sat in the stands at the great wooden amphitheatre that had been built next to the fortress at Carnuntum, and they often held games where savage beasts from the wilds of Africa and Asia were let loose on a band of sorry Christians. Murdered for nothing other than their beliefs.

'No, I won't believe it. He can't be!' Longus shook his head fervently, refusing to accept it. 'We all know what Christians do. They eat flesh and drink blood, there's no way Calvus would get involve with any of that.' The Italian winced in disgust, just imagining the despicable rituals the followers of the strange cult were said to partake in.

'Well I'm telling you, brothers, he has been laying there, talking gibberish about how his Lord was going to cleanse his soul and deliver him to Heaven. He asked his Lord to forgive him for his sins, and to welcome him into his embrace. I'm just glad the old healer ain't got no Latin, would have been a bastard to try and explain! Imagine what Taurus would say if he found out?' Habitus reached across the table for an empty cup and the jug of ale, he poured himself a cup, and nearly choked on his first sip. 'What in Jupiter's name is this horse piss?'

Libo smacked the Syrian on the back, 'You never had a good German beer before? Even with all your years' service? You've been missing out, brother!'

The Romans roared back into laughter, jokes about the length of Habitus' service being common and always raising their spirits, except Habitus'.

The greybeard Syrian was about to respond when Bucco got up from his chair and marched round the table to where his comrades were sitting. He leaned over Albinus, planting his huge hands on the young man's slight shoulders. 'So, Chief Haribert has very kindly decided not to kill us all.' He paused, and Longus let out a sigh of relief, as did the others. Although Longus sensed the news wasn't over just yet. 'However, he does have a little job he would like us to do for him, call it payment for all the men we killed earlier tonight.' The veteran's dark eyes shone on the firelight, smoke from the hearth swirled around his back. Longus suddenly felt the hall becoming very hot and clammy.

Despite this a chill ran down his sweat-soaked spine. When Bucco had that look in his eye, the one he was giving Longus right now, it could only mean one thing. The eight tent mates were supposed to have been making their way quietly through Germania to the north, avoiding the locals and stealing away Albinus' kidnapped fiancée. So far, Calvus had been forced to chop his own fingers off, and they had slaughtered a sizeable number of tribal warriors. And now it seemed, things were going to get a bit more … bloody.

What would Taurus think?

43

IV

First Spear Centurion Taurus stood rigidly to attention on the grass carpet of the parade ground floor. The remnants of the Fourteenth Gemina stood in dressed ranks before him, each man trying not to shiver as the bitter winter wind bit at their bones. It swept off the banks of the River Danube to their rear, sending icy gales up the hems of their belted, thigh-length tunics.

There were four legions on parade, with Governor Bassus on his way from the fortress to inspect the troops and take their oaths of loyalty to Augustus Marcus Aurelius and his Caesar Lucius Verrus. The First Adiutrix had been moved east from Brigetio, a small fortress in-between the larger cities of Carnuntum and Aquincum. Taurus had taken a liking to their Legate, Publius Helvius Pertinax. At forty years of age, the son of a freedman had surely reached the pinnacle of his military and political career. Sons of former slaves were not regularly given commands of legions. Taurus thought he could still see the vault in his step every time he walked, as if he couldn't comprehend how high he had risen.

Next to the light blue shields emblazoned with the winged horse Pegasus, the proud symbol on the front of the Adiutrix's shields, were the First Italica, a new legion, the first to be raised from men inside the Italian borders since the time of the great Augustus. The raw recruits shivered in the morning cold, their white shields as clean as the new-issue tunics they wore underneath their gleaming mail shirts, the small interlocking iron links having so far avoided being pierced by the point of a blade. A dark and grizzled boar decorated the front of their shields.

Last in line were the Second Italica. Even newer then the former, they had been raised in haste as Emperor Aurelius sought to strengthen his forces on the Danube. Their red shields were beautifully decorated with Romulus and Remus, the founders of the eternal city being suckled at the teat of the she-wolf.

It wasn't the gleaming new armour that kept Taurus looking at the newly formed legions, or the wispy, pale faces of the young recruits: it was their equipment. The legionaries had been equipped with spathas – swords that had until now been solely used for the cavalry. They wore the long, straight blades on their left hip, rather than the right where the men in Taurus' legion wore their shorter gladius. Their footwear was also different: they wore closed, leather hobnailed boots, which Taurus looked enviably at, his own open top sandals being almost unbearable to wear in the winter months.

'How can those swords be better than ours?' Taurus said as he continued to stare at the two newly formed legions. 'The whole point of the short sword is that it's better in close quarters, when the shields are locked together and you've got no room to swing a long blade. That's how we've fought for hundreds of years! You think they've been trained differently?' He glanced back at Abas, his optio, as he spoke.

'No. I watched them go through some drills yesterday, was the same routine we do. They were raised on short notice apparently, men conscripted straight from their farms, so maybe they didn't have enough of these to go around?' The optio raised his own scabbarded gladius, which hung from its belt on his right hip.

'Just don't make sense, does it? Why change a winning formula?' He rubbed his beard, just starting to turn more grey than red. It had earned him the nickname the silver fox, at least when he was out of earshot.

'I don't know, sir. Let's just hope they can fight well with them,' said Abas, a twinge of nerves in his voice.

Taurus turned to face his optio. The bald Greek looked as ageless as ever on the dull winter's morning; he was freshly shaven, his skin olive-coloured, free of lines or scars. He could have passed for a recruit, such was the purity of his skin. He frowned, nervously studied the two newly formed legions.

45

Taurus thought the same thing but decided to keep his doubts to himself. He turned back to his own men, the pitiful few that survived. Out of the five thousand that had marched into battle against Balomar and his horde, only fifteen hundred remained. They had been grouped together and made into three cohorts, all nearly at full strength. They had only been able to form so many cohorts thanks to the arrival of the stragglers from the Thirteenth Gemina. Centurion Ulpius Bacchius had led the remnants of his century proudly into the fortress of Carnuntum under their eagle a few days before. His men were the only known survivors from a raid on Dacia by the Iazyges and the Naristae; the legions summer camp at Tibiscum had been completely destroyed.

Taurus eyed the former First Spear of the Thirteenth Legion as he forced his way through the ranks of the waiting men of the Fourteenth and marched smartly towards him. He had taken to being demoted fairly well, given the circumstances. Taurus had given him the highest position he could, making him the princeps prior of the First Cohort. Bacchius therefore commanded the second century in the cohort, and was junior only to Taurus himself, the primus pilus, or First Spear. Taurus had made sure the second century was made up of all the survivors from Bacchius' old century, hoping it would help the man to settle in to life in his new appointment.

'Centurion,' he nodded as the man saluted smartly in front of him, 'how are your men?' Taurus still had mixed feelings about his new centurion. He was jealous of him, in many ways; Bacchius was one of the few men that made Taurus look small, and he had to crane his neck to look him in the eye. Then there were his undeniable good looks, it seemed over twenty years of marching with the eagles had not worn his face the same way they had his own. Bacchius had light green eyes, that swirled, moved, the colour growing lighter than darker with the sun. They reminded Taurus of marble. His nose was long, broad and strong, full lips surrounded a mouth full of gleaming white teeth. He was freshly shaven, as he always was, his face pale and smooth beneath a crop of short black hair streaked with grey.

'As good as they can be, sir. The shame is still there, the embarrassment of defeat. But they will fight well come spring, you can count on that.' He stood rigidly to attention as he spoke, eyes fixed on the point just above Taurus' head.

'You can drop the formalities, brother, no need for that when it's just us. Don't worry about the lady over there.' He hooked his thumb over his shoulder towards Abas, who mumbled a cursed reply.

'Right, sorry First Spear. Still getting used to my new position.' Bacchius' eyes lowered to his sandals. Taurus thought how he would feel if his legion were wiped out and he had been thrust a rung back down the ladder. Not that he had ever risen through it, making the extremely rare jump from soldier to First Spear, at the insistence of his predecessor. *Praise Jupiter for old Silus. Always did the right thing by me. Am I doing the right thing by his son?* Letting Albinus and his mess-mates go north had not been an easy decision to make, but Taurus had felt the lad would have gone alone if he'd have tried to stop him. That he couldn't have allowed.

'Don't look so downbeat, brother, no one here blames you for your legion's defeat. It won't be long before the emperor orders the Thirteenth back up to strength, especially with the prospect of a long war with the tribes. You'll be back as First Spear of the Thirteenth soon enough, mark my words. Until then, enjoy your time with the Fourteenth Gemina!' Some years before, when the divine Augustus made the Roman republic into an empire by crowning himself as the first emperor, Rome could call on over fifty legions spread across their frontiers. It was Augustus himself who made the much-needed change and reduced the number of legions by half. The Fourteenth had earned the name Gemina, when it had been merged with another legion.

'Thank you, First Spear, I hope you're right. I have a favour to ask, on behalf of me and my men.' He paused, shifted nervously from left foot to right. 'Would we be able to stand and march under our eagle? I know it is being kept safe in the shrine room within the principia, but it would mean a lot to the boys to have the eagle with us when we next go to war.' Taurus saw the hope in the man's eyes. He knew only too well the hurt it must have caused to see the Thirteenth's eagle retired to the dark room in the centre of the Fourteenth's headquarters. He couldn't imagine the shame of seeing his own eagle left in the dark indefinitely.

'Of course, brother. I would deem it an honour for our eagle to fight alongside yours. You have an aquilifer?' The aquilifer was the legion's eagle bearer, an honoured station; they carried the beloved bird wherever the legion went.

'Yes. A young lad named Cato. The battle at Tibiscum was his first under his wolf skin, not one to remember.' An aquilifer fought without a shield, a wolf skin lined their helmeted head, and the eagle itself was held instead of the scutum in the left hand.

'He fought beside his First Spear, saved him in battle and whisked the eagle away to safety when all was lost. I remember you introducing him to me now, that sounds like a man who should be proud of his achievements, don't you think?' Taurus thought of his own aquilifer, Vulso, and whether he would fight with such courage when the time came.

'I suppose, yes. He is a good lad, will make a good officer, if he survives long enough.' The conversation trailed off, Bacchius' humble words sending both men deep into concerned thought. 'Do you not need to ask the legate if we can bring our eagle?'

'You can ask him yourself, he's right behind you.' Taurus nodded to the east where the new legate of the Fourteenth was pacing slowly in front of the First Cohort of his legion. He saw the two senior centurions, nodded, and made towards them.

'Sir.' Both men rasped a salute as he walked closer. He waved a hand, signalling for both men to be at ease.

'Morning, brothers. How are the men?' Legate Marcus Valerius Maximianus stood proudly in the morning chill, resplendent in a bright white cloak and matching crest atop his helmet. Underneath he wore the same bronze muscle cuirass he had worn as a tribune, and still carried the same plain gladius, having chosen not to ordain the eagle-headed parazonium he had been awarded upon his promotion, following the death of Legate Candidus against the tribal army the previous summer.

He was a good appointment, Taurus thought. His military experience was vast, unlike most senators who were commissioned into roles commanding huge armies they had no idea how to lead. He had fought in more battles than Taurus was ever likely to see – from Britannia to Asia, on land and sea.

48

He was a steady hand for the legion, the right man to rebuild and lead them into war. 'As good as they can be, sir. It has been a difficult winter for us all.'

It had been late summer when they had set off on that fateful march to meet the tribes. Legate Candidus had ordered that the artillery was to be left behind, men to take minimal rations; he was confident his victorious army would be home by nightfall. He couldn't have been more wrong.

Taurus didn't know what had driven the man to decide to fight in the front line at the centre of the Roman formation. In the previous actions he had overseen since taking command of the legion, he had left the actual command of the battle to himself and Maximianus, and had always sat atop his horse well back from the front line with the colour party.

His decision to lead from the front had been the talk of the fortress throughout the winter. Roman legates usually only fought beside their men when on the brink of defeat, with the legion fighting a last stand; never from the onset of battle. But Candidus had. Some said it was the Marcomannic king Balomar himself who had led the charge which broke the Roman centre, although Taurus hadn't been able to see that from his position on the left flank.

All the First Spear had been able to do was to order his men to form square and march doggedly back towards Carnuntum, fighting every step of the way. Maximianus had done the same from the right flank, and together the two officers had spent that night looking on from the fortress walls as the city of Carnuntum was put to the sword. Both men had led the remnants of the legion into the city the next day, it had been a scene Taurus would never forget.

'Indeed it has, brother. I don't think I've ever seen a more subdued Saturnalia than the one just passed.' He paused, eyes turning to scan the massed army awaiting the governor. 'What do you make of these two new legions? Seems strange to see legionaries with cavalry swords eh?' Taurus thought he spoke with genuine interest. He was after all a military man through and through.

'Was just saying the same thing to Abas here.' Another thumb gesture towards the optio. 'Let's just hope they can use them!'

'Yes, indeed. They look like their shivering.' Maximianus hissed. 'Fucking

49

recruits, need to learn to wear their spare tunics under their armour – nothing worse than spending a whole morning on parade in the depths of winter. Especially next to this wind tunnel of a river!' Both centurions laughed. Taurus himself was wearing four tunics beneath his mail shirt, plus a pair of bracae under them. Whilst Roman soldiers were not allowed to wear trousers, like the tribes north of the river, they did get away with the shorter wool skin garment that stretched to just below the knee. He also had strips of wool stuffed beneath his arm and leg greaves, but not even Abas knew about that.

'You will have to get Pertinax to get his centurions on the case, sir. He'll have half of his men in hospital with frostbite by lunchtime.' Again, more laughter.

'Speaking of hospitals, Taurus, Felix tells me you have reported eight of your century on sick leave, but they aren't on the roster at the hospital. Look into it after this will you?' Taurus gulped. He had been required to report Albinus and his mess-mates as sick when he had filled in his last roster for his century. He'd hoped the small anomaly would go unnoticed. Clearly it had not.

'Err, yes, sir. Will do.' Taurus began to sweat, despite the cold. Bacchius looked at him quizzically.

Trumpets announced the arrival of Governor Bassus. The man arrived without much fanfare, walking through from the door of the amphitheatre, where he had been breaking his fast, and up the stairs onto the raised wooden platform that been constructed especially for today.

'Come, brothers, let's get this over with and get back into barracks. It's freezing out here.' Maximianus walked towards the raised platform, Taurus and Bacchius following close behind. Abas made his way back to the legion; only the senior centurions from each legion were allowed to stand with the army's commanders on the platform.

Taurus climbed the stairs and paused to look upon the stone statues of Augustus Aurelius and Caesar Verus. He had never met either man, so had no idea if the masons had done a good job recreating their likeness. *Guess I'll find out soon enough.* The two emperors had travelled north with the Praetorian Guard as far as Aquincum, where they had congratulated the city's forces on holding off the tribal army, who had scuttled north before winter took hold of the land and provisions ran dry. From there they had travelled back to Rome, but were making the journey north in the spring.

The centurion knew that the gathered men would be expected to rebuild the ruined city of Carnuntum, sweep clear the battlefield of the dead and broken equipment. Pannonia would need to appear to be a province in control, a nation ready for war. He had overheard Bassus saying just that to Maximianus and Pertinax the day before, that there was much work to be done. He was glad that the Tenth Legion had not been summoned to take the oath with the others. Their legate had delayed when the messenger from the Fourteenth galloped to their fortress at Vindobona, due to some personal grudge between him and Candidus. Over three thousand men had died because of that grudge. Legate Decimus was still in disgrace, and Bassus had already informed him that his men were to play minimal part in the war that was to come.

Taurus snapped out of his trance as the governor began to speak, his voice loud and booming, scything through the winter air. He coughed slightly, clearing his throat, as he prepared to renew his vows to the emperors and Rome. He wondered briefly what Balomar was doing in the distant north. Was he too gathering his tribal leaders together, renewing vows of friendship and brotherhood? Taurus thought it likely. Whatever happened come spring, he knew it would not be a quick and easy victory for the legions.

V

January AD 169 – Germania

The hearth's fire warmed his skin. The harsh ale bit the back of his throat as he struggled to swallow it down. *How much of this shit have I drunk?* His feet sweated in his leather boots, lined with sheep's wool. He had already discarded his thick bearskin cloak, and it lay slumped on the floor at his feet. He closed his eyes, scrunched them shut, rubbed at them furiously before wrenching them back open and squinting into the fire's dancing flames. They were still blurred. 'My lord? Are you okay?' A hushed voice in his ear.

'Fine. Fine. Just drunk, Adalwin, that's all.' Balomar, High King of the untied tribes of Germania, slumped lower in his chair. 'What is it?' His captain hadn't moved, still knelt by his side. He looked concerned.

'The chieftains are waiting. You said you would address them all tonight. We need them, my lord, if we are to fight again come spring.' Balomar sighed, rose unsteadily to his feet.

'They don't need addressing, my friend, they need bribing. Silver is the only thing that will see them march come spring. Don't object, Adalwin, we both know it to be true.' The king lurched, nearly fell, but Adalwin caught him before he embarrassed himself.

It felt as though they had been on the road for the whole of winter. Well, they pretty much had. The tribal army's hasty retreat from Italy in late summer felt like a lifetime ago, their resounding victory over the Fourteenth Legion in Pannonia even longer than that. Despite all the success the tribes had enjoyed the previous year, Balomar was already sick of trying to persuade the petty chiefs to march under his banner once more.

He had at first gone home once he had re-crossed the Danube into Germania. But his return to Goridorgis had been cold. His Roman bed slave, Aelinia, was desperate for the king to make her his queen. She had been ruling like a tyrant since he had left her on the road from Pannonia, where he had been attending a peace treaty with governor Bassus, on the false pretence of pleading for peace on behalf of the tribes. *How I'd have longed to see that greasy man's face when he heard I had re-crossed the river and ripped one of his legions to shreds.* He smiled drunkenly. He didn't smile enough these days.

So, he had suffered his bed slave's complaints for no more than two weeks, before sending her west to a winter hall whilst he toured the tribes and garnered support for the new campaign. It had been tougher going than he feared. At the failed siege of Aquileia, he had let his temper get on top of him. He had grown tired of the Quadi king Areogaesus and his barbed comments, his whispered treason with the chiefs behind his back. Alexander had been no help. The eastern soothsayer had been the architect of the whole campaign. He had wanted to use the tribes as a distraction. He wanted the Roman people in a state of fear, to lose faith in the emperor and the senate that governed them. He sought to drape himself in purple, to be king of Rome, and Balomar was one of his pawns. The German was sure there were many others.

But when the easterner had suggested that maybe the king of the Quadi was right, maybe they should let the chiefs vote for what they wanted to do, Balomar had taken the head from Areogaesus' shoulders in his rage. After that, it was all he could do but to lead his vast army back across the Alps, through Pannonia and into their homeland. The emperor Aurelius had been travelling north with his Caesar Verus and a fresh army, and Balomar knew his men would not fight a fixed Roman formation after that. His campaign was over for the year.

But he had hoped the chieftains would be eager for another year of raids and plunder. Instead, it seemed they were happy to sit in their halls, wait for the Roman emissaries to knock on their door, and gladly accept their bribes for peace. Balomar knew he could not allow it to happen, knew Alexander would not allow it to happen. *If I do not rally the tribes for war, that bastard will find another man who will, and that will be the end of me.*

He had agreed to side with the Abonoteichon originally as, like many other chiefs, he had become frustrated with his tribe's treatment at the hands of Rome. His people were depleted by plague, famine ruled in the lands north of the Danube, and his pleas for aid to Rome fell on deaf ears. The empire that ruled most of the known world had more people than it could count; more farms, cattle and sheep then it would ever need; would not lift a finger to help their closest neighbours in their time of need. It sickened Balomar to his core.

Let alone the fact that it had been years since Rome had bothered to pay the promised tribute. A cart of gold, delivered at summer's end, that's what they were supposed to receive. A cart of gold to stop their spear points turning south and keep them pointed at their fellow tribesman. Rome had thought the tribes weak, depleted from internal wars, too tired to rise up and face the might of the empire. Rome had been wrong.

Or had they? He stood drunkenly at the head of a small, rectangular table. The chiefs of the nearby tribes sat in sombre silence, each man's eyes fixed on the Marcomanni king. *Inspire them. Feed their thirst for spear fame.* That was the plan – the one he and Adalwin had discussed as they travelled east to Carrodunum, capital of the lands of the Sidones. Their chief, Euric, sat nearest to Balomar on the right-hand side of the table, his brow creased in concern.

The same could be said of Dagar, chief of the Osi, or Boric, chief of the Avareni. All in all, there were ten chiefs crammed into the small, round hall that passed for Euric's home. The Sidones were not a big, nor a great tribe. But Euric was well respected amongst the leaders in eastern Germania, and Balomar knew gaining his support would be vital to his cause.

Balomar was enraged that Valao of the Naristae and Bandanasp of the Iazyges had refused his invitation to join the other chiefs at the gathering. The two men were vocal in their reluctance to risk another year fighting the eagles. Their raids on Dacia and down through Moesia and Thracia and into Greece the previous year had filled their coffers with more wealth then they could have hoped to imagine. They had in fact, made it farther south than Balomar, nearly reaching the great city of Athens, before being forced to turn back north and west to meet with Balomar and the rest of his army.

They had rebuffed the almost pleading message Balomar had sent them to meet with him and chiefs at Carrodunum. Valao had at least explained that it would take years for him to recover from the losses he received at the hands of the Romans, and that he had no need for further provoking the feared legions. Bandanasp had just said no.

So he stood at the head of the table, facing the chiefs of ten of the smaller tribes from the east. He knew if he could band together the lesser tribes, he would still have an army to reckon with. He took a deep breath, stifled a rank sour burp into his beard, and begun to talk.

'Chiefs, warriors, brothers. I thank you for joining me here this night, and I thank Euric for graciously offering to be our host.' Euric made a muttered comment about his winter stores running thin and ale being on half rations for the rest of the winter, which earned a laugh from his fellow chiefs. Balomar forced a smile, and hoped it looked genuine. 'I have gathered you here tonight to talk of our plans for the spring, for the retaliation we can expect from the Romans.' Balomar was worried by their initial reaction, each man's gaze falling from his to meet the rim of his ale-filled cup.

'They will come with iron and fire, brothers, of that there is no doubt. We gave them such a crushing defeat last year that they will have no choice but to cross the Danube and try and force the initiative in our lands.' Still the chieftains kept their eyes fixed on the table top. 'You know what I say? I say we march our armies south, we meet them at the great river and we keep them pinned on the south side. No good can come from letting them cross. You all know what will happen. Does any man here want to see his wife raped, his children sold into slavery? We all know what Rome does to her defeated enemies: she wipes them off the face of the earth!' He crashed his fist down onto the wooden table top, but in his drunken state, he misjudged the power of the blow and sent ale flying through the air to splash in the chieftains' beards. From the corner of his eye, Balomar saw Adalwin wince and shake his head slowly.

He let the silence hang in the air, counted his heartbeats to twenty.

55

The men were still brushing ale from their beards. 'Well then, my friends, what do you have to say?' He sat down slowly, thought of pouring himself another cup of ale, then decided he'd had more than enough.

A man stood at the end of the table, furthest from the fire's warmth, his face shrouded in shadow. He was Adalwolf, chief of the Sideni tribe, from the northern shores of Germania. The Sideni had long since been swallowed up in the vastness of the Suevi, a tribe that ruled nearly all the north, but some tribes had been allowed to keep their own rulers and customs, as long as they gave up the asked-for tribute each year. 'There is only one question any of us need answering, Balomar, King of the Marcomanni.' His dark eyes burnt into Balomar as he spoke. He was slight in height and build, but his voice cut through the smoke-filled haze like a sharp blade through flesh. 'Will the Quadi march with you once more? With the Quadi we can stop the Romans crossing the river and ravaging our lands. With the Quadi we can field a force strong enough to meet the dreaded eagles in open battle. With the Quadi we are strong, without them … ' His point was clear, his tone threatening.

'And it's not just the Quadi,' another chief found his voice. 'I was told to expect Valao from the Naristae, and Bandanasp from the Iazyges tonight. I see neither man in this hall. Have they, too, turned their backs on you?'

Each man seemed to have something to say now. Angry voices raised in Balomar's direction, he flinched away from the pointing fingers and menacing faces. Their cacophony was intimidating, as endless as the green plains to the north. The great king of the Marcomanni, the man who had done what no other had in over a hundred years, he who had forged an alliance of the tribes with men who despised each other to the very core, slumped back in his chair and rubbed his eyes with his hands, a sudden wave of weariness washing over him.

After a time, the chieftains quietened. Balomar could feel the mood of the room; the tension at the table was palpable. He took a moment to think how he must look to these chieftains; he was bone-tired and drunk, travel-sore and lonely, deflated and humbled, despite his victories last year. The Marcomannic king thought of the spinners – the three sisters who weave the fates of men. *Those bitches have woven me a terrible fate. To be on*

56

the edge of glory, on the verge of eternal spear fame. And now I must watch my dreams turn to ash. He started at a loud voice to his rear; powerful, deep and booming, it galvanised the ale-weary men at the table.

'Noble chieftains, warriors, brothers. My lord and I come here to you this night to celebrate our great victories this last year. Who would have thought the leaders of the people of this vast nation would ever come together and fight under one banner, let alone defeat one of Rome's dreaded legions in battle? But we did. *You* did. But what was the point of it all, if we do not continue the fight. Tell me, wise and noble leaders, why did you choose to lead your men against the eagles? There must have been a reason, share it.' Adalwin finished his speech by spreading his arms wide, inviting the seated men to speak, but none did. Balomar raised his head and looked each man in the eye, desperate for one to speak, to say anything, just to break the awkward silence that had descended in the hall's gloom.

'Very well, I will bite.' Euric rose to his feet, left hand rubbing his long yellow beard as he thought. 'As I'm sure you are aware, my tribe has been embroiled in a long and bitter fight with the Cogni, a tribe based just a day's ride to the west of here. The cause of this conflict was my marriage to Haribert's sister, Freyja. Contrary to what the man might tell you, I did not steal her in a raid, she came to me freely.' He paused, tears welling in his eyes. 'We were in love,' he said in a voice not much above a whisper.

'She ran away when her father passed away. We had waited until the old man was dead, both knowing full well he would not have agreed to give her over in marriage to me. He and my own father had somewhat of a chequered history, but that's a story for another day.' His voice got stronger now, a sad smile on his face. He was remembering his father, Balomar thought. 'So, old Gundahar went to feast with the Allfather, and Freyja ran to live with me here. The following years were the happiest of my life, I can tell you.' His smile was vast now, it seemed to brighten the dim hall.

'But the happiest day of all was when he told me she was pregnant with my child. King Balomar, you are yet to experience the unbridled joy of fatherhood. Let me tell you now, it truly is the greatest thing a man can achieve in this world. The pregnancy was tough for Freyja. She was only small, slim-hipped and narrow-waisted, all the old women in the tribe whispered that her birth would be one of the hardest they would ever see. In truth, it was much worse than any of them could have imagined.' The tears came back now; he buried his face in his beard and took three long shuddering breaths as he struggled to compose himself. Balomar himself felt a burning sensation behind his eyes – any fool could see where this story was leading.

'The pains started during the night. It was summer, ten years past. I was shut out of my own hall, sent out into the cool night air. All night I paced the muddied streets of our small town. No mead or ale could quench my thirst, or dumb my wits against the screams of agony coming from within these very walls.' Balomar shifted uncomfortably. *Gods, tell me she didn't die in the very hall this man has feasted me in.* 'The sun rose, redder than the dye that coloured my trousers. I had never seen it so red, so deep, and I haven't since. I stood and basked in its glory, praying furiously to the spinners, begging them not to take her from me. But the old hags paid me no heed.' His tears fell in droves, hitting the wooden table top with soft splashes. So numerous were they, that two round puddles soon formed on the dark wood.

'I was only allowed to see her once it was over, after her body had been cleaned, the bloodied rags burnt. I will never forget the paleness of her face, the blue of her lips, how cold they were on mine when I leant in for one final kiss. But even in her death she had granted me one last gift, a final piece of joy: my daughter. I named her Freyja, after her goddess of a mother.' Again, the chief of the Sidones broke down in floods of tears. They forged two streams through his beard, either side of his quivering mouth. Balomar, though saddened by the tale, was beginning to wonder when Euric was going to get to the point.

'I took her body to Budorgis, seeking peace with Haribert. In my distress, I thought our mutual loss would bring us closer together, bind us in some sort of brotherhood. Instead, the cur tried to murder me in my sleep. We have been in a state of war ever since.

'I joined this army, agreed to fight against the Romans, in the hope that Haribert would too, and that finally my people and his could find some unity by fighting against a common enemy. But, on hearing that I had pledged my spears to Balomar, Haribert turned the invitation down. I was worried last summer when I left my lands with my warriors, that he would take the opportunity to raid my people and punish them for what he perceives as my crimes. But, thanks to Donar, he kept his spears in their huts. Although he did come here and spent an afternoon with his niece, and she says they got on well.' Euric's voice trailed off, his story at an end.

The awkward silence resumed around the table. Hard-bitten warriors shot each other quizzical looks over the rims of their cups, not used to hearing a man speak with such emotion. Adalwin broke the silence. 'Thank you, Euric, for a truly stirring tale. It puts what we fight for into perspective. We can defend our loved ones from Rome, but no one can protect them from the will of the gods. I met your daughter earlier on this evening; she does you great credit my friend, I found her intelligent and beautiful.' Adalwin nodded his head to Euric, who returned the gesture whilst wiping the last tears from his eyes.

'And what a reason to fight,' Adalwin continued. 'Raise your hand if you only agreed to fight the legions for the opportunity for coin and plunder?' He smiled when the rest of the chiefs all raised their hands 'This man,' he said, pointing at Euric, 'fought only to forge a friendship with his brother chief. To unite his people and Haribert's, and form a lasting peace with his neighbour. Can you see how this war could help to unite our people – to make us stronger? A united Germania is something that Rome cannot ignore. It is not us in the wrong here. All we want is some respect, for the emperors on their throne in distant Rome to think us strong and worthy allies. To share the vast wealth that consumes their empire. They will never listen if we give up now.' He finished there, rested a hand on Balomar's shoulder. The king wondered if he was meant to speak now, but the ale and the heat from the fire had made him drowsy, slowed his wits, and he could think of nothing to add.

Time dragged by and the silence stretched into the night. Balomar embraced the warmth of the hearth, the rich fragrance of roasted boar that danced up his nostrils. He felt his eyelids go heavy, his chin sag on his chest. 'Well fuck it!' Balomar jumped from his seat, bloodshot eyes burning as they wrenched open in surprise. 'If Euric's in then I am. Too long have my people drifted away unnoticed in the north, it's time we got us some respect, too. Not to mention coin!' Adalwolf stood and raised his cup to Balomar. 'Our spears may not be many, our armour worn and full of holes, but the men of the Sideni will be at your side, Balomar king.'

Balomar felt his tiredness lift like a cloud uncovering the sun. *Maybe the spinners haven't deserted me yet.* One by one, the chiefs round the table followed suit, standing and raising their cups to the king, each man making an oath to the Allfather to bring their spears south come spring.

The Marcomanni king took each man's oath in turn. When the last was done, he turned to a beaming Adalwin. The two locked eyes, and Balomar fought the urge to run to his captain and bind him in a bear hug. He knew all too well his faithful friend had saved his campaign, and possibly his life. He raised his cup, and silently mouthed his thanks to the one man he knew he could always rely on.

VI

The wind tore at her face. It snarled in anger at pale skin as she stood, hunched behind her shield. Her hair was lank, heavy with sweat, staining her face in lines running from left to right. She huffed out a heavy breath, trying in vain to blow the errant hair from her stinging eyes.

'Shield up, Licina! Straighten that spear, your opponent is to your front, not by your side!' Heide's voice renewed Licina's concentration. Hefting the shield in one hand, with her right she brought her spear tip to the front – it had been lagging to her side, the leaf-shaped point dragging in the snow.

She had reacted just in time. Her opponent leapt forwards with a growl, her own spear arcing from high to low. Licina saw nothing but a hint of black shadow against the white backdrop, but it gave her just enough warning to raise her shield to meet the spear. The tip bounced off her shield boss with a spark and clang.

Her opponent backed away and the two circled each other warily, panting heavily. Licina studied her opponent over her shield rim, which was getting heavier with every thumping heartbeat. This was not the first time she had faced Gisila in the circle, in fact this was the longest she had lasted without being put flat on her back. Gisila was bigger than Licina, in height and breadth. She had a longer reach and could land her blows with greater power. Heide had told Licina that Gisila was the perfect sparring partner for her, for if she were to join the shieldmaidens in battle, she would be

61

facing fully grown men in the shield wall and would therefore have to get used to fighting bigger and stronger opponents.

Still they circled, the women around them cheering for their favourite. Licina thought she saw two onlookers exchanging coin as bets were placed on the likely victor. She wasn't surprised to see it was Ruga taking the coin, it seemed there was nothing the blacksmith's daughter would not take a bet on. Distracted, she didn't see Gisila's lunge, low, aiming for her knees. Licina yelped in pain as the edge of the spear head scraped through her woollen trousers and sliced through skin. Hot blood flooded down her left leg; she focused on keeping the pain at the back of her mind, using adrenalin to force it from her thoughts, just as Heide had taught her.

Deciding to try and grasp the initiative, she leapt into the air, using her uninjured right leg to propel her up and forwards. Swinging her shield out wide with her left arm, she used the momentum of her body to hammer down her spear with her right. It smashed into Gisila's raised shield, tearing a hole through the wood at the top. The point stopped inches from Gisila's face. She stood in stunned silence, staring at the leaf-shaped point in amazement.

'You stupid little girl! Are you trying to kill me!' Gisila screamed, her accent thick and guttural. It was the voice of a man, Licina thought, a warrior.

'I … I'm sorry. I didn't mean to hurt you, Gisila.' Licina thought her own voice sounded pathetic in comparison. 'But you did cut my leg, it's bleeding badly.' She stooped to show the heavy cut through her torn trousers, hoping that was reason enough to have nearly driven her spear through her opponent's face.

'Bah!' Gisila waved her hand in frustration. ''Tis nothing more than a scratch! You will not last long with the shieldmaidens if you can't take a wound and keep your senses! Heide, it was your idea to bring her here, she's your new playmate, you sort her out.' With that she was gone, pushing through the sphere of shields, Licina's spear still lodged in the wooden boards of her own.

The gathered women tried unsuccessfully to hide their smirks as Licina met their eyes. She wondered what Gisila had meant by the term 'playmate'.

'All right, ladies, show's over! Everyone back to the grove, we eat at sundown. Do what you wish until then.' Heide walked slowly towards Licina, who felt even more like the foreigner she was as the circle of smirking women disintegrated around her. 'Well done, Licina! You were amazing today!' There was no scorn or mocking tone in Heide's voice, it was genuine, as was the touch on her shoulder. 'Come, let's get that cut seen to, looks nasty.'

Together they walked behind the others, back off the frozen plain, towards a lone crop of woodland, a black hollow in an otherwise world of white. 'Didn't feel like it went well. I don't understand what I'm supposed to do, Heide. When I lose I'm ridiculed for being weak, and when I win, I'm told I'm too aggressive!' Licina threw her arms up in the air, clearly exasperated.

'You're new, the girls are just getting a feel for you. You're doing well. This is what, you're third time away with us?' Licina nodded, eyes downcast on the snow. 'And you're getting better with our language. It's just a matter of time Licina, you'll soon be one of us.'

'What did Gisila mean by playmate?'

'Huh?' Heide slowed in her stride, her face in a scowl.

'Gisila said I was your new playmate, what did she mean?'

A pause of silence, and Heide rubbed her neck; Licina sensed her mind trying to frame the right words. 'You are aware that us ladies have taken a vow to not have children?' Licina nodded. 'Well some of us have decided to … stay away from men all together, if you get my meaning?' Another nod. 'But even with that vow, it is natural to get … urges.'

The last word hung in the air. Licina felt herself blush. 'So some of you … keep each other company? Rather than having a man to … keep you company.' Despite the wind and the cold, Licina's cheeks burned.

'Yes. It is nothing to be embarrassed about. I believe it makes our bond stronger. Will make us fight harder together when the time comes. Love is a powerful emotion, it can drive you to achieve great things.'

'So Gisila thinks that you and me … ' Licina took a step to the right, away from Heide. It was involuntary, and quickly became one more thing to be embarrassed about.

'Hey! Don't look so offended! I'm a desirable woman.' Heide winked, and laughed at her friend's awkward demeanour. 'The girls just assume that since you're new and we have become such good friends, that … you know.' The rest didn't need to be said.

63

'And Gisila, is she a former *playmate* of yours?' Licina emphasised the word, curious to know.

'Well, yes. In fact, we have only grown apart since you came to our lands.'

'Ah!' Licina had thought as much, and now having it confirmed made it easier to understand why Gisila seemed to have taken such a foul attitude towards her. 'So she hates me then, right?'

'Maybe. But she is far too stubborn to ever admit why. Don't worry about it Licina, you have done nothing wrong. And anyway, I have a surprise for you tonight.' Licina paused, a questioning look on her face. Heide laughed. 'Don't panic, it doesn't involve you and me sharing a blanket. Unless of course you want to?' Another wink from Heide, a deeper blush from Licina.

Night fell quickly out in the wilds of winter. The black sky was full of low hanging cloud, obscuring the blue light of the moon. Licina shivered in her bearskin cloak, wrapping it tightly round her slim body. She stood back from the others, who were gathered in a tight circle, arms interlocking, all facing towards a stone-built well. The Well of Urd, they called it. And in its depths, the fates of men could be woven. Some could be lifted from slave to lord, others from king to beggar. It was said to all hang on what was woven in the gloom.

Licina watched in awe as the sisters of the sword chanted in unison, their voices high-pitched, soft in tone at first but growing louder as the chant wore on.

'Urd, mistress of the Fates, join us.

Verdandi, mistress of the present, join us.

Skuld, mistress of what is to come, join us.'

Louder and louder the chanting rose, until it reached a piercing crescendo, so loud Licina scrunched her face in pain and pulled her hood tighter about her ears. Suddenly, they stopped. The silence was absolute, although Licina felt her ears ring, such was the power of the sisters' voices.

'The Norns are with us, sisters.' Heide stepped forward from the huddle of cloaks, pulling back her hood and exposing her pale skin to the night's chill air. Her breath was heavy on the dark sky, long trails of steam streaking towards the heavens. Licina felt her heart beat harder. Those eyes. Crystal blue, like the purest water, they gleamed in the torchlight. Licina took two deep breaths and tried to force the image of Albinus from her mind, but his face was as unmoving as a mountain when facing an easterly wind. The mop of light brown hair, like a small clasp of wet straw. His button nose scrunched up in concentration as he studied the summer's crops that swayed in the gentle breeze. A taut mouth, thin-lipped, but with a smile that would have illuminated this dark and dreary night. And those eyes, Heide's eyes. If you had met them both, you could have been forgiven for thinking they shared a father, although Licina knew it to be impossible. She didn't think she had ever pictured his face so strongly.

Heart still racing, cheeks burning, a growing wetness between her thighs, it was all she could do to not groan out loud. Heide's eyes met hers, and she felt her knees shake like a new-born foal. It was an age before she even realised Heide was speaking, all she could hear was the blood pumping in her ears.

'The Norns are with us sisters. They honour us with their presence this night. They who decide the fates of gods, of kings, stand with us. Bring forward the sacrifice, we shall show them we are worthy of their presence.'

Licina stood frozen as the lifeless trees as all eyes turned to look upon her. *Sacrifice? Surely not …* And then two women pushed past her, in their midst a groaning cow, reluctant to meet its fate. This time Licina's knees very nearly gave way, the wave of relief too much to bear. *By all the gods, I thought they were looking at me!* She sighed heavily, her breath choked with emotion, and smiled at her own stupidity. When she looked back towards the huddled sisters, her eyes caught Gisila's. The shieldmaiden smirked; she had clearly seen the pantomime of emotion on Licina's face.

The cow was dragged to the well. The light grey stone came up to the cow's underbelly, and the sisters struggled as they dragged the beast until its neck was directly above the dark water lurking below. Licina watched as Heide drew a slim dagger from beneath her cloak. She came up behind the cow, as if concealing the blade from its wild eyes. Again, the animal groaned, pulling on the leather leash that was wrapped tightly round its neck. The cow knows, Licina thought. Her mind thrust her back to the last sacrifice she had witnessed: Saturnalia, the previous winter, another dark and freezing night, Silus standing bare-headed in the moon's glory, robed in blue, offering sacrifice to one of Rome's most beloved gods. The piglet had not known what was going to happen. It had spent its last moments on earth sniffing the earth for food. Its mother had though. Licina could still remember the squeals.

Just like on that night, she scrunched her eyes shut as the blade moved towards the animal's throat, though this time she did not have Albinus' chest to bury her head in. She heard the squelch as the blade penetrated the skin; the rasp as the edge was pulled from left to right; the snap of arteries and the crunch of gristle; the splash of hot blood on the dark water. She didn't open her eyes again until she heard the crash of the carcass hitting the snow-covered ground. The cow hadn't made a sound.

'Oh glorious sisters, lords of gods, masters of our fate, accept our sacrifice and hear our plea.' Heide's cry was repeated by the others, and again their collective screams hurt Licina's ears. 'We offer you this life so you may preserve our own. Watch over us in the battles to come, see that we may live to defeat our enemies.' Again, the gathered shieldmaidens repeated the cry. 'And if you have woven our deaths, let them be clean. Let them be glorious, defiant in the face of our foe. For there could be no better fate than dying victorious on the battlefield!'

Licina found herself taking a step back, confused thoughts whirling through her mind. *See that we may live to defeat our enemies? No better fate than dying victorious on the battlefield?* Licina had often heard veterans of the legions talking round the fires at night, when she was an innocent girl living happily with her parents on their colonies farm. They spoke of the cruel fate they had been given, having to live to watch their once formidable bodies waste away as they waited for their cot death. They spoke of the envy they felt for the men who had died in their prime, sword in hand with their front to the enemy. These were the men that were remembered, immortalised through the years as veterans told exaggerated tales to new recruits of long-dead comrades' skill at arms, their bravery in battle and the foes they had slain.

To Licina it brought to mind the war god Hercules, and the twelve labours he was said to have suffered. Or the Christ god Jesu, who was said to have died on the cross to save all of humanity. She wondered if these gods had just been ordinary men once, whose legend had grown far and wide from one man to the next, the tale becoming greater and more extravagant with every telling. Is this how gods were made? With a small smile, she wondered how long it would be before the men of the Fourteenth Legion were worshipping Silus as a god, as men had looked upon him with the same reverence whenever he had walked past.

There was a silence in the small grove now, the women bowing their heads in prayer around the stone-built well, the carcass of the cow still bleeding on the snow. Again, Licina wondered who the shieldmaidens' enemy was, and if there was a battle impending. She knew that the Heruli, the tribe she was living with, had a difficult relationship with their northern neighbours, the Suiones. The land of the Heruli was known as Gotland, and covered the southern coast of the frozen country she had journeyed to. North of them was Svearland, the home of the Suiones. Licina had heard tales of raids taking place on both sides of the border, cattle seized and the odd man killed, but she had seen no evidence of war breaking out. Although it was winter, she mused, the land was thick with snow, the mud tracks these people called roads were impossible to find, let alone follow. Perhaps when the sun grew warmer and the snow began to melt, she would discover the truth.

A hand on her shoulder startled Licina, and she jumped and gasped in surprise. 'Sorry, sister! You were in a daze. Everything okay?' Heide was beside her, hood pulled back over her face. Her right hand was covered in dark blood. It streaked down her cloak and had formed a stain on her boot.

'Fine, thank you. Just thinking.'

'Of ...?'

Licina paused, wanting to frame the words correctly. 'You spoke about defeating your enemies, being victorious in battle. Who are you planning on going to war with?'

'You have heard of the Suiones to the north?' Licina nodded. 'They were raiding our lands at the end of autumn just past. There is a village, Scurgum it is called, right on the border where our country ends and theirs begins. Our chief, Sigivald, was visiting the village with his eldest son, Reiner.

Sigivald, as I'm sure you have seen, is old. This winter is his sixtieth, and he knows he is not long for this world. He had taken Reiner north with him to ensure that he was seen by the people, that they would know who it is who will rule them when Sigivald passes into Wotan's Hall.' Licina nodded, sensing a bitter ending to the tale was approaching.

'They were feasted in the hall of Erwin, the village's elder, honoured and praised as they ate and drunk their fill. When they were asleep, when the hearth's flames had smouldered to embers and the hounds were snoring in their beds, the raiders struck.' Licina felt a cold chill run down her spine – she knew all too well the feeling of raiders forcing their way into your home whilst you slept.

'But this was no mere cattle raid. These men knew who they were after. Breaking down the doors to the hall, they stormed inside, bare iron shining blue in the moonlight. They say Reiner fought well, before the axe cleaved his chest. Unarmoured, he had stood in defiance in front of his father and cut down the first four men that attacked them. But there were too many in the end …' Heide's voice trailed off, her tone full of anguish. Licina thought of Fullo, standing in the doorway of his family home, sword bared and bloody as he fought in vain to protect his mother and herself. *Turda, what I'd give to have you here with me now.*

'But Sigivald escaped? How did he get away?' Licina was stunned. It had been weeks now since she had arrived at the lands of the Heruli, this was the first time she had heard the tale. She worked the dates out in her mind, and realised that this raid could only have just happened when she first set foot on the shingle beach.

'Erwin and his men rallied and drove the raiders off. They saved Sigivald, but were too late for his son.' Licina could see the ice in her friend's eyes; she stared off into the distance, her mouth curling into a snarl.

'So, come spring, there will be war with the Suiones?'

Heide nodded. 'Sigivald sent men to speak to his brother, but they were sent back without being granted an audience. They have never got on well, Dagr and Sigivald, but I never thought it would come to this.'

'*Brothers?*' Licina was shocked, it was clear in her tone. She almost shouted the word.

'Gods! I forget you are new to our lands! Yes, the two are brothers. Once, long ago, when my grandfather was still a young man, their father was king of both Gotland and Svearland. He ruled the two tribes and their peoples for over fifty years. On his death, he left the northern lands to Dagr and the southern to Sigivald. It is said he made them swear a blood oath to never go to war with each other. It would appear they have both forgotten that now. Our people were great once, we were strong and feared. Now, we are just two small tribes set to fight out a petty war.'

Licina stood in stunned silence, her breath heavy on the freezing air. 'I thought only in Rome did people go to war over jealousy and greed, but it seems it happens wherever you go.'

'There are many wars within the empire? Roman fighting Roman?'

'There used to be, when the empire was a republic and the senate ruled. The first emperor was a man named Augustus. He rose to power to avenge his uncle, Julius Caesar, I assume you have heard of these men?' Heide nodded.

'Caesar had conquered the province of Gaul, sailed to Britannia and had never been defeated in battle, or so they say. The senate grew wary of him, fearful of his reputation and the huge army he had at his disposal. They ordered him back to Rome, to come back without his troops and stand trial for crimes against the republic. He refused, of course. Hungry for power himself, he marched on Rome with all his might, and fought a long and bitter war with a man named Pompeius Magnus. Caesar won in the end, was named dictator of Rome.'

'What happened?' Licina could see her friend was eager to hear the rest of the story. She smiled to herself; it felt good to be the one with something interesting to tell, rather than listening eagerly to anther of Heide's tales about her strange gods.

'He was murdered. In the senate house, by his fellow senators. They say not one of the assassins died a natural death. Augustus took his uncle's army and hunted them to the ends of the earth. By the time he was done, there was no one strong enough to oppose him, and he was named Princeps, Father of Rome. There have been emperors ever since.'

Heide breathed out heavily, a breath she had not been aware she was holding in. 'Wow. It is frightening, do you not think, how many people are willing to die for one man, one leader. It is no different here, except our armies are tiny compared to yours, and our wars fought for much less reward!'

'But you are free. You have no emperor or governor taxing you, telling you how to live your life, invading your lands and tearing down your homes to replace them with their own, only to charge you to live in them. Your destiny is your own, and that should be cherished. Trust me.' There was power in Licina's words; she had not realised the strength of the emotions she had buried deep within her.

'Have you ever seen it? Rome?'

'No. Never been further south than Pannonia, where I was born. Can't say I've ever had the desire to. They say a thousand thousand people live in Rome. Can you imagine so many people in one place? It must stink!'

Heide laughed. Then there were raised voices, loud and harsh. The words too quick for Licina to understand. 'What's happening?' She said, nervous.

'It is time to offer the blood to Yggdrasil,' said Heide, her voice pious.

'Huh?' Licina rolled the word on her tongue, but couldn't grasp its meaning.

'The tree of Yggdrasil – its roots go down into the underworld, its branches reach up to the heavens. It connects the living to the lands of the gods.' Heide was already moving, gesturing for Licina to follow.

They walked through the throng of shieldmaidens, up to the well itself. Licina stepped warily round the carcass of the dead cow. She felt silly, but she was worried it would suddenly move. One of the women thrust a bucket into her hands. It was simple, carved of wood, handleless, so she had to grip it by the sides. Heide motioned to the well, and with an uneasy gulp Licina realised what she was being asked to do.

She stooped over the well, the iron smell of blood filling her nostrils. Again, it brought back nightmares of last winter, of bearded raiders with bloodied spears; green-cloaked men snatching her and throwing her over a horse. She tried to block the thoughts from her mind.

In went the bucket, the bloody water soaking her hands and the sleeves of her tunic. Lifting it out, the dark water shone a deep red in the dim moonlight. Licina looked around questioningly, unsure what she was meant to be doing. To her surprise, it was Gisila who gently touched her arm and led her away from the well to a nearby tree.

70

It was as old ash tree, its roots protruding from the ground, thicker than Licina's waist. The bark looked black in the night, as if Jupiter had scorched it with a thunderbolt. *Or Donar.* She remembered where she was. Looking up, Licina could see the sky beginning to turn a light blue, a darker undercurrent of deep purple. The tree's branches seemed so high they could almost touch the sky. They, too, were black and lifeless.

Gisila knelt on the frozen ground beside her. Licina copied the gesture. Her ears were filled with Heide's high-pitched voice behind her.

'Wotan, lord of the gods. Donar, bringer of thunder ...' On and on she went, calling on every one of her gods to bear witness to their sacrifice, 'The Norns, sisters of the Fates, masters of our destiny, be with us now as we offer you the blood of life. Accept this offering and know that we are yours.' Her prayer was repeated by the gathered shieldmaidens, who were all on their knees, eyes to the ground with their hoods masking their faces.

Silence. 'Gisila,' whispered Licina, 'what am I supposed to do?'

A snort. 'Just tip the blood onto the trees roots, quickly!' Her reply was hissed, but without the anger Licina was expecting. Gently, careful not to spill any onto herself, Licina tipped the bucket and watched as the bloody water spilled onto the snow and roots. Too late she realised she was kneeling downhill from the roots, and grimaced as she felt the wetness on her knees as the blood trickled down the incline. And then it was done.

Gisila rose slowly to her feet, eyes still downcast. Licina followed suit. Still it was silent. Licina heard a bird squawk overhead, then another.

'Sisters!' It was Gisila who spoke. 'Wotan has sent his ravens to witness our blood offering. He shows us his favour! We will be victorious in battle, our enemies will flee before our swords!' A great cheer erupted from the gathered women, loud and piercing. 'Our lord also shows favour to our newest recruit, surely we cannot deny the favour of the gods. Licina has been honoured by our lord, welcomed into the ranks of the shieldmaidens. She has shown her valour and skill in the circle, and come spring she will get the chance to show her prowess in battle!' Another roar, loud and deep like rolling thunder.

Licina looked to Gisila in shock. The warrior-woman met her stare with a smile that was pure evil. *She knows what she is doing. Make out I am*

71

favoured by the gods, then watch as I am cut to pieces in some worthless battle in the spring. Licina shuddered, suddenly feeling very cold and alone.

The sun chose that moment to begin its ascent into the sky. The first rays burst through the leafless trees, bathing the gathered women in glorious red light. Licina thought of her father, and how he would greet the rising sun each morning. *Apollo, unconquered sun. Lord of light, master of the bow. We pray for your eternal glory.* Her father had been a keen bowman, and had often taken Licina out hunting with him, much to the dismay of her mother. Perhaps, she thought as she embraced the warmth of the sun's first rays, Apollo could watch over her as well. She felt she would need all the protection she could get.

VII

The night's wind was harsh on Rullus' skin. His beard tugged left then right, strands of long red hair dancing in the wind in front of his eyes, and he struggled to brush it all back under his helmet. The moon was full and bright, its light guiding the small party of men clearly as they crept through the brush that surrounded the village.

Carrodunum, capital of the lands of the Sidones, was asleep. Not a soul stirred as Rullus pulled back the branches in front of him to stare out into the night. A hall sat in the middle of the village, surrounded by smaller homes and other buildings. Rullus saw a building that looked like a smithy; a huge iron anvil sat outside the door, smoke loomed from the building where a raging forge would always be kept warm. There was a granary to the north of the hall, the building raised on wooden stilts so the grain wouldn't get damp in winter.

The smell of rawhide from the building nearest to Rullus indicated a tannery, where leather would be worked into sword sheaths and shield covers or stitched over cloaks to keep the rain out. Rullus sensed a presence to his right and turned to see the crystal blue eyes of Albinus as he crawled up next to him.

'See anything, brother?' he said as he too peered through the branches. Rullus continued to stare at the younger man, a smile fixing his face. It amazed Rullus how different this young soldier was to the cowardly boy

73

who had joined the Fourteenth not even a year ago. Fullo had told him that Albinus had spent his entire childhood trying to distance himself from Silus and what the centurion had stood for. It was ironic that his death had caused the son to follow in his father's footsteps. Rullus thought the old man would be smiling in Hades as he watched over his son, proud of the man he had become. Rullus knew he and his mess-mates all were. They all felt the same paternal instincts towards him, which was why they had agreed to venture into Germania with him in the first place.

'Nothing, brother. No walls, no guards, barely any buildings! I am glad it is this place we are to attack and not the one we have just left!' Budorgis, home of the Cogni had been a far more formidable town. Walled and garrisoned, the Roman soldiers would have been unable to simply walk in as they would be able to here.

'Seems strange, does it not, that the Cogni have requested we do this for them? I mean, how many men did Haribert have within his hall alone? Let alone on his walls and standing guard at the gates?' Albinus was fast becoming known for being the thinker of the group; he had a keen intelligence and intuition which would serve him well in his life in the army, Rullus thought. As long as he stayed alive.

'Maybe he does not want him or his men to be seen here? He said before that he alone of the tribes of this region did not follow Balomar in last year's fighting. Would make sense for him to want to keep a low profile, especially with war looming again come spring.' He wouldn't admit it to Albinus but Rullus, too, was concerned at the task they had been set by the chief of the Cogni.

Haribert and Bucco had talked for what seemed an age in the chief's hall, two nights previous. They had reached an agreement: the Romans would do something for Haribert, and the chief in turn would provide men to act as guides for the Romans as they continued their journey north. It seemed fair, especially when you considered Rullus and his friends had killed a fair number of Cogni warriors. They had sent them to their gods last night, their bodies buried in the ground rather than burnt on a pyre, as was the Roman way. No great stones or marble structures marked the graves, a sight that was common outside every major fortress or city throughout the Roman

74

empire. They were just buried together in a mass grave. It seemed undignified to Rullus; these men had been warriors, they would have been proud to fight for their tribe and chief. It seemed disrespectful to their families to watch their loved ones thrown into the dirt without any seeming care of affection. 'We come from the mud, then when we die, we return to it.' Haribert had shrugged his answer to Rullus' question.

The sight of the bodies being dumped in ground brought to mind the standard bearer's past, his mother. He had no memory of her, but knew she was from a tribe much like the Cogni. Had her body been thrust into a pit when she died? For she was surely with her gods now. Rullus himself was over forty years old and approaching twenty years' service under the eagle. He had no 'Familia', no fancy three-barrelled name like the upper classes – the legates and tribunes who had commanded him throughout his army life. He could just remember being called Rullus as a child, a name given to him in the small hostel he had been brought up in, back in Carnuntum. He was similar to Taurus in that respect, he thought with a sense of pride. Both men had grown up the hard way. Life on the cobbles had taught them many things, forged them into natural soldiers, even before they had taken the oath.

Rullus blushed, involuntarily reaching up a hand to stroke his growing red beard. He had known it would make him look like his First Spear when he had begun to grow it, but had always denied that it was the reason why. Deep down, he knew it really was. He worshipped his centurion, would die for him, just like he had Silus.

'There, a man moving in the shadows. Can you see?' Rullus snapped out of his daze, his eyes following Albinus' pointing hand. There was indeed a man stumbling in the darkness. Rullus could make out a shaggy mane of blond hair and yellow trousers, hear the man curse as he tripped and nearly fell.

'Someone's been at the ale! If Fortuna's with us brother, every man in there will be in the same state!' Rullus said as he stifled a laugh, watching the drunken man fall violently into the hall. The crash of timber as he ripped open the door reverberated around the silent woods.

'Shall we go through the plan one more time?' Albinus had a nervous edge to his voice, and Rullus noticed for the first time how tense he appeared. He could see the younger man rubbing the inside of his mouth with his tongue, exploring the fresh scar tissue where a spear had ripped into his face during the summer's fighting. It was easy to forget the young man had only seen combat a couple of times. Rullus could well remember the fear he felt the first few times he fought a man, a fear he still felt, not that he ever let it show.

'Sure. How's the cheek?'

'Huh?'

'You're rubbing at it with your tongue. Didn't the medicus tell you to leave it alone?'

'Yes, but it's been months since then. Still hurts like crazy, I thought the pain would have gone away by now. And I'm still getting used to chewing on the other side of my mouth, keep forgetting I'm missing half my teeth!' Albinus had lost six teeth from the left side of his mouth, although he could have lost a lot more. The spear tip had exploded into his jaw, but luckily his reactions had saved his life. The medicus had said that had it gone just a little further in, he would have choked to death on his own blood. As it was, Albinus had continued to fight for the remainder of the day, leading the men in the front rank of the retreating square as they fought their way back to Carnuntum. *He's more like his father then he will ever know.* Taurus had recommended him for an award for valour in battle, but it was to be a surprise for him when they returned to the legion. *If we return.*

'So anyway,' continued Albinus, 'the plan—' A flaming arrow shot into the sky, arcing over the rear side of the hall.

'That's the signal, let's go!' Rullus was off, not waiting to see if Albinus followed. He hunched over as he ran, keeping as low to the ground as he could. He felt naked without his shield, but speed was to be the key tonight, and carrying a cumbersome scutum would have slowed them all down. His sword already drawn, the bare iron glimmered in the moonlight. Ten paces, twenty, and they were past the first huts. Some didn't even have doors, just a crude canvas curtain to keep out the night's chill, Rullus was conscious of the crunch of his hobnailed sandals on the frozen mud.

A noise to his right – the grunt of a man snapping awake. Rullus slowed,

76

pointing to Albinus with the tip of his blade the hut the grunt had come from. The young legionary didn't hesitate, burst through the canvas door and Rullus heard the wet slap as a gladius sliced through flesh and bone. Rullus stopped and counted the beats of his pounding heart; Albinus was out the hut before they got to ten. He nodded to Rullus, but said nothing.

On they went, the hut drawing closer. The heat as they passed the black-smith's was welcoming, the smell of heated iron rich in Rullus' nostrils. He was tempted to barge in, if only just to enjoy the warmth for longer, but he ran past its doors without pause.

Movement to his right, the gleam of a naked blade, and Longus appeared from the gloom, trudging casually down the mud road as if he was out for an evening stroll. Libo was behind him, his blade dark with blood. 'Brothers,' the Numidian whispered, his breath thick on the night air, 'any trouble?' Rullus and Albinus shook their heads in unison. Rullus nodded his head toward the blood on Libo's blade. 'It was nothing,' he said, pausing to wipe it on the mud, 'just a poor barbarian who chose to take a piss at the wrong time.' Rullus watched as Libo and Longus shared a grin and tapped each other on the shoulder. The standard bearer shook his head but smiled; a legionary's sense of humour was all kinds of wrong.

The four men moved in a tight formation, making for the doors of the hall. More men emerged from the darkness, first Fullo, then Bucco. Habitus came from the left, an arrow notched on his small bow. They paused outside the doors to the hall, the same ones in which Rullus had seen the drunk man fall through not long before. Each man breathed heavily, their breath misting the air. No one spoke, just shared nods confirming each man was ready.

'I'd just like to point out,' whispered Habitus, 'that if this door is locked we're fucked!' A pause of silence, then grunts and cackles as each man suppressed a laugh. Nothing like a cheap joke to ease a soldier's nerves before combat.

'It's not,' Albinus replied, 'we saw someone go through it earlier. He was blind drunk, let's hope the others are too!'

The plan was simple. They were here to rescue Haribert's niece and bring her back to the Cogni, her mother's tribe. Her father, Euric, was not a good man and had ill-treated her since the death of his wife, or so Haribert said. The two tribes had been in a state of war for several years now, and Haribert wanted to rescue his niece and keep her safe among his people, a task he was apparently unable to do himself, hence why they were here. The major downfall of the plan was also simple: they had no idea how many men were inside the hall. And there were only seven of them, Calvus still being unconscious on a straw bed in Budorgis. Haribert had provided two mounted guides to take them to and from the lands of the Sidones, but they had been instructed to stay out of sight whilst the Romans entered the town itself.

'What d'ya reckon? Nice and slow or flatten it and pile in?' Bucco gestured to the door.

'It was you that got us into this, brother, so your choice!' Libo's tone left no room for argument. The others nodded. Bucco gulped, stepped forwards, and creaked the door open. It edged inwards, revealing nothing but blackness.

Adalwin sighed in frustration. All around him drunk men snored and farted. The sound made the ground shake and the smell brought tears to his eyes. He needed to piss, but the remnants of the hearth were warming his bones and he had no desire to step out into the winter night. *At least the snow has stopped.* Seven nights they had been at Carrodunum, longer then he had wanted to stay. Balomar, however, had been insistent. The promise of warriors from the gathered leaders had rejuvenated his spirits, and Adalwin was pleased to see some colour return to his king's cheeks and the smile return to his face. Adalwin did not think he had seen his king eat since he had returned to Goridorgis from his hunt in the north, chasing the ghost of the runaway Roman slave, Licina.

But for seven days he had watched in pleasure as Balomar gorged himself on anything in sight. He broke his fast on hot oats, bread and cold meat for the midday meal, and whatever roasted meat was on offer for dinner. That, combined with a lethal amount of ale, had seen the king return to his former spirits.

Adalwin turned over in his sheepskin blanket. It itched through his tunic, leaving long thin red marks all over his body. He looked as though he had been attacked by a cat. He hated cats. Sighing again, he rolled back, facing away from the hearth. Balomar was this side of him, arse facing towards him. The king farted, loud and long, the sound bringing to mind a pig being sat on by a butcher as they struggled to hold it steady as they reached round its neck with their blade. The smell brought to mind the stink of a pig's bowels when opened by the butcher's blade.

He sat up, deciding that braving the cold to piss was better than smelling his king's arse. He groped in the darkness for his trousers, shivered as the cold bit at his bones when he threw away the blankets. A flash of light to the right caught his attention. The door to the hall had been opened, and a man crept silently through, quickly followed by more.

Adalwin froze, one leg in his yellow trousers – the colour of the Marcomanni – the other bare in the darkness. The men fanned out, their footsteps making a light thud on the wooden floor. *Men back from their shift on watch?* He tried to remember if a watch had actually been set. He had said to Balomar on their arrival that he had been uncomfortable staying in an unwalled village as anyone could just wander in when the sun was down and darkness ruled the land. He thought harder, running through the night's events in his mind. *There wasn't a watch.* A flash of naked iron glinted off the hearth's embers.

'Get up! Get up! Arm yourselves!' He heard the first wet thump as the shadows began to slaughter the men at their feet. Around him, the sleepers began to stir. 'Get up you whoresons! Intruders! Protect the king!' Balomar had only brought ten men with him, insisting he needed no more to travel through Germania's heartland. Adalwin had hand-picked the men himself, the hardest and bravest of the king's household troops, his hearth warriors. They were the few who earned their coin from war; it wasn't a duty to fulfil that kept them from ploughing their fields.

They were the first out their blankets, fumbling for their iron in the darkness. Adalwin stood over his king, one leg either side of his great bulk. He hefted his hastily grabbed spear in his hand and wished he knew where his shield was. 'Adalwin, what in the gods' name are you doing?' The king was groggy, the ale clouding his thought box. He stumbled to a sitting position, nearly cried aloud when his face hit Adalwin's bare arse. *Fucking serves you right,* the king's captain thought.

'We're being attacked, my lord, get up quick!' Balomar responded quickly to that, shaking the ale from his head he rose unsteadily to his feet, clumsy hands finding the hilt of his sword.

And then there were men all around them – Marcomanni, Sidones, Osi and Avareni, they had all rallied to Adalwin's call. The hall was almost pitch black. He could just make out the shadows as they hacked and slashed their way towards him.

'Who are they?!' A cry from behind him, voicing the question at the front of everyone's thought box. 'Who cares,' someone snarled, 'just fucking kill 'em!'

A heartbeat later they were defending for their lives. Adalwin tried to count the shadows but had no time to go past five. A huge man attacked him. Adalwin had always prided himself on his height, but this man dwarfed him. The man's blade flashed in the gloom. Adalwin thrust his spear shaft up in hope and was relieved to feel the blade bite the centre of the shaft. It was cleaved in two.

Taking a step back, now with a wooden shaft in his left hand and the leaf point in his right, he squatted down and leapt at his opponent. He feinted high with his right and hooked the wooden shaft up with his left, a raking cut that started on his assailant's knee and finished on his groin. Had it been with the leaf-shaped iron it would have been a death blow. Although even with just the splintered wood, Adalwin was encouraged by the sensation of warm blood spilling down his arm. He danced forwards on the balls of his feet, hopping from left to right as he sought to dazzle his opponent with his speed. This time a feint with his left and a jab with his right, the blade rebounding of an armoured torso.

His opponent staggered back, edging further towards the hearth's embers, a sliver of light revealing the man's appearance. His skin darker than the night, all Adalwin could see of his face was the whites of his eyes under his helmet's rim. The man grimaced in pain, there was a flash of teeth, and then he launched himself at Adalwin. A feint with the man's sword then a crushing blow found Adalwin's cheek as his assailant's fist connected with awesome power. Adalwin fell back, hitting the man behind him, friend or foe he did not know. He used the body to propel himself forwards, growling in anger as he dived in for the killing blow. His spear point rebounded off the flat of a blade. He swiped his left arm in anger, the splintered edge of the wood cutting deep into the dark man's face. His assailant screamed in pain. Adalwin didn't hesitate, following the blow with a jab to the neck with his spear tip, rejoicing in the familiar sensation of iron penetrating flesh and the sucking noise a man's skin makes as he pulled the blade back out. Blood gushed from the wound, a deep red glow in the blackness. The man dropped back onto the hearth without a sound.

'I've got her! Let's go! Let's go!' Habitus crouched with knife in one hand and bloodied gladius in the other. He swivelled on the balls of his feet, leapt over the corpse behind him and sprinted for the door. He was the first there. Sheathing his blades he drew his bow, notched an arrow and waited in the shadows to cover his brothers.

He counted them off as they shuffled past. First Fullo, blood spattering his face. Then Longus with a grin straight from Hades. Rullus' great bulk was next – he patted the Syrian on the arm as he passed. Bucco laboured to the door, a bundle wrapped over his shoulders. 'Fuck me, she ain't dead, is she?'

'Had to do something to stop her trying to fight me! Come, brother, let's go!'

'No Libo yet, brother!'

'He's dead! I saw him fall!'

Libo? Dead? 'Or Albinus!'

Bucco stopped, cursed, and launched the wrapped bundle out the door. 'Someone get her!' He sprinted back into the hall's darkness. Habitus cursed under his breath and followed. The hall stank of stale ale, sweat and blood. It had smelt a lot worse than when they had first entered, the stink of open veins seeming to have over powered the aroma of reverberating bowels.

The dead were everywhere, a hazard in the gloom. Habitus skipped over two corpses before someone grabbed at his feet. *Not a corpse!* He thrust down with the arrow, punching through the now dead man's eye. Moving on, he notched the bloodied arrow to the string and let it fly at a whirl of movement to his left. There was a thump as the body hit the timber. Too dark for the bow now, he slung it back over his shoulder and ripped his sword from its sheath. A man screamed as he charged him. Habitus side-stepped the assault and slashed the blade down the back of his attacker's neck. A spray of claret spattered his face.

He was confronted by a ring of blades, all bearing down on him. But Habitus noticed none of the men were looking towards him, all eyes diverted to their left. Looking to his right, Habitus stifled a scream as he saw Albinus locked in combat with a barrel of a man. His torso was huge, arms bigger than Habitus' thighs, great wide legs rooted to the timber, yellow trousers glowing in the dim firelight. He had a huge great beard, a hint of red, wild eyes bulging from the sockets. He whirled his longsword in a savage arc that Albinus just dodged, the thrust forwards with his own blade catching nothing but air.

Habitus despaired. The man was both broader and taller than Albinus, and his blade twice as long. The Syrian could see no way the young legionary was going to be able to step inside the longsword's arc to do any damage.

Another lunge from the barbarian, this time from high to low. Albinus side-stepped it neatly and flew in with his sword outstretched. There was a howl of pain as the gladius ripped through the big man's bicep. Spears moved in the darkness, a press of bodies around the big barbarian. Habitus stood transfixed, his brain unable to tell his body to move. Bucco was more alert. He took advantage of the distraction and grabbed Albinus by the arms and hauled him back towards the door. 'Jupiter's shining cock, Habitus! Help me!'

The Syrian woke from his daze and sprinted to catch up with the big Pannonian. They reached the door in no time, falling through it in a wave of flesh and armour. Habitus breathed in deep the night air, a vague smell of pine welcome on his nostrils after the heavy stink in the hall. None of the three men paused in the moonlight, the distant shapes of their comrades entering the woods to the west ahead of them as they sprinted to catch up. Roars of anger loud in his ears, a crash as men forced their way out the hall, Habitus didn't dare look back.

VIII

January AD 169 – Legionary Fortress of Carnuntum, Pannonia

Hobnailed sandals clanging on the cobbles, Taurus marched briskly down the paved road. He nodded curtly to the sentries standing guard outside the entrance to the Principia, and passed through the pillared portico into the inner courtyard.

It was bustling within, slaves and clerks running through the throng, each man and woman focused only on their own tasks. Taurus paused, taking a few heartbeats to absorb it all in: the day-to-day hustle of the army, the only life he had known. He tried and failed to envisage a life without it, shaking his head and rubbing his eyes. Could he settle down, find a wife and farm a patch of land? He didn't think so, but then he imagined Silus having the same thoughts as he approached the day of his discharge. But Taurus still had ten years until that day dawned, and the prospect of a long and drawn-out war with the tribes to survive.

He shook his head, clearing it of thoughts and dreams of the distant future. He moved through the courtyard, pausing by one of the stone pillars to let a clerk loaded with scrolls and tablets pass. The man mumbled his thanks, bowing his head as he did. Maximianus, he knew, would have scorned him for letting a mere clerk have the right of way. Life was all about discipline for the legate – and respecting your superiors. Taurus was all for it, especially with the men of his cohort. But sometimes it paid to not be an arse.

83

He turned right when he got to the rear, into a shaded corner under the red-tiled rooftop. The sun never managed to kiss the cobbles with its warmth, and it was noticeably colder than the rest of the courtyard, even with the great brazier roaring and smoking. Again, he nodded to the guards – two men from his own century – and passed through into the darkness of the shrine room.

The place had always held a special kind of magic, a presence in the air, as if the gods themselves were standing guard over the precious golden birds and their standards. Taurus shuddered in the gloom, his breath misting the air in front of him. Telling himself it was just the cold, he walked slowly until he was in the centre of the room, which was lit only by four wicker candles planted a few paces apart in front of the arrayed standards.

Taurus sunk to his knees, mumbling a prayer to Jupiter, Best and Greatest as he did, thanking him for allowing him to serve his beloved eagle. He would know it anywhere, would be able to pick it out in a room full of eagles gathered from every legion across the breadth of the empire. It stood proudly in the lamplight, the orange flicker of the flames shimmering off its polished edges. As always, Taurus marvelled at how something so beautiful could be moulded from a slab of gold. Its wings were gilded, each swirl of feathers exquisitely carved; a short neck atop a round body, huge eyes that seemed to pierce straight through him, to know what he was thinking, feeling; a beak set in what could have been a frown, an imperious expression that Taurus thought made the bird look even more impressive.

Stepping forward, he smiled as he saw the familiar notches in the gold, remembering how they were made. There was one just under the right wing, taken in a battle in the east of Germania. The Iazyges had raided into Dacia, killing and raping as they went. The Fourteenth had been sent into their lands to wait for their return; they had crushed them on their own turf. The Fourteenth's aquilifer at the time – Taurus struggled to remember his name – had been wounded early in the fighting. Taurus had been in the rank behind him, and had leapt forward and snatched the legion's symbol as the man fell to the ground. Heartbeats later he had been in the front rank, and had used the golden bird to block a spear thrust that was destined for his throat.

Taurus smiled wider as he remembered Silus raging at him when the fighting was done, cursing him for putting the eagle in danger. 'What was I supposed to do? Just stand there and die?!' His retort had earned him five lashes, and taught him a valuable lesson about army life. *Juno's tits! What was that man's name?* Still he couldn't remember, it seemed a very long time ago now.

A disturbance behind him, the slap of hobnailed feet on the cobbles, and Legate Maximianus entered, head bowed in reverence. 'Sir!' Taurus snapped to attention, feet clicking together, arms locked by his side.

'At ease, brother. I apologise, the sentries didn't say there was anyone in here. I shall leave you to your prayers.' The legate turned to leave, his white cloak glowing a shade of blue in the lamp light. Rank didn't matter when a soldier was praying to the eagle; only officers were allowed to enter the guarded shrine, but no one could then order them to leave.

'It's okay, sir, I'll go. I was just leaving anyway,' Taurus lied as he made to leave, nodding his head as he passed his commanding officer, but Maximianus stopped him with a firm hand on his shoulder.

'Stay, brother, pray with me.' Taurus was unsure, uncomfortable doing something so personal with a man he had no real relationship with outside their professional capacity. The centurion nodded, reluctant but not willing to disobey, even if it wasn't an order.

Both men turned to the altar and kneeled, each man keeping his head bowed and eyes closed. Taurus was uncomfortable, suddenly wanting to be away from the room. He had never spent much time alone with Maximianus, and wondered if it was intimidation he felt, but shook it off. *Ain't no man who can put me in a corner.* He exhaled heavily, thinking if it would be impolite to leave. Had he stayed long enough?

'You seem tense, brother, what ails you?' The legate's words were quiet. He hadn't moved, head still facing the carpeted floor.

'Just a lot going on, sir – new recruits to train for the spring, Bacchius and his lads still settling in, paperwork overloading my desk. Nothing out of the ordinary though.' Taurus had been recruiting heavily in the last few weeks, desperately trying to get the legion to near full strength for the coming campaign. So far he had got the numbers up to four cohorts, which was nothing short of a miracle given that conscription was never popular. But, needs must.

But most of the young lads he had dragged in were soft; they snivelled in their armour and shook with the wind. Taurus knew they would not be ready to fight come spring, and that a lot of them would die the first time they saw combat, but there was only so much he and his officers could do.

'Speaking of paperwork,' the legate continued, 'Felix and I still have not received any word as to the whereabouts of your eight missing men.' Taurus felt his heart thud like thunder in his chest. His ears were red hot and for a moment he was concerned they might actually be bleeding. 'How much easier would your life be if you had eight of your most experienced veterans in your cohort to help settle in the fresh meat?' Maximianus was looking at his First Spear now, an eyebrow raised in question.

Taurus grunted, clearing his throat. Maximianus raised a hand. 'Don't bother to tell me they're ill, First Spear. I've had Felix make some enquiries. He tells me one of the cavalry auxiliaries saw young Albinus tethering a horse back in November, but the lad wouldn't tell him why. And then, according to this auxiliary, you barge into the stables, the other seven men of his contubernium at your back, and send them all trudging off north over the bridge. What are you up to?'

Taurus said nothing, shame and embarrassment consuming him. He felt his face go red. 'I … I … err …' It wasn't often the First Spear of the Fourteenth Legion was dumbfounded.

'Spit it out, brother! Whatever it is I'm hardly going to string you up on charges! We both know the legion would be lost without you!' Again, Taurus blushed; it was rare praise from the legate. He took a deep breath, and told the legate everything. There was a long pause of silence when he was done.

Eventually, Maximianus broke the tension by barking a laugh. 'Ha! This young man Albinus, he has made some effect on you, eh?'

'Yes, sir, he has. He is so much more than he thinks. You should have seen the wounds he took in the battle against the tribes – a dislocated shoulder and half his face ripped off by a spear. And still, Abas tells me, he fought like a lion in the square as we cut our way back here. The lad seems to have spent his entire childhood resenting his father. But Silus' death has brought out everything in him the old man would have wanted him to be. He would have been so proud to see his son handle himself the way he did against the tribes.'

'He impressed me, too, when I took him and his friend Fullo over the river to scout for their army.' It had been Albinus who had first encountered Balomar and his force. He had been over the river the day after he had learnt it had been a girl matching Licina's description that had escaped from Carnuntum. He had set off to search for her, but had found a horde of barbarians instead. 'He is intelligent, slow to speak but quick of mind. I could see him following in his father's footsteps. Do you know I wish I'd met him.'

'Silus?'

'Who else! How long since he left the legion? And still all anyone speaks of is him! He must have been some man.'

'He was. Truly fearsome, he didn't even have to speak to the men in his cohort, just the way he looked at you would either have you standing taller than the gods or shrivelling into your mail.' Taurus laughed, a smile of affection fixed his face. 'He was the greatest I ever served with, the greatest I ever will serve with. I try every day to live by the standards he set, to lead by example and accept nothing but perfection from my men.' Taurus looked down as he spoke, unsure if he was living up to the high expectations he installed in himself.

'You are the finest First Spear a legate could ever hope to have. I really mean that. You are the first man out on the drill field of a morning, and the last to leave. And as for your handling of your cohort in battle!' Maximianus shook his head with a wry grin upon his face. 'Although you sometimes go … a bit over the top shall we say? You always lead from the front, always the first to wet your iron. The men see that, and respect it.' Taurus knew the over-the-top comment referred to the battle the legion fought to defeat the tribes from the original raid onto Roman lands last winter. A full legion's strength of barbarians had crossed the Danube and laid waste to the farming settlement run by Silus. The former First Spear had died trying to protect the citizens within, so had all his men.

So blinded by rage, Taurus had pushed his cohort hard as the battle lines drew together, forcing them so far forward they were nearly cut off from their neighbouring cohort. Taurus himself had felt the raw emotion of the battle so strongly he had been blind to the danger, and had pushed into the enemy ranks on his own, slashing and hacking a bloody path across the field until he met with a crop of woodland. It had been a miracle he hadn't been killed.

The centurion nodded slowly, flushed with the praise from his commanding officer. 'So you are not angry at me for sending my boys north?'

Again, the legate smiled. 'I fear it may be a fool's errand, and there is a chance they won't return. But you let your heart rule you, make the decision for you. I think you did the right thing, the gods only know what would have happened to Albinus if you hadn't.'

'But I may have killed eight of my own men! At least, that's how it feels right now.'

'Don't be hard on yourself. You never know, they might bump into Balomar on their journey north. It would save us a job if they could fill him with iron!' Taurus laughed politely.

'You heard any news of the tribes?' said Taurus, seeking to move the conversation on.

'I have. Apparently the Quadi have agreed to ally themselves to us, their new king not being a fan of Balomar. Must have something to do with him taking the head of his predecessor! They have agreed to let us cross into their lands, which will give us a bridgehead for an assault.'

'So the army will march north?'

'Almost certainly. And our esteemed Augustus will be here to lead the advance in person. I'd waged that Balomar and his little friends will be pissing in their breeches when they hear there are nearly twenty thousand men let loose in their homeland come spring! Bring it on, brother, bring it on.'

'So let me get this right,' said Balomar, sitting astride his huge black stallion. 'You believe, that the men that attacked us back in Carrodunum were Roman. And that one of their number was *probably* a man named Albinus, who is on his way north to a place called Rugnum, where he believes his lost love Licina – also my former slave – is being held captive by the local

88

tribe.' He rode with no hands on the reins, letting the horse pick its steps over the rough, boggy terrain.

'Well … yes,' said Adalwin, aware it sounded presumptuous at best.

'And you think this because when you followed the girl to the north, you saw her being manhandled onto a ship that sailed out across the grey water. And the man that threw her on there is our old friend Alaric, who we both thought was dead until now.'

'Yes.' Adalwin felt his cheeks glow red as he saw the amused expression on his king's face.

'And Alaric told you …' Balomar didn't try to conceal his laugh, '… the noble and trustworthy gentleman that he is, that he had unfinished business with this Abinus, and that he had bribed a Roman merchant to deliver a letter to the young legionary. This letter would state it was from Licina, and that she was being held at this northern place, and ask Albinus to come and rescue her?'

'Yes,' said Adalwin, a tired strain to his voice.

'And you believed him?'

'I did. It is the type of thing the old loner would do.'

'And, assuming this is all true of course, you believe that this Abinus will be stupid enough to fall for Alaric's trick? That he will come galloping through winter to save the women of his dreams?' The king barked a laugh as he spoke the last words. He jaunted in the saddle, the horse slipping on an ice-covered stone. He winced as a lance of pain burst up his arm, where the deep cut from the sword in the dark had pierced his bicep.

'All I'm saying, my lord, is that we were attacked by eight Roman soldiers—'

'We don't know they were Roman!'

'The dead man, the black man, he was definitely Roman. I know none had shields but all had mail, Roman-style helmets and fought with their stupid little short swords. They had to be Roman!'

'Okay.' Balomar chewed his captain's words over in his head. 'So, they were Roman. How do we know they are going north? They made off with that girl, so in my mind they had come from the Cogni. They weren't there to kill me, I doubt they even knew who I was! No, they were there for her. The forming of an alliance perhaps? The Romans get back the girl and the Cogni side with Rome come spring?' It was the only thing that made sense to Balomar.

'Maybe. But why prioritise an alliance with the Cogni? They are far away from the border, a tribe of no real consequence. There are at least a dozen other tribes that it would make more sense for Rome to target. Just doesn't feel like the reason.'

'Well what then?'

'I don't know. A chance meeting on their journey north perhaps? Get the girl back in exchange for a guide north?'

The conversation ebbed away. They were riding east from Carrodunum into the territory of the Iazyges. Balomar had requested a meeting with Bandanasp, their chief, and he had agreed to meet. They were on the plains now, two days into their journey. The wind was ferocious; it bit into their bones and caused the horses to sway with its motion. The snow hadn't stopped since the previous evening, and although it hadn't been strong enough to lay, each man was soaked through, heads nestled in hoods as they shivered in their cloaks. There were just five of them now – Balomar, Adalwin and three of the king's warriors. Seven of the ten they had brought with them from Goridorgis had been killed in the night raid at Carrodunum.

Balomar frowned with fear and sadness as he thought of the men. It would be hard when they finally rode back through the wooden gates of Goridorgis, facing the expectant faces of the wives and children of the dead men, eager to welcome their loved ones home. He had never been any good at delivering bad news. Adalwin would volunteer to do it for him he knew, but there were some things a king should do himself.

A sudden commotion began to his front, raised voices and the rasp of swords being thrust from their scabbards. Cursing the wind and snow, Balomar threw back his hood and squinted into the distance. Two of his men were ahead, iron bared as they spoke with four horsemen, each with a spear readied in his palm. Urging his giant stallion on, he pushed through his men to confront the newcomers.

'I am Balomar, king of the Marcomanni. Who are you to challenge me on the road?' Road was a bit rich, he thought even as he spoke it. *Oh to have the flat cobbles of Rome.* The path they had been following was mud, of sorts. It was sleet mixed with gravel and dirt, and to call it treacherous was polite. Put that together with the winding valleys they were travelling through and it was thanks to the gods that one of the horses hadn't lamed itself on a loose rock or puddle of slush.

The men were from the Iazyges, and had been sent east to meet the king on the road and guide him to their chief. Without delay, Balomar ordered them to lead the way. He was cold, wet and hungry, and wanted to be on the road no longer than was necessary.

The snow had stopped before nightfall, and as the sun set Balomar found himself sitting in a lavishly decorated hall, surrounded by slaves, fine wine and fresh meat. He shared a glance with Adalwin, full of contempt, then fixed his face into a smile as Bandanasp entered the hall from his private quarters to the rear.

The hall had a rich aroma of freshly cut timber; looking around, the king could see the light shade of the wood on the walls, confirming that it was newly built. He thought of his own hall in Goridorgis, half the size and the wood blackening with decay. A wave of envy washed over him, and anger. *How much gold did this weasel keep from the raid on Dacia?* The chief of the Iazyges had told him that the carts he had brought back from the east contained everything he had pillaged on their raid. Balomar's surroundings told a different story.

He watched as slaves wrapped in gold-fringed cloaks served wine and ale to the revellers at the tables. Saw the sparkling silver eating knives resting on serving trays of shimmering bronze. A beautifully woven tapestry hung from the eastern wall, and Balomar gazed upon a figure whom he assumed was Apollo in his golden chariot pulling the sun up from behind a dazzling blue ocean.

On the high table where he sat in the place of honour at the right hand side of the host, was a vase of bluest glass, engraved with swirling flowers and blossoming trees, and inside which were chunks of gold, glowing red behind the glass. *My gold.* He stared at it, hands shaking in rage. He knew he needed to control his temper. On more than one occasion already this winter his anger had cost him the support of potential allies. But he didn't care.

He glanced down the hall, to where Adalwin, sitting on one of the lower tables with the remaining men of his household guard, also glowered in spite. The king watched as his captain looked round the hall, making sure there were no eyes upon him, then swiped his hand across his throat, his feelings clear.

And then Bandanasp was at his side, a broad smile fixed to his heavily bearded face. His straw-yellow hair ran free and wild past his neck, eyes a light shade of blue. His nose was full and rounded, with a thick-lipped mouth that had many missing teeth. He was robed in deep purple, a thick gold torc around his neck; rings covered the skin on his fat fingers. His skin would be pale, if he wasn't so flushed with wine and the warmth of the hearth. 'Brother!' He spread his hands out wide, sweeping them back in to grab at Balomar's shoulders. 'I hope your journey was as good as it could have been at this time of year?'

Brother? Balomar wanted to rip the man's hands from his shoulders, vault from his chair and scoop up one of those precious silver knives, and rip it across this whoreson's throat. *Brother? I am the only king in this hall!* He looked back down to Adalwin, who smiled sickly at the outraged look on his king's face.

'*Chief* Bandanasp, son of Euric, lord of the Iazyges and loyal allies of the Marcomanni, you seem to be doing well for yourself.' He rose slowly from his chair. He was a full head taller than his counterpart, and a great deal broader. He felt his hand itch for the leather-wrapped grip of his sword, which he had surrendered, as all men did, upon entry to the hall. He watched in pleasure as Bandanasp winced slightly, then licked his lips uncertainly.

'I am, lord king. I have spent *my* share of our summer's venture well, don't you think?' He bowed slightly, his purple cloak falling back behind his hips revealing a short sword belted on his right side. The hilt was gold.

Balomar bit his tongue, literally. The familiar metallic taste as blood welled in his mouth, and he swallowed it back. He sucked his teeth at the pain, grimacing. He had not spent his whole share of the gold, but what he had spent had gone on food for his people to last the winter, fresh clothing to keep them warm. He hadn't spent a drop on himself. He was a king, a leader, and nothing without the people he ruled. He had promised them last spring when he launched his plan for war with Rome that things would get better. And he had stood by that promise.

'I see you have spent it lavishly, and quickly. I would not say well.' His tone was gruff, dismissive and curt. He'd meant it to be.

'Oh?' Bandanasp pursed his lips, a flicker of anger in his eyes, but it was gone in a heartbeat.

'I walked through your gates to see soldiers standing guard in nothing but tunics and thin cloaks. I saw people on your streets with no shoes; they seemed to have no shelter for the dark and cold nights. Three people dropped to their knees as I passed and begged for food. I felt sympathy for you then as I rode through that hovel.' He paused, shaking his head in shame. 'I, too, just last winter had people I could not feed and clothe, who glared at me in anger and envy whenever I rode down to my gates. I fretted all through the long, dark winter, and insisted on letting as many of them into my hall as I could squeeze. Was all I could do.' He shrugged, sad eyes remembering the toughest months of his kingship. 'You see you may not know, chief, but I wasn't born a king. I wasn't raised in a grand hall, with slaves to dote on my every need. My father was a blacksmith, as good an iron worker as you will ever meet. He forged my sword for me when I reached manhood.

'You see in the Marcomanni, leaders are not born, they're made. Our old king was a cruel man, selfish. He was hated and feared. When he died, the people gathered at Goridorgis to crown a new king, who would lead them into better times. That man was me.' He leant right in to Bandanasp, until his breath warmed the chief's cheeks, stabbing fiercely with his finger at his own puffed out chest. 'I made a promise to do what is right for my people, not just for me. I did not enter this war with Rome out of personal greed, but out of necessity. We live in a time of famine and plague, where as many people die of empty bellies as they do of the sickening disease. Last year, when the sun finally melted the snow, and the trees began to blossom, I swore to Wotan I would never see another winter where my people suffered the way they had. Never again would I allow them to starve or freeze to a lonely death. I'm here for the good of the people, all the people of the tribes. And I thought my brothers leading our other tribes felt the same way. And then I came here and saw you.'

The hall was silent, the cracking of the burning logs on the hearth the only sound. People stood with mouths wide open, shocked at the exchange between king and chieftain. In his anger, Balomar didn't notice the watching crowd. 'You, Bandanasp, son of chief Euric, son of some other chief, have never gone hungry, never wanted for anything. And here you stand, in your grand new hall, robed in purple and covered in gold. MY FUCKING GOLD!' Spittle flew from his mouth to speck Bandanasp's cheeks, who stood rigid in fear. 'You sicken me. Your people starve and freeze whilst you live like a king in the warm. You are no king, no leader of men. You are a son of a whore, a worm, and it gladdens my heart that you will not ride with me come spring. I have no need of curs like you.'

Without another word, the king turned and stormed past the crowded benches towards the door. Adalwin and his men got up hastily to follow, grins fixed their faces.

'Wait!' Bandanasp finally found his voice. 'You need me, Balomar!'

'Why would I need a weasel like you?' Balomar roared like a lion, full of gravel.

'Because I can get you the Naristae, all of them!'

Balomar paused, his anger subsiding as his interest piqued. The Naristae were the only tribe in southern Germania who could put as many spears in the field as the Marcomanni, apart from the Quadi, who Balomar could no longer call allies.

'How?'

'With a marriage, brother,' the chief of the Iazyges said through a sickly smile. 'Your marriage.'

IX

Snow fell in flurries. It whirled in the wind and lashed her face. Squinting through its murk, she paused, listening for the screams, the clash of iron. All she could hear was the storms howl.

A crack of lightning; an explosion of light; the low growl of thunder. Licina stood alone, lost, at the mercy of the gods. She staggered forwards in the snow, booted feet squelching and sliding as she struggled through wretched terrain. Her sword still bared, she had yet to use it in anger; shield shaking in her left hand, eyes flittering left and right. A scream came, but from where?

She stood, still as a rooted tree, eyes closed as she focused all her energy on finding her sisters. The shieldmaidens, they were out here somewhere, lost on this frozen plain, and they were dying.

Men had attacked, when winter had taken a turn for the worse. They had streamed from the dark forests to the north, laying waste to all in their path. The chief was sending an army north, or so the story went. But Heide had not wanted to wait for the men. They were the shieldmaidens, warriors of the Fates, they would repel the raiders.

So north they had gone, running like night shadows as they streamed across the frozen land. Until they had found them – a small party of men, black cloaks and shields, the glisten of mail as the pale winter sun reflected its light. That had been the day before. They should have attacked straight away, Licina knew. But Heide had wanted to wait, let the shieldmaidens recover their strength and rest a night. They had woken to the fury of Donar.

As she stood, frozen in her tracks, there came another snap in the air and a burst of light below the angry black clouds. The thunder was so close Licina could feel the ground shake when it snarled. *This truly is the land of gods.* Even as she thought the lightning struck again, a white light that plummeted like a spear from the heavens and cracked into the snow ahead of her.

And there they were: a huddle of brown cloaks, surrounded by black shadows. She stumbled through the snow, battled against the howling wind. She could hear it now, the clash of iron, the raised voices, shouts of triumph and screams of despair.

Twenty paces away, she could make out the individuals. Heide stood front and centre, no shield, sword in one hand, spear in the other. Gisila was next to her, shield and spear working in savage unison. Even as she watched the warrior woman raked her spear tip through a bearded man's throat.

In their midst now, a sudden ferocious blood lust upon her, she leapt into the fray. Crashing her shield into a black cloak, she lunged forwards with her sword and felt the edge bite his mail. The man staggered back, face set in a snarl as he growled in anger. He regained his footing and made his own lunge. An axe head shone as he swung it back over his head and sent it crashing down towards Licina's skull. She raised her shield, blocking the blow, but the force of the impact sent sharp pain shooting up her arm. She screamed, stepped back and dropped her shield to the ground.

The black cloak smelt blood now, victory near. He smiled as he vaulted forwards, sending his shield boss smashing into Licina's face. Light exploded behind her eyes, the crunch and twist of bone as her nose snapped, blood welling in her mouth. She spat claret on the white carpet as she fell to the ground, head indented in the snow.

Get up! GET UP! She knew she was dead if she didn't, but she couldn't make her body follow her mind's command. Her left arm, elbow to shoulder, was an torment of pain. It seemed to flow with her blood, up to her shoulder, before shooting down past her elbow. The snapped bone of her nose felt numb, which was a relief, but she wondered if that was because it was buried in snow. It was quiet with her head buried beneath the surface, the battle a distant roar, as if it was being fought in another land.

She thought of Albinus, wondered if he'd made the hopeless journey to the north of Germania only to find himself at the sharp end of Alaric's blade. She prayed to all the gods, Roman and not, that he had stayed at home, with his friends in the legion. She smiled into the mush, cold on her teeth and lips. *Live my love. Live and be happy.* She waited for the chop of the axe that would end her life.

Muffled voices, distant, like echoes in her mind. Shouts and screams, wails and cries. Hands on her back, under her arms and on her shoulders. A cold palm on her face, the spasm of pain after the slap. The burn of red skin against the icy wind. She opened her eyes, just for a heartbeat. Heide was shouting, her face a vicious snarl. Blood-spattered cloak and mail, matted in her yellow hair. Licina tried to speak, to ask what was happening. All that came out was a croak, her throat burned. She felt dizzy, the light faded with Heide's face. She tried to fight it, to climb out from the impending darkness, but it swallowed her. She didn't feel her chin slap against her chest.

Her eyes snapped open, she sucked in air, almost choking as it froze her lungs. It was dark, black shadows of pine rising towards clouds that rolled like the waves. Snow was falling in flurries, carried on a southerly wind. It slapped against the bare skin of her face and seemed to stick. She tried to rise, shake off the white powder that covered her, but her arms had no strength, and she slumped back to the ground. Snowflakes flew into the air like dust, a white cloud erupting in the blackness of the night. A cry of alarm, the pad of booted feet on the snow, breath warm on her neck, cold palms on her face.

'Licina! You're awake at last!' Heide's voice, weary yet joyful, she sounded like a cat had scratched her voice box.

'Where am I?' Licina's voice was just a whisper, an intense pain in her throat. Her nose felt funny, tingling in the cold. She reached up her hand, probing gently. White hot agony ripped through her, the pain in her throat made worse by her scream.

'Don't move my love, don't move. You were knocked out by a shield thrust, your nose is broken. You've been in and out of consciousness for four days now!' Tears wetted Heide's cheeks, her wet eyes glowed like gem stones. Her smile was dazzling.

'Four days?' Questions came and went in her mind: Had they won the battle? Was everyone else alive? Where were they? Did she just call me 'my love'?

'Hush, hush, be quiet now, rest. We can talk later. I will get you some food and water. It will hurt to eat and drink, but you must. You've had nothing since you were wounded.' With that she was off, scuttling away into the darkness.

Licina lay back and looked up at the whirling cloud. There was a certain beauty in its savageness. It danced like a wild cub, tumbling and leaping, answered to no master, bowed to no god, and bit like a battle-hardened wolf.

Soon Heide was back with a flask of water and a simple meal of bread and cheese. The bread was rock hard and stale, the cheese half frozen. Licina did her best to chew without the pain becoming so intense she wanted to vomit, and nodded as she listened to the tale of events from the last few days.

The shieldmaidens had taken heavy losses in the battle against the black cloaks. Licina could remember nothing of the day of the battle, let alone the fighting itself. 'We lost you in the first fight, not far onto the frozen plain. We pushed them back and we pursued, which was our mistake. When you found us again we were outnumbered and nearly surrounded. It was the will of the Fates that we survived.'

'How did we get away?' Again, her voice was no more than a croak.

'We ran! Dragging you with us of course! You were face down in the snow. We made a circle of shields and backed away. The black cloaks seemed to have no heart for the hunt, thank the gods. We are back in the forest now, by the well. The chief rode by with his army two days ago. He seemed angry that we had started the battle without waiting for him.' Heide paused, frowning. 'His warriors thought it funny that a bunch of women had attacked armed men. They won't find it so funny when they come across the corpses we left behind.' There was a touch of pride in her voice.

'What do we do now?' asked Licina, wincing at the agony in her throat and nose.

'Wait. Let the brothers fight it out, let winter turn to spring, then we'll see.'

'What?'

'Who's left alive, who rules. Then we'll know where we stand.'

Licina frowned, confused. There seemed to be so much she wasn't aware of, so much she wasn't being told. Why would the shieldmaidens need to know where they stood? They lived in the lands of Chief Sigivald, he was their lord and they lived under his protection. Surely they stood with him? She looked at Heide, who knelt with her head bowed and eyes closed. What were the Norns showing her? What fate did they have instore for her and the other women?

Will this cursed winter ever end? His green cloak was soaked with the flurrying snow, the metal clasp digging into his neck as the waters weight dragged the cloak ever down. His black hair, usually slicked back and tied in a neat bun atop his head, was wild and curly and freezing water streamed down the curls to numb his face.

The Thracian was well used to cold winters, the lands to the west of Byzantium being well known for their harsh climate, but this winter it seemed had lasted a lifetime. It was mid-February now he reckoned as he cantered along the cobbles atop a giant black stallion, probably already past the Ides. But still the snow tumbled onto him day after day, still the winds were thwart with ice and hale, the landscape barren and lifeless. Back home, the racing factions of Byzantium would be getting ready for the Equirria, the first of two days of racing dedicated to Mars. Chariot racing was a religion to many of the poor that lived in the empire's major cities; the factions were not just teams, they were the law. Protection rackets, wine smuggling, robbery, assault, you could get anything you wanted if you knew where to ask.

Cocconas had always followed the Greens, the team so famously loved by the Emperor Nero. There had been a driver during his childhood, a slim but muscled Egyptian called Medhu, and Cocconas had worshipped him as much as the man himself worshipped the sun. He had worn a golden cuirass under his deep green cloak – the cloak Cocconas himself wore had been cut from the same cloth. His skin was bronzed and his hair deep and dark. He had been the lord of the race track, unbeatable on the sand-made straights. He wondered if the Egyptian still lived, or whether he had met his end atop his chariot, green cloak whirling behind him as he yanked the reins and whipped his stallions as they dragged him round the sharp bend. It would have been a fitting end for the man, he thought.

The Equirria had always signalled the end of winter and the arrival of spring. He could remember standing atop his stool and marvelling at the sun as it glinted off Medhu and his golden breastplate. A fresh aroma of pollen would fill his nostrils, pockets of pink and purple appearing in the trees as the budding flowers began to creep out from their winter hiding holes. It was a day of new life, new beginnings, always one of his favourite of the year.

But this year it appeared the day would not be marked by a warming sun or the fresh colours of spring; it promised to be another dull day of slate grey clouds and barraging winds. Winter, it seemed, was not yet ready to release its grip upon the land.

He looked about him, squinting through the haze. He was travelling south and west, although there was no sun to confirm it. A faint smell of salt wafted on the breeze, the only sign he knew he was edging closer to his destination. His master was at Aquileia, a stone fortress of a city at the tip of Italy. It was the city that in the end had defeated Balomar and his marauding barbarians, as they had discovered they were no match for high stone walls topped with Roman artillery.

Alexander of Abonoteichos had spent the winter in Italy, first travelling south to Rome and then slowly making his way north. He had originally wanted to seek passage with the emperors when they marched north in the spring, but the unfortunate incident with the lions the previous autumn had put an end to that. His master had decided to stay clear of the Augustus Aurelius and his Caesar Verus until enough time had passed for the needless deaths of Roman soldiers to be forgotten.

Cocconas smiled. He wished he had been present when the men of the Fourteenth Legion unleashed two wild lions atop the great bridge at Carnuntum and tried to throw them over the side. From what he had heard, at least one had survived the fall and had swam out the great river and attacked the waiting legionaries. The reports as to how many men had been killed before they struck the lion varied, but it was widely thought at least ten men had lost their lives.

The Thracian's thoughts returned to his recent mission, yet another trip across the northern frontier and into the wild land of Germania. A trip to Bandanasp, a short and sweet meeting in which he had persuaded the chief to meet with Balomar and suggest a marriage to the daughter of the ruler of the Naristae. It had been a blow to his master's plans when the king of the Marcomanni had struck the head from Areogaesus' shoulders, ending the alliance between the Marcomanni and the Quadi. Alexander needed Balomar to have another army at his back come spring. He needed the war to continue if his vision was going to come to fruition. Cocconas had been tasked with keeping it alive.

Once again Cocconas's hand drifted to the leather pouch hidden within his tunic. A sizeable amount of crushed nightshade lay within; he prayed to all the gods it was still dry. He didn't know when or how his master was planning on poisoning the Augustus and his Caesar, but he knew it couldn't happen unless he delivered it to him safe and dry.

Emperor Alexander. The thought filled him with both glee and dread. His master was both cruel and unforgiving. He possessed a thirst for blood that was rarely quenched. He would threaten and manipulate all that stood before him, and as he had proved on more than one occasion, would not hesitate to order a man's death if it would benefit him in some way. Cocconas tried to picture the old man robed in purple, sitting atop a golden throne in the imperial palace atop the palatine hill in Rome. He thought how unsuited his master would be to the role. Alexander was a loner, a quiet man who often preferred his own company to that of others. He rarely removed the hooded cloak from his face; all most people got to see of the soothsayer was his thin lips, a few small yellow teeth and his white beard. He had aged so much in the last two years, the constant travel and scheming had worn him down until his body had shrunk within itself and his skin turned ash grey. His limp was also worse. Cocconas had seen him only the past autumn as he struggled to rise from his bath, his left leg swollen and red.

How old is he anyway? He had been a greybeard when Cocconas had first set eyes upon him, a long ago distant summer's day in the great Greek city of Athens. Already he had stunned the world by proclaiming the arrival of a new god, and then revealing the snake Glycon. Cocconas chuckled into the snow; how anyone still thought the snake to be a god was beyond him. It wasn't even the same snake as the one that Alexander had 'hatched from an egg' all those years ago. The first one had bitten Alexander on the arm, apparently, and he had been bed-bound for over two weeks. Only a local doctor saved him, but only by using an antidote from the poison made up from the snake's blood, so it had been killed. Of course, the doctor was put to death as soon as Alexander was well; it wouldn't do to have word spread around that the founder of the new great god in the east had nearly been killed by the deity he had created.

Through the snow Cocconas could make out the slate grey walls of Aquileia, the red-tiled roofs within. More worries began to swirl in his mind, his heartbeat growing more rapid now his destination was insight. *How is Alexander going to get the support of the legions? Where does he plan to be when he makes his bid for the purple?* East would make sense, his father-in-law was the governor of Asia. Cassius, a man Cocconas knew to be his masters ally, was the governor of Syria. And Senator Avitus, governor of Bithynia, had long been in Alexander's pocket – something about him and young slave boys he would rather keep quiet. Yes, Cocconas thought, the east would make perfect sense. The governors would declare for him, their legions would follow suit. And once he had made a miraculous and sudden peace with Balomar and the coalition of tribes, ending the war in the north, then the Danube legions would follow suit.

Then there's just the Rhine legions, the two in Britannia, one in Spain, one in Africa, Egypt. Sweat trickled down his brow, an icy dread spread from the base of his spine. Too many legions, too many ambitious senators. The years of civil war after the death of Nero should be a reminder to all: no good can come when Roman starts killing Roman.

Avidius Cassius would be the key, Cocconas knew. At a time of plague and famine, so much would depend on who held the grain ships from Egypt. Feed Rome, hold Rome. Simple. Cassius would be tasked with seizing control of the ships and ensuring their prompt arrival at the eternal city once Alexander had one arm in the purple, but could the man be trusted?

He was entering the city gates now – huge great beams of timber, turned black by the constant barrage of ice and hale. A welcome brazier in the gatehouse, Cocconas removed his hood and slowed his horse as he passed, revelling in the warmth. The wind didn't reach the small passage, and it felt good to have a solid ceiling above him, even if it was a wooden battlement lined with archers, arrows pointing tip first at the people entering the city.

Through the inner gate and into the city itself, the aroma of stale shit and piss hit him like a shield boss – frozen sewer passages in need of a good clear-out before the spring. People were everywhere, thronging to and thro as they fought their own mini-battles for superiority on the cobbles; a market to his right, a parade of temples to his left. He jerked his horse away from a light blue litter, a muffled complaint from the slave holding the front left corner. The litter jerked, a scream from within, a hand flying out the curtain to grip the wooden base. 'Careful, you maggots! I'll have you all whipped!' A mumbled apology from the slave, and then the litter was past.

Into the market, he caught fresh smells of spices and herbs, newly baked bread, steaming on shelves as the bakers sweated at their ovens. Too much to resist, Cocconas bought a fresh loaf and some salted ham, devouring both in heartbeats. He tried to think of the last time he'd had a decent hot meal, Bandanasp's hall perhaps?

His horse's hoofs rang loud on the cobbles as he cantered up a hill into a quieter sector of the city. A posh tavern on a corner, a swinging sign with the mark of Apollo above the door – he had reached his destination.

He threw the reins of his horse to a waiting slave, slipping him a bronze coin to ensure the stallion was well fed and watered; it had served his master well this winter. Into the tavern, the rush of warmth was a pure joy. Shedding his cloak, handing it to another waiting slave, he scanned the crowded room, eyes seeking a green cloak that matched his.

In the far right corner, just out of reach of the brazier's light, three green cloaks, brown circular patches embroidered with a snake, he had found his master.

He moved through the packed benches, dense with smells of wine and roasted meat. He wondered momentarily if he should have stopped at the bath house to freshen up before presenting himself, but he was already late and Alexander valued promptness. Leaving the brazier's warmth, squinting through the smoke that rose from it, he nodded to the first of the green cloaks to spot him. Clasping hands with another, he took the seat offered to him, and opened his mouth to ask where Alexander was. His question was answered before he had even asked it.

'Ahh, Cocconas my friend.' That whisper, the husk of it rasped straight through him. 'We were just discussing your imminent arrival, we have much to catch up on, you and I.'

X

February AD 169 – Germania

Mist swirled all around them, shadows lurked in the murk, breath steamed the air to his front, and Albinus ran like he had never run before. Albinus hated running, especially in armour. His chain mail rattled and clanked against his torso, the neck guard at the back of his helmet had now drawn blood on the base of his neck. Each time he bobbed his head it roared in pain. All that he could cope with, had been trained to ignore. But his feet, now that was a whole different kind of agony. He could feel the blisters rip and rub beneath the leather straps, the pain so great he thought he might vomit. The excruciating ache at the soles of his feet were worse, and he knew as soon as he stopped they would cramp up. With the weight of his armour and equipment all pushing down into the soles, the hobnailed sandals offered no protection against the rough and hard terrain he scampered over.

His shoulder screamed at him every time he put his right foot forwards. He had dislocated it in his first battle, when his sword had got stuck in the base of a barbarian's spine. It seemed to be worse in the winter, when the cold seeped right into the joint and the bone roared in disapproval. His jaw ached so much he thought it may be on fire. He knew if he were to gaze upon his reflection the scar would be bright red and livid. The swollen gums from his missing teeth pulsed with every step. He kept managing to forget he had no teeth to chew with, and then cutting the gums back open with his food. The metallic taste in his mouth told him they were bleeding now, and he spat claret on the frozen ground.

Ten days now they had been pursued, since the attack on Carrodunum – ten days of running and fighting. There were six of them now, left from the eight who had set of from Carnuntum at the start of winter. It felt like a lifetime ago.

Their guides had been true to their chief's word, and had stayed with the group, guiding them along a nameless river to the north. They had stayed, and been killed. Three nights ago, their pursuers had attacked their makeshift camp, really nothing more than a few piled-up logs as a perimeter and a fire. The two guides had been the first to die, arrows filling their torsos with holes.

Since then the Romans had ran by day and stood wearily on watch at night, not daring to light a fire for warmth. They were all tired now, freezing and hungry. They had handed the girl over outside Carrodunum, a quick exchange for supplies for the bundled girl. But those supplies had either been lost or consumed, and the group had no time to hunt or scavenge.

This is it. The thud of booted feet on the path behind him, grew louder with every heartbeat. The small party of Romans had reached the end of their stamina, no reserves of energy left to keep them going. Tears welled in Albinus' eyes even as he ran: Libo dead, Calvus unconscious, abandoned in a barbarian hall – all because of him.

I'm not going to reach you, my love. The thought broke his heart: to have come so close, to have survived everything they had, only for it to end now, on some frozen pathway in the middle or nowhere.

A touch on Albinus' shoulder. Looking through red tear-rimmed eyes, Bucco nodded and slowed, his hand still firm on his shoulder. 'Halt!' the veteran ordered, the others all stopping gratefully, stooping over with hands on knees as they sucked in lungsful of air. 'That's it, I ain't running no more!'

Mumbles of agreement followed amongst the coughs and gasps. Albinus rose from his knees, feeling his heart rate slowly subside. 'You should all go,' he said quietly.

'Huh?' Fullo looked up sharply, his scarred forehead glowing silver in the moonlight. 'We're not leaving you, brother.' Grunts of agreement came from the other men.

'You're all here because of me! In this mess because of me! Libo is dead, because of me! And Calvus may well be too. I couldn't bear it if … if …' He couldn't continue, and hot tears steamed as they fell down his frozen skin.

'Well, fuck that!' Habitus hawked and spat. 'I'm here, brother, because I chose to be. Ain't nowhere else I'd wanna be than right here, sword in hand, standing with my brothers.' The others roared their agreement.

'Too right! We're brothers ain't we?!' Bucco stood tall and thumped his fist to his chest. 'I deserted your old man last year, left him and my mates to die so I could go and find you, and bring word to the legion.' It was Bucco's turn to pause, his own tears welling now. 'I loved your father more than I ever loved anyone else. He believed in me, trusted me to keep you safe. And I've failed him.' Protests followed from the others, but Bucco silenced them with a motion of his hand. 'I have, I made him a promise, and I can't keep it. But I'll be damned to Hades if I'm going to leave you here to die! If anything, you should go on, find Licina, leave the army, live long and be happy.'

'As Mars as my witness I will not run off into the night and leave you here! You're my brothers too. Losing my father and Licina, joining the army – I could never have coped without all your support. I know you only did it in memory of my father, but still … I'm grateful.' Again, his blue eyes glistened with moisture, his small button nose scrunching up as he fought back the tears.

'Juno's bleedin' tits! When did you lot become such a bunch of tunic lifters! If you're gonna run, then run! If not, draw your swords and face front!' Rullus roared as if he were screaming at a cohort and not five men. But he was right.

The rumble of feet sounded loud in the darkness, harsh barked words of command as the barbarians swooped in for the kill.

'How many are there d'ya think?' Fullo licked his lips, a nervous twitch in his wrist as he rolled his sword.

'Odds about two to one I reckon.' Longus stared into the darkness, hunched behind an imaginary shield.

'Not the worst odds I've faced in my time.' Bucco's tears were gone now. He looked every inch the veteran, sword steady in his hand, ready to kill. 'Habitus! Got any arrows left?'

'Aye, brother! I'll try and even the odds a bit!'

The first twang of the bow, a thud and scream pierced the blackness.

Albinus stood shaking, trying to calm his nerves. He'd passed out before the battle in the summer. His head had swum and his legs gone wobbly, so he prayed to Mars to give him the strength to stand firm now. He prayed, then sprayed vomit all over his sandals.

'Good gods here we go! Someone catch him!' Small chuckles of laughter at Longus' cheap joke – a soldier's joke. Nothing like laughter to calm a man before battle.

White faces appeared in the darkness; shining mail under dark cloaks, bare iron glinting off the moonlight. Another twang from the bow, another barbarian was face down in the mud.

Albinus thought of his father, the invincible Silus. *What would you have done? How would you win?* The answer struck him like a well-thrown spear. He remembered being a boy, sitting next to his father as he regaled the gathered revellers round his fire of some long distant battle. His cohort had been badly outnumbered, lost on the wrong side of the Danube. Surrounded on all fronts, his men set in a square, he had started to bang his sword on the boss of his shield, screaming a war cry as he did. His men followed suit, the noise like thunder, Silus had said, the ground shook like Hercules himself was charging into the fray.

'MARTIAL AND VICTORIOUS! MARTIAL AND VICTORIOUS!' The Fourteenth Gemina Martia Victrix – the Fourteenth twinned, martial and victorious. These honours had been awarded to their standard long ago, when they had still been known as the Fighting Fourteenth. The screams had been deafening. The barbarians had been shaken, their resolve gone before the first sword swing. Silus and his men had carved through them like a butcher's blade through fresh meat.

More faces appearing in the gloom, Albinus didn't hesitate, didn't wait for the nerves to get the better of him. He had no shield to rasp his sword with, but he had his voice.

'MARTIAL AND VICTORIOUS! MARTIAL AND VICTORIOUS!' Bucco grinned, a thing of pure evil, and he, too, quickly took up the cry. The others followed suit, each intake of breath followed by a louder shout.

The barbarians paused, suddenly unsure of themselves, and another fell to the twang of Habitus' bow.

'THE FIGHTING FOURTEENTH!' Albinus waved his sword in the air, brought it down in a savage arc towards the stumbling barbarians, then charged.

A slate grey sky, black swirling clouds, but a yellow tint coloured the land, Apollo not willing to relinquish his grip on the sky. The town of Rugnum lay within Albinus' sights, small and peaceful, looking tranquil and vulnerable beneath the violent sky.

Albinus lay flat on his belly, chin resting on his hands as he surveyed the darkening landscape. Fullo lay next to him, a fresh cut on his arm from the brief fight with their Sidone pursuers the week before.

Albinus' charge had broken them, before he had even swung his blade. Habitus had thinned them out with his bow, the other five had cleaved a bloody path through the rest, leaving no survivors. Fullo had been the only one wounded, miraculous given they were outnumbered and fighting under a winter's night sky. Seven days' hard marching, made easier by the pillaged supplies they had liberated from their attackers packs, had taken them right up to the estuary where the river met the sea.

They'd stood and marvelled at its banks. Of their tent party, only Calvus had seen the great expanse of water before, having braved its waves when he crossed the narrow sea from Britannia to Gaul. For those standing there, it was their first experience. No one had spoken, they all just stared in wonder at the great expanse of blue on grey, the silver tint as the sunlight shimmered on the skimming waves. Albinus had heard people describe it before – the endless surf, bobbing off over the horizon. The strong smell of salt was so powerful just breathing would dry your mouth. None of their words did it justice.

A local sailor had pointed them in the direction of Rugnum, and off they had gone, along the shingle until they had spotted their destination. Finally, they had reached Rugnum. Finally, Licina lay in touching distance.

'Argh!' Fullo winced as he shifted his weight off his injured right arm. The cut was short but deep on the base of his wrist, and it joined to the one he had earned fighting the Cogni.

'You okay, brother?' Albinus didn't take his eyes off the town.

'I'll be fine. Seen anything yet?' The others of the tent party were taken it in turns to sleep, just behind where Albinus lay in a small wooded grove, out of sight of any guards or watchmen, not that there seemed to be any.

'Nothing. The place looks half deserted. I was expecting walls, a garrison, a strong chief of some kind, not some sleepy little fishing village. This can't be the right place, can it?'

'It is, brother, according to the locals we've spoken to anyway. Not two miles west of here is the start of the Amber Road, and this is where it all washes up. They pick it from the beaches and wheel it south by the cartload, just to trade with us.' Both men were silent for a moment, each remembering the trade they had helped their fathers with over a year ago: the Romans in the cage; Aelinia and her brother. Aelinia had spoken to Albinus, begged him to help. Her brother had lain wounded, sword thrust to the side. He could still picture the sweat on his ashen skin. But Albinus had left them to their fate, choosing to accept his father's orders. He and Fullo had seen the girl again, riding at King Balomar's side as he exited Carnuntum, homebound from the peace talks with the Roman governor Bassus. It seemed she had done well from being sold into slavery. Albinus wondered if her brother still lived. *What had been his name?* He fought to remember, but all he could picture was his face as he lay dying. *He can't have survived long after that.* Sadness sitting heavy on his shoulders, he thought it was no wonder the girl had taken her chances and stuck with the barbarian king; Rome had done her no favours.

And what of Alaric, the one-eyed old rogue who had seemed to have had previous with Silus and Vitulus. Neither man had mentioned him on their journey home, and Albinus had not thought to ask. The man had seemed a low-life, cunning and wicked. It satisfied Albinus to think of his father staring him down, taunting him for the defeat the barbarian had suffered at his hands. *I must ask Bucco how he took that bastard's eye.*

Albinus smiled to himself, memories of his father warming him inside, even with the howling winter wind skimming off the endless sea. *Are you proud of me father? Proud of the man I have become?* He snorted a laugh. He was not yet seventeen, and most certainly not yet a man. But was he? He had bedded a woman, fought and killed in the shield wall, proved his prowess and courage to his brother soldiers. Is that what made you a man?

'What you laughing at?' Fullo's face set in a quizzical frown.

'I was just thinking … are we men?'

A pause. Fullo still wore the frown. 'Well, I don't know about you, brother, but I've definitely got the required parts—'

'No! I don't mean male, I mean men! Are we men? Or boys?'

'Men! No doubt.'

'Why?'

'We're soldiers! Take the oath, become a man. That's what father always used to say to me.' Fullo's logic was always so simple, always so self-assured. Albinus wondered if would cope if Fullo were to fall in battle and leave him on his own.

'I remember the old man saying something similar to me. Not that I ever listened.'

'No. Your quiet life of farming and raising a family isn't quite working out is it!'

Albinus smiled, and thought back to simpler times: barley swaying in a late summer's sun, the back-breaking days of the harvest, reaping until he could reap no more.; the cluck of chickens waking him in the morning, the whines of the hounds as they struggled to break into their pen; the stench of manure, pungent, but the smell of home nonetheless. 'Do you think Hanno survived?'

'Who?'

'The slave that father freed. From Carthage. He managed the land, used to soak us in water from the mill when we'd been running through the fields and woods all day.'

Fullo grunted a laugh. 'He was a good man, I hope he made it. There were many good people, too many of them didn't.' They shared a sad look.

'That's why I'm here. No farming for me, not until I've had my revenge!'

'Aye to that! So what's your plan? When do we move in?'

Albinus thought, nose scrunching, eyes squinted. He gazed once more upon the seemingly sleepy coastal town. 'Not sure yet. Need to keep a look out for a while longer, see what happens. I'd have thought if she were here we'd have seen her by now.'

The sun lowered in the west, blood red and strong, its heat burning away the blackened clouds. Albinus still lay watching, the red rays now causing him to squint as he continued to gaze at the small town. Fullo was long gone, replaced by a dozing Bucco, head drooping towards the tall grass.

Warmth. It felt strange to feel the sun's heat after so long. Spring was coming, and soon they would have to dash south to make it back to the legion in time for the upcoming campaign. Taurus, Albinus knew, had been more than lenient in letting the eight men leave their winter camp and sally off north on some hopeless personal mission. *Eight men won't be coming back.* No one had spoken of Libo's death, their desperate run north; evading their pursuers, then the subsequent battle, had not left time for reflection. A stab of guilt in his chest, Albinus bit back a sudden rush of tears. Libo had been a twenty-year veteran, approaching his retirement. He had served under Silus, and was infamous throughout the whole legion, not just the First Cohort. He had been robbed of his fame and retirement, in some meaningless skirmish in the dead of night in some godless hall in the middle of nowhere. *And it was all my fault.*

Hands squeezed his shoulders, a pressurised grip. 'It wasn't your fault lad.' said Bucco, as if he was reading the younger man's mind.

'Course it is! He'd never have been here if it wasn't for me! He'd have been tucked up safe and dry in Carnuntum, whoring his way through the winter. Instead … ' Albinus couldn't stop the groan and another rush of tears, hot on his cheeks as he sobbed uncontrollably.

'He was a fighter, a warrior. He'd never have been happy living on some farm in the country. He told us all that often enough himself. He was born to fight, and he died fighting. A warrior's death, he would have been happy with that.' Another squeeze on his shoulder, but it did little to comfort him.

'Thank you, Bucco. I don't know what I'd do without you.' Albinus didn't think he'd ever spoken truer words. Fullo was his best friend, his brother in all things. But Bucco had quickly filled the hole left by his father's death. He knew he would have never have survived the training, let alone battle, without Bucco's support and guidance.

'You're stronger than you think, lad. Jupiter's cock you're so like your father, sometimes I think you are him! I nearly saluted you the other day after that fight in the woods. The way you started shouting, screaming your war cry, that was Silus all over.' Albinus studied the older man, looking for a hint of sarcasm, but found none.

Chuckling, he replied, 'It amuses me that I seem to have spent most of my childhood trying not to be my father. But the older I get, the more people tell me I remind them of him.'

'It's true! I know you had your differences, but your old man was a good 'un. One of the best men I ever knew. And when we get back home, you're gonna take his name.'

Albinus gaped for a few stunned heartbeats. 'You think I'm ready? I'm still only sixteen!'

'You're a man, lad, Fullo too. We're gonna see you initiated to the bull, let you in to the secrets of Mithras. We'll do your naming ceremony with him watching over us. That way he'll know who you are, and watch over you, as he did your father.'

Didn't do Silus any favours in the end! Some things are best left unsaid. Albinus just nodded, thinking with dread to the cold, dark dungeon under the granary back at his father's farm; the terror he had felt the one time he had gone down the stone steps. Mithras dwelt in the darkest corners of the land.

He tore his gaze away from his father's friend, looking back out towards the village, bathed in the red light of the setting sun. Movement caught his eye, a flash of bared iron. A man was moving through the mud-made streets, sword in one hand, a hooded captive in the other.

Albinus gasped, not daring to believe. 'Jupiter, Best and Greatest!' Bucco was already on his feet, racing back to wake the others. The man with the sword walked slowly round the outskirts of the village, as if parading himself and his captive. He wore a hat, faded black, the edges drooping down to partially cover his face. But his identity was never in doubt. An eye patch covered his left eye, a shaggy brown beard masking his face and drooping down to his waist. A black cloak, glimmered mail underneath. He wore heavy padding on his shoulder, as if he was still recovering from a wound. A black pommelled sword, the bared blade the same length as his legs, was so long it dragged on the dirt behind him as he walked.

Abinus rose to his feet, mouth still open in shock and horror. *Alaric.* The slave trader. The barbarian with a grudge against his father. *What is he doing here?*

Never ask a question you don't want to know the answer to.

His captive struggled and Albinus heard a muffled scream. A female, she was struggling with the bonds that held her hands behind her back. Alaric led her as if she were on a leash, a rough bit of rope stretching out from behind her back. Albinus watched as the barbarian tore the hood from the girl, revealing a long luscious flow of golden orange hair.

'LICINA!' He didn't realise he'd screamed; didn't know he was pulling his sword from its scabbard; couldn't control his legs as they charged down the gentle slope into the village.

Bucco had woken the others. They charged behind him, screaming his name, desperate to pull him back. Albinus didn't hear his brothers, didn't care if they were with him or not. He was consumed with the desire to kill, the lust for blood. Gone was the timid child, the coward who would hide whilst others practised with spear and shield. Dead was the boy who was too afraid to stand up to his father, to meet his icy eyes and speak the truth. That boy had died on a cold winter's morning when his world had been torn apart. Left was a man – a killer – trained in ways of sword and spear, muscles hardened by months of relentless drilling, mind sharpened from his first taste of battle. His courage would not fail him.

The gods only know how quick he covered the ground, long slim legs propelling giant strides as he leapt down the slope. He snarled in anger as Alaric threw Licina to the floor and whirled his sword in a savage arc, a toothless smile fixed his face. 'C'mon then, pup! Come an' die like your daddy!'

The words didn't register, the insult not hitting home. Albinus jumped the last three paces, gladius held behind him, his thrust so quick the iron didn't have time to catch the sun's rays.

114

A clash and rattle of metal on metal rang out, the iron point of Albinus' gladius rebounding from the barbarian's mail. 'You gotta do better than that, boy!' The Roman didn't take a breath, but leapt again and lunged for the throat, an instant kill. Alaric darted right, the blade missing by a hair's breadth. Albinus off balance, all his weight on his right foot, Alaric turned on the balls of his feet, sword held high above his head; he hammered it down with all his strength, aiming for the dull iron of Albinus' helmet.

The Roman was too quick. He ducked and rolled, back on his feet in a heartbeat, sword point licking out and punching a hole in Alaric's thigh.

'Aaaarrgghhh! You little cunt!' A rush of dark blood, thick and heavy on his black trousers. 'You'll pay for that!' Keeping the weight off his injured left leg, the German danced forwards, sword moving from left to right, then low to high, he sought to distract the Roman into making a mistake.

Albinus ignored the whirl and flash of the blade, his father's voice filling his mind: *Never watch the sword. Always the eyes lad, always the eyes. The sword follows the eye, watch the eye, you anticipate the sword stroke. Watch the sword, and it may already be too late.*

Now the Roman ducked and dodged, but his eyes never left Alaric's. He was out of reach of the wounded man, and knew he only had to take his time. Another flash, a rush of wind on his face. He didn't flinch. Alaric had over-reached, getting desperate, feeling the life blood ooze out of the deep wound in his thigh. He staggered, screamed as his full weight landed on the injured leg. Collapsing to the floor, he was trying to rise as the touch of cold iron on his neck sent a rush of fear down his spine.

XI

February AD 169 – Germania

Alaric knelt in the mud, panting, the point of the blade pressed against the base of his neck.

'Don't … you … move.' The Roman's voice was iron-hard and unbending. Alaric had been expecting a boy, the same frightened child he had seen just a year before – the boy who would not meet his eye and seemed more afraid of his own father than he was of him. It would seem that boy had died with his father. The man who stood before him now had bettered him in single combat, fought with skill and courage, and his anger poured off him in droves. It was intense, powerful, a tide of fury and rage, and Alaric was aware it was coming for him.

Raised voices now, Latin-tongued; armoured men streaming down the slope, shouting their war cry as they burst into the nearby huts, swords raised as they searched in vain for Alaric's men. But it had been a long time since he'd warriors sworn to his sword.

He had been a great man once – a king-maker, tribe destroyer. People had spoken his name in fear. He had been a nightmare told round camp fires at night, whispered threats to naughty children: 'Behave or we'll send for Alaric to come and get you!' Now, now he was just a sad, lonely, bitter old man, who lived only for vengeance.

Alaric had thought killing Silus would leave him with a sense of fulfil-ment, righting old wrongs and completing his revenge on the man who had taken everything from him. It hadn't. The bitter taste in his mouth had beome stronger, repulsive and sour. Silus' death was not enough; it was not enough that he and his men had perished in the snow, their bodies left to freeze as the crows feasted on their cold flesh.

Even in his moment of glory, Silus had managed to leave his mark. Alaric had swung his long sword high, bringing it back down with savage force to cleave into the centurion's skull. He could still picture the arc of the blade, the strain on his shoulders and thighs as he fought to keep his balance, the feeling of pure joy as the edge bit through bone. He had not seen the spear point in Silus' left hand, only felt its jarring impact as it ripped a bloody hole in his shoulder.

The German had fled, scuttling off into the north, a blood-splattered trail on the white snow behind him. Two weeks of stumbling through the wilderness, feverish and delirious had brought him to the farm of his father, a man he had not seen for many years, and wasn't even sure was still alive. The old man had taken him in, coaxed the fever from his body and cared for him until he was healthy enough to carry on north. He had planned to go home, to his own small farm and his wife and two children, but the Fates it seemed, had other plans for him.

The gods delivered to him Licina, the flame-haired lover of Silus' child. And of all the people for her to have been travelling with, it had been the wounded gladiator he had been paid to take from an inn in Gaul. – the boy he had given to Balomar.

The sight of the girl had brought back the blood lust, the need to punish Silus' shade. He'd formed his plan in a heartbeat, a wicked scheme to bring down the centurion's son and reunite him with his father in Hades. Although it seemed everything was not quite going to plan.

He winced as he shifted the weight on his knees, leaning heavily on his right to avoid his wounded left. 'You're pretty good with that blade, boy.' He hawked and spat, winced again at the blood mixed in with the phlegm.

'You'll find out just how good in a minute. Fullo, watch him.' Alaric watched on as another young man came over, blade bared, and stood over him. He looked up at the newcomer, seeing the setting sun wash over his face, a scarred forehead glowing white in the red light.

117

'I know who you are, boy. I remember you. You're Vitulus's lad, although if I didn't know better I'd say you'd eaten him! Fucking size o' ya!' The young Roman looked down in disgust, leering at the kneeling German. 'Shut your mouth, you whoreson.'

'Fair enough.' Alaric muttered, looking past Fullo to Albinus as he tenderly lifted the red-haired girl to her feet, brushing away her hair to gaze upon her face. *Someone's going to be upset ...*

'It's not her!' Cries of confusion and anger. Alaric chuckled.

'WHERE IS SHE?! WHAT HAVE YOU DONE WITH HER?!' A snap and crunch, the breaking of bone and cartilage – Albinus' sword hilt connecting true with Alaric's nose. He slumped to the floor face first, biting his tongue with toothless gums until it bled to stop himself from crying out. The strong metallic taste of his own blood filled his mouth. He spat it out, grinning. 'You really think it was gonna be that easy?!' Another snap, this time a lightning bolt of white hot agony shot through his head from the back. His head hit the floor so hard that if he'd had any teeth left, they would have been loose on the mud. He raised his face, still grinning. 'Let me up, boy, and I'll tell ya all about it.'

The Romans took a step back, a circle of snarls and swords surrounding him. He reached for his own blade, comforted by the familiar feel of the worn black leather-wrapped hilt. *If you want to dine in Wotan's Hall, you got to die with a blade in your hand.*

He staggered into a sitting position, dizzy, face sagging to the floor. The sword thrust to his thigh had severed his artery, and he could feel the pulse of his lifeblood as it poured out, hot and sticky on his leg. He knew he was not long for the world, offered a short prayer to the Allfather and promised himself to make Albinus suffer as much as he could before his last breath.

'How'd you end up in the army, boy? Last time I met ya you didn't exactly strike me as the type.' His voice was hoarse, a dying rasp. The dizziness came again, stronger this time. His stomach heaved. He didn't see Albinus shrug. 'Was it after your precious father died? Ha, if looks could kill! Now scarface over there is a soldier born.' He nodded his head at Fullo, who subconsciously rubbed his forehead. 'But you? Just don't seem natural. S'pose you wanna be like your father eh? The invincible Silus, lord of the

118

battlefield, slayer of the tribes! What a cunt he was. Turns out he weren't so invincible after all!'

He laughed in pure joy at the look of rage on Albinus. 'You wanna know how he died, boy? I'll tell ya if you want?'

Silence. Alaric saw Albinus' eyes moisten. 'You were there.' It wasn't a question.

'Oh, I was there, boy. I was there when we crossed the river in the dawn, and let me tell you, fording a river that wide in the middle of winter is not fucking pleasant! Still waiting for one of me balls to drop back down! But it was worth it in the end. Your old man and his troops made a fair fight of it, gotta credit 'em for that. Formed a wedge and charged us! Couldn't 'av been more than a hundred of 'em! Numbers told in the end though. He was wounded when I found him, been charged by a horse and catapulted through the air. Sort of pissed me off to be honest, wanted all the credit for meself.'

He kept his eyes fixed on Albinus as he spoke, and couldn't keep the smile from his face.

'I came in slow, wanted him to know it was me see. Then I raised this blade and crashed it through that maggot's skull, cleaved like a melon dropped from a cart.'

Alaric cackled a laugh as tears streamed down Albinus' face. The Roman snorted a cry, then gathered himself and spoke. 'He got you though, didn't he? Even at the moment of his death, he still hurt you. I found his body the next day. There was a patch of flattened grass next to it, soaked in blood. Your blood.' He pointed at Alaric with his sword.

'Aye he got me, the whoreson. Thrust through me shoulder with a spear, was in and out of fever for weeks, thought the gangrene might have set in for a while.' Wound rot killed as many warriors as death blows. 'But I made it back to me old daddy's farm, and he fixed me up good. I was just about to set off for home, finally see me wife and sprogs now I'd gone and got my revenge, but guess who turned up at my old man's doorstep?' He watched in pleasure as the colour drained from the young Roman's face.

'Yeah, you know who! Running north she was, escaped from old King Balomar's household. But I bet ...' he paused to laugh at the sky, '... I bet

119

you'll never guess who she was with?' He watched in glee at the confounded look on the legionary's face. 'You remember when we met on the Amber Road? I had two Romans in a cage, being carted off to be sold?' He smiled as Albinus nodded. 'Well I gave 'em to Balomar, good will gesture and what 'av you. Well, Julius, think that was his name, was with her. He'd helped her escape, brought her north on his own. And let me tell ya lad, he'd gotta hard on for your girl!' He couldn't help but laugh aloud again as Albinus' anguished face turned back to rage, his skin redder than the sun's dying light.

'Oh yes! And it's some hard on an' all. I should know, I watched her ride it like a prized stallion. Never heard a woman scream out in pleasure like that before, I'd wager you ain't either!' He barely felt the crunch of the Roman's fist on his temple. Truth be told, he could barely feel anything now.

'What? You thought she was gonna wait for you! Some skinny little whelp? You sorry bastard, and you came all this way—'

'You're lying!' Two of Albinus' friends were holding him back now, his fists and boots making circles in the air.

'Not a word, lad, not a word. The two *lovers* ...' another chuckle at his use of the word, '... wanted to acquire passage over the sea, apparently your young lady held a passion for seeing new lands as well as Julius' cock.' The legionaries were struggling to hold Albinus back now, he was bellowing in anguish, red-faced and puffy. Alaric didn't care, he was already a dead man.

'So, I got them passage on a ship, gave the lad a good beating just for old times' sake, then sat down and wrote you a nice little letter. Been waiting here for you ever since.' He could sense his voice becoming weaker. Every heartbeat was an effort, a convulsion. His sight was going, the world becoming a pristine sheet of white. Voices filled his ear, screams of rage, but they sounded distant, like they were being screamed through a wave. 'You bastard! I'll kill you!' Alaric smiled. *You already have lad.* He sank onto his back, stars on white were all he saw. His right hand still on his sword hilt, he concentrated all his strength on gripping the leather hilt tight. Had he lived well? No. Been good to others, treated people fairly. Certainly not. Had he proved himself in battle, forged himself a name in iron and blood that was feared and respected? Yes, and to him, that was what mattered. A whimper of a heartbeat, his time almost at its end, he pictured his wife and children one last time, and sent a swift prayer to the gods to watch over them. They had done nothing wrong.

Another convulsion, but there was no heartbeat this time. His lungs caved inwards, airless and flat. His last thought was panic, as the sword hilt was ripped from his grasp. He had no strength to get it back.

Rullus picked up the dead man's sword, flexing his wrist and swinging the blade. 'Got some weight to it, this.' He dropped it, unceremoniously, to the ground.

'Why did you take it from him?' Asked Longus.

'This lot believe you can't get into Wotan's Hall when you die unless your holding your weapon. Given the circumstances, it felt right to deny him the opportunity.'

Albinus wasn't listening as Rullus and Longus filled the tense silence. He was pacing, frantically. His mind a whirling mess, he tried to slow his breathing, calm himself down, but he couldn't.

He marched over to the red-haired girl, still standing where he had left her. She appeared shocked and terrified. 'Who are you?' Albinus screamed at her face. 'What are you doing here? Where is Licina?' The girl choked back tears. She spoke animatedly, hand gestures on outstretched arms, pointing to Alaric and then to one of the huts. She spoke in German, and Albinus grew more agitated as he failed to understand what she was saying.

'Anyone know what she's going on about?' He turned to his comrades.

'Says she has been kept prisoner by Alaric since the end of summer. Says he turned up to their town, killed her father and moved himself into their home. She says ... she says he raped her every day, kept her hands and legs tethered, and has been parading her round the outskirts of the town three times a day for the last few weeks. Must have been waiting for us I guess.' Bucco trailed off, his voice cracking with emotion.

A sombre silence fell, the Romans unable to meet the girl's eye. 'Bucco, tell her that ... tell her she's free now, that the man who did this to her will never hurt anyone else.'

Bucco stumbled over the right words, awkward and apologetic. At his signal, the group moved away from the girl, north through the settlement until they were at the point the shingle met the sea.

Albinus slumped down to his knees and looked out across the infinite expanse of water. *She's out there somewhere. In the new lands, where no one knows her name or her past. Just like she always wanted.* He knelt in silence for what seemed an age, staring unblinkingly across the sea.

There was a ship to their left, sitting at anchor a short distance from the beach. Albinus watched as the man who appeared to be the captain shouted and grunted as his men loaded barrels and amphorae into two small row boats to bring them onto shore.

A cough behind him, Bucco clearing his voice. 'Hate to bring this up now, lad, but winter's nearly over. The sun is getting warmer, first signs of life in the trees and bushes. The First Spear will be expecting us back.' Albinus slumped, chin falling on his chest. He knew his friend was right, there was no way he could cross the sea and continue his search for Licina. He was no deserter; he would not abandon his legion when they needed him most. 'I know Bucco.' Tears trickled down his cheeks, he looked up and was shocked to see how dark the sky had become. 'We'll begin our journey south tomorrow. Head back the way we came, pick Calvus up on the way.'

No one doubted or questioned the young man's right to make decisions for all of them. He had more than earned their respect in the last months. 'C'mon then,' said Habitus, hauling Albinus to his feet by his shoulders, 'let's find somewhere to get some sleep eh.'

Albinus nodded, took one last look across the water. The moon was out now, its pale light glistening silver on the waves. He realised he was cold, his breath steaming the air. Shivering, he turned to walk back into the town, but stopped dead in his tracks. A man stood behind them, black-haired and dark-eyed, his skin a reflection of the pale moonlight. He took a small step towards the group before speaking.

'You may not remember me, but I know you. Your name is Albinus … Albinus Silus, correct?'

Albinus nodded, stunned.

'My name is Julius, Julius Decanus. We met once before. I was wounded, caged with my sister. You were with your father, trading for amber. Correct?'

Albinus just nodded.

'And you are here for Licina? But found Alaric instead?' Another nod from Albinus. 'And yet you are alive, I'm assuming—'

'He's dead.' Albinus muttered, still in shock.

'Yes. Err, good. Good for you. Licina is—'

'North, across the sea, I know. Alaric told me she was … with you?'

Julius's turn to nod. 'I was with her. She settled in quickly with the local tribe there, is enjoying her life. I did not, I missed home, the empire. So I got the first ship back once the sea lanes opened.'

'You left her? All alone?' Albinus was struggling to control his emotions. He wanted to hate this man, to draw his sword and run him through. He had slept with his betrothed, taken advantage of her loneliness. At least in his mind that's what had happened. But Albinus had left this man for dead once, locked in a cage and destined for a life of shackles and beatings, that was if he survived his wound.

A glance to his left showed him Fullo remembered Julius too. His scars were an angry red and he scowled as he fingered his sword hilt. Albinus shook his head slightly. Fullo got the signal and relaxed his posture.

'She is not alone. She has friends, powerful friends who can protect her and guide her. She's happy, free, for the first time in a long time. I tried to persuade her to come back with me, but her mind was set. What will you do now?'

Albinus took a moment before replying. 'I must go back south. We are soldiers, and we must be back at base for spring and the campaigning season. Although I cannot leave here without sending Licina some sort of message.'

Albinus saw a slow smile appear on Julius's face as he looked out on the darkening shadow of the ship, still sitting at anchor in the deeper waters. 'I think I can help you out with that my friend.'

XII

The first signs of spring were in the air: the smell of pollen was in her nostrils, spots of pink, yellow and purple dotted the green landscape. The sun warmed her face as she sat atop a small rise in the sweeping landscape, a rare moment of peace in a life that had become almost total war.

The battle in the depths of winter had just been the beginning. The raiders had grown bolder, boosted by their early victories, and eager to gain more plunder they had raided deeper into Gotland.

Sigivald had met them at the banks of a gushing river. Shield wall formed, he'd stood with his hearth warriors and waited for the raiders to attack. Attacked they had, and sent the chief scurrying back for the south coast, counting his dead and licking his wounds.

Since that terrible defeat, the defence of the land had turned to the shield-maidens and any local farmers brave enough to stand in line with their pitch-forks and hoes. It had been bloody and desperate, but not wholly unsuccessful.

The day before, the shieldmaidens had set an ambush, waiting within a small thicket of pine. There was a small but sharp slope that separated the trees from the mud road. The women warriors had lain in wait, iron bared, hearts pounding, listening to the trudge of booted feet on the road.

At Heide's signal, they had burst from the cover of the trees, screaming their war cry. The slope gave them an advantage in height, which coupled with surprise, was enough to see them win the day – not one survivor from the black cloaks from the far north. But all the women knew there would be more.

A call from Heide, and the convoy reluctantly clambered back to their feet. Hefting spears and slinging shields over shoulders, they made ready to continue the journey south.

Licina rubbed tired eyes, trying to remember the last time she had slept longer than an hour. The dead stalked her dreams. They begged her, cursed her, grabbed hold of her and wouldn't let go. In her mind they were still alive, the men she had slain. She could picture them clearly, clearer than her parents. Last night it had been the first man she had killed in the ambush the day before. Well, not quite a man – a beardless youth, cheeks glowing red in the early spring chill. His eyes had been as dark as his cloak, full of reluctance and fear. He had been screaming in terror when she was still ten paces away. Only the cold edge of her blade had silenced him.

But he could talk in her dreams. In her dreams he told her his name, Sigurd. He spoke of his elder brother, who lost a leg defending his home from raids from Sigivald's men; of his sister, raped and beaten on the same raid; of his father, a scowling, bitter old man, determined to avenge the hurt his family had been caused.

Last night he had struck her, a clenched fist across her face. He'd screamed and bellowed, cried and raged as he begged her to bring him back. Who would look out for his sister now? Or his poor old Ma, now he and his father were confined to the halls of the gods. She had woken herself with her screaming, shocked to find her face speckled in hot blood – her blood. Heide had told her she been speaking the dead boy's words in her sleep, that writhing and wriggling, she had hit herself in the face.

She had heard the whispers from the other women, noticed the distance they were keeping from her. Licina had been a loner once, a troubled girl locked within her own mind. She had no wish to fall back within those gloomy depths, to have people say she was cursed by the gods. But that was exactly what they were saying. 'Völva', that was the word they used.

To be a Völva was to be connected to the gods, your mind intertwined with theirs. Licina was certainly not that. But she knew someone who was. She approached Heide as she trudged through the dew-covered grass. Her straw-coloured hair was matted with blood, a fine bruise round her left eye.

'You are troubled, Licina.' She hadn't turned around, or shown any sign she knew Licina was approaching, let alone what was on her mind. 'The girls are saying you are a Völva, your mind linked to the gods. They say those gods are tormenting your dreams, bringing the dead back to life. They say you are cursed, destined to live a life of misery.'

Licina was expecting one of her friend's mocking smiles, a nudge or a wink as she turned to face her. She got nothing but a blank stare. 'How do you know what goes on in my mind?'

Heide moved forward, bringing Licina into a light embrace. 'Because I am what they say you are. My mind is joined to the spinners. I see the fate of the people around me.'

Still no smile. No hint of humour or jesting. 'I know what you are, Heide.' Licina swallowed nervously, not wanting to ask the question, but she knew she had to. 'What do you see in my future?'

'I have told you before, as you stood and watched Julius sail out on Freya's sea. I cannot see your future. It is clouded.'

'What does that mean?'

'It means your future will take you far away from these lands. I cannot see the fates of people who are not tied to our land, to our gods and beliefs. They are hidden from me the way a mountain conceals a lake. You will leave us soon, that I am sure of. Although to where I cannot say, but you will be smiling when you sail, full of hope and happiness.' Heide closed her eyes and ran the palm of her hand across Licina's forehead. 'Yes, soon now.'

Licina felt dizzy, light-headed suddenly. It felt as though a part of her left when Heide pulled her hand away – part of her strength, her reserves. She sunk to her knees, gasping for breath. 'What did you do to me?'

'I looked into your mind, Licina, into your soul.'

'And what did you see?' Still gasping, Licina struggled to her feet.

'Love. Pure and untouchable. Albinus still has your heart. You will go to him soon I think.'

126

Albinus still has your heart. He always has. 'How can I go to hi—'

'Hush, Licina. Soon, your questions will be answered,' Heide said as she turned away, continuing her inexorable march south.

So many questions. How can they possibly all be answered?

Spring was in full blossom and the sun warmed Licina's cheeks as she made her way down to the small harbour. Julius was already aboard the ship – the same one that had brought them here in early winter.

The shieldmaidens' journey south had continued uneventfully. Licina had arrived on the south coast footsore and hungry. She hadn't even noticed Julius lurking in the doorway to her small hut, and he'd had to cough politely to get her attention.

But she felt tired no more; hope and excitement filled her every step and thought. She was going home, going to him. *Albinus.* In the joy of reading his message, of having Julius confirm he was both alive and searching for her, she had cried a river of tears, as a years' worth of emotion released itself from within.

Her stomach was full of butterflies, nervous tension that fluttered every time she breathed. *Will he still want me? Love me?* She wondered, too, how she would react when she saw him. Julius had said he was scarred, a livid line down the side of his face. His eyes had been cold as iron, his hand rarely straying from the pommel of his sword. None of this sounded like the Albinus she had known and loved. She thought that maybe it was just Julius trying to throw some doubt into her mind.

She stopped suddenly, throwing the bundle of clothes she had been thrusting into a small leather bag to the ground. *What must Julius be feeling?* The man had left her for their homeland earlier in the year as he had grown dismayed by the fact that he was in love with her but she did not return the feeling. Upon landing in Germania, the first person he had come into contact with had been Albinus. *Sick. He must feel sick.*

The fact that he had returned to the far north at Albinus' request spoke volumes for the way he still felt about her. Despite himself, he had felt compelled to help her out in any way he could. A pang of guilt washed over her like heavy rain. She would make an effort with him on their journey south, ensure he felt valued and respected. The man had done so much for her, it was all she could do to repay him.

She filled her bag, lifted it onto her shoulder, was about to turn and leave when there was a knock on the door. Heide stood half masked in shadow, her straw-coloured hair like a light in the room. 'Your fate lies away from here, but you already knew that.' she said and smiled. It was infectious. Licina smiled back as she dropped the bag back to the floor and embraced her friend.

'I was going to come and see you before I left,' Licina said as she pulled back from the embrace. The shieldmaidens locked eyes, their faces a hand-breadth apart. Heide's kiss shocked Licina. 'Oh!' was all she could say as Heide pulled her lips from hers. 'That was ... unexpected.'

'Was it,' followed by another kiss. 'You know who I am, the company I like to keep. I like your company, it's a shame I'm not going to be able to enjoy it further.' Heide could not keep the laugh from her voice.

Licina blushed. 'Well ... I ... err ... thank you.'

'For the kiss?'

'No! Well kind of. For everything. Without you, I would never have been so happy here. I'd have spent the whole time wallowing in self-misery, wondering about Albinus and the fate I had left him to. Instead I have had an adventure, one I always dreamed of as a child. It has been ...' she paused, searching for the right word, '... magical, in so many ways.'

The two women walked out into the warm spring air, birdsong serenading them overhead. 'I am glad I met you, Licina. I have a feeling we may even meet again. Our fates will cross at some point, I feel it in my gut,' Heide said as she embraced Licina one last time.

Licina was in tears as she made her way through the busy shingle beach, row boats coming in and out from the ships docked out in the deeper water. She hadn't the courage to face the other shieldmaidens and say her goodbyes – too many memories from the fierce fighting in the last few months. She thought she might wilt and stay under the pressure of their glares. She was leaving them at a time when they were more desperate than they had ever been for a strong right arm behind a practised blade, their fight would be long and desperate. She hoped they prevailed.

Julius stood swaying in a row boat, two gruff-looking oarsman to his front and back. He beamed at her as she made her way through the shallows, one arm clutching her bag as the other lifted the hem of her cloak. 'Where's your shield?' he jested as she slung her bag into the small raft, causing it to wobble on the waves.

Her only reply was to poke out her tongue as she clambered into the small boat. It rocked violently as she planted her feet, causing Julius to stumble and fumble for a grip on the rail. 'What in Jupiter's name have you been eating?' he stuttered as he righted himself.

'You cheeky bastard! You're looking a bit rounder in the belly yourself than when we first set off for the north!' She settled down into the cramped wooden bench in the centre of the boat, Julius sitting next to her.

The short journey was made in companionable silence, just the splash of the oars and the odd count or warning from the man in the stern. They clambered out of the small craft, up the rope ladder onto the ship that would take them back to Germania, and Rugnum, where they had set off from last winter.

The ship turned slowly and set out to the open sea, Licina looking back on the land that had become more than a refuge to her, a place where she had come to feel like home after so long of being a stranger in foreign lands.

The shingle glistened in the spring sun as the ship glided further into the deep blue. The fading sight of the small wooden huts that had seemed cold and unwelcoming when she first set down on the shore now had her welling up with tears. There was a flash of yellow in the distance, a waving arm just visible. Licina raised her own in reply as a final goodbye to Heide. The gods themselves only knew if it was their fate to meet again. Licina desperately hoped it was.

PART II

A CLASH OF IRON

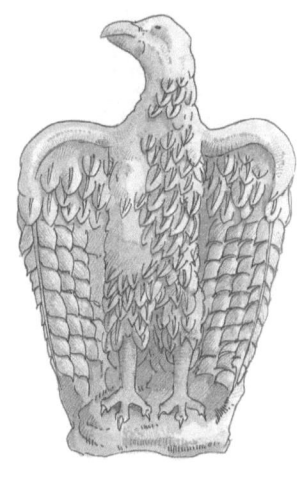

July 169–September 171 AD

XIII

The heat was formidable, the windless courtyard a furnace as the summer sun roasted him. Surrounded by trees growing fresh olives and figs, Alexander sat uncomfortably on a small stone bench, and sweated. He regretted wearing the loose-fitted silk trousers, but his left leg had swollen horribly, was almost green as the grass it was so filled with pus. He did not want to present himself to the emperors with something so vile and revolting on show.

He had shed his green cloak not even half way through the cobbled streets from his tavern room to the palace, slinging it over his shoulder to reveal a pristine white toga, edged with purple and gold. It was a risk to wear purple in the divine emperor's presence, as the colour was usually strictly reserved for those who sat upon the throne. But, he figured, it wouldn't be long now before his saggy old arse was seated on the gilded throne he craved.

As he sat and sweated out the wine he had drunk with his breakfast, he pictured the pure purple cloak he'd had made, sat in a chest with the rest of his belongings just a short walk down the road. He yearned for it, with every beating of his heart. All the men that had stood against him throughout his rise to prominence, those who had slandered him to his face or whispered behind his back, would soon come to regret their misplaced derision and lack of respect.

Soon, he would be master of the world, a vast army at his back, and he wouldn't waste it the way he had seen previous emperors. *Fools. If I'd been running the empire for the last thirty years, we'd control all of Germania, and the Parthians would be a distant memory.*

The snake writhed on his arm, hissing at a small bird that had dropped to the grass to feed. It slithered forwards, hoping to sneak up on the bird unobserved. Alexander tightened his grip on the snake, causing it to turn and hiss as him. A shiver of fear ran down the old man's back, the sweat momentarily turning to ice. One of his earlier 'Glycons' had damn near killed him once, plunging its fangs into his arms. His whole arm had been purple for a month. It was the only thanks to the talents of a nearby healer he had pulled through. That had been one of the few times Alexander had regretted ordering a man's death.

Despite his transition from an apothecary into the fraud he had largely become, Alexander still held in wonder the men who could turn strange plants and herbs into liquid that could seemingly bring people back across the River Styx. Their knowledge and ability was truly awe-inspiring. And then there were the men like him and his master when he was a young man, making dodgy concoctions that glowed a pleasing colour, and fobbing them off to the plebs as miracle cures, able to solve any health issues one could possess. And then quickly scampering off to the next town before anyone could accuse them of treachery. *Those were the days.*

The plague had proved to be very problematic for Alexander. Even now, approaching five years since the first deaths, it was hard to find a city or town across the length of the empire that didn't stink of death and decay. Graveyards had more than doubled in size, and it was a common joke wherever he went that the best trade to be in these days was as a stone mason: everyone needed a tombstone. The problem for Alexander was that everyone around him expected him to come up with an answer. 'Fix it, Alexander! Give us an antidote! Pray to your god, ask him for a cure!' Of course, he hadn't the slightest idea how to cure the plague, they may as well have asked him to dim the stars. And his 'god' was going to be no help at all, as he had invented the whole thing himself.

He had, he thought smugly, deftly avoided giving a straight answer to the demands of the plebs and senators alike. 'My lord will give us a sign,' he proclaimed as he paraded his snake to the masses on his journey north from Rome. Although he hadn't yet worked out what that sign would be. *As soon as people stop dying,* he figured, *I'll think of something and let the 'divine' Aurelius have it read to the plebs in Rome. Or maybe when I'm proclaimed emperor?*

'The Augustus will see you now,' said the shadow of a gruff praetorian standing over his shoulder. The soothsayer jumped, inwardly cursing himself for being so lost in his thoughts he hadn't heard a fully armed soldier rattle towards him.

He clambered slowly to his feet, wincing at the shooting pain in his left leg. He followed the praetorian, but at his own pace. He'd be damned if he was going to let some stuck-up soldier, with ideas and opinions far above his station, dictate the tempo. In the limited time he'd spent around the Augustus and his imperial court, he had come to detest the 'hangers on' as he called them – the guardsmen and the chamberlains, the eunuchs and the whores. Each thought themselves better than they were, simply because of their close proximity to the power of the world. *All will be different soon, just as soon as I reach the purple.*

He limped through a lavish corridor, soft Persian rugs beneath his feet atop a marble floor. Beautifully finished mosaics adorned the walls either side: Romulus and Remus suckling the wolf's teat, in a dark and dense forest; the goddess Diana sat atop her blue tinged moon, engulfing the twins in a pale light; on the other side the war god Mars, reaping his way through what appeared to be the Carthaginian army, their one-eyed leader Hannibal wincing in fear as the god's mighty blade ripped into his flesh.

It was all propaganda, the Abonoteichon knew. The twins were never really suckled by wolves – if they'd even lived at all – and he was quite certain Mars wasn't present on the plains of Africa when Scipio had defeated the legendary Hannibal. Come to think of it, he was fairly certain the Carthaginian general had survived and fled back to Carthage. Still, it made for good art work.

Up a flight of marble stairs and through another lavish corridor brought him to a gold-plated door flanked by two more praetorians. One wore a transverse crest stop his helmet – horse hair died a pure white, marking him out as a centurion. 'Alexander of Abonoteichos, he's expected, sir.'

135

Alexander's escort offered a salute, hooking his thumbs in his belt. He stood at rigid attention as he waited for his commander's reply.

Alexander resisted the urge to sigh in frustration as the centurion gave him a dour look. 'You searched him?' he asked the guard who had shown him up. 'No, sir,' the guardsmen replied in surprise. The centurion approached Alexander, tucking his vine stick into his belt and flexing his fingers.

Alexander held up the palm of his hand, halting the centurion. 'How dare you, soldier!' he proclaimed in an outraged voice. 'I am Alexander of Abonoteichos, dear friend of our beloved Augustus. I am a man of the gods, a soothsayer, if you like. It is an insult to the dignity of my position that you would think I would approach our beloved Augustus and his Caesar armed. Do I look dangerous to you?' A pause. 'Well, do I?'

The centurion, humbled and abashed, muttered his apologies. He did make a gentle enquiry as to what was in the glass jug the Abonoteichon gripped in his right hand. Beautifully crafted blue glass, corked and sealed with the insignia of a snake atop the cork, it was the main reason for Alexander's supposedly surprise visit to the Augustus. 'A gift, centurion. The finest Falerian, brewed and bottled in Baiae. I could uncork it if you like, you could sample some? Although I fear our divine Augustus may be somewhat disappointed.' More mumbled apologies, a hesitant gesture to stop Alexander removing the cork. 'Well then, if that's all centurion, let's not keep the Augustus waiting any longer.'

The golden door was pushed open, well-oiled hinges making no sound as it swung inwards to reveal a room of sheer beauty. The marble floor glistened and winked in the sun's rays, the open sun ports in the ceiling letting the dazzling yellow glow flood the room. Statues of stone and marble were tastefully dotted round the large open space; plants of varying heights and colours gave the room the full aroma of summer. Stone porticos surrounded the east and south edges, the lack of walls allowing a gentle breeze to float and whirl, heavenly after being sat in the airless courtyard with just the glare of the sun for company.

The Augustus sat on a wooden desk in the north-west corner, small stone weights holding down a pile of papyrus as he scribbled on another with his quill. The hobnailed boots of the centurion rang off the marble floor. He stopped smartly in front of Augustus Marcus Aurelius and snapped a salute, standing in silent attention until the man who ruled the civilised world put down his quill and raised his head. 'The noble Alexander of Abonoteichos, here to see you, Divine Imperator Marcus Aurelius Antoninus Augustus, and the Divine Imperator Caesar Lucius Aurelius Verus.'

Alexander studied the Augustus as the titles were shouted at the walls by the centurion. It amused him that he thought Aurelius looked bored as his full name was spoken aloud. *How many times a day must he have to wait for some poor bastard to ring off all those names? When I rule, I shall simply be known as Alexander. After all, they say even the great Macedonian himself let his inner circle address him by name.*

With a sudden start, Alexander realised the room was silent, and all eyes from slave to emperor alike were on him. He coughed politely, hoped is face wasn't flushing red, stepped forward and sunk to his knees, groaning as his weight fell on his infected leg. He stayed there, prostrate, his nose an inch from the marble, as he waited to be asked to rise. The silence stretched out for what seemed an age.

'Rise, my friend.' It was not a strong voice that spoke; not deep, or full of authority. It was the voice of a thinker, a philosopher.

Struggling to his feet, Alexander rose and looked upon divinity. Wearing just a plain white tunic, devoid of fancy decoration or elaborate trimming, Aurelius glowered at his guest. Dark eyes stared disapprovingly under a curly crop of dark hair. His beard had small clouds of white at the edges; it looked unkept and wild. 'Alexander, I have been waiting for your visit for some time. Ever since some of my legionaries lost their lives releasing two live lions into the River Danube, in fact.' He spoke with no spite or sarcastic humour. He merely stated a fact. Alexander's prophecy had been a catastrophe for the Fourteenth Legion, who had lost men putting down the rogue lions as they attacked them at the river's edge. It had been done on Alexander's advice, a way to appease the gods, to rid them of the cursed plague and the ravaging raiders to the north.

Alexander struggled to suppress a smile. He had of course thought up the most ridiculous thing he could imagine when Aurelius had written to him and asked for a way to appease the gods. The tears of laughter he and

137

Cocconas had shared when they had heard of the deaths could have filled one of the great bath houses in Rome.

'Divine Augustus,' Alexander bowed his head in mock reverence, 'I have indeed come to beg my forgiveness for the disaster that befell the brave men of the Fourteenth Gemina. It must have proved to have been a very tough period for the legion, coming straight after their total defeat by the northern tribes.' His voice was an icy whisper on the close air, and he could almost hear the sharp intake of breath from the slaves and eunuchs that stood around the emperor.

'Total defeat? I have just returned from Carnuntum. They did not, to me at least, appear to be a legion in crisis. Unless you are better informed then I?' said Aurelius, his voice taking on a firmer tone.

Careful Alexander. No point getting yourself killed. 'My apologies, most divine one. I merely meant that after suffering from such a huge battle, having the lions turn on them and attack must have been very difficult. Especially since I hear their legate was killed in the attack. They have a new legate now I presume?' The Fourteenth were undoubtedly the strongest military presence along the Danube, and the one that Balomar had feared the most. Without making it too obvious, Alexander was keen to find out as much as he could about what was left of the legion and who commanded them.

'You are well informed again, Alexander. Though quite what Legatus Candidus thought he was doing fighting in the front rank is beyond me. The man had never been a soldier, never truly at home in armour. He was the perfect administrator, kept his fortress clean, men paid, fed and equipped, roads in good condition. But repelling a foreign army? No, that would never have been his strong point. We have been victims of our own hubris, Alexander. Too occupied, we have been with trying to repel the plague, keeping our eastern border secure, that we had quite forgotten the north. A mistake we shall not make again, I hope. Maximianus leads the Fourteenth, an equestrian, I know, but a good man, an experienced soldier. This war could well be the making of him.'

'Well, colleague, you shan't be worrying about the east for many years. I made sure of that!' Alexander had not thought there anyone else present, but turning into the sunlight he saw the Caesar Verus standing atop a small

138

podium on the southern portico, a golden muscle cuirass fit snuggly over a body that had well and truly run to fat. A balding old man, tray of paints in one hand and brush in the other, was carefully and slowly painting a likeness of the Caesar. Alexander caught a glimpse of his work, and thought how thinner, tanned and better looking he appeared on the canvas.

Verus stood down from the podium, waving the artist away. 'Gods below, I must have been standing there for hours! Are you hungry, colleague?' he said as he strode over, bright blond hair sprinkled with gold dust dazzling in the sunlight.

'My dear Verus, you had been on that podium no more than an hour. And you ate your fill before ascending it. And as for you being responsible for the downfall of the Parthians, I'm sure Governor Cassius and Legate Priscus would be delighted to hear how you won battle after battle, crossed the Euphrates on a bridge of boats and slaughtered near on seventy thousand Parthians in a single day.' Again, the Augustus' voice held no malice, he spoke as if he were correcting a child. He might aswell be, thought Alexander.

'Well, they … err … acted on my orders. Anyway, that was just one of Cassius' most recent triumphs.' Verus snorted as he spoke. Aurelius was quick to respond.

'Are you referring to his recent conquest of my wife or that of our friend Alexander's daughter?' asked the emperor, in the gentlest of tones.

'Err …' Verus stumbled, shocked that his superior knew what he knew. Alexander, too, stood aghast. Though he figured that if he had spies watching the people closest to Aurelius, it made sense for the man himself too as well.

'I apologise, Alexander. I assume a man with your reach is already aware of Cassius and his affairs?' Aurelius said, turning his attention to the gaping Abonoteichon.

'Yes, Divinity. My daughter had always had a rather …' he searched for the right word, '… unhealthy appetite when it comes to men. She plays a dangerous game I fear, if her husband were to find out—'

'But he already knows my friend.' Aurelius butted in, his voice still as soft as a summer's breeze.

'He does? But my daughter … she is in no danger? Rutilianus wouldn't dare harm—'

'Have no fears, friend.' Aurelius held up the palm of his hand, seeking to calm Alexander. 'Governor Rutilianus is older than us both. Run to fat and more concerned with the wealth in his coffers than the engagements of his wife.' Sounds a bit like you, Alexander thought as he stood in silence. He had of course been aware of Cassius and his affairs with both his daughter and the emperor's wife. But to hear it from Aurelius himself, that the man knew his wife was sleeping with a senator behind his back and had done nothing to reprimand him, shocked Alexander. *I will not be so forgiving when I am in power.* Alexander would have had Cassius by the balls by now. Chained up in a cell beneath the Palace in Rome, torturers making his every waking moment agony. He'd planned to do it anyway, for seducing his daughter. Although he was fairly certain it would have been her that had done the seducing. *She always was destined to be a whore.*

Verus, hoping he had been forgotten, was slowly backing away from the Augustus, out onto the portico. 'Verus, colleague, where are you going now?' The Augustus said, his tone still mild and pleasant.

'I was just excusing myself, give you two some privacy.' He bowed slightly – the second most powerful man in the world, humbled at the feet of an old man in a plain robe sitting at a desk you would think to find a brothel accountant.

'Leaving already? Alexander has brought us a gift, seems to be more your taste than mine. Why don't you take it with you, I'll join you for a glass later.' The Caesar's eyes lit up as he spotted the blue glass jug in Alexander's hand. Alexander stepped towards him, jug held out in his hands. He realised he hadn't considered the probable fact that Verus would sink the lot before Aurelius could get the opportunity. He momentarily regretted throwing all the nightshade into one jug. *Never put all your eggs in one basket. Even an old dog can learn new tricks.*

The Caesar grasped the jug, raising it to the light and licking his lips in anticipation of tasting the deep red liquid within. With a bow to Aurelius and a nod of thanks to Alexander, he scurried off without a word, a blaze of gold dust flittering down onto the marble in his wake.

'Now, my friend, that my esteemed *colleague* has gone, sit with me so we can talk.' The emphasis on the word colleague was not lost on Alexander.

Aurelius had adopted Verus and named him Caesar at the request of the deceased Emperor Antoninus. No one among the Senate and the elite in Rome had actually thought Aurelius would do it; any man with half a brain could see Verus was completely unfit to rule. If Aurelius were to die and power transfer solely to him, it would thrust the empire back into the dark days of Nero or Caligula – vile men who used their power to rape and steal and further their own ends. *Unless there was someone else, ready to step from the shadows.*

'I had thought to write to you soon and request you attend me. I must say I was surprised to learn you were in Italy, you were in the north last I heard?'

Alexander knew he had to tread carefully. The fact the Augustus knew he was in the north at the time of the German rebellion may seem a little too convenient for any frumentarii agent digging into the whos and whens of the last year. The frumentarii were a network of spies, loyal to an unnamed prefect who answered only to Aurelius himself. They had been mere wheat collectors up to the time of Emperor Hadrian. But he had seen their worth, them being the people who regularly made contact with farmers and merchants across the breadth of the empire, and he had put them to better use. Ever since, any scrap of information that may be of vague use to the Augustus had found its way back to Rome.

Alexander suppressed a shudder. The thought of the man in front of him already being aware of his plans had unwillingly crossed his mind numerous times: being dragged off to a dark cell, damp patches over cold cobbles, iron manacles digging into his wrists and ankles; the icy touch of the blade at his neck, the burning agony of hot pokers on his chest. He sweated profusely, could feel it dripping down his nose even as he nodded, dimly aware it had been some time since Aurelius' question, and he was yet to answer.

'I was, Divinity. A quick tour through the provinces on my way from the east. The plague seems to have affected the people more there than anywhere else I've been. I had hoped to help ease people's suffering. The sight of a god can do miraculous things, after all.' As if on cue the snake slithered from within Alexander's toga, raising it head and hissing at Aurelius. Two unnamed praetorians rasped their swords from scabbards, stepping forward to cover their Augustus if the snake attacked. Aurelius waved them away with an easy flick of his hand.

'Your god has grown, my friend,' said Aurelius, as he reached out a tentative hand and stroked the back of the snake. 'You were present at the meeting between Governor Bassus and the barbarian king?'

On your orders. 'I was, Divinity,' Alexander said, preparing for the inevitable question.

'What did you make of this Balomar? What sort of man are we facing here?' He stared intently at Alexander, his gaze as strong and impassive as the sun's glare. The older man found it hard to meet.

'Uncouth, as you'd expect. Built like an ox, he was intimidating, intelligent. Barbarians we call them; I think it does some a disservice,' Alexander said, his words slow, methodical, practised.

'I agree. I have met many a man from over our borders who have been delightful company. You know I once spent an entire day discussing philosophy with a man from India? From India! You'd have to travel all the way through the Parthian empire, and then some to reach it! But there he was, sat across from me as you are now, his grasp of Latin perfect.' Aurelius paused, and Alexander noticed the frown upon his face. 'We have stopped learning, my friend, stopped expanding and experiencing new cultures. I fear one day the world will leave us behind.'

'We are the world, Divinity. Masters of it. At least the best parts. You are worried this Balomar and his armies may be the start of things to come?' Alexander thought the notion of the empire being left behind ridiculous. Although it troubled him to hear the words from the Augustus. For all that he despised him and coveted his throne, he knew the man was no fool.

'Maybe. Possibly. My spies north of the river speak of vast armies, countless numbers of people on the wild plains to the north and east of Germania. All are travelling south and west, in search of better lands. It will be some years before it poses a significant problem for us, but it is coming. And our armies are not what they once were, as the Fourteenth Legion can now attest to.'

'You are just back from the northern borders? How was it?' Alexander said, unable to stop himself leaning forwards. This is what he needed to know – facts and numbers he could relay to Balomar. Aurelius motioned to an unremarkable wooden stall. Alexander sat down slowly, trying to hide his wince as the pressure in his leg sent a shard of agony rippling through him.

'I was impressed actually.' Alexander's heart sank a little. 'Carnuntum has been rebuilt, the Fourteenth Gemina nearly back up to strength. The Thirteenth Gemina, who I'm sure you're aware were nearly wiped out in Dacia, are with them. I have ordered them to be brought back up to full strength and sent back to Dacia to garrison Apulum. Then we have the two new legions from Italy, who appear to be shaping up well, although still untested in battle. I have ordered them south to rebuild the defences around the Alps, under the command of Pertinax. Have you met him? No? A quite brilliant man. He's had some trouble with Cassius, something to do with outstanding debts, but I'm sure that will blow over. Claudius Fronto has command of the Fourth Flavia and Seventh Claudia in Moesia. Another good general and, as I'm sure you're aware, a dear friend of mine.

'Elsewhere I have removed Legate Decimus of the command of the Tenth. Caesar's own Tenth, in disgrace for not marching quick enough to aid the Fourteenth. What times we live in!' Aurelius looked down and shook his head. 'Pontuis Laelianus has been given the command. Again, he is untested, and in the inevitable war to come giving him his own command is a risk, but Vindobona is close enough to Carnuntum for the Fourteenth to support him. Also, I have removed Governor Bassus and sent him east. Claudius Pompeianus, another dear friend of mine and a man who served with distinction in the Parthian wars, has moved north to govern Pannonia. He will be the strong arm we need, a man with a taste for blood and a nose for victory …'

This revelation hit Alexander like a hammer blow to the heart. He felt its impact as he slid down his stool. Pompeianus going north was a game-changer. The man, by all accounts, was a born soldier, a keen strategist who had earned his reputation cutting the Parthians to shreds. Aurelius was still talking, something about the Fifth Macedonia in southern Dacia, but Alexander's mind was already whirling, plans taking root in his thought box. *Pertinax, have you met him? Some trouble with Cassius … gambling debts … Fronto … a dear friend of mine.*

' … so all in all we have nine legions ready, plus a few thousand auxiliaries scattered across the Danube. We shall prevail my friend, never fear.'

Alexander nodded. The confidence he'd felt when entering the imperial palace was slowly sapping away. Verus had gone off with the poisoned wine, the defence of the northern frontier had been strengthened. And worst of all, no attacks had come from Balomar this summer, and he had received no word. There was much work to be done.

XIV

April AD 171 – Germania

(Two years later)

Trudge, trudge, trudge. The army moved at a steady pace, dust clouding the air from the dried mud roads. Trudge, trudge, trudge. Albinus was glad he was in the front rank of his legion's column, the dust spiralling around him was torture. His throat was raw and felt cracked like the sun-baked mud he walked on, his eyes lined a crimson red and stinging like he'd been stung by a bee. The gods themselves only knew what it must have been like for the men at the rear.

Four legions marched in the unseasonably warm spring sun, over twenty thousand men, plus thousands more auxiliaries. The dust clouds would be seen for miles. The hooves of the cavalry thundered in his ears, messengers galloping up and down the line to keep the high command up to date with the latest news from the front.

Four weeks they had been marching. Four weeks of nothing but the foot-destroying trudge of the march; the back-breaking labour of building a full marching camp each night – trenches dug for the wood of the walls, defensive ditches in front of them, lilies carved from smaller branches and forced into the mud using human shit as a lubricant. It was Albinus' first taste of life on campaign, and not for the first time in the last three years since signing up, he was sincerely regretting it.

145

Trudge, trudge, trudge. He marched on the far right of the column, level with the front rank, as was his given place as the First Century's tesserarius, or watch officer. Taurus marched to his front, his face set in a scowl as always. Rullus was just behind him, the cohort's standard proudly hefted on his right shoulder.

'Fucking dust is crazy eh?' said Fullo, scarf wrapped round his face, squinting into the dust.

'Sure is, brother! Can't believe how warm it is. Gonna be horrid come summer if we don't get some rain!'

'How much longer we marching for then? Feels like we've been at it forever! Be glad when the old Germani finally decide they want a ruck!' Fullo scratched at his face. Albinus watched as the white, livid scars appeared on his forehead, the red clay from the dust being wiped away.

It had been nearly three years since Albinus and the rest of the Fourteenth Legion had stood in battle and fought Balomar and his horde. Albinus was still having nightmares about that day; the scar on his face still burned whenever he thought of the spear point bursting through cheek, tearing skin and rupturing tissue as it dislodged his teeth. The pain in his right shoulder still got so intense it would lock in place and only with the help of his tent-mates and a considerable amount of wine could he dislodge it again. For all that was horrid about the monotonous march through the scorching wilderness, nothing it could throw at him would be worse than the bowel-clenching, bladder-filling, heart-thundering feel that shuddered down your spine when a barbarian horde charged at your shield.

'Aye,' he muttered, not wanting to appear cowardly in front of his friend. There was something else that caused him to be muted in his reply, something Fullo didn't know. The enemy were in sight, not a day's march from their position. Albinus was a junior officer now, a promotion awarded to him upon his and his tent-mates return from their winter journey through Germania over two years ago. He was still not fully acclimatised to his higher status. But it meant he was privy to information legionaries were not, and Taurus had briefed him on the plan of attack the night before.

The enemy were waiting, on ground of their own terms, in land they

146

knew best. But the Augustus Marcus Aurelius was not deterred. He had ordered the attack.

This time tomorrow the Fourteenth and the three other legions would be knee-deep in blood, pushing their way up hill into a heavily fortified defensive position. Albinus felt his bowels go loose, the rumble as nervous gas moved lower. He winced as heartbeats later, he heard the groans and moans of the legionaries, all demanding to know which bastard had farted in their faces. One positive of being an officer, even if only a junior one, is that you were above suspicion.

'You okay, brother? Been very quiet today?' Fullo had the sense to sound casual in front of the other men, but Albinus could see the suspicion in his eye.

'Fine. Just had a crap night's sleep, can't wait for today's march to be over!' His bowels jerked again, more vile gas leaking out to poison the trailing soldiers' nostrils. He hated lying to his friend, knew he would hate it even more if their positions were reversed. He also knew it was necessary.

'Been up all night ain't he! Tugging off thinking of that bit o' stuff he's got waiting for him back home!' said Habitus as he chewed on some hardtack. Albinus marvelled at how he could eat something so dry amidst all the dust, his throat hurt enough as it was. He smiled shyly, thoughts turning to his wife.

It had been a shock when Julius had turned up at the gates of Carnuntum with Licina. Albinus was of course aware the man had agreed to go and get her, but he had never dared hope she'd actually agree to come back with him. But she had, and their reunion had been full of emotion and passion. She was different now, scarred in body and mind by her experience as a slave and her journey into the frozen north. But she was his Licina, as beautiful as spring's blossom, and his heart beat only for her. He hadn't summoned the nerve to ask about her experiences in the distant north, or how she had come by the vicious scars that crisscrossed her body. It was enough that she was back where she belonged, with him.

'Leave him alone, you old rogue!' Bucco pitched up in Albinus' defence. 'And when you address our tesserarius, you call him sir.' He spoke with authority, a gravelly edge to his tone that had always sent Albinus scurrying for the shadows.

147

'Too right! Unless you want the last watch every night for the rest of the month!' Longus piped up from the far end of the line, always quick to pitch in when it was someone else's turn to be picked on. The last watch was the one they all hated. Better to do the first and get to your bed late, or one in the middle when you knew you would still get a decent rest before the trumpets announced the dawn. But the last made for one long day: up before the crows, and still having to dig trenches with the rest as the sun was in descent. And if you ended up fighting that day? Better to be a rear ranker: a tired soldier was as good as dead when the iron clashed and blood flew.

'Why you all picking on me? Every day you lot find something to pick at! If Libo and Calvus were still here they'd have something to say about the abuse I get! I've been doing this shit over twenty-eight years now—'

'Here we go again!' Rullus didn't even turn around, eyes to the front as he shifted the standard from his right shoulder to the left. A long time they had all been listening to Habitus complain about his missing paperwork. Every year it got harder not to laugh when the legion was paraded, and the year's discharges read out by the legate. The old Syrian would mutter and fume as the realisation that he would have to survive another year campaigning dawned on him. It had been tough on the men of the contubernium, losing both Libo and Calvus in such a short space of time. They had commissioned a headstone for an empty grave for Libo in the cemetery in Carnuntum. Carved from the finest stone, it was a fitting tribute to a demon soldier. Calvus had survived the fever that threatened to consume him. But he was unable to continue active service in the legion, with the fingers of his left hand no longer on the end of his hand. He had been discharged, and had stayed in Carnuntum when they marched north. He had promised Albinus he would keep Licina safe.

'I'm telling you, the clerks lost the pap—'

The thunderclap of hoofbeats, the shaking of the ground as an alae of cavalry galloped past carrying bloodied spears and lances, the wounded being herded back in the middle of the pack. The men of the Fourteenth fell silent as they watched the horsemen pass, the sight of fresh blood dampening their spirits, wiping the banter and camaradrie from their tongues.

'Easy there, brother!' Taurus stalked from his position to wave down one of the rear rankers. He wore the same died horsehair crest running from left to right across the top of his helmet, a metal harness atop his mail, previously polished, now dull with blood. 'At ease, decurion,' he said as the cavalry commander snapped a salute from his horse. 'What goes up there?'

The conversation that followed was lost to the harsh sounds of the horses, men and metal that moved back and forwards along the column. Albinus watched as the decurion gestured frantically with his hands. *Ditch, wall, spears.* He guessed what the man was saying, didn't like the conclusions he came too. After a while Taurus nodded and waved the man on, returned to the marching column, his face a mask of concern. 'Centurions to me!' Taurus bellowed, moving off to the right of the column so it could continue to advance while he paused to speak to his cohort's commanders. Albinus felt his bladder fill as his mouth ran dry., the twitches in his hands, the chill down his spine. This was it. Battle was upon them. He looked left to his friends, all marching now in dim silence. Battle was upon them. *And I haven't told my friends. What sort of man am I?*

Balomar clenched his teeth through the pain as he pulled back from the front of the fighting. It was nearly dark now, the sun's yellow turning red as it dipped behind the forests to the west. He grinned, but to his men it looked more like a snarl. Red was an appropriate colour for today.

The Romans had come in mid-afternoon, when the sun was at its hottest. Balomar had set his defences well, spent the whole of winter preparing the ground. They were on the top of a gentle, sweeping valley. Thick forest either side protected their flanks. He had got his men digging ditches in random positions across the valley floor, then filling them in with leaves, twigs and small branches. He had hoped with the scattered leaves across the green carpet they would go unnoticed by the first Romans to advance on them. And sure enough, the Roman cavalry had charged straight into them, the sound of horses' legs snapping could be heard from atop the valley.

Repelling the cavalry had been easy after that. A volley of spears, quick sally out from behind their rough wooden walls, and they had sent them packing. The four legions that followed, however, were proving a much tougher nut to crack.

They had come on slowly, their metal-covered bodies filling the valley. Balomar had marvelled at seeing so many men brought to face him. The fear he thought the Augustus must feel was great, considering he had decided on a hasty march north with such a huge army.

Their supplies were running low, if the messages he had been receiving from Alexander were anything to go by. He was there somewhere, probably in the mass of colour and standards that marked out the command party at the rear of their force. The Augustus Marcus Aurelius rarely let the Abonoteichon stray from his side since the unexpected death of the Caesar Verus early the previous year. Well, not entirely unexpected; the only surprise for Balomar was that Aurelius himself still lived. Despite his alliance with the soothsayer, it had amused him to see the older man's plans not working out the way he had intended. The man was always so sure of himself, confident and arrogant. It would do him no harm to be knocked down a peg or two. *As long as the old goat keeps his promises to me.*

The Fourteenth – the legion that held the biggest grudge against Balomar, as he had all but ended them as a fighting force two years previous – had attacked first. Drafted back up to full strength, with even slaves and gladiators amongst their ranks, they had come on slowly, filling in the pits as they went, a solid, dense hedgerow of spears and shields.

They had paused at the larger pit, dug out across the entire length of the German line. It had been filled with sharpened wooden stakes, which the legionaries had methodically cleared, all whilst under the constant barrage of spears and stones. The Romans had responded by bringing forwards a unit of slingers – men with dark skin that wore no armour or helmets. Their small leather slings had whistled as they whirled them above their heads. Balomar's men hadn't known what hit them when the first wave cut through the air at such pace they were invisible. Men just fell, seemingly at random, with snapped bones and holes for eyes. It had been unnerving.

It had taken all of the king's nerve to stand in line with his men, to not flinch as the whistle of stones skidded past his face. Men fell screaming all around him, blood flying from small round holes. But he had stood, roaring his defiance, and his men had stood with him. It had been more than two years since the tribes last fought. And his army today was smaller than the one that had crossed the Danube. Two years of keeping the peace and making deals, he wasn't going to let a few stones ruin the work he had done.

The Fourteenth had retired after the stakes had been cleared and their men run dry of javelins. Next had been the Tenth, with a point to prove after leaving the Fourteenth to their fate when Balomar had attacked. They'd come on quick, spurred on by their legate and centurions. Pontuis Laelianus was their legate, or so Alexander had told him. *Stupid names these high-born Romans have.* He was apparently inexperienced, never commanded in the field. It showed in the way he threw his men against the German spears. Gleaming spear points atop their small but sturdy wall, it had been easier than slaughtering cattle.

The Germans were retiring as the sun was setting. Balomar stood panting, blood pouring down his right arm. The wound he had taken in the night fight at Carrodunum had been reopened with a lucky throw from a javelin. He clenched and unclenched his right hand, wincing at its stiffness. Gulping from the water skin at his waist, he walked slowly along the front of his defences, praising the men as he went. Adalwin fell in step next to him, and the two shared a nod. 'Your arm okay, lord?' Adalwin asked, a concerned nod at the leaking blood.

'Fine, my friend, just a scratch,' lied Balomar, hoping the pain didn't show on his face. 'We've done well today. Must have killed thousands.' He motioned with his left hand at the blood-soaked field the other side of the wall. A flood of bodies covered the grass for the first fifty paces down the gentle valley slope. The Romans were retreating to the south, wanting to put a safe distance between themselves and the Germani before making camp.

'Be a lot of pissed off men down there tonight. Tomorrow could be a long day.' Balomar didn't reply to his friend, just grunted his agreement, watching the backs of the retreating legions.

'Seemed quite easy today, do you think? I mean I know we lost men, and that they nearly broke through a couple of times, but …' Balomar paused. Something concerned him, a nagging doubt fluttering through his mind. Like a spider who had sought to weave its web upon his head, you can never quite shake the thing off. 'But, it all seemed a bit half-arsed from them. One legion brought up at a time, only two legions actually fought in total ... Thoughts?' He would never share his concerns with any other than Adalwin. The captain of his guard and his oldest companion, he knew he could be honest with him.

'You have chosen the ground well, my King. A narrow front, the ground littered with pits. They have to march up hill, get through the ditch, then reach over the wall to attack us. They can only attack with one legion at a time, no room for more. Unless they're gonna march through the trees, and no legion cou—'

A whistle through the trees to their rear, the snap of slingshot crunching bone. More high-pitched screams as more stones cut through the air so sharply it bled. Balomar dropped down to his knees, growling in frustration. *How are they behind us?* He'd set chief Euric and the Sidone tribe as a rearguard, not because he thought he'd need one, but because he doubted the quality of his troops. It seemed his doubts had been well founded.

Can't just lie here all night! He leapt up and drew his sword in one fluid motion. 'Marcomanni! On me, charge them!' He was already running as he yelled, eyes locked on his first target. He felt Adalwin at his shoulder, but had no idea if any more of his warriors followed. He didn't care, he was angry, embarrassed. He'd slaughter them all or die a warrior's death. *I'm coming, Allfather.*

It had, of course, been Taurus' idea to loop round the back of the barbarians and hit them in the rear. Albinus had thought his terrifying afternoon over when the First Cohort's horn blower had relayed the retreat from the command party.

It had been all he could do to not shit in his loincloth as he'd made the slow descent down the defensive ditch to rip the stakes from the mud, spears and rocks turning the sky black above, dying men moaning and grabbing his feet beneath him. The ground was slick with dark blood, the clash of iron hot in his ears. He'd never been so grateful as when he saw the slingers advance through the cohorts and unleash their missiles on the barbarians. The noise of the flying stones had drowned out the cacophony of the battle, its song high and painful to hear.

Wearily they had trudged off as the Tenth advanced to take over. The men of the Fourteenth were so tired they couldn't even bring themselves to jeer the cowards who had abandoned them in their time of need. The two legions had needed separating at one point on the march north, such was the animosity between them.

Albinus had just slumped down to the hard ground when Taurus had called him to his feet, briefly going through the plan. Just the First Cohort, and a century of slingers. Albinus hadn't even had time to sip from his water skin before he was back on his feet, getting men into line and off marching again.

The barbarians had a rearguard in place, a small clutch of desperate looking warriors, lounging in the sun as they waited for news of the day's fighting. They were dead before they knew they'd been killed.

They stalked through the thick woodland, grateful of the respite from the setting sun, the ground crisp underfoot, with muttered curses from centurions as twigs snapped and men tripped. Then the slingers whirled into action, stones hurtling at the unsuspecting barbarians faster than a lightning bolt.

Roars of fear and defiance, swords and spears raised in anger, Taurus got the men into line, and they charged. So did the Germani.

They met at the edge of the trees, where the crimson light met the darkness. Albinus stood on the far right of the line, Fullo to his left. They took down the first barbarian they saw together, Fullo ramming him with his shield and Albinus sticking him with his sword. The next man was a greybeard, too tired from a day spitting Romans on his spear. Albinus feinted low with his gladius; the old man just got his shield down, but had no answer when the younger and fitter Albinus reversed the thrust, whipped his sword over the shield and carved into his neck.

Spinning for his next opponent he saw Fullo knocked to the canvas by a giant. A great two-headed axe splattered red with crimson was raised over his head as he thought to split Fullo's skull in two. Albinus let out a cry, too far away to stop it. Time slowed, his mind went blank. He had one

153

chance. *Pretty sure this won't work.* Adjusting the grip on his short sword he threw it overarm, the blade spinning and whirling as it tumbled through the air. The hilt bounced harmlessly off the giant's chest. *Bollocks.* It did, though, cause the giant to pause, which gave Fullo enough time to kick him in the balls and scramble to his feet. Two legionaries appeared from the woods to finish him off.

Swordless now, Albinus ripped his pugio from its scabbard on his left hip, ducked behind his shield and advanced forwards at a crouch. Grouping back up with Fullo and the rest of the line, blood pumping in his ears, he deflected a thrown spear with his shield, stuck his dagger in a man's thigh without breaking stride.

Almost at the wall now – a small, crude timber barricade – he wondered why the legions had not been able to break through all day. A roar to his right and a mass of charging barbarians answered his question. Yellow trousers – Marcomanni then, Balomar's own tribe – they formed a sort of wedge, with a man Albinus assumed to be their king at the tip. A barrel of a man covered in metal, a huge iron helmet ordained with bronze wings atop his head, his sword longer than Albinus's arm, he snarled as he charged, eyes fixed on Albinus.

Albinus just had time to duck behind his scutum. His left arm shuddered with the impact as the great sword rang off the iron boss at its centre. Forced down to his knees, he braced himself once more as another blade bit into the linden board. The shield gave in, wood chips plastering Albinus' face. He let out an involuntary cry, his imminent death turning his bowels to water.

'THE FOURTEENTH!' A loud cry in his ears ... blurred visions of sandalled feet running past him ... a clash or iron ... screams of victory and despair ... hands on his shoulders, hauling him to his feet ... left arm numb, legs a wave of agony, he was pushed back, up against the barbarian wall.

'Thought we'd lost you there, lad!' Bucco at his shoulder, pushing him over the wall. 'Thousands of the goat fuckers now! Time to leg it!' Without another word Bucco thrust Albinus over the wall, his pugio slipping from his hand as he fell, hands scrambling in the blood. *Got to find the hilt.*

'Leave it, little brother, we gotta get the outta 'ere!' Habitus with his

154

hands on his back, pushed him down the slope. Up the other side, crimson blood stained the grass, dead men and rusting metal everywhere, running into the darkness, men laughing and cheering as they went. Albinus was still trying to recover his senses, blood pounding through his head, he could hear his heartbeat through his armour.

'FOURTEENTH! MARTIAL AND VICTORIOUS!' Taurus started the cry, quickly taken up by the rest of his cohort. The barbarians weren't pursuing, too shocked by the sudden attack on their rear. Albinus spat blood, and wondered where it came from. He was running from a battle without his shield or sword – he didn't feel victorious.

'Albinus, lad!' Taurus clamped his arm in a vice grip. 'What do you think of our opponent then? Big cunt ain't he!' He was grinning from ear to ear, blood pouring from old cuts on his scarred lips, his red beard darkened with claret, mail coat more crimson then the plume on his helmet.

'What?' Albinus managed to stutter out.

'Balomar! You just fought the enemy king in battle! Without a sword as well! You wait until the legate hears about this!' Albinus' vision blurred, he staggered, but Fullo quickly propped him up, Bucco at his other shoulder, Habitus, Rullus and Longus all at his back, all wanting to shake his hand or pat his shoulder. Then he was off his feet, hands on his back and arse as they hefted him high off the ground. 'SILUS VICTORIOUS!' The cry from his tent-mates, quickly taken up by the men around him.

It was a strange feeling, hearing his father's name spoken out loud after all this time. *No, my name.* An even stranger thought. He was no longer a child, no longer the squeamish boy he had been when his father had lived. Gone was the child named Albinus. Sitting atop those shoulders, half blind, dizzy and nauseous, was a man named Silus – Albinus Silus. The soldier.

Torchlight appeared up ahead, great wooden gates in between two towers. Through the gates they went and into the vast encampment that housed four legions. Legatus Maximianus stood beaming with pride, embracing Taurus warmly as the cohort marched smartly back through the gate, Albinus still held high.

Lowered back to the ground, Albinus saluted his legate unsteadily, his eyes wandering to a man draped in purple atop a white stallion. The Augustus

Marcus Aurelius had been a constant presence on the march north. It was well known within the army he blamed the Germani for the death of his colleague, the Caesar Verus. A heart attack had been the official version of events read out on the corners of every city throughout the empire. But everyone knew treachery was suspected. His dark eyes bore into Albinus, who should have averted his own. But he stood transfixed. Dark curls shot with grey blowing wildly in the night breeze, a short-cropped beard white against a sun darkened face, the emperor, ruler of the known world and father to all its inhabitants, smiled at Albinus before giving him a nod and kicking his stallion back into the camp.

Albinus still stood, stiller than a mountain, shocked that the most powerful man in the world had given him a smile. He didn't realise he was now looking at the man that had been behind the emperor. Cloaked and hooded in green, his face was masked by the night, hints of a grey beard round his shadowed chin. Stumps of yellow teeth showed as he gave Albinus a sneer, before lurching his own jet-black stallion round and following the emperor.

XV

Calvus followed the newly paved road that ran along the river bank. The air smelt like spring, growing grass danced in the breeze, birds flew overhead, bees buzzed in and out of purple, pink and yellow flowers. The small floating islands in the middle of the great river had bloomed a glorious green, their light reflecting off the dull waters. It was a glorious day, the pale blue sky cloudless, the sun big and warm. It should have been enough to cheer his spirits, put a smile on his face and a whistle on his lips.

It wasn't. It didn't.

All morning he had been following her – the skinny girl, with the long sweeping legs, sandalled feet and a wicker basket swaying at her hip. The rest of her was masked by an old legionary cloak, a once proud red now a dull brown, hood up to obscure the view of her hair and face, as if she didn't want to be recognised. Calvus watched her intently as she walked slowly through the small riverside market, stopping here and there to view small pieces of cheap jewellery or to haggle over the price of freshly caught fish.

Twice Calvus saw her delve into a money purse tied to a belt around her waist. Each time she produced a small bronze coin – an as – and handed it over to the merchant. Each time, Calvus noticed, she received nothing for her coin.

Further into the hustle of the market she went. A tall man on a wooden dais was selling slaves; skinny Africans, skin darker than the night sky, they

157

looked as though they hadn't been fed in weeks. *Poor bastards probably haven't.* He studied the slaves, seeing a resemblance in their features to his lost friend Libo, and he sent a quick prayer to his shade.

He watched as the hooded girl paused by the slave merchant, too far away to hear what she called up to him. The merchant stopped his shouting mid-flow, stooped down and muttered something to the girl. Calvus stopped by a fish merchant, not wanting to get too close, or bring any attention to himself.

'All right, brother, what ya after?' Calvus looked up into the eyes of the merchant, seeing the same scarred look behind the smile, and spotting a fellow veteran. He assumed the man saw the same in him.

'Nothing, brother. Just looking.' He looked back to the girl, moving slowly off from the slaver, basket swaying at her hip.

'Trout for an as, eel for two and a catfish for three. Rare bit o' fish that is, and you won't get a better price anywhere else ...'

Calvus had already moved on, stalking his prey as he treaded light-stepped through the throng. The slaver had quite an audience now, a semicircle of potential buyers, up to six deep in places. Calvus cursed under his breath as he forced a path through, using his fingerless left hand as a rod to steer people out his way, right hand firmly on the hilt of the dagger under his cloak.

Halfway through, he could just make out the hood of the girl's cloak as she exited the crowd, into the open space beyond. He cursed as the thought of losing sight of her set his heart racing. He'd promised he'd follow her, keep an eye on her. He was being paid for this, his first assignment, and he was already failing. His employer was not a man to let down. It wasn't just the money though: he had a personal obligation to the girl, an emotional interest in her wellbeing. He just wished he could reach out to her, let her know he was there for her.

More urgency now, he pushed at the massed people firmer, shoving into backs and treading on toes. A woman squealed in fright. Calvus just pushed her harder, she stumbled forwards, dropping the sun shade she had been holding above her head.

'Hey! Excuse me, yes you! That's my wife you just pushed. Apologise this instant!' *Christ on the cross, give me a break.* He muttered an apology, turned his back on the man quickly, eager to be on his way. 'I said excuse me!' The man grabbed Calvus by the shoulder, spinning him back around. Calvus knew the type of man he was facing, didn't have to give him a good looking-over to know – just the tone of his voice, the cut of his toga. Not a senator, not someone important, but someone who thought they were important. A banker, Calvus guessed, a man with money and sense of status rather than a man with any actual status. *A cunt.*

Calvus hated cunts.

In one fluid motion the Briton spun on his toes, grabbing the banker's left shoulder with the stump of his fingerless hand. In his right was his dagger, the sharpened iron reflecting the sun's light as he shrugged his cloak off his shoulder. Two quick thrusts to the groin and the man was as good as dead, he just didn't know it yet.

Not pausing, he didn't want to have to answer difficult questions to the patrol of legionaries carelessly observing the market. He sheathed the blade and shuffled off quickly, lowering his head and throwing up his hood. The woman screamed behind him, a cry quickly taken up by those around the stricken banker. People streamed past him, eager to be away from the dying man and his panicked wife.

Calvus cast a wary glance to his left and right, but saw no soldiers pressing towards him. Pausing in his stride, he looked intently for the light brown hood, the basket at her hip. His heart thudded in his chest, exhilarated by the quick kill, anxious to lock his gaze onto his target.

Thud, thud, thud. People streamed past, soldiers shouted and the woman's grief-stricken wails grew louder and more desperate. Thud, thud, thud. A green cloak sped left, a red one right. A white one streamed towards him, a red one away from him. *Where are you? Come on, come on.* A flash of orange to his left, a flame haired girl being dragged away from a stall by a tall man in a deep green cloak, a flood of recognition sparked within him. *Is that ...?* In the distance, disappearing between two white-stoned buildings, the flash of a brown hood before it disappeared into the shadows.

Bless you, Jesu, you're all right after all! Forgetting the flame-haired girl he approached the alley at a gentle run – no good going hurtling around the corner, no way of knowing what's there. Approaching the white walls, topped with red-tiled roofs, he tried to peer into the alley, gauge what lay in wait. Darkness was all he saw. The floor was damp, brown puddles in places; it stank of piss and shit.

A door to the left and one to the right. The one on the left had no mark or signs, just the plain dull colour of unpainted wood. The one to the right was dark and looked to be mouldy, an erect phallus nailed to the wall above the door. The door was swinging shut. Calvus sighed. Of all the places he thought this job would take him, a brothel would have been bottom of the list.

He entered the alley, nose scrunched against the smell, pausing at the door, wary looks to either side to make sure he wasn't being followed or observed. *Knock? Or just go in?* Every brothel in the empire had different ways of doing it. There had been one back in Londinium where you'd had to pay the fare on the door, without even getting a peep at what was on offer. He weighed his options. Barging open the door and getting kicked out before he'd got a foot in wouldn't help his cause; he thought it better to play it safe.

Two knocks, a short pause, an elderly lady, stooped spine and round belly, opened the door and ushered him inside, into a small corridor, blandly decorated and dimly lit by two flimsy candles. He passed through a side door and into a better lit reception room. There was a worn blue couch and two folding wooden stools that wouldn't have been out of place in a legionary's campaign tent. He sat on one of the stools, always more comfortable there than on a couch. The old lady hobbled to a small desk in the corner of the room, slumped down on her own chair and ushered Calvus over with a wave of her hand.

'What you after?' she said, blunt as a rusty blade.

'Well, what you got on offer?' Calvus scanned the room, looking for other exits. The girl must have gone somewhere. A dark red curtain on the wall to his front rustled, followed by the stamp of booted feet as an unseen person walked by.

The old lady sighed. 'Don't beat around the bush, mate. We got what every brothel in town has. Depends what you fancy – boys, girls, a full-on fuck or a quick fondle. Now, what do you want? I got other customers waiting.'

Calvus glanced round at the empty room, silent but for the flicker of the candle flame. 'You do?' he asked, arching a sarcastic eyebrow. She made no reply. But she gave him such a look that could bring thunder from the cloudless sky. Calvus' turn to sigh. He thought about his options, didn't like the conclusion he came too. The girl he followed, she was no prostitute, that he was sure. So, there was no point asking for a girl, hoping to catch one who'd just gone on shift. He also knew brothels had a tendency to keep the girls and the boys in separate quarters of the building, so if he asked for a girl he could end up in a separate part of the building to his assignment, assuming she hadn't asked for one herself. He sighed again. *She wouldn't have. Jesu's shining cock!* The curse seemed appropriate, considering what he was about to ask for. *Glad Habitus ain't here to see this, I'd never hear the end of it.* 'A boy, please,' he muttered, feeling the vomit climb up his throat.

'Sorry? I didn't quite catch that?' The old woman lent in towards him, face to the side so her right ear presented itself. He saw the smile on her face.

You're enjoying this aren't you? 'A boy I said! I want a boy!' It came out louder than he would have wanted. The old lady smiled, showing the stumps of her yellowing teeth.

'Well, that's all you had to say,' she said, lifting herself up from the wooden chair and waddling towards the red curtain. 'Follow me please.' She didn't look back as she made her way down another narrow, dark corridor. Grunts and moans, the stink of sweat and sex – it had been a while since Calvus had spent the evening in a brothel, been a while since he'd had the coin. Not much work for a retired soldier with a fingerless hand.

The prostitutes were kept in what appeared to be more like booths than rooms. Big, burly guards, scarred and fearsome looking, patrolled the small corridor, every now and then thrusting their heads through the dark curtains to the booths, ensuring the punters were behaving themselves, not damaging any of the merchandise.

Through another doorway they went, into a smaller corridor, only two booths here. 'Don't get much custom for boys, so just got the two, and one of them's with a punter at the moment. Curtain on the left, he's all yours. We charge by the hour, I'll take payment on your way out. Oh,' she said as she turned to walk away, 'don't try anything funny, got my guards here patrolling. They'll sling you out in the gutter if they think you're up to no good.' Calvus nodded as she waddled off, her massive girth making it a struggle for her to fit in between the narrow walls.

With a cautious look at the waiting bodyguard, Calvus entered the booth, feeling foolish and sheepish. A boy of no more than twelve sat on a wooden bench, puppy eyes quivering in fear. He moved off the bench and took Calvus by the hand, moving him onto it and kneeling before him. *Fuck. My. Life.* Calvus tried to ignore the boy and focused his gaze through the curtain, into the booth opposite.

His view was dim, hindered by the flickering light of a few candles and the thickness of the curtain. He could make out the hooded girl, see the outline of her nose and lips as she spoke with someone … could hear whispers, faint on the air, but they just sounded like a gust of wind from so far away. A man stepped into the candlelight, tall and well built. He wore no hood, but was covered in a thick cloak. His hair looked to be slick with oil, eyes narrow, face covered by a shadowy beard.

Calvus leaned forward, as if by moving the short distance the whispered words would become clearer. He didn't notice the kneeling boy wince, his small hand up his thigh, under his tunic, creeping into his loincloth. A candle flickered and went out, a waft of breeze, rustle of the cloak as the guard poked his head in. 'What the fuck you looking at,' Calvus muttered. The guard gave him a look that promised blood, before turning towards the other curtain. Calvus shifted to the right, peeping round the side of his own curtain, hoping to get a look through the gap into the other booth as the guard ducked his head in. There was a muted conversation with the bearded man, who nodded, the clink of coins changing hands, the grind as the guard rubbed them together as he made off down the corridor.

Calvus dared not move, or take breath. The whispers were more urgent now, frantic and desperate. He watched as the bearded man grabbed the girl, a hand on each cheek as he pulled her face to his, a long and passionate kiss. *Oh baby Jesu no! No!*

The man pushed the girl back, away from him so hard she hit the wall, the back of her head colliding with a violent thump. Without another word the man was off, thrusting back the curtain and stomping down the corridor. Calvus could make nothing of his face, hooded now in a cloak. It took another moment for him to realise the man had the wicker basket, the one the girl had brought in. *What in God's name is going on here?*

He sat in silence, unsure whether to follow the man or stay with the girl. His heart urged him to reach out to the girl, but he knew he couldn't. He pondered, knowing he had to make a quick decision. If he went with the man and was discovered, his cover would be blown, his employer not happy. It was something he didn't want to risk. The girl had been his mission, for both himself and his employer. He would stay with her, ensure she was safe. Sniffs and sobs came from the booth now, the girl crying when she thought there was no one to listen. Calvus tensed, fighting increasing the urge to go and comfort her. *Don't be a fool. You're the last person she wants to see right now.*

She was up after a short while, brushing down her cloak, pulling her hood tight and making off down the corridor. Calvus stayed rooted to the bench, counting the beats of his heart. He had to leave it long enough for her to get out of the building, but not long enough for her to disappear down the alley. A spark of pain in his groin, he looked down to see the boy flicking at his limp penis. 'Did I do something wrong, sir?' asked the boy in an anxious voice.

'No lad, you did great,' said Calvus, giving the boy a reassuring pat on the shoulder before adjusting himself and making for the exit.

The old lady was back at her desk as he passed through the red curtain, the bodyguard nowhere to be seen. He fished in his money purse, flicking the old wench a gold coin. She caught it, tried to hide her surprise at the weight and colour. 'A denarius, very generous, you've barely been here half an hour!'

'What can I say, he's a good lad! You should pay him more.' Out into the alley, the light that had appeared so dim when he had entered was now bright and dazzling.

Calvus looked left, then right, spotting the brown cloak and hood bobbing deeper into the narrow walkway between the clutch of buildings. He set off at a slow walk, aiming to maintain the distance. He chewed over what he had seen – the merchants in the market, the hushed rendezvous with the man in the brothel, the basket containing God knew what. Cursing, he wondered why it had been him who been approached for this job, and why did it have to turn out to be her? He already knew why him, an out-of-work soldier desperate for coin, but her? In truth, it hadn't taken much persuasion to get him to do it. And the offer of coin helped. But what about her? What could she have got herself into?

He chewed so hard on his lip it began to bleed. Blood dripped down his stubbled chin, but he barely noticed. *What are you up to?* was all he could think. *And what in all things holy am I supposed to do to help you?*

Licina shed her cloak as she walked through the door to her small apartment. She slumped down on the straw mattress in the corner of the one room that consisted of her world, tears welling in her eyes. Life without Albinus had been hard, harder than she could have imagined. It felt an age since he had marched off north, but it had only been a matter of weeks. She had received no letters from him, though he had promised to write as often as he could. She had no idea if he was even alive. Had the Romans found the barbarians and brought them to battle?

She had taken a job as a laundry maid in the basilica at Carnuntum. She worked in and around the heart of the city's home of law and order, washing clothes and changing bed sheets for the officers and clerks alike. There was a tribune in charge, Appius Scaevola, a snob of a man who thought too much of himself. He was tall, dark-skinned with slick black hair. He had taken to wearing a cropped beard, a style adopted by many since Aurelius had risen to the purple. He was loose with his tongue, reading aloud messages from the front. The Governor of Pannonia and general in command of the main army was Claudius Pompeianus, who was clearly not a fan of the tribune. Scaevola would read aloud the harsh and sarcastic orders he received from the general, benign things such as coin needed to pay the troops, mules and carts to replace ones lost on campaign, horses to replace the ones slain in battle. The tribune thought himself above such simple and boring tasks, and was instead spending the coin he had been set aside on a lavish statue of the Augustus in the forum of Carnuntum. It was shrouded in secrecy, this statue. Tarpaulin covered the whole thing, stretched around wooden scaffolding. He would state that none would witness the statue until 'his' Augustus was present. It was the way he said 'his' that piqued Licina's interest. Surely the Divine Aurelius was everyone's emperor?

Once he had read aloud the belittling letters from his commanding officer, he would then dictate his own to his great friend Avidius Cassius, governor of Syria. In these dictations he would openly mock the general as well as Aurelius himself. He once called them 'two toothless old men, rambling about the German country side like lost sailors, hungry for the sea.'

Licina would wince, head down obscuring her disapproving expression. Surely the Augustus would have spies here, listening, observing what this man was doing with the free rein and imperial coffers he had been given? It would appear not – that or the Augustus was a very tolerant man.

Despite the long and thick cloak that hid a body she had come to understand was desirable to almost every man she met, she could feel the man's eyes upon her – dark eyes, darker than the purest soil. The tribune would devour her when she walked past him, his dark eyes undressing her, hands shifting unconsciously to his groin, mouth open, saliva visible. Licina would rush, thrusting dirty laundry into her wicker basket, running from the room, out the door and into the hustle of the forum. It didn't matter how many times she visited the newly rebuilt public baths in the city centre, the glint, the hunger in those dark eyes always made her feel dirty.

The tears at these thoughts were almost gone now. She picked herself up from the mattress, collected the cloak and threw it on the back of the door. She thought of writing to Albinus, telling him of the tribune and his dark lusting eyes. She knew it would be a mistake, knew her love would come rushing south to spit the man on the end of his spear. She smiled at the thought. There really was nothing he wouldn't do for her. But how far would she go for him? She stroked her belly as she thought, her mind wandering. Would Heide have tolerated it? She would have gutted the man by now, she knew.

A knock on the door made her jump. Gathering her composure, she called for the visitor to enter. The door opened slowly and Calvus poked his head round the carved wood, a bland smile fixed to his scarred face.

Calvus, she knew, had found it tough no longer being a soldier. He was lonely, missing his brothers in the army. He often visited unannounced, Licina thought purely for the fact he had nothing else to do.

'Hi,' she said as Calvus moved into the room, closing the door behind him. 'Not seen you for a few days, you been okay?' As he moved closer, she caught a scent of cheap perfume, tainted by sweat and sex. 'Have you been in a brothel?'

Calvus drew up, a look of embarrassment flashing across his face. 'I ... err ... got a job. Earned meself some coin, and yes, spent some of it in a brothel.' His cheeks flushed red. Licina tried to hide her amusement; a veteran soldier, combat hardened, embarrassed at having to admit to his friend's wife he'd paid for sex. She laughed, unable to hide it anymore.

'Good,' she said, 'I'm glad. Life must be tough for you right now, I'm glad you've found some work. What are you doing?'

Calvus, still flushing redder than the purest rose, spoke slowly. 'Got some work down at the markets by the river. Just lugging boxes really, nothing fancy. Coin's coin though, will help keep a roof over my head.' Licina knew Calvus had been living in the fortress still. Allowed by the primus pilus Taurus, he had been allotted a small room in the First Cohort's barracks, fed twice a day and given odd tasks to do around the fortress.

'You can't stay at the fortress?'

'Not long term, no. The legion will be back at some point, won't be room for me then. Gonna save all I can, hopefully rent somewhere in the city when the lads come back.' He sat down awkwardly on the straw mattress. Licina noticed for the first time there was blood on his tunic, just above the right hip, and encrusted in the fingernails of his hand. 'I saw you today, at the market. You were too far away to call too, what were you doing down there?'

He didn't make eye contact as he spoke, though the words were said lightly enough. Licina felt the sweat begin to drip on her forehead, an intense pain at the back of her head, her belly suddenly tense and full of butterflies, a vile taste in her mouth. 'I was just browsing, picked up a fish for dinner. You want some?' She picked up the fish wrapped in brown paper, offering it to Calvus. 'There was some sort of commotion at the market today, a man was stabbed. Did you see anything?'

166

'No, first I've heard. And sorry but I can't stay thank you. I have plans with someone tonight, an old army friend. Another time perhaps?' An awkward silence presided, neither finding the right words to break it.

'Well I had better be going. Just dropped in to make sure you were okay. Is there anything you need, anything I can do for you?'

Licina stood, willing her heart to stop racing. Hands still clasped to her belly, she saw Calvus look at her hands and frown, as if he were confused, or considering asking a question he might not like the answer to.

'No, I'm fine thank you, just lonely, same as you I guess. Do come back, won't you? Stay for dinner, would be nice to have some company.' She moved to open the door for him. He paused at the threshold, his hand grabbing the hem of her cloak that hung on the back of the door. It was one of Albinus' old ones that he'd left behind when he went to the north. Brown stains covered the bottom of the cloak, as if it had been dragged through a dirty puddle.

Calvus showed her his teeth, or what was left of them, as he gave her a weak grin. 'Might wanna get that cleaned. Albinus won't be happy when he gets back.' He left without another word, left Licina standing alone in her small room, hands still rubbing her belly.

XVI

'Steady boys! Hold the line! Push, push!' Optio Albinus Silus stood behind his century as they pushed the Roman line forward. The fighting had been intense for most of the morning, the Romans taking heavy casualties.

They were assaulting Eburum, a small hilltop fortress of crude wooden barricades atop a steep slope. It was the home of the Batini, a small and inconsequential tribe. But they had forsaken the terms of their peace with Rome and sent warriors to fight in Balomar's army, therefore they must be punished.

The General Pompeianus had detached Maximianus and the Fourteenth Legion to deal with the threat, thinking one legion would be enough to suppress a small tribe in a foolish revolt. He had, it would appear, significantly underestimated the tribe's numbers, and those of its allies.

Uphill they had been fighting all morning, the relentless summer sun scorching, roasting them under their armour and weapons. Albinus stood at the rear of his century, palm itching for the grip of his sword hilt, rather than the long wooden pommelled staff that was his badge of office. It kept catching on the underside of the silvered ring he had been given on his promotion, purely decorative and to mark his rank. He'd found it hard, being promoted. Moving to another cohort and century, away from his brothers in the First Cohort, who had made his transition into the army as seamless as it could be.

He was in the Sixth Cohort now, Fourth Century. Good men, he had to admit, but not up to the standards of the First Cohort. Less than a month he had been there, and this was his first engagement as the century's second-in-command. Their centurion, Marcus Valerius was a good man, if a little to quick to lead with his vine stick rather than by example. He was a veteran of over twenty years, more than ten of them as a centurion, and Albinus could see the bitterness in him that he had never risen past the Sixth Cohort, or got the chance to command a whole cohort himself.

He had left the day-to-day running and drilling of the century to Albinus, who had at first found it daunting, but then had quickly taken to the role, building bonds with the men under his command. One of those men was Julius Decanus, who had signed up with the Fourteenth after bringing Licina back from the distant north. He had wanted to stay away from Albinus and his friends, thought it was a blessing when he was assigned to the Sixth. Barracks at the other end of the fortress to the First, place in battle line the opposite end, neither man had thought they would have to see each other again. After all, a full-strength legion of over five thousand men was a mobile city in itself, a mass of men and metal – and cohorts tended to mingle only with themselves.

But now, Julius stood directly in front of Albinus, matted in blood, having just rotated out the front line. Albinus moved forwards and tapped him with his staff, ordering him to take on water whilst he could. The battle was going well, Albinus thought. The natural defences around the hill top made an assault very difficult, but the poorly armed and armoured barbarians were slowly having to give ground; it was only a matter of time.

Albinus saw the red plume of his centurion as he stood in the front line of his century, shield high, sword thrusting in and out. A wave of fear washed over him as he thought he would have to relieve him soon; centurions always fought in the front rank, but no one could expect them to stand and fight there all day, the man would need a break. Scanning the front line he could see other helmets crested with two feathers, where other optios had pushed forward and relieved their tiring centurions.

He was just about to push his way through and give his commanding officer a break when he heard something, felt a change in the battle: a rumble on the ground, soft but steady, like distant hoofbeats; a cry in the air, then another. He spun, turning his back on the battle. At the bottom of the slope stood the supply wagons, surrounded by the cavalry that Maximianus had declared redundant for the uphill assault. The wounded were trickling down the slope to the small tents set up by the medics and the surgeons. Slaves with stretchers carried the dead and the dying from one tent to another, depending on the surgeon's verdict of their survival chances. And behind all this, the trees were alive with warriors. They streamed from the thick forest, wave after wave of iron-bearing barbarians, screaming their barritus as they ran.

Tribune Vindex led the cavalry, and was quick to react. Albinus watched open-mouthed in shock as Vindex got his men mounted, formed them into a rough wedge and charged.

'Horn blower, to me,' said Albinus as he motioned with his staff. The man ran over, bronze instrument held awkwardly in both hands. 'We need to turn the back four lines round to march down and face those bastards.' Albinus pointed at the approaching barbarians, surrounding and cutting down the exposed Roman cavalry. The horn blower paused, uncertainty written all over his face. *You know we need to give the order, but you don't want to take it from me.* Albinus could see and understand the soldier's indecision. He was just a junior officer, not a tribune or a centurion. The horn blower was wondering if a mere optio had the authority to order such a manoeuvre. He hesitated, his instrument half toward his mouth. 'Come on, man! Romans are dying, we need to alert the legate to what's happening!'

Even as he spoke the cavalry's willowing dragon standard fell to the dust, a hearty cheer erupting from the barbarian horde. The horn blower didn't move, he just stood, stuttering.

Albinus didn't waste any time. Telling Julius he was in charge, he set off, sprinting from the line to find the legate and warn him. The Sixth Cohort were on the far right of the line, attacking the south bank of the hill top. The legate would be attacking the western banks with the First and Second Cohort, unable to see the approaching barbarians that were about to take them in the rear.

Sweat streamed down him in droves as he ran, his helmet a furnace,

170

armour an anvil on his back. His breath came in rasps, feet blistering with every step, lungs on the verge of collapse. The colour party were up ahead, the legion's eagles resplendent in the sun, Maximianus in his white-crested helmet, the sun's rays reflecting off his polished bronze cuirass.

'Sir,' he rasped, hands falling to his knees as he stopped and heaved in air in front of the legion's commanding officer. He didn't notice the pommelled staff drop unceremoniously to the floor, where it had slipped out of his sweat-soaked palms.

'Optio Silus, what in Jupiter's name is happening for you to rush here like this?' The legate asked, no sign of panic in his voice.

Albinus gasped out what he had saw. Maximianus and his officers leant forwards, struggling to make out the young man's words. Once he'd got the bulk of it, he didn't waste any time. 'Come, optio, you're with me!' and he was off.

Albinus gulped warm water from the skin on his hip, and fastening the stop back in place he was off after his legate. He looked up at the sun as he started off again, almost dismayed to see it was not yet midday. There was a lot of daylight left, and a lot blood to be spilt before it turned to darkness.

'I don't care what you *think,* tribune! Your legion was routed, disgraced in front of the enemy! I'm sending you west and that's final! The Rhine is quiet, the tribes bordering the river are causing us no hassle. It will do you or your legion no harm to spend some time there, recover your losses and your flagging morale. Dismissed!'

Legatus Maximianus marched briskly and angrily from the command tent. His cheeks flushed in anger, breath ragged, he looked as though he had just marched from the battlefield, not the army's headquarters.

Taurus stood to attention just off the via principia that ran through the centre of the marching camp. Maximianus noted his usually formidable First Spear was keeping his eyes on his boots, not willing to bring them up and see the fury in his superiors.

'Centurion,' he nodded to Taurus, who fell in step alongside him. 'Well, that was a fucking disaster!'

'What happened, sir?' asked Taurus in a cautionary tone.

'The *esteemed* General Pompeianus has accused *me* and *my* legion of cowardice! Cowardice! Running in the face of the enemy, he said! As if he has a clue what happened!' Maximianus hawked and spat. He stopped, sucking his teeth as he drew in the cool evening air. The legate had been unable to turn his legion to face the new threat to their rear in time. His retreat, though, he had thought a masterstroke.

Calling back the First, Second and Third Cohorts from their position, hidden round the bend at the opposite side of the hill fort, they had marched in perfect formation to surprise the enemy on the flank, freeing space for the rest of the legion to march away in ranks rather than the rout it so nearly was.

He had been so careful in his report to the Augustus and his general. But it seemed his tactical manoeuvres had gone unnoticed.

'Something's amiss here, Taurus,' he said, teeth now gnawing his gums.

'How so, sir?'

'I don't know. But someone is working against me, I can feel it. I don't know who and I don't know why, but this all feels as if its been some sort of set-up.'

'I don't follow, sir? I know we ended up in the shitter, but that could have happened to any legion. We did everything proper – scouts out in all directions for miles around us. The enemy just used the ground, their local knowledge, and had an ambush planned. Can't anticipate that, sir.' Taurus shrugged as he spoke. Maximianus envied his ability to let the weight and troubles of command wash over him. Every set-back was personal to the legate, every defeat a hammer blow.

'Think about it, First Spear. We were ordered to march directly to Eburum, no artillery, no auxiliaries for support. The general had limited intel on the tribe or their manpower. Why send us? There were other legions closer, why not send them?'

Taurus shrugged, 'Fucked if I know, sir. We're the Fighting Fourteenth though, right? Martial and Victorious and all that, maybe the general thought we were the right legion for the job.'

Maximianus shook his head. 'No, mark my words, there's more to this than meets the eye. Someone has a hard on for us, maybe me personally.

And I have no idea who.' He spat again, mumbled a curse to the gods. 'Let's talk of other things, before I drive myself crazy with conspiracy theories. How many did we lose?'

Taurus didn't hesitate, didn't need to consult the wax tablet under the crook of his arm. 'Eight hundred dead or missing, four hundred wounded, give or take. The surgeons reckon at least one hundred of the wounded won't make it, another fifty will never fight again.'

'Juno's tits! That's over two cohorts out of action! What about centurions?'

'Twelve dead, one wounded. Surgeon says his marching days are over – took a spear just above the knee.'

Maximianus winced. *Rather be killed then crippled, any day.* 'Which centurion?'

'Marcus Valerius, Sixth Cohort, Fourth Century.'

'I don't know him, not by name anyway. Who's his optio? Can we promote him? At least that's one quick fix.'

'Well, him you know actually. Albinus Silus, my predecessor's boy. He's only just made optio, not been a soldier long! Probably a bit early, sir.' Maximianus nodded. He turned, looking past Taurus to Abas, who was never far from his centurion. Maximianus lowered his voice, 'The time may have come to finally force your deputy into a promotion. The Gods themselves know he's more than ready for it. Why not swap him with young Albinus, that way you can groom the lad into the officer we need him to be.'

Taurus blinked, surprised. 'Albinus, optio of the First Century, First Cohort? He's very raw, sir—'

'I seem to remember being told you were thrust straight from the ranks into your position?' He arched an eyebrow at Taurus, who nodded. 'Because Silus knew your worth, so did Felix and the legate for that matter. Well, if I'm not mistaken young Albinus has all the makings of a fine officer, let's make sure he fulfils his promise, eh.'

He turned back and carried on down the road. 'Come on, First Spear, let's get back to the legion, I need wine!'

Things happened very quickly in the days that followed. The Fourteenth were shipped off west, the surviving men crammed into barges that crept along the Danube. Disembarking the barges at Castra Regina, they made their way on foot through Moesia until they came to Germania Superior.

Rumours were rife amongst the soldiers. Some said they had been sent there as a reward, a welcome break from the fierce fighting they had been constantly thrown into over the last months. Others said they were being punished, that their commander had fallen out of favour with the emperor, and they had been outcast to the remote Rhine frontiers.

This was the theory that stuck. All the men knew of Maximianus and his famous friendship with the General Claudius Fronto. The general had been a favoured friend of Aurelius himself, so men thought it wise they followed a leader that had close links to the emperor's inner circle. Fronto, though, had been killed a few weeks before the Fourteenth's defeat at Eburum, and soon after they had been sent away. The men were starting to smell foul play amongst the upper class, and they weren't happy.

Albinus trudged along the mud road alongside his centurion. Taurus had been in a foul mood since they had set on the barges at Carnuntum. Albinus kept thrusting his superior side glances from the corner of his eye, unsure whether to broach the subject on all the mens lips.

He turned back to view the front rank of the First Cohort, where Habitus and Longus gave him encouraging nods.

'Sir,' he finally plucked up the courage. 'Can I ask a question?'

Taurus blinked, shaking his head as if waking from a daze. 'Huh? What is it, lad?'

'Are we being sent here as a punishment? For the defeat at Eburum?'

Taurus scowled, 'Now why would you say that?' he barked.

'Just the men, sir.' Albinus recoiled, inwardly cursing himself for letting his tent-mates put him up to this. 'They're saying that now General Fronto is dead, Maximianus has fallen from favour with the emperor. There's talk we've been outcast from the war, that the legion is no longer trusted. Just wondered what you knew is all.'

Taurus spun on the spot and marched directly to Habitus. 'Did you put him up to this, you old goat?!' He whipped his vine stick from his belt, holding it an inch from the Syrian's face.

'Me, sir?' Habitus pretended an offended expression. 'But since you've brought it up …'

Longus sniggered, Bucco firmly elbowing him in the ribs to silence him. 'And you!' Taurus turned to Bucco. 'I'd expect better from you!'

Bucco shrugged. 'We got a right to know, sir. We ain't done nothing wrong from what we can see.'

Taurus calmed, lowering his vitis. He sighed. 'Well since you're a bunch of old nosey laundry maids, I suppose I can tell you what I know.' He fell back into step next to Rullus; the standard bearer looked to be feeling quietly pleased with himself for avoiding a dressing down. 'We're going to Mogontiacum. The garrison there has gone east, and us and the First Adiutrix are going to replace them.' Moans and groans from the men as Albinus heard his centurion's words repeated to the men further down the line. 'Now, I don't know the exact reasons why, but I know the legate ain't happy. You all know him and Legate Pertinax were close to General Fronto, and that Fronto and Pompeianus were from different parties in the Senate. So, it stands to reason tha—'

'We're fucked then!' Rullus winced as Taurus' vine stick followed his ill-advised remark.

'We're not fucked, well, not completely. We're just in the dog-house a bit. We just need to go to Mogontiacum, keep our heads down, and we'll soon be recalled to Pannonia to stick it to the tribes.'

Albinus noticed for the first time Legatus Maximianus riding a chestnut mare to the right of the marching column. His face was an ashen grey, pale green eyes almost hidden beneath red rims. He drank heavily from a wine skin as he rode, consumed by grief for his friend and anger towards his enemies. *I have a horrible feeling, that whatever it is we will be doing on the Rhine, it won't be keeping our heads down.*

Maximianus slumped on the wooden folding stool, his brain addled by the wine. He had drunk all the way to Mogontiacum, and hadn't stopped when he'd got there. Pertinax slumped next to him, heavy-eyed and yellow-skinned; he looked more like a beggar than a senior officer.

Didius Julianus looked upon his colleagues in disgust. Previously a proconsular legate in Africa, now commanding the Twenty-Second Primignenia on the Rhine frontier, he snorted. 'Colleagues, look at the state of the two of you! I came here tonight to see two old friends, hoping for a joyous and laugh-filled reunion, and what do I find …?' he arched his eyebrows in question, '… two moping little boys, sulking as they feel they have fallen from favour!' He laughed, a deep and reverberating noise, his expansive waist shaking as he did. He was olive-skinned – his father from Italy, his mother Africa – and he wore a tight, well-cropped beard round his saggy jaw, his hair styled in the way of the Augustus. He had been raised in Rome alongside Aurelius himself; after Aurelius' mother, Domitia Lucilla, had taken accountability for his upbringing and education.

'Easy for you, *colleague,*' Maximianus slurred, 'not all of us were Aurelius' playmate growing up! Had to earn our positions, weren't just given them!' Pertinax tried to suppress a laugh, hiding his bared teeth in his wine cup.

'Playmate? Well excuse me! I didn't ask for the esteemed Domitia to take me into her household, and the Augustus was already a grown man when I went to Rome! Jealousy will get you nowhere, my friend. I suggest, if your wine-fuelled brains can handle it, we talk about how we can improve your standing with the Augustus, and get you back on the front line where you deserve to be.'

Maximianus snapped his head up at that, his intrigue instantly piqued. Pertinax stopped sniggering, his face taking on a serious scowl. 'You have a plan, colleague?' He asked, mouth still formed in a frown.

'I don't, friends, no,' Maximianus and Pertinax shared an angered look. 'I don't need one, not really. The Chatti, it would seem, have done the thinking for us.'

A red dawn broke on a cloudless sky. It turned the shimmering waters of the River Rhine claret and orange. Birds chirped their morning song and the trees rustled with the light breeze. Summer was always Abelard's favourite time of year. Autumn and spring meant nothing but back-breaking labour on the modest patch of land his father owned, back west in the country, in a small farming village, not half a mile south of the Chatti's foul-smelling and overcrowded capital. He hated his visits to

Alefum; the fortress offered no comforts, just left the rank taste of rotten food and open sewers in his mouth.

Twice Abelard had been across the great Rhine, into the stone-built fortress of Mogontiacum. Each time he had been astounded at the scale of the stone-built walls, the ingenuity of vast gates and underground sewage systems. Great arched aqueducts gave a constant supply of fresh water, so much of it that they even heated it and filled great baths for washing.

All day, he had spent in the great oval bath house once, marvelling at the domed ceiling, the elaborate tapestries and mosaics that adorned every wall. The fact that most of them had depicted the Roman legions killing his kin had left a bitter taste in his mouth, but he could appreciate the quality nonetheless.

Now, as he took in the sights of the circling birds, dancing through the sky above the small green islands that dotted the central flow of the river, he wondered again about the decision his tribe had made to go to war with Rome.

The Chatti were no longer the force they once had been. There had been a time when their numbers and spear fame had been felt enough to tackle Rome on their own, but that was back before his grandfather's time. Now, they were a shadow of the tribe they once were. Their numbers depleted by tribal wars and the ravishing plague, they felt there had been no choice when emissaries from King Balomar of the Marcomanni had come calling.

So here he was, armed with just a spear, armoured in a tin pot helmet, patrolling the river bank, waiting for the inevitable attack from the blood-thirsty legions. Ten thousand men their chief had managed to raise. Men from the nearby Tencteres and Ucipetes had volunteered, though that was to be expected as they were under the Chatti's rule and paid them tribute.

Though we have done nothing with them. The frustration gnawed at him, nibbled like a small hound. Abelard was still a young man, not yet in his seventeenth year. He wore his yellow hair long and unbounded; his wispy beard danced in the breeze and flew into his mouth and nostrils. He longed to cut both off, to be rid of the lice if nothing else. But he couldn't, not until he had first shed blood for the tribe in battle. He hefted the heavy spear in his right hand, his grip clammy on the ash shaft. The leaf-shaped iron point glimmered in the morning's early rays as he prayed to the Allfather today would be the day he got to earn his way to the god's hall by spilling Roman blood.

He passed another warrior, patrolling the river in the opposite direction. They paused for a few heartbeats, exchanged friendly conversation about the weather and such. The man wore a deep blue tunic and trousers, marking him out as a member of the Tencteres. Abelard himself wore a faded red, the colour of the Chatti. The other man moved off south as Abelard kept moving north. His thoughts drifted to his mother, who would be standing at the door of their small farmhouse right now, praying to all the gods for her only son to come home safe. His father would be telling her to stop fussing, reminding her it was his rippled muscles and gleaming arm rings that had attracted her to him in the first place.

Abelard smiled at the thought, a hint of a tear in his eye as he thought of his family. It would be good to get back to them soon.

A disturbance in the air, a zip and a whirr as something flew inches above his head, strands of yellow hair flying up in the breeze, a scream from behind him. He dropped to a crouch and spun on his heels. The man in the blue tunic was on the grass, claret pouring from an arrow wound in the back of his neck.

He looked towards the river, which moments before had been the epitome of tranquillity. Barges filled the river, obscuring the water completely. Long and thin, they had a boy on the front of each with a large pole, testing the depth of the water as the soldiers behind him rowed. An older man stood at the rear of each craft, steering oar firmly in hand as he guided the vessels across the current.

Abelard felt his heart race, the noise like thunder in his chest. His legs went to mush, like a lame plough horse when his father slit its throat. He staggered, dizzy, breath coming in panicked gasps. He didn't want his beard gone, could live with lice in his greasy yellow hair. He just wanted to be home, sowing and reaping the year's meagre harvest with his father, listening to his stories of glory and plunder from his younger years; wanted to feel his mother's hands on his cheeks, her soft lips on his as she kissed him goodnight as the stars lit up the night sky; the smell of pine as the morning dew shimmered in the pre-dawn air; the simple beauty of earning an honest living out of the ground.

An arrow thumped into his chest, punching through his rib cage like an axe through rotten wood. Blood erupted from his mouth, choking him as he fell to the mud. Red shields, white shields, blue shields – they formed a wall of wood and metal along the river bank. A man stepped out of the line, two red-dyed horse plumes atop his helmet, red shield, gold decoration in his left hand, a giant pommelled staff in the other. He walked towards the dying Abelard, who lay choking on his own blood. Abelard looked into the Roman's eyes, the purest blue, tinged with ice, like a frozen lake. Something lurked underneath, hard and unmoving as iron, but with more bite.

Abelard tried to plead for his life as the wooden staff crashed into the side of his head. His world went white, stars upon stars as the dizziness subsided, his regrets fading away; he drifted upwards, towards the pure endless whiteness.

XVII

Albinus wiped the blood off his staff on the grass. The young barbarian, dark blood matted in his straw-coloured hair, shuddered and twitched as he died. He looked up from the corpse and surveyed the landscape: greener than the lands that bordered the Danube; sweeping valleys, as endless as the sea. Good land, he thought, better than the lands in Pannonia. He wondered why Rome had never pressed on this side of the river; it had been a province once, occupied by the legions and governed by Rome – until a man called Arminius had united the eastern tribes and massacred four legions in the Teutoburg forest.

This is why we can't let Balomar win. This land, those trees, the smoke rising from hearth fires obscured by distant forests: it should all be Rome's. It had been Rome's, the greatest empire the world had ever known. But they had let it slip through their fingers, got complacent. Hubris was a dangerous thing, and Rome had been guilty of that with these lands and people.

At the noise behind him, he turned to look upon the vast sight of three legions disembarking from hundreds of small boats. Taurus walked up to him, his armour glistening in the summer sun, his red-crested helmet freshly brushed, sword bared in his hand. 'Optio Silus, get the First Century formed into column and ready to march. We ain't hanging about! The legate wants us back across the river by nightfall.' Albinus saluted and ran over to where his century were stretching and fastening armour, ready for the march.

180

'First century, form column!' he shouted in his best parade ground voice, which wasn't a patch on his father's. He worried it was too high-pitched, that he sounded like a squawking crow when he raised his voice. But the soldiers responded well enough.

Time seemed to stop; the wait for battle hadn't got any easier for Albinus. He'd only finished off the yellow-haired boy as he thought it would help ease his nerves. But his full bladder, dry mouth and shaking hands told him they were still there, white-knuckled grip on his staff, a quiver in his bottom lip.

After a time, the wait was finally over. Legatus Maximianus trotted a fine white stallion across the front ranks of his legion. His white-plumed helm shone, bronzed cuirass polished to shimmering perfection beneath a spotless white cloak. 'Men of the Fourteenth Gemina!' His voice was the roar of a lion, bitter and full of gravel. 'We march for battle, to restore our honour, and bring further glory to our eagle!' The men roared in return. The golden eagle swayed in the front rank as men reached out to touch the aquilifer, who staggered and swayed from the shoves in his back.

'I have only one question, brothers. ARE YOU READY FOR WAR?!'

'READY!' came the swift and savage reply.

Maximianus laughed. 'Gods! Am I going to battle with a bunch of old farm hands?! I swear a group of children could make more noise than that! I said: ARE ... YOU ... READY ... FOR ... WAR?'

'READY!' The ground shook as four thousand men screamed at the tops of their voices. Birds darted from nearby trees, startled by the noise. It reverberated across the landscape, sending shockwaves through the valleys. Albinus laughed, his fear subsiding as he felt his blood rise. The men seemed to group closer together, the chanting and shouting drawing them in, bringing them closer together as a unit.

The march through the German countryside was short. They passed abandoned farms, tools still laying in the fields where terrified farmers had dropped what they held, scooped up their children and ran for the safety of the nearest trees. Vast, dark columns of smoke appeared on the horizon as the barbarians warned each other of the Roman army's arrival.

Through a patch of small woodland they emerged, the trees alive with the

181

sound of wildlife. Into the sun, Albinus squinted at the shock of light after the murk under the trees. A wall of noise struck the marching Romans, a mass of German warriors roaring and screaming in defiance at the advancing legionaries.

'Jupiter's balls!' Fullo exclaimed from the front rank, 'there's a lot of the whoresons!' No one else spoke. Albinus tried to whirl spittle around his desert-dry mouth, to no avail. Habitus hooked his small bow from his shoulder, fitting the string and notching the first arrow from the quiver on his back.

'Optio, to the rear,' said Taurus, readying his own shield, checking the chin strap of his helmet.

Albinus gripped Fullo in the warrior's embrace, each wishing each other luck. Bucco gripped him in a bear hug, making him promise to stay safe. 'I am your superior officer you know!' he exclaimed as he wriggled free.

'Aye you are,' replied Bucco, 'but I've not forgotten my promise to the old man. I don't intend to break it.'

Albinus nodded to the men in the century he knew as he watched them march past. They were on the far right of the marching legion – the place of honour. He stood at the back of the double strength century, numbering just one hundred rather than the one hundred and sixty it should have. There wasn't a single century in the entire legion at full strength, but the first had taken more losses than most during the season's fighting, as they were always the first into the fray.

'Form up!' he bellowed as he tried to swagger behind the line, the way he had seen Abas do time and time again. He thought of the Greek then, looked left along the line to see if he could spot him, but the Sixth Cohort must have been over half a mile away.

He found it frustrating, standing at the rear. All he could see was the standards and the eagle above the men's helmets; he had no idea what was going on at the front. He turned behind him to see the centurion of the Fifth Century, he nodded to Albinus who returned the gesture. He tried to remember the centurion's name, but couldn't; so many of them had died in the recent battles, it seemed all the surviving ones had been promoted to fill the holes.

The noise louder at the front now, Albinus' heart thudded in his chest, not particularly fast, but heavy and consistent, like a blacksmith's hammer on the anvil. 'Martial and Victorious!' Right across the ranks of the Fourteenth the cry was taken up, men smacking pila on their shield bosses, the noise like cracks of thunder.

BANG. BANG. BANG. 'ROMA!' *BANG.* 'ROMA!' *BANG.* On and on it went, Albinus joining in with his staff. He was vaguely aware of whistles being blown in the front, the men of the First Century hefting their first pilum, gaps in the tight ranks appearing as each man made ready to throw.

Shadows filled the air as the first rank threw, then the second, third and fourth. Each line dropped to their knees once they'd thrown, giving the men behind them a clear target. And then there was the enemy. Line after line of whirling and throbbing barbarians, armoured or bare-chested, spears waving towards the sun. The whistle of the darts was shrill as they raced up to the circling crows, before arcing down and raining iron on the howling mass of savages. With a wet crunch and a splat they tore the German front ranks to shreds. Blood flew in the air, some dark like wine some light and bright like crushed rose petals.

'Get up! Up men, ready second javelins!' Albinus stalked the line, prodding men with his staff as he shook them back into life. Taurus' whistle blew again, and again the Roman javelins rained terror on the helpless barbarian horde.

'Swords! Draw swords!' Again Albinus butted soldiers with his wooden pole, pushing them forward, keeping the lines straight as they advanced over the crippled and dying barbarians. The front ranks were into them now, the shoving match of the shields had begun. The advance halted, and the Roman line began to get pushed back.

The centurion from the Fifth Century was right behind him, his breath hot on Albinus' neck. 'Want a hand, brother?' He motioned to the rear rankers of the First, digging in their heels and sliding backwards on the blood-soaked ground.

Albinus nodded, 'Sir,' he said and without another word the front line of the Fifth slammed their shields into the rear rank of the First. Suddenly the First stopped sliding back, and inch by inch they begun to gain ground as the legion gathered momentum.

Albinus stood without a shield, crushed in the throng. He roared and waved his staff to encourage the men forward. Soon they were in a rhythm: 'ROMA.' Push. 'ROMA.' Push. They trampled over the dead and the wounded screamed for mercy, water, for their mothers as the Romans stamped on their windpipes or thrust swords through their hearts.

A man grabbed Albinus' foot, hands like ice on his legs. Albinus lifted his leg, tried to shake off the grip, but the dying man held on firm. He screamed at Albinus in his barbaric tongue. Albinus for a moment felt sympathy as he looked down onto the beardless youth, probably of a similar age to himself. Hardening his eyes, the young optio raised his pommelled staff and sent it crashing into the young man's nose. Bone shattered and cartilage tore as hot blood splattered Albinus' leg. The barbarians grip went limp, and Albinus trudged on.

Whistles again pierced the air, and centurions across the front rank signalled the change of ranks for the first time in the battle. Across the line, the front rankers turned their bodies side on, shield protecting them as they left pockets of space for the second rank to step into. They then quickly retreated through the formation until they were at the rear.

'Everyone okay?' asked Albinus as he saw Fullo emerge from a huddle of cloaks and shields. Fullo nodded, wiping blood from his face with the hem of his cloak. Bucco appeared, then Habitus and Longus. Rullus was still next to Taurus in the front rank, the cohort's standard swaying in the air.

The men took the opportunity to take on water, eat some hardtack and empty their bowels. They had maybe an hour's rest as each rank took their turn at the front. Albinus kept his eyes on Taurus, expecting a messenger to run back from the front any moment and ask him to relieve the centurion. But Taurus was not like other centurions; the only way he'd leave the front was wrapped in his cloak.

But suddenly, the red crest of the First Spear's helmet disappeared. It swayed, then fell right, like a tall tree fallen prey to a woodcutter's axe. Panic swept through the ranks; like a plague it engulfed each soldier in turn. Eyes started darting to the rear, steps taken backwards instead of forward.

'Albinus! Albinus get up here!' Even over the cacophony of battle Rullus made himself heard. Without hesitation the young optio forced his way to the front. The Roman advance had stuttered as Rullus stood over his fallen centurion who bled heavily from a wound in his right arm.

Albinus felt the eyes of a hundred men on him. Barbarians whooped not five paces to his front, their blood lust heightened by the demise of a Roman officer. With renewed courage they rallied and charged the Roman line, men jumping from deep in their ranks to climb over their comrades and get at the Romans.

As always, Albinus didn't notice the sickening fear in his stomach subside, couldn't see what other men saw. The ice blue eyes turn hard as iron, thin lips set in a snarl as he took in a deep breath and roared: 'FIRST CENTURY REFORM THE LINE! SHIELDS UP, SHIELDS UP YOU MAGGOTS! THROW THEM BACK, THROW … THEM … BACK!' If Silus could see his son now, as he gazed back over the River Styx, he would have shed a tear in pride.

Albinus' men responded. Shields went back up with the snap of wood as they re-joined and once more formed an impassable line. A repetitive dull thud as barbarian iron hammered the linden boards, found them as immovable as stone. 'Right, ladies, let's finish these curs!' A cheer went up as Albinus raised his staff. He stood, still without a shield, in the front rank of the Roman formation, Rullus on his right shoulder, snarling and screaming at the enemy. There was movement to his left as Bucco forced his way alongside the son of his former commander. 'Made your old man a promise, didn't I? And here you are, in the front rank without a fucking shield! Mithras help me!'

Albinus laughed, a sickening noise that made the nearest barbarians recoil. Fullo appeared at his right shoulder, covering him with his own shield. A rush of air by his ear; Habitus was at his back, another arrow already knocked on the string. My 'Familia'. He would fight with his brothers, die with them if necessary.

Without waiting for an order, the Roman line pushed forward, shield bosses smashing into unprotected faces and bellies, swords licking out like snake tongues to effortlessly steal a life. On and on they went, Albinus using his staff as a spear, the pommelled end breaking noses and jaws as he jabbed it at man after man. He thrust it forward again, against a barrel of a man facing him, thick arms lined with warrior rings. He caught the staff and heaved it towards him. Albinus was caught in two minds: let his grip go or play tug-of-war in the midst of battle. In the end, he let the big barbarian yank him forward. Bucco screamed and reached out and grabbed the back of his cloak. It ripped, but slowly enough to allow more hands to get underneath his chainmail and pull him back.

Still Albinus gripped the staff, fingers incapable of letting go. Pain flared in his shoulder, intense and blinding, then the joint went pop and his world went white. It had happened to him before, the very first battle he had fought. The doctor who had popped it back in had said it would happen again, but Albinus had all but forgotten about it; the grievous wound he'd taken in his face during the same battle had been more of a problem for him.

But now the pain returned, he screamed and yelped as his hand let go thes and he fell tumbling to the blood-soaked ground. Bodies around him, booted feet stepping over his body, he was vaguely aware of it all. He couldn't move his hand, couldn't feel it either. 'Can you hear me, lad?' Bucco's voice in his ear. Albinus couldn't reply, just nodded. 'We're gonna get you to the rear. Can you stand?' Albinus nodded again.

Bucco pulled him to his feet, but waves of agony rolled from his shoulder and spread throughout him. He staggered, vomited, wiped his mouth and vomited again. Pulling himself upright, he scanned the front line of the battle, where the fighting was deadlocked. 'I need to stay, Bucco. Who's gonna lead the First if Taurus is injured?' he said, wincing through the pain as he did.

'Don't think you need to worry about that, lad,' said Bucco, gesturing with his head to the far right of the battle line.

Blue shields appeared over a small ridge, each depicting a proud white Pegasus on the front. Albinus watched as the First Adiutrix legion, commanded by Pertinax, formed a giant wedge and tore into the exposed flank of the German army. The men of the First shouted and cheered as they watched their enemy melt away like thawing snow. Cheers came from the far left, where presumably the Twenty-Second Primignenia were doing the same.

'Come on, lad,' said Bucco, gently tugging Albinus away from the battle, 'our work here today is done.'

Balomar slapped his thigh in frustration. *Another defeat.* He watched as the two legions engulfed the German army and wrapped up the flanks. The German warriors were caught like fish in a net; they wriggled and swarmed from one side to the next, but in the end there was no escape.

'My King, we should leave.' Adalwin at his shoulder, his voice urgent, face a mask of concern.

Balomar sighed, hands rubbing his beard. 'Yes, my friend. Come, let's go. There's nothing we can do here.'

There was a deafening silence in the small party of horsemen as they made their way back west. The tension was palpable, Adalwin not wanting to risk a conversation with his king, fearing his wrath. Balomar strove to keep his raging emotions under control, lest he say something he may later regret.

The king's mind whirled – angry thoughts, dark thoughts, thoughts of defeat and hatred. The season's campaigning had started well enough. Balomar had gained the support of the Naristae through marriage, and they had brought with them not just their own vast numbers but those of their surrounding tribes. His army had been huge, too numerous to keep in one location.

So he had split them up. Bandanasp taking the forces in the east, striking south into Moesia and even killing the Roman General Claudius Fronto. In the German centre, north of Pannonia, Balomar himself commanded with the support of the Naristae and their chief, Valao. It irked him that he hadn't replicated the success of Bandanasp, who was fast making his name as a war leader and a man to follow.

Some of the smaller tribes had even quietly deserted his army and moved their warriors east to fight under the chief of the Iazyges, thinking there was more plunder and glory to be had. Whispered words round camp fires spoke of how the Allfather had blessed Bandanasp with his favour, how his warriors were certain to earn a place in his great hall. Balomar felt his face flush red with anger at the thought. Was it not he who had first united the tribes? He who had led them to glory two years ago, striking as far south into Italy itself. And now it seemed that all he had built was slowly coming apart at the seams. This latest setback, he knew, would not go down well with the chiefs when he told them. *But do I have to tell them?*

Enlisting the support of the Chatti had been his idea, one that hadn't been supported by all the tribal chiefs. They were an unruly people, their own chief Gisbert a bitter and disliked character. Too many times he had staged daring raids on his neighbours, hoping to win back some of the lost glory of his tribe. *Well that's never coming back now.*

It had cost him a fortune in gold and cattle to get the man to raise his men and those of the tribes under his protection. It had proved to be a waste of both good coin and fine cows.

At least I may be able to get someone more agreeable to lead the Chatti, he thought as he bounced along atop his black stallion. The horse was a constant reminder of the debt he owed Alexander of Abonoteichos, and wondered if that was the reason the old conman had gifted it to him in the first place. *Damn that man to Hel. I should never have let Aelinia push me into all this.*

Aelinia: another of his problems; his former bed slave had become a constant nuisance since he had married. He had moved her back to the slave quarters at the back of his hall, but she had not taken it well. His wife's first night in her new home in Goridorgis has been one to forget: a great feast in motion, the benches packed with ale drunk tribesmen, amidst the wrestling bouts and drinking competitions between the warriors of the Marcomanni and Naristae, Aelinia had thrown a jug of ale all over Saxa. The cacophony in the hall had dropped to a deathly silence. Men shuffled on the straw as they crept back to their benches. Saxa looked helplessly toward her father; Valao had jumped to his feet in a rage, howling in anger at the insolence of the slave. It had taken all of Balomar's diplomacy to calm the chief, and to prevent him from spilling Aelinia's blood in his hall.

He sighed. Life had become complicated, too muddled for a simple mind like his. 'What shall I do, Adalwin,' he asked, looking to the one man he could call a friend.

'My lord?' said Adalwin.

'What am I going to do?! I have enough trouble as it is keeping Valao and the other chiefs on board. I've got Bandanasp in the east winning victory after victory. And now this …' he motioned behind him. 'Another defeat in the west! What shall I tell the men when we get back?'

Balomar watched as Adalwin chewed his cheek, seeking the right words. If there was one man whom the king could rely on to give him an honest answer, it was Adalwin.

'Tell them the truth. The Chatti were weak, their leader a fool. He stumbled into an ambush and got wiped out. You want to fight a defensive war, the chiefs want to go south of the river and attack. Use this defeat to your advantage. If we fight on our own ground, on our own terms, we can win. If we take the fight to Rome, allow them to choose their ground, bring their artillery into play, we die.' He spoke with certainty. Balomar saw the two hearth warriors nod in agreement, though they pretended they weren't listening.

'You think they will listen? Most are lost in the tales of glory from Bandanasp's men in the east …' He trailed off, sighing. 'Why did we start this war, Adalwin?'

Adalwin frowned. 'Because Rome treated us like fools. They neglected to pay our tribute, turned us away when we asked for aid amid the plague. They thought us weak, we seek to prove them wrong.'

'Correct. Second question: haven't we achieved that now? Could we not plea for peace, come to some agreement with Rome and her generals?'

Adalwin was sipping from a water skin. He spat out the liquid in surprise and coughed. 'Are you serious? After all we have achieved, the victories we have won? We would be foolish to back down now. Plus, you would lose face with the tribes. You are the leader, the man they call High King. To back down shows weakness, and the tribes won't tolerate a weak leader.'

Balomar nodded. He turned his head and watched the sunlight roll off the green valleys to the north. It was a sight that would normally have brightened his mood. Today he found it just made him darker.

XVIII

Licina worked her way through the forum. Surrounded by stone porticos, a thriving market was in session on the sunlit cobbles. She wore just a sleeveless stola, and still the intense heat made her flush as she frantically wafted herself with a small fabric fan. The stola had been a gift from Albinus on their wedding day. Beautifully woven from wool, it stuck to her back and thighs and she could feel the intense burn of a heat rash appearing on her lower back. She had discarded the palla she'd left her apartment with. All respectable Roman women were supposed to wear them, but she could not bare to cover her head and shoulders with the thin rectangular cloth.

Her belly was swollen, so much now that it was impossible to hide. She was sick every morning, on edge constantly throughout the day. It had been some time since she had first saw Calvus notice the gentle curve, but it had taken him weeks to build the courage to ask her. *Yes, I'm pregnant. Of course it's Albinus'! No, no I haven't told him.*

His letters to her had been rare and sparse in detail. He had fought in a defeat to some tribe or other, and his legion had been sent east in disgrace. That was all she knew, and all she wanted to know. She couldn't bring herself to tell him about the baby in her replies. He would worry, want to return home. What if it made him do something reckless in battle? She was of course well aware of the difficult relationship her husband had held with his own father; would he panic that it would be the same with his child? No, she thought, better to wait until he is home.

But when would he be home? She sucked her teeth as she battled to fight the whirling thoughts from her mind. Had she contributed to his being sent east? *No,* she asserted to herself as she forced a path through the throning crowds, *I did what I had to do, what any wife would do.*

As they always seemed to when she was out walking alone, her thoughts drifted to Heide and the shieldmaidens, and the life she had left behind. How had the war ended? Which brother had triumphed? She wondered if she regretted her decision to abandon them in their hour of need and run back south to Albinus. She knew if he had been here then she wouldn't even be pondering the question. But the long, enforced absences cast doubt on her mind.

She paused at a stall, cheap bronze and metal brooches on display. She stood and enjoyed the gentle breeze that drifted through the shade, offered by the great tarpaulin-covered statue being erected by Tribune Scaevola. The merchant eyed her as she picked up a brooch, a small silver fish with a crude clasp. 'Afternoon, beautiful,' he said as he slid over to her like a snake who'd spotted a mouse. 'See anything you fancy?' Licina didn't know what repulsed her more: the man's sickly wink or his rank mouth, yellow tongue and toothless, black gums.

'No,' she said and made to walk off. The merchant grabbed her, slipping a small piece of parchment into her hand. 'He said you'd be along.' With that he was off.

Licina took a few more steps, gingerly unfolding the parchment and cursing at the hurriedly scribbled words. A giant oil lamp, metal-made, round and imposing stood outside the great temple to Jupiter. She scurried over, sandals flopping on the flagstones, and threw the parchment in. She stood on the steps to the temple and scanned the crowds, looking for a familiar face. Panic began to flutter in her belly; her heart rate quickened, the beats coming fast and firm in her chest.

A hooded man, dark-skinned and black-haired stood across the forum. His dark green cloak soaked up the sunlight, his eyes poured into her. She let out a gasp; staggered and slipped into the protection of the crowds. She kept her head low, cursed herself for not keeping her palla; her flame-red hair was not common in these parts. She worked her way to the edge of the forum, slipped behind a stone pillar, and stood panting in the shade of the portico.

Why is he back? He told me that was it! She sunk to her knees, intense pain in her belly. Her breath coming in gasps, she fought to bring it under control. Slow, deep breaths, and the pain subsided. She began to relax, ignored as she sat in the shade outside an official-looking building. *At least I got away from him.*

'Hello, Licina,' a deep voice from above her shoulder. 'Allow me to help you up.'

Calvus stalked the shadows, like a leopard he prowled, keeping downwind of his prey. He'd followed her to the heart of the city, head hidden under a cloak despite the heat. Sweat trickled down his unshaved skin. He had been shocked to see the whiteness of the hair in the water's reflection when he'd splashed his face that morning, an unwelcome reminder that he was no longer a young man.

Weeks now he had been following the girl, but he had got no closer than the day in the brothel; learned nothing, to his shame and the anger of his employer. The days since had begun to blend together. He would rise early, disguise himself in some sort of hat or hood, and pretend to be a beggar or a merchant selling fish on the corner of the street where her apartment was. He would wait for her to leave; watch carefully the way she held herself, the swell of her belly as she walked slowly through the overcrowded streets.

Day after day, and nothing more interesting to report than the acquisition of a new dress or a trip to the market for fresh food. He came to know the routine of the street: the baker that opened his shutters every morning, just as the rising sun kissed the red-tiled roofs, whistling a tuneless tune as the tantalising aroma of oven-baked bread wafted up Calvus's nostrils and set his stomach grumbling; the tanner that rolled out his barrel of fish oil, great sheets of cow hide rolled in bundles awaiting his treatment; the hammer of the blacksmith as it hit the anvil, soft iron being forged into blades and utensils, his looker of a daughter, young but busty, setting up the stall at the front of the shop, the prices varying depending on how wealthy the potential customer looked.

But now, here she was in the heart of the city, head bared and resplendent in the sunlight, as if she hadn't a care in the world. The man who always accompanied her still wore a green cloak, hood fastened securely over his face. The pair stood in the shade of a stone portico, the official emblem of the imperial mint set above a great pair of wooden doors. Calvus thought it seemed an odd place to meet.

The traffic in and out of the building was heavy. with toga-wearing men surrounded by groups of ex-gladiators, purses bulging with chinking coins as they went about their business. Calvus stopped and leant up against a stone pillar from a portico on the opposite side of the forum. His view was obstructed by the hustle and bustle of the market in the open square, but the distance made sure he wouldn't be noticed.

He watched as he approached her, his lips as hot as her hair as they locked in a passionate embrace. They spoke frantically, him gesturing wildly with his hands. She shook her head, lips quivering as she tried to back away. Calvus fought the urge to cross the forum and break it up. His body willed it, knuckles burning white as he gripped the hilt of his knife. He forced himself to stand as still as the stone portico, breath coming in hot rasps as rage whirled like fire within him. *Jesu watch over her. Keep her from harm, see her safe and I will bring her into your flock. This I swear.*

The time was getting closer, he knew. But he needed evidence, a confession from one of them. But first he needed proof; once he could prove their treason he could take them to his employer, then he could wet his blade.

A litter passed through the forum, slaves lifting heavy wooden poles in each corner as someone who was too posh to walk was carried by. Calvus cursed, losing sight of his prey. He slipped from the portico and darted through the crowds. Bodies pressed in around him. He muttered curses and used his fists as batons as he barged a path through the masses. His hobnailed sandals clattered on the cobbles. Throwing back his hood he jumped to catch sight of the green-cloaked man still ahead of him.

Ducking back down and shoving the last of the people out of his way, he staggered into a clearing, breathing heavily, sweat sliding off him like rain off a roof. Hands on knees, he regained his breath and looked up at an approaching green cloak, a flame-haired girl being dragged in its wake.

'Well look who it isn't,' smirked the green cloak. The man threw back his hood and leered at Calvus. 'Ex-legionary Calvus. What brings you to the more civilised part of town? Don't you have some brothels to visit? Stables to muck out? Fish to sell?' He snorted as he spoke, looking past the flame-haired girl to two red-cloaked legionaries, who laughed at his joke.

Calvus ignored the jibe, eyes firmly locked on the flame-haired girl. She met his eyes briefly, her own wide with terror. He nodded slightly, giving her a tight-lipped smile. 'Tribune Scaevola, sir. Good to see you, sir. It is a beautiful day.' He saluted and stood to attention.

Scaevola laughed, a pompous sound. 'It is indeed, Calvus. How's retirement treating you? I've heard some interesting stories. I never knew you were so interested in the grain collection in the province?' He arched an eyebrow as he spoke, and a crooked smile fixed his dry lips.

Calvus wasn't listening, eyes still fixed on the flame-haired girl, the wide panicked eyes, the swell of her belly. 'Ahh,' said Scaevola, looking from him to her. 'Do you two know each other? Old friends? Yes, yes I can see it in your eyes, Calvus. Well fear not, my friend, she's coming home with me. But don't worry, I shall ensure she is kept busy. You could even come and visit her yourself, although there may be something of a queue.' Again he cackled, throwing his head back and laughing at the sky.

Calvus stared at his exposed throat, imagining the wet thud his knife would make if he rammed it through. His hand shook on the hilt, rage thrashing like a caged lion within him. He fought to bring his emotions under control, watched on helplessly as the tribune grabbed the girl and dragged her in his wake. He barely felt the shoves from the two soldiers as they barged past him. For an age he stood there, thought box shuddering with indecision. The sun was blood red and half obscured behind the rooftops when he finally moved off with purpose, thunder in his eyes and murder in his heart.

XIX

July AD 171 – Fortress of Goridorgis, Germania

Raised voices ahead of her, fire behind her, Aelinia stalked the shadows, head shaking from front to back like a lost puppy listening out for its mother. It had been the work of moments to set the freshly laid hay in the hall aflame. That had been simple, easily thought and easily executed. It was only now she fully appreciated what the hardened warriors said round their benches at night: planning and executing a raid is easy, it's the getting out that's hard.

She crept through the side streets and alleys of Goridorgis, shivering in the moonlight. No matter how hot the summer sun got in this part of the world, the nights were always bitter and each breath misted the air. She cursed as her bare foot snagged a loose stone on the path.

She ran her hand along the wooden beams that made the fence as she ran, counting them down until she reached the stables. The smell of horseflesh and fodder was hot in her nostrils; cold air steaming off the horses' flanks. Old leather in her hands felt callous and dry as she threw a saddle over Balomar's prized black stallion. It had been gifted to him the day Licina had arrived. *My life changed for the worse that day.*

She still bore the scar on the back of head where her own brother had knocked her out cold. *All to save that whore.* She'd thought little of her brother over the last couple of years; her thoughts were consumed with keeping her king satisfied and his spears pointed south toward Rome – toward the empire that had abandoned her, left her for dead, to sell her body for food. But now she was going back, tail between her legs; she was going to run back to the very people that had disowned her, like a lone wolf that thought it had outgrown the pack, only to find the road much harder on her own. Tonight she went back to her pack; she just hoped they didn't eat her alive.

For the first time in an age, she prayed to Roman gods as she mounted the stallion. *Juno, guide me home. Fortuna, watch over me, grant me fortune, make their spears fall short.* She kicked the stallion and it charged out the stables, doors left swinging in its wake. A desperate look over her shoulder told her the hall was fully alight now. Balomar's voice was clear in the night air as he roared and raged, ordering his warriors to put out the dancing flames. A haze of red and orange to her rear, there was nothing but darkness to her front.

She rode down the main slope of the fortress at a gallop, hoofbeats making the ground rumble, a consistent dull thud on the mud. She hadn't planned how she was going to get out the gate, but her luck held out. A night patrol was just entering at the run, the gates thrust open hastily as the men ran towards the ball of light in the black sky.

People everywhere, panicked voices as the fortress' inhabitants were awoken from their slumber to the lung-squeezing smell of thick smoke; the creak of the gates as they opened. Licina's heart beat faster than the galloping stallion.

A guardsman challenged her as she approached the gate, she didn't slow or hesitate, galloped straight into the approaching column of men, who jumped to the side at the last moment to avoid being trampled. Aelinia caught a fleeting glance of Adalwin as she sped past, his face a mask of fury beneath his nose guard.

The open air smelled fresher and cleaner. Out of the gate she sped and into the starless night. Her breath steamed the air as her heart slowed, the adrenalin wearing off. She paused at the edge of the forest, yanking on the reins to turn the stallion back. She gazed at the place that had been her home since Rome had left her and her brother for dead.

It surprised her that she felt nothing: no sorrow at leaving behind the people that had taken her in, treated her as one of their own; the man that had thought to fuck her, only to fall in love with her. Not for the first time she wondered if she'd made a rash decision. Had jealousy driven her to this madness? She had of course known that Balomar would have to take a wife, and that despite her best efforts between the sheets that wife would have to come from the tribes. But it had still hurt when the king had arrived back at Goridorgis with Saxa, the daughter of the chief of the Naristae; seeing Saxa's long golden hair, full curved breasts, curved hips and flawless legs, Aelinia had known at first glance she was beaten.

Thrown from the king's bed, forced back with the slaves she had previously lorded over, she couldn't bear to stay there any longer. The whispers, sniggers, snorts in the cramped room they all shared – she didn't need a fire's light to tell they were aimed at her. The day before Saxa had asked her – ever so sweetly – to fill in the old latrine pits at the rear of the king's great hall. That had been the last straw.

She turned back her horse and shuddered at the cold as she made her way into the darkness of the forest. Her path was set, and she had a long road ahead of her.

Three days' riding took her south to the Danube. Her mouth as dry as kindling, lips cracked like old bark. Her belly growled in hunger, some sour berries she'd found on a bush being her only nourishment since her flight from Goridorgis. Through forests and over mountain passes she had ridden, no real idea of where she was or where she was going. She kept the sun to her right and prayed to the gods she was going south.

She heard the rush of the water before she saw it. Smelt the freshness in the air. The stallion was as tired as she, and it slumped at the river bank and drank greedily from the green glinting waters. She fell from the saddle and knelt next to the horse, greedily slurping in handfuls of water, not caring that she was downstream of the beast's tongue.

Once she'd drunk her fill, she looked across the river, squinting through the floating green island at the signs of life on the other side. She could make out the tops of a fortress; see the slanted wooden roofs of the towers, gleaming iron helmets and blood red cloaks of legionaries consigned to roast on guard duty.

She looked left and right, searching for a bridge and finding none. Her mind worked back to the time she had visited Carnuntum with Balomar, negotiating for a farce of a peace treaty. Also the time she had raped Licina, and been knocked cold by her own brother. She rubbed the scar on her head and willed her mind to forget that night. Only the gods themselves knew why she had done what she did. As a woman who had been raped herself, just the memory of her actions made her sick to her stomach.

She struggled back to her feet and resolved to find a crossing. Hazarding a guess at the location of the fortress across the rippling water, she clambered back atop the stallion and steered his flanks so he faced west.

Watch officer Tullus cursed under his breath. His shift had not begun well and seemed to be getting worse by the hour. To start with he had trodden in horse shit on his way from his barracks room to the northern gate. His centurion had already been waiting in the shaded courtyard beneath the wooden walls, and had promised him latrine duty for a month if he still stunk like shit at the end of his shift.

Then after the first hour the legionary assigned to flip the sand clock had forgotten his duties. So now they had no real idea of the passing of the time, apart from Tullus' extended walks over to the east gate to check on the progress of their water clock. The north gate were the ones responsible for the trumpet signal at the end of each hour. Tullus knew full well he would get more than latrines if the passing of the time was not properly recorded. So in between each trot to the east gate, he had been rigorously smacking the side of the glass sand clock, hoping it would encourage a few more granules to fall through the narrow gap to the bottom.

And now it seemed, some random whore had turned up at his gate and was refusing to leave. The gates would have been kept open if it wasn't for the ongoing war with the tribes north of the river. In disgrace as they were, the Tenth still maintained wartime routines and had all gates shut and barred at all times.

'I said fuck off!' shouted Tullus, his right hand still smacking the glass. He glanced nervously towards the sun, trying to judge its arc. In truth, he had no idea how far it had moved. Like most other soldiers, he was entirely dependent on the routine and timings of army life, which because of one of his men was completely out of sync.

The girl shouted something back, inaudible from Tullus' height. She looked dreadful, clad in a loose-fitting dress half torn and shabby, wild dark hair like a mane down her back. She wore no shoes, seemed to have no saddlebags on her horse, which was magnificent. Tullus was no lover of horses, but he enjoyed a day's chariot racing as much as the next man. Even from this distance he could see this horse was made for racing. It stood a full head taller than the girl, its black coat gleaming in the sun. Thick muscle on its flanks, it snorted and stomped in impatience.

Tullus glanced nervously along the wall. He'd sent a man scurrying across the battlements for another check on the water clock. He was sure the hour must be up by now, and his sand clock was still half full. A quick glance left and he nearly shit his breeches: his centurion was walking towards them with Tribune Macro, a man with whom Tullus had had one or two bad experiences. *Fortuna, please, I beg you!* He turned back to the girl, 'Look I don't care what you want! You need to piss off, sharpish!' He gestured with his hand, a shoeing motion, which had served him well with locals right across the empire.

Again she shouted something in reply, muffled by the stamping hooves of the horse. 'Please love, just go the fuc—'

'Watch officer Tullus! I do hope your boots are cleaner.' Centurion Hilarius smirked as he approached, a swagger in his step as he looked to show off to his superior. *Bollocks.* Tullus looked down at his right boot, the black leather still smothered in brown shit. Despite the name, his centurion wasn't known for his great sense of humour; punishing his century seemed to bring him the most joy in life. Someone had once told Tullus that you herded sheep with a stick, you led men from the front. His centurion would have made a great shepherd.

'Sir!' Tullus snapped, saluting and standing to attention. The tent party he had with him did the same. The tribune frowned as he looked at the sand clock, checking the levels at the bottom and looking up at the sun. 'I could have sworn it was later than that.' Tullus felt his bowels lurch. Thankfully the girl took the attention off of him.

'Who's this then?' asked Hilarius, leaning over the battlement.

'Just some civilian, sir. Been trying to tell her to get lost, but she ain't getting the message. Think she came from over the river, so not sure if she speaks the lingo.' The centurion nodded absently, turning away and looking down onto Tullus' boots. He was about to berate the watch officer when the tribune cut in.

'Is she saying barbarians? Army? Look she's pointing! Jupiter's tits, I think she's trying to tell us there's an army on their way!' He turned to Tullus, 'Open the gates, man! For Mars' sake open the damned gates!'

Tullus and his men took the steps two at a time, heaved the locking bar from the gates and swung one open to let her in. She fell through the gateway, collapsing in the shade and sending small clouds of dust spiralling into the air.

As the girl lay choking on the dust, Tullus could just make out the word 'water' as she coughed and spluttered. He handed her his own water skin, and she drank greedily as his centurion and tribune came down the steps at a more dignified pace than he and his men had.

'Has she said anything?' Tribune Macro asked as he approached her. Tullus shook his head. He moved to the girl and clasped her gently by her shoulders. Tullus watched as she slowly came back to life, revived by the powers of the cool water.

'Balomar,' she stammered. 'I have information about Balomar, his armies and his plans. I was his slave … escaped … ran here.' She collapsed into the tribune's arms, exhaustion getting the better of her.

'Centurion, get her to the hospital immediately, and alert me the moment she is awake.' Hilarius saluted and ordered two men to take the girl. Tullus was still watching her, so didn't notice Macro appear at his side. 'Why in the name of the gods did you leave her out there, watch officer? I've half a mind to put you on latrines!' Tullus fumbled his thumbs in his belt, trying his best to keep his head straight and eyes pointed dead ahead. His bottom lip quivered as he sought a reply, judging if the tribune's question was rhetorical or that he was expecting an answer.

A commotion on the battlement above them. The man Tullus had sent to the east gate came back, screaming for the horn blower to sound the new hour. 'We're late! Very late! Quick, before someone notices!'

Tribune Macro and Centurion Hilarius both snapped their heads from the shouting soldier to Tullus, who once again felt the overbearing urge to visit the latrines. 'Not having the best day, are you Tullus,' said Hilarius, the smirk still fixed to his face.

XX

August AD 171 – Germania

Albinus sighed in frustration. Life for him had been hard since Taurus had been wounded in the fighting on the Rhine. He was now in temporary command of the First Century, which at full strength would be one hundred and sixty men. As they were they numbered at just under a hundred, and many of those were new recruits. There were tent parties made up of slaves that had been conscripted to help the war effort; gladiators that had taken the oath rather than risk their lives on the arena sand; youths that would have normally been too young to be accepted. Right now the army didn't much care who signed up, they just needed the numbers.

Their victory on the Rhine had not gone unnoticed by the Augustus, who had quickly called them back to Carnuntum and sent them north across the Danube. They were now two days' march north of the river. Albinus strolled along the battlements of the marching camp the legion had built that afternoon. He thought back to his first effort at fort building, in the woods south of his father's farm. He smiled. He had once thought the crude and flimsy walls he had helped construct were the most formidable defences he had ever seen. Though since the campaign against the tribes had begun, he had partaken in the building of more marching camps than he could remember, and had the blisters on his palms to prove it.

He squinted against the last rays of the setting sun. Fullo was the newly promoted watch officer tasked with the men on duty on the western gate, and he was frantic with worry when Albinus arrived.

'Albinus! Jupiter's balls, brother, help me! I have so much to do I don't even know where to start!' Albinus bit back a retort. He thought of the pile of tablets on the small desk in his tent he had yet to browse, the reports he needed to write and send to the legate's staff. He wished Taurus would hurry and recover.

'What is it, Fullo?' he said, reluctantly.

'I need a watch word, how do we decide what they are? And the response? Can we re-use a word?' Fullo was frantic with panic, his fingers rubbing at the scars on his forehead.

'Just make it up, Fullo, it can be anything you like!' Fullo stood staring at him, his face set in a frown. 'Oh Juno's tits, pass me that amphora,' and he motioned to a small clay amphora of wine sitting atop a wooden table.

Fullo passed it over with a small chunk of chalk. Albinus scribbled on the side. 'There, the watch word for your shift is 'The Tenth' the response is 'Tunic-lifters'.' It got a cheap laugh from the tent party of soldiers who stood at the gate. Albinus knew he could get in trouble if the legate or one of the tribunes found out, but he was too tired to care.

He left the laughing soldiers and made his way down the steps onto the via principalis, and thought of diving into the principia and seeing if he could see the camp prefect, Felix. The old soldier had been a huge help to Albinus in the last few weeks, even drilling and inspecting his century so he could try and keep on top of his administrative duties.

He paused outside the principia, oblivious to the traffic that trudged past him on either side. He made to enter the great tent that housed the officials that kept the army moving, then thought better of it. Would his father have gone running to his superior officer every time he was stressed or had too much to do? Would Taurus? It was a question that didn't need answering. He carried on down the road, then turned off and passed through the tent lines of the First Cohort until he reached his tent.

Well, it was Taurus' tent really, but since he was still in his hospital bed Albinus had used the space whilst he filled in. He was therefore shocked when he pulled back the flap to see his First Spear sitting by the brazier, right arm strapped to his chest in a sling.

'Sir!' Albinus snapped to attention, saluting before standing stock straight with his thumbs hooked into his belt.

'At ease, lad,' said Taurus as he struggled off the small folding stool he had been sat on. Albinus relaxed his posture, unhooked his sheathed sword from his belt, sighing in pleasure as the weight was released from his hip. Surprising, how heavy the short swords were, he wondered how the Germani coped with their long swords, which were more than double the length of the Roman gladius. 'How's it going?' asked Taurus, giving the wax tablets on the desk a quick scan.

'Okay, sir, I think. I have some admin to catch up on, but the lads are holding up all right.' He shuffled nervously, expected a dressing-down from his superior. He sought to fill the silence when Taurus didn't reply, 'How's the wound, sir? Healing well I hope?'

Taurus laughed. 'Yes, lad, it's doing fine. Finally been discharged from that horrible hospital bed. I'd hate to think of the number of men who have died on that rank straw cot they threw me in. I swear even the fleas had lice! You would, of course, have known that if you'd have come to visit me.' He shot Albinus a hard stare.

Albinus blushed. 'Sorry, sir, it's not that I didn't want to, just had so much to do! I don't know how you keep it all together, sir!'

'Ha! I don't really. I have you to do most of the books, and I get the other centurions to help me out with drilling the men. Felix normally does the odd bit for me as well, so I can spend most of my day running around for Maximianus! He came and visited me by the way. So did Bucco, Habitus, Longus, Fullo ...'

'Okay, okay, message received!' Albinus held up his hands in defeat. 'Next time you're grievously wounded in battle I'll make sure to visit you every day!'

'Well, let's hope there's not a next time, eh!' said the First Spear as he slumped back down on the stool. 'The gods know wounds never used to hurt like this.' He winced as he rubbed his right arm with his left. 'Must be getting old.'

'Old, sir?' Albinus had never thought of Taurus as old; to him his centurion was as immovable as time itself, sturdier than the strongest oak.

'I must be thirty … something, I guess. Not sure really,' Taurus rubbed his nose as he thought. 'Can't remember what year I signed up now.' He laughed again, slapping his thigh. 'Best years of my life have been in this legion. You know this was your father's tent?'

Albinus was speechless. He looked round again at the leather walls with a new-found reverence. 'Surely not? How often are they replaced?'

'Replaced?! The army don't replace what ain't broken, lad! No, it was good enough for the old man, and it's served me just fine.' Taurus rubbed the leather with an affectionate palm, as if the memories would rub off and surge through his veins. 'See my chest over there?' He motioned to a plain wooden chest by the cot. 'Open it.'

Albinus followed the order without thought. He pulled back the brass clasp on the front and lifted the lid, momentarily shocked by the weight. The contents were masked by an old cloak. He cast Taurus a questioning glance. 'What am I looking for, sir?'

'You'll know when you see it, lad.'

Albinus thrust aside the cloak. There was a small amphora of what he assumed was wine, two wooden cups, on old bowl and matching spoon, and a sword. He gasped.

'Didn't think I'd let it out of my sight did you?'

'Can I …'

'Course! It's yours by rights anyway!'

Tears welled his eyes, blurring his vision as he gently lowered a shaking hand into the chest. The feel of the handgrip – so familiar but so different. No wood or bone was used to hilt this blade, but the purest ivory. He raised it from the chest, ran a hand over the red leather scabbard, trimmed with gold. The pommel was crafted into the shape of an eagle's head, the work beautiful, the detail flawless. Albinus rasped the blade from the scabbard. It showered the room with a dazzling white light.

'My father's sword,' he muttered to himself. Tears burst from his eyes and streamed down his face.

'A parazonium, to be exact. Our very own legate Maximianus wears one very similar to that on his left hip, you may have noticed. Though only when in his parade armour. Shows just how lucky your father was to be awarded it, usually reserved for the upper classes they are.'

Albinus wasn't listening. A thousand childhood memories whirled through his mind, dipping in and out of the misty haze to bring joy, sorrow and anger in equal measure. Suddenly he was a boy again, tugging at his father's hand as he raced to show him a tree. 'Look father, there! That tree, with the three trunks coming out from the ground, that can be our fort!' Then he was hiding under his mother's skirts as his father raged at his cowardice, after one of the other farm boys had given him a beating. There had been two sides to Silus: he had been firm but loving whilst Marcia had lived, able to show emotion and praise his son to the heavens; but he had turned into the drillmaster, reverted back into the officer when she had died. It pained Albinus to think his father had never fully recovered from his loss, that he'd died with a part of him still missing.

'Your old man loved you, Albinus, more than you'll ever know. He used to chew our ears off with tales of your younger years, before he retired. All he ever wanted was for you to be happy.'

'All he ever wanted was for me to be a soldier.' Albinus scoffed, rubbing tears from his eyes. 'Well, guess he got his way in the end.' He sheathed the blade, as if by shutting it in its scabbard he could lock away his memories.

'And what a soldier you turned out to be! Got to admit, wasn't sure you'd make it to start with. Never been so happy to be proven wrong.'

'Don't feel like much of a success.' Albinus put the sword back in the chest, threw the cloak back over it and closed the lid.

'You can take it, if you want.' Taurus motioned to the chest. 'It's yours.'

Albinus shook his head. 'No. I'm not ready, not by a long way. What was it you said to me, when I first signed up? I've got to earn it. I haven't done that, not by a long stretch.'

'Well, I dunno. You've been promoted to optio, fought in … how many battles now? Got yourself one mean scar on your face, took on the most powerful man outside the empire in single combat, and ran the First Century of the First Cohort in the finest damned legion Rome can put in the field! And the men respect you, and you've made enough of a name

for yourself for Maximianus to take note of you. I could go on and on!'
He slapped Albinus on the arm.

'No. I didn't do those things, Silus did. I'm Albinus Silus, the only thing
people respect about me is my name. And I hardly fought Balomar in single
combat, you were all around me, and all I did was duck behind my shield!
And no one's really sure it was even him! Not like his face is on any coins!'

'None of that matters, Albinus! It's all about reputation, and you have
it. I swear thanks to Abas most of the legion think I'm some sort of god!
That I can fight all day, get an hour's kip and get up and do it all again!
Heard one recruit saying once that I never fought with a shield as I didn't
need one!' He chuckled to himself as he made for the tent flap. 'The men
think you can do something, that elevates you in their eyes. The trick to
it is to not get found out!' He lifted his wounded arm and smiled. 'Like I
did!' With that he was off, out into the warm evening air, leaving Albinus
to ponder his words.

Licina huffed and puffed as she dragged the bulging laundry sack through
the corridors of the basilica. Her back was in ruins but still she pulled
the bag which was filled with cloaks, tunics and other garments from the
officials that worked within. Not for the first time, she wondered at the
arrogance of the seemingly higher classes, that they were unable to wash
their own clothes. Most of the men that worked within the building were
young, not long freed from their tutors as they adventured from Rome out
into the provinces to cut their teeth in their chosen profession. *Wouldn't
hurt them to bring a servant to do their washing for them.*

She dropped the sack in a doorway to a small office at the back of the
building. The windows had been left shuttered up here. Even though the
sun was bright and strong outside, the corridor was dark, and dust matter
sparkled in the slivers of light that shone through the gaps in closed doors.

She arched her back and sighed in pleasure, knees cracking as her legs
straightened. She hadn't long left now, if her dates were correct. *And still
I haven't told him.*

She had been overcome with joy when word had spread that the Fourteenth
Legion were returning to their home in Carnuntum from their exile on the

Rhine. For days she danced through the markets, spending lavishly on fresh sheets, new dresses, fine wine and exotic herbs, all for the dinner she planned to cook when her husband finally walked through the door.

She had stood atop the walls and looked on in horror as the legion had marched straight from the barges that had brought them up-river and over the great bridge into Germania. All she had got was one apologetic letter, explaining that they had been ordered straight north. They hadn't even got one night together.

For days she had been fuming. Storming the streets like a wild boar, she moved people and carts from her path with force, no one yet willing to face the wrath of a heavily pregnant woman. How dare he not visit! What sort of man would not take but an hour to check on his wife, his pregnant wife! She knew her anger was ridiculous, though it did nothing to quash her wild and unstoppable emotions. For one, Albinus had no control over where the legion was sent and when; and second she hadn't even plucked up the courage to tell him she was with child.

Not for the first time she questioned the wisdom of her decision. She was all alone in the city, had no friends to speak of. The one person that had always made an effort with her was Calvus, and he had been oddly aloof as of late, always working, quick with excuses as to why he couldn't stay long when he did visit. She had also noticed he looked at her with an expression something like suspicion. She banished the thought from her mind. There was no way he could know, and anyway, she'd done nothing wrong.

She was just readying herself to continue dragging the sack full of laundry when she heard raised voices from behind a nearby door. She paused, head snapping left and right to see if anyone else had heard. *Just go. There's no need, you've done everything he asked of you.*

Against the will of her mind her feet took her to the doorway. It was pulled to, but not shut. She squinted through the slim gap, seeing the outline of an ageing man, his back to her, being berated by a man standing over the chair he sat on. Her heart raced as she recognised the standing men. Slick black hair and a green cloak, remnants of a black beard on his chin: *Tribune Scaevola.* The sight of the man sent chills down her spine. Her advancing pregnancy had done nothing to stop the man's lingering glances at her, his inappropriate touching of her thighs and arse whenever she walked within arm's reach. He was a predator, sick and twisted and a traitor to boot. *But then so am I now.* Did it make you a better person if you passed on information you knew could help save a loved one? Even if you knew in doing so betrayed your country, and the one you love so dear would never forgive you if they found out? These thoughts she had pondered a lot, and not enjoyed the answer to.

Yet still she pressed her face into the sliver of light, careful not to disturb the door. 'Where man? You must tell me or I swear I'll—'

The old man in the chair squealed in terror as Scaevola rasped a knife from its scabbard. Licina involuntarily leant back, the door moving slightly from the pressure of her hand. She held in a gasp and felt her heart roar in her chest. Adrenalin pumped through her, spasms of pain in her belly. There was a moment's silence on the other side of the door. Any moment Licina expected it to be thrust open and her earwigging revealed. But nothing happened.

'Tell me,' Scaevola went on, obviously satisfied the door had been moved by the jarring of the chair the squealing man sat on.

'All ... all I know is ... is the legion are under-provisioned. The Tenth had got word that the Naristae were on the move, the Augustus has ordered the Fourteenth and the First to intercept and destroy them.' The man quivered as he spoke, hands locked together as he begged for mercy.

'Fuck! How long ago was this?'

'Th- ... three days ago. Please, I have a family!'

Scaevola threw the man to the floor, stepped over the body and wrenched the door open. Licina was pacing down the corridor, laundry sack wiping the floor of dust behind her. Scaevola didn't speak as he stormed past, but did pause to gaze longingly at her breasts. Once he had gone from sight, Licina slumped to the floor in exhaustion, the adrenalin wearing off. As the pain in her belly subsided and her heartbeat slowed, she thought about what she had heard. *The Fourteenth ... Albinus ... ambush the Naristae ... low on supplies.* Her mind whirled and she choked back vomit as she thought of what she had to do. *For Albinus. I'm doing it for Albinus. But what if I get him killed?*

'I'm telling you what I've been told! Listen to me man, you must get word to your master now!'

'My master will already know. He is in a far better position that you to be able to influence the emperor's decision.'

'But will he? Will he be able to? This could swing the balance in our favour. It is the opportunity we have been waiting for!'

Calvus kept his head down and tried not to breathe. The tavern was quiet, eerily so and the slightest noise could alert the whispering men to his presence. They sat on a large circular table, a thin curtain giving the pretence of privacy. Calvus sat alone on the nearest table on the other side of the thin curtain, his back to the two men.

'How did you come by this information anyway?'

'I have one of his slaves. *His* slaves!'

'How—'

'It doesn't matter how, it just matters that I have! Cassius sends word from the east, he is ready to advance at a moment's notice. Now is the time to strike, surely your master sees that?'

'He sees, friend. And will strike when he is ready. We must tread carefully. There have been too many near misses in the last years. To top it off there are even whispers the frumentarii are keeping tabs on us.'

Calvus tensed, his senses prickling. 'Pah! I have the tribune of the frumentarii in these parts in my pocket. I assure you, friend, we will get no trouble from there.

Sweet Jesu, who died on the cross, let that be a lie. The conversation died to an inaudible mutter, then the two men quickly parted ways. He watched as two green cloaks and matching hoods left by different doors. One man he knew for sure, the other seemed familiar, but he struggled to place him. This is what I have been waiting for, he thought as he sipped cheap vinegar wine. Finally he had evidence he could take to his employer, and bring this whole unpleasant business to a close. The last weeks and months had taught him he wasn't cut out to be a spy; he was a fighter, liked his enemies to his front and a good blade in his hand. Cloaks and daggers was a game for cowards and politicians. He resolved to play no further part in it. He rubbed the stumps of his missing fingers, and planned his next move. *I must do what it best for her.*

A knock on the door startled Licina from her half sleep. She sat up blinking grit from her eyes. Another knock on the door. She pulled back the curtains, letting a flood of white moonlight into her small apartment. *Gods, who wants me at this hour?* Wearing just her nightwear, she groaned as she rose to her feet and waddled over and opened the door. 'Calvus? What hour is it?'

'Third of the night I believe. Sorry to call on you so late, but I wanted to check you were okay.' She watched as he fingered the stumps on his left hand nervously, an awkward expression on his pale face.

'Come in.' She pulled back the door and gestured inside. 'I've not seen you for an age, are you okay?'

'I'm fine, fine,' he mumbled as he staggered in and slumped down onto a small wooden stall. He smelt of sour wine and meat, Licina wondered what back street tavern or brothel he had frequented that night.

'Can I get you a drink? Food?' He turned down both requests, still fidgeting with his hands. 'Of for Juno's sake, Calvus! You clearly have something on your mind! Spit it out man!' She felt her cheeks flush red as she raised her voice, knew the old man in the apartment next door would be tutting to himself through the paper-thin walls as she did.

'I need to talk to you about something. About, the work I've been doing. It's … complicated, what I've got myself mixed up in.'

'Okay,' said Licina, sitting herself with difficulty at the end of her cot. 'Tell me.'

For what felt like moments but turned into hours, Calvus regaled her with his story. From brothels to forums, markets to taverns, he told all he had seen and heard. 'And the worst thing is, I've done all this on the orders of a man I'm now not certain I can trust with the findings. What should I do?'

Tears streamed down Licina's face. His tale was harrowing and filled with sorrow. Silently she cursed the evil that wound its way into the world, and remembered the shieldmaidens to the far north, the spinners they

211

worshipped and the great tree that rooted the worlds together. *Fate brought Calvus here this night. He has told me this for a reason. To give me the chance right my wrongs.* A stream of tears became a torrent as she thought of her husband in the north, fighting on the behalf of men who cared not whether he lived or died. *And I have reduced his chances of survival.*

She sucked in a deep breath, 'Oh, Calvus. We are both fools. Pour yourself some wine, I have my own story to tell.'

XXI

Albinus felt his belly grumble as he stood in position behind the First Century. It had been two weeks since they had last received supplies from south of the river; two weeks of hunting and scavenging in a land picked clean by the enemy. And now they had to fight.

Things had gone from bad to worse for the Fourteenth Legion ever since they had returned from the west. Ordered straight from their barges across the bridge at Carnuntum, they had been frustrated by the enemy every time they had tried to give battle.

It had become a game of cat and mouse, marches and counter-marches. But despite the advanced fitness and discipline of the Romans, they had been unable to trap their foe in a snare. To make matters worse, it seemed someone was revealing details of supply routes and dates to the enemy, who were leaving trails of black smoke and chopped-up corpses whenever the Romans tried to supply the legion. Albinus knew it was the same for the other legions scattered across the south of this vast country, but it didn't make him feel any better.

Discipline was flagging, legionaries were now openly slack in their duties. Two men had been executed the day before for falling asleep on watch, and ten men had been flogged for talking back to their centurion. Desertions had tripled in the last two weeks. Men began to whisper that the emperor was cursed, that the gods had deemed him unfit to rule. Albinus had even

213

heard some men suggest Alexander of Abonoteichos should be raised to the purple, that he and his snake god could restore glory to the empire. Thankfully for Albinus, he had heard no such folly from the men in the ranks in front of him.

The First Cohort had been an example to the rest, doubling their efforts, openly scorning the other cohorts for not keeping to their high standards. And their reward for that? They were to take the brunt of the enemy attack today.

Word had got to Maximianus that the warband of the Naristae – the tribe they had been hunting – were to pass through the lands of the Marcomanni as they ventured east. They were the one remaining tribe – apart from the Marcomanni themselves – who were capable of causing Rome damage without the assistance of their cousins. Destroying them was an opportunity the Fourteenth's legate was not going to let slip.

Maximianus and Taurus had chosen the ground well, Albinus thought. They stood on a gentle slope, in a wide-open field. There were no clumps of trees or plants to get in the way, no marsh or streams to get bogged down in– and best of all, no thick forests for the barbarians to hide in. The grass plain was covered on one side by large rocks; taller than a man they stood, making it impossible for an ambush from there. To their right were mountains, one small track being the only pass through. Behind them were more fields, the odd farm with the burnt remains of crops black dots on an otherwise green landscape.

The sun was just descending from its highest point and Albinus was beginning to wonder if they were going to stand waiting all day when the scouts came galloping back, arms waving frantically. Every man knew what that meant: enemy in sight. The low chatter of the waiting soldiers grew to shouts and hoots as the men became aware they were to fight. Albinus didn't think he had ever seen the legion so desperate for the iron storm, the lottery of life and death. Even he felt a tremor of excitement in his veins, the blood pumping quicker, fingers tingling with anticipation. *About time.*

His belly growled again. He thought of waffling down the last bit of salted meat in his pack, but the horn blowers blew the signal to ready for battle.

At once Albinus reacted, marching down the rear rank of his century, barking orders and prodding men with his wooden staff. Around him men hoisted their breeches for one last piss; squatted and shat brown water as their bowels quaked in fear. At one time this would have horrified him, he would have felt the same needs himself. But he was a veteran now, an officer, hardened by the shield wall and well used to the smell of blood on iron. His courage would not fail him again.

He stood behind a new recruit – a youth with a shield shaking like a leaf in the breeze. Two old gladiators stood either side of the young lad, but neither man sought to encourage or comfort him. Albinus raised his staff and cracked it round one of the gladiators' head. 'What the fuck?!' the man exclaimed as his brain rattled from one side of his skull to the other.

'What do you think you're doing, soldier?' screamed Albinus with as much gravel as he could muster. 'See this lad here …' he grasped the youth by his shoulder, '… he's about to experience his first battle. And what are you doing to help? Offering advice? Helping to check his helmet and armour? No! You're standing there in silence, minding your own business!'

'Ain't my fault if the boy can't put his own fucking helmet on!'

'It's your duty to help him, soldier! You're not in the arena now, there's no more single combat for you. This is the army, and in the army you're only as good as the man that stands at your shoulder. Now, do you want your shield partner to be shitting himself as he stands in the front rank with you? His shield quivering like a piece of old cloth?' The old gladiator looked at the youth with eyes filled with shame. Albinus could see he'd got through to him.

'No, sir, I don't.'

'So what are you going to do, in the time left to you before the enemy arrive?'

The soldier nodded. 'I know what to do, sir, sorry.'

Albinus walked off with his heart thudding in his chest. The ex-gladiator was twice the man he would ever be, in height and breadth. He had also witnessed him practising with the sword at his belt, and knew he wouldn't last a heartbeat if he decided to draw it on him. Not for the first time, he marvelled at the undisputed power his rank gave him over the men under his command.

As he paced away he heard the chink of metal and the low murmur of

215

the ex-gladiator as he spoke to the lad and checked the strap on his helmet. Albinus smiled, pleased to have been able to do something helpful for the recruit. He remembered his own first experience of battle, the heightened nerves he'd felt in the wait before. Still smiling, he recalled how he'd vomited on his shield and passed out. He owed a lot to the men of his tent party, who had seen him through that day. To Taurus as well, who even offered him the chance to move back from the front line. He hadn't, of course.

He paced to the end of his century, on the far right of the Roman line. The First Cohort stretched out behind him: five double strength centuries – over forty ranks of men ready and waiting for the battle to commence.

Rolling away, as far as the eye could see, were the rest of the legion, each cohort ten ranks wide, with the first century from each at the front. Legatus Maximianus had decided no cohorts were to be kept in reserve, therefore each would take its place in the battle line.

Albinus stood on his toes and looked to the rear as the artillery were brought forward, so that they stood on a small ridge behind the last century's of each cohort. There was a noise like rumbling thunder as they were dragged to position on small wooden carts by unwilling mules. As the mules were driven off Albinus watched on in wonder as teams of specially trained auxiliaries opened the wooden sides of the carts until they were folded down on the ground like leaf petals, and quickly assembled the carroballistae within. The cart then became a wooden platform for the machine to rest on.

The carroballistae – or 'scorpion' as they were commonly referred as – were something like giant bows, two-armed, with giant coils of sinew rope powering the bolts or stones forward. Albinus was yet to see them in use, as it was rare for a legion to take them out into the field on campaign. He was looking forward to seeing what they could do.

Averting his eyes to the front and through the rows of helmets and trumpets and standards he could make out the first of the enemy snaking into the field. He imagined what they must be feeling: the fear of seeing the enemy in the place you least expect them to be.

Taurus had been doing his rounds earlier in the day, telling the men the Naristae were just as tired and hungry as they were, after all, they had been running away from the legion for as long as the legion had been chasing them. The First Spear always seemed to know the right words, speak the right way to raise the morale and confidence of his men. Albinus was acutely aware he didn't possess those skills, but he was doing his best to learn fast.

A white stallion galloped into view, Maximianus looking resplendent in a bronzed cuirass and white-plumed helmet. He'd ditched the white cloak he wore around camp and was caped in a standard issue legionary cloak. Albinus watched as he dismounted and threw the reins to the nearest soldier, and went to stand next to Taurus.

Albinus shifted from foot to foot, cursing for not being able to hear what the men were saying. It was none of his business of course, but he was curious none-the-less. But then men were shouting his name, and Taurus was waving frantically for him to come forward.

He was there in heartbeats, saluting smartly to the legate and standing to attention with his thumbs hooked into his belt.

'Optio Silus, good to see you, young man,' said Maximianus, slapping him on the shoulder. 'Stand at ease, brother, and listen very carefully.' Albinus stood in awed silence as the legion's senior officer filled him in on his plans for the battle. 'Do you understand what I've told you?' the legate asked. Albinus nodded slowly, still shocked to be taken into confidence. 'And do you understand why I have told you? What you will need to do?'

Albinus paused, running the legate's words through his head. 'Yes, sir. We will do what is ordered, and at every command we will be ready.' Again, he saluted smartly and watched as the legate leaped atop his horse without another word.

'You ever fought in a boar's snout before, lad?' Albinus hadn't noticed Taurus appear at his side.

'No, sir. But we've done it on the drill field plenty of times. The lads will be fine, I'm sure. You want me to stay at the rear? Will be hard for me to relieve you if I'm way back there ...' He motioned to the rear of the century.

'Stay in the centre, where you can get a grip of the men on either flank. I'm not sure there's gonna be any relieving; those of us that start in the front are gonna end in the front, or die there.' the First Spear said grimly.

'Are you sure you're fit enough to fight, sir? That arm can't be fully healed yet surely?'

'Ha! I like you, Albinus, I really do! Thanks for your concern, but I'll be just fine. The legate thinks this is the best way to break them, and who am I to question him. One of the scouts said there were roughly ten thousand of the goat fuckers, so should be one hell of a fight!'

'Yes, sir,' replied Albinus uncertainly.

'Right, they're coming, so get your act together and be ready to lead these men should I fall.' The two men embraced in the warrior grip, arms locked together, before Albinus moved toward the rear. He passed Rullus who gave him a wink and a smile, as well as some sort of remark about him being a teacher's pet. He embraced Fullo and Bucco as he passed them, briefly explaining what was to happen. Each man nodded in turn. Habitus spat in disgust when he heard. 'Can't we fight at the rear with you?' piped up Longus, a mischievous grin on his face.

The trumpets blew before Albinus could reply. He sprinted to his position and checked his helmet and armour one last time. Through the gaps in the ranks he watched as the Germani moved forwards uncertainly. They hadn't been expecting to fight today, and like Taurus had said, they would be just as hungry and tired as the Romans were. Slowly they came on, the man Albinus presumed to be their chief stalking the front line of his men, screaming and shouting in his hoarse language, sword raised above his head.

Then the barbarian cry began – the 'barritus', so someone had named it – a chorus of screams that rose in volume from low to high back to low again like the rolling waves of the sea; a continuous sound, as if none stopped for breath. It was chilling to listen to. They stood in disciplined silence whilst the enemy shouted and hollered. The recruits were easy to spot now. They were the ones that quivered in the light breeze, fidgeted with swords and armour and shifted from foot to foot. They looked round questioningly, wondering why the veterans weren't touching cloth like them.

It would have been normal for the Romans to respond in some way. Cries of 'ROMA!' were hushed quickly by angry centurions and lightning thrusts of their vine sticks. The legate had been specific in his orders about the men remaining silent until the last possible moment. The ground began to shake as the Germani picked up the pace, two hundred or so paces out now.

A horn blower in the centre of the Roman line blew one short note on his trumpet, the first of three expected signals. Albinus didn't take his eyes from the front but far behind him he heard the auxiliaries load the first bolts into the ballistae. One hundred paces now, another note blasted through the air. 'Draw swords!' Albinus joined in with the other officers as each man in the legion tucked away his pila and drew their gladius from their right hip. There were some looks of confusion in the ranks, men looking towards their nearest officer in question. Albinus strode into the rear rank of his century, snatching a shield from the nearest soldier. 'On the next trumpet, lads, smash your blade against the shield boss, just once.' He handed back the shield and moved back to his position, smiling with the men as they understood what they were to do.

The third trumpet blew. *BANG.* Five thousand men in unison crashed iron into iron. The sound was like a thunderbolt from the gods, deep and loud enough to wake Hades in the underworld. The Naristae were startled, terrified and shocked. Their charge broke down to a standstill, warriors' heads flicking frantically to the rear. Albinus watched their chief as he raged at his men; he must have been furious after taking the time to build their courage for the charge.

Legatus Maximianus made sure the enemy had no time to ponder their courage. He had waited until they were in reach of the artillery to give the signal, and now he made it rain iron on the hapless barbarians. With nothing but a twang, a storm unleashed on the warriors of the Naristae. Black iron bolts ripped through the air at blistering speed to take two or more men to the gods at once. They tore through mail and bone like an axe through rotted wood. Still the barbarians didn't move, just stood and died as volley after volley flew from the ballistae. Eventually the Naristae chief roused his men from their quivering fear and dragged them toward the Roman line. The bolts kept raining death but the Germani sprinted through the hail. Thirty paces out and the cry went out to 'Ready pila!' Each man sheathed his sword and gripped the shaft of their pilum, waiting for the order to let it fly. When it came each rank took their turn, until each of the First Century's ranks had spent the last of their missiles.

Albinus watched on in awe and disgust as the combination of pila and ballistae bolts destroyed all in their path. He thought there couldn't have been a single warrior left standing from the front ten ranks of the Germani, even their chief was gone from his sight. The following warriors had to pick a path through the forest of the dead and dying. It slowed their pace and destroyed their momentum, but still they came.

Then the last trumpet the officers had been waiting for sounded loud and true. 'Form wedge! Form wedge on me!' The towering voice of Taurus echoed through the century, months of training paying off as the men responded without thought.

Albinus pushed his way into the centre of the triangular formation, his height serving him well as he looked atop the helmets either side, pointing and shouting to make sure each man held his place right in the line. The move was repeated across the breadth of the Roman front, transforming their line into a giant saw, making less clear targets for the oncoming barbarians to charge into.

Heart thudding, hands shaking, Albinus gripped his staff tight and began to feel the old ache in his right shoulder. *Haven't even swung my blade yet.* He couldn't recall ever feeling the pain before a battle; it was usually tender for some days after, but that was because he had been using the arm to swing his sword. The scar on his cheek itched, he clenched a portion of gum inbetween his remaining teeth and rubbed frantically at it with his tongue, to no avail. He pictured Licina's face, and prayed to Mars he would live to see her again.

The Germani hit first on the opposite flank, the cacophony of battle distinctive and loud even from that vast distance. They closed with a whimper when they limped up to the First, the foremost men dying before they had even raised their blades. Albinus watched Taurus, with his wooden whistle fixed between his teeth. He could hear the snarls and growls as the centurion went about his business with grim efficiency. Bucco stood at his shoulder, his old segmented cuirass making him easy to distinguish. Habitus was at his back, his bowstring quivering after taking its latest victim. Albinus tried to spot Fullo in the crush but couldn't make him out. He resolved to duck his head and heave with the rest as they pushed back the incoming torrent of flesh and iron.

The pressure was intense. A man shoved his shield into his back as he braced against his staff and heaved with all his might into the man in front of him. The pungent stink of leather, sweat and blood filled his nostrils, burnt the hairs as they slithered through and into his lungs.

All around him men screamed and roared, the tip of the wedge flowing forwards and back as the opposing armies sought to sweep the other from the field. Albinus noticed after a time that the Romans hadn't gained an inch, but he was moving further and further forwards none theless. Before he knew it he was behind Longus, who stood hunched behind his shield with a crimson sword hanging low to his right. He was panting like a dog, sweat streaming from under his helmet. 'Move over!' said Albinus as he stood behind. 'Take a breather, brother.' But Longus just shook his head.

Albinus could only look on in despair as his friend reacted too late to a feint high to his left, Longus was unable to bring his shield back across his body in time as the spear ripped into his chest, plunging through his heart and tearing a hole in the back of his mail. He dropped to the earth without a sound.

Roaring in incoherent rage, Albinus leapt over Longus' corpse and smashed his staff into the German's face. Wielding the wooden badge of office two-handed, he brought the pommelled tip back and drove it into the next man's midriff. He stepped forward. Swinging the staff left to right, he hit three men in one motion, swivelling on the balls of his feet,; he caught the next man on the shoulder and the one after went down seeing stars after taking a hit in the chin.

He was lost in his own rage. The red mist had descended and the blood joy had him now. Out from the protection of the Roman wedge and the solid rectangular shields, he fought the tide of iron with just his wooden staff. He was seemingly immune to the thrusts and hacks of the axes and broadswords the Naristae approached him with. His eyes were a bright blue fire, his scarred face fixed in a snarl.

Further into the fray he staggered. Mindlessly swinging and clubbing, he carved out a bloody path. He was oblivious to the screams of Taurus and Bucco and Fullo as they desperately tried to bring him back from the battle madness. He didn't feel the battle change, didn't sense the barbarian horde stop in their relentless charge against the impenetrable Roman formation. Horn blowers across the Roman front sounded the advance; the ballistae started firing bolts once more. One sped past, a hair's breadth from Albinus' face; he didn't feel the rush of air, nor see the three men the bolt took with it to the earth.

The bolt's flight opened up some space to his front. He stopped, panting, slowly regaining his senses. A flick of his head left and right told him he was surrounded. He daren't risk looking behind to see how far back his century were for fear of being cut down. *Shit.* He couldn't remember ever being in a more vulnerable position. Time seemed to slow as thoughts of his father filled his mind. *Is this what it was like for you, at the end? Alone and surrounded, with nothing but your sword.* A flash of iron to his left and he ducked just in time as a blade whooshed past above him, clipping the two plumes that adorned his helmet. He rose from his crouch and hurled his staff at his attacker, who recoiled when struck by the heavy wooden beam. Rasping his sword from his scabbard on his right hip, Albinus stepped forward and in one fluid motion drove the blade straight through the unarmoured man until he felt the tip explode from his back. Hot blood ran down his arm; his shoulder was on fire, the pain spreading to his elbow as he twisted the blade and tugged it back. Red cloaks at his shoulder; rectangular shields, bronze-trimmed with gleaming white Capricorns painted on the front, his friends were here. 'Albinus, get back behind the shields you halfwit!' Taurus' voice was in his ear, his voice box cracking and croaking from the constant strain of shouting.

Nodding, Albinus let himself be guided behind the wall of shields, Fullo and Bucco grabbing his arms and slapping his face. 'By the Gods, lad, that was something to see! You must have taken down over ten on your own! Your father would be proud!' said Bucco as he handed him a dead man's shield and wiped the blood from around his eyes. Albinus just nodded again, suddenly bone weary.

Screams of defiance to their front, a man in a great cloak of bear stepped forward from the retreating Germani: their chief, Albinus assumed, though he didn't know the man's name. He wore a helmet trimmed with gold, had a great blond beard that ran halfway down his blood-soaked mail. In knee-high boots that were now dyed red, he charged the Roman line without waiting to see if his men followed. They didn't. He got within five paces of Taurus and the front rank of the Fourteenth before there was the low rumble of a charging horse and Legatus Maximianus, hanging from his saddle, his spatha hanging low in his right hand, swiped the blade once and the gold-trimmed helmet toppled to the floor, the head still encased within.

Silence spread like the blood on the grass. The chieftain's eyes still moved within the helmet, Albinus watched the amazed stare they maintained, until the life extinguished, like a lantern left out in the rain. With a roar of triumph the Roman line surged forward as one; men released from the cage of fear and discipline that binds them in battle, they mobbed the remaining German army, hacking and stabbing with endless energy and enthusiasm.

Albinus didn't know how long he fought for. Surely there was no greater joy in killing when the enemy had lost their courage. With ease he smashed with his shield and stabbed with his sword, laughing and shouting with Fullo and Bucco as the three men carved a joy-filled blood path through the enemy.

A horn sounded the halt; it was repeated three or four times before the men responded. Maximianus on his white stallion rode through the front ranks. Waving his sword in a great circle he screamed in a hoarse voice for the men to stop. The barbarian horde kept running toward the distant trees they had emerged confidently from earlier in the day, their dead and wounded left forgotten on the battlefield. Survival was their only thought now.

But the refuge of the dark forest would be ever denied to them. Light blue shields stepped from the canopy of the trees, horns blew and banners were raised. The First Adiutrix had come to join the fun, Legatus Pertinax on horseback leading the cavalry into the melée. The Fourteenth cheered again, their work done for the day. Victory was theirs, their honour restored under the emperor.

Abinus grinned and hugged Fullo, no words needing be spoken. They were both just happy to have survived. Pulling away from the embrace, Albinus turned to see Bucco consoling a grief-stricken Habitus. Guilt and sadness washed all the joy from Albinus, as in a moment he realised he had forgotten Longus. Rullus walked over and joined the four men as they barged through the ranks of the rear centuries to find the body of their friend. No one spoke, no one cheered or boasted of their actions. All the joy from the victory had gone, masked in grief, as the moon rises in the evening to mask the light of the sun.

PART III

THE GRAIN MEN

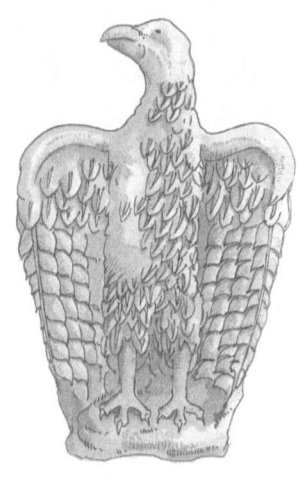

September–December AD 171

XXII

Calvus stood in the shade of the great wooden gates, sucking his teeth in impatience. 'And you're certain the young master is expecting you?' the major-domus asked for the third time. Calvus sighed, rubbing his temples.

'Yes, boy, I'm sure! I wouldn't fucking be here otherwise would I?! Now, is the *young master* here or not?' Calvus watched in pleasure as the major-domus recoiled at the word 'boy'. The upper classes of Rome's society were not known for the good treatment of their slaves, using the term 'boy' to address them was not the worst way to treat them, but stung their small pride nonetheless.

'I hesitate to remind you that I am no slave, I am a freedman in the employ of—'

'Yeah, yeah, well I ain't here to see the big man himself, it's his son I'm after. Now, you gonna leave me standing here all day or what?' said Calvus, spittle flying from the gaps between his teeth.

'My apologies, dominus. Please step in the side gate and I will take you through to the tribune.' The major domus gestured to a gate just wide for Calvus to shuffle through if he walked side on.

'You want me to go through the slave gate?' He shouted up to the freedman, who stood atop a ladder at the rear of the main double gates, sweating in the late summer sun.

'Well, I'm not going to the hassle of opening these great things just to

227

let you in.' Even from the distance, and with the sun in his eyes, Calvus could see the smirk on his face.

'And what if I was wearing one of those uniforms?' said Calvus, gesturing to the two legionaries standing guard at the gate. 'You'd open it then wouldn't you, you turd! You know how many years I fought under the eagle? First Century, First Cohort, Fourteenth Martial and Victorious, and damn proud! Now open this fucking gate!'

Heartbeats later one of the main gates swung open, the two legionaries stamping a salute and standing to attention as Calvus strutted through. 'Too fucking right,' he muttered as he passed the youths, who couldn't have signed up more than a year ago. Wish I could have spent my years guarding some rich bloke's house, he thought as he entered the courtyard. The major-domus offered him a short bow as he approached, muttering a small apology for any insult he may have caused. Calvus brushed him off with a wave of the hand. 'Where is your master? I've important business with him and you've cost me enough time already.'

The freedman scuttled off, gesturing for Calvus to follow. He looked around appreciatively as he walked down the wide cobbled pathway that lead to the front doors. It was a patchwork of colour: blue, green and purple flowers under a canopy of fig trees; bronzed water fountains and braziers dotted the greenest grass Calvus thought he had ever seen. Up a small flight of stairs they went and into the shade of a stone portico, two more legionaries either side of the great double doors, and into a light and airy vestibule with marble under foot and tapestries adorning the walls to left and right.

A small wooden podium sat up against one wall. Calvus looked at it questioningly. 'For when the dominus is in residence.' The major-domus answered the unasked question. 'For when he holds the salutatio with his clients.' Calvus nodded, only half understanding. The salutatio was held every morning, and was the chance for the clients of a wealthy and well-connected senator to come and offer morning blessings, catch up on gossip with other clients and take the opportunity to ask a small favour of their patron. Given the stature of the man whose house Calvus stood in, he guessed the list of clients would be substantial, but he lived in a different world to them, and had no real understanding of what it was they did or discussed.

Through the vestibule and into the atrium; Calvus stopped and gasped, for the room held such wealth and beauty that he couldn't begin to comprehend what it all must cost. The floor was polished marble, which gleamed and reflected the sun's light that poured in through the compluvium – a square opening in the roof, slanting inwards, that allowed rain water to fall into an impluvium, which in turn was a shallow rectangular drain pool, surrounded by colourful mosaics. The water would drop into the drain pool, where it would then be transported through several pipes, before ending up in a giant cistern. The cistern would be somewhere in the slave quarters of the building, where it would be kept atop a roaring fire, which would heat the water within, giving hot water for baths and underfloor heating. Calvus had heard men speak of all this before, but had never appreciated the complexity and ingenuity of it all until now.

He stared open-mouthed at the lavish couches that sat alongside a giant cushioned chair ordained in bronze. He thought it looked suspiciously like a throne. Under the giant chair was an iron strongbox, a dark key-shaped hole at the top. Within would be kept the owner's most valuable possessions. He wondered briefly at the value of the contents of that box, and why anyone would choose to keep it on display. *Guess everyone ain't where I'm from.* His thoughts drifted back to his old life before the legions: dark nights, quick fingers and purses full of coin. Of Aife, and her—

'Dominus, this way please,' said the major-domus, dragging Calvus from the abyss of his past.

They passed through the atrium, over mosaics depicting the war god Mars, who stood on a field of sand wielding a blood-drenched blade with an eagle head pommel, as he fought and killed men ten times his number. Again, his attention was caught as they approached the family shrine to Juno and Vesta, the mother of gods and the goddess of hearth and home. A small candle was lit within, and always would be. He slowed, wondering if he was meant to approach and burn some of the petalled incense that sat in a small clay bowl beside the candle. A nudge from the major-domus corrected him and he carried on.

All the doors to the left and right were closed, but Calvus could hear hushed voices from within as the household slaves went about their daily business. Soon he was out into a large portico, which surrounded the inner garden of the property. A shallow pool with large arched waterfalls was the main attraction. Each wall was painted with a wild animal in their natural habitat; it made the space feel bigger than it was. Round the portico, past the kitchen and bath houses, until the major-domus stopped at a small, insignificant-looking door. He knocked and waited for an answer. 'Enter,' was the muffled reply.

Through the door they passed and into a sparsely decorated study, plain grey walls and just a small wooden desk and some papers the only décor. The room was given light by another rectangular hole in the ceiling, and a corresponding drain pool beneath. At the desk sat Marcus Avidius Pompeianus, eldest son of Claudius Pompeianus, Governor of Pannonia and commander of the emperor's army in the war against the German tribes. 'Calvus, my dear friend,' he exclaimed as he looked up from the small pile of papers on the desk. 'What an unexpected delight. Come in, my friend. Krateros, fetch another chair would you.'

'You sure you want to see *him*, master?' Krateros, the major-domus, raised his eyebrows.

'Yes, quite sure. A chair, now please.' He left and quickly returned with a small wooden folding stool. Avidius was about to reprimand the man when Calvus held up a hand and said the stool was fine. He sat down and waited for the freedman to close the door before speaking. 'Good to see you, sir. I'll get straight to the point, I believe I have gathered enough evidence to support the theory you came to me with.'

'Really? That is brilliant news. And do you believe my theory to be correct?'

'I do, sir, yes. I can't *fully* prove it, but there's enough there to arrest him on I think.' Calvus said with more authority than he felt.

'Okay,' said Avidius, leaning back in his chair. 'Do tell.'

So Calvus told it all from the beginning: The flame-haired girl, the green-cloaked man; their meetings in markets, brothels and forums; he finished his tale with the tavern a few nights before, and the other man in the green cloak who had been with his prey. 'The other man I half recognised, but can't place where from. He was dark-skinned, not African-like, but tanned. Eastern, I'd guess. And he had some sort of patch on the back of his cloak. It was brown, some sort of symbol on it. But I couldn't get close enough to make it out.'

Avidius leapt to his feet in excitement. 'Was the man tall? Yes. Was his hair long and dark? Slicked back in a top knot? You think so? Well think, man, think!'

Calvus closed his eyes and concentrated. He thought back to the tavern, the flickering light of the lamps, the thin partition curtain, the voices within. 'I don't know, sir, I'm sorry.' He sighed, feeling he had let his employer down.

'No matter, Calvus, no matter. You have done an exceptional job. I have to say, I wasn't expecting much when I first hired you, but First Spear Taurus was insistent that you were the man for this sort of work.'

'Taurus? He knows about this?' Calvus was shocked. He had never thought his old centurion thought much of him at all, let alone that he'd put him forward for work once the army had pensioned him off.

'He knew the kind of work, but not the details of course. What we do is based on secrecy – on absolute secrecy. We are sitting in a house full of lavish reception rooms and studies, and yet I meet you in a room locked away in the back corner, with no luxuries within at all. Why is that, do you think?'

Calvus didn't reply at first. But the silence gave him the answer. 'No slaves,' he said. 'All the slaves are within the house, going about their duties. There's no need for any to come this way unless you command them. And no slaves means—'

'No prying eyes or sharp ears. You have it, Calvus! There can be no secrets where slaves are concerned, they gossip like you wouldn't believe. Now you are of course aware of who I am, but do you know exactly what it is that I do?'

Calvus scowled, considering the question. 'You're frumentarii – grain man, right?'

Avidius lifted his chin and howled loudly. 'Grain men, yes that's what we are! And what is it grain men do?'

Calvus was still scowling; he thought the man was trying to make him feel stupid. 'You are responsible for the grain supply for the army.

You're picked for your local knowledge of the province you are sent to, and you use that knowledge to buy grain from local suppliers.' He grew red as Avidius laughed again. 'Sorry sir, but are you gonna tell me what's going on here?'

Avidius calmed his laughing, chest heaving with the effort. 'I'm sorry, my friend. Officially you are correct, the frumentarii were formed many years ago, tasked with the assignment of ensuring that each legion across the empire had a reliable and constant supply of grain. Unofficially, in the time of the Divine Emperor Hadrian, it was felt there was a need for an official spy network across the empire. Too many plots and scheming senators and Generals, you see. So, who better than the men who were experts of the provinces they were stationed in, who knew everyone from the local governor to the poorest farmer. Us, of course. This is our real purpose, our mission in life. We uncover plots against the empire or indeed the emperor, and take them back to the Castra Peregrina in Rome, for our glorious leader to stamp them out before they become a major issue.' Calvus noted the tribune was studying him as he spoke, judging his reaction.

'I see,' he said, nodding his head slowly. Like all soldiers, he had heard of the Camp of Strangers on the Caelian Hill in the south of Rome. And like all soldiers, he had grown to detest the men that wore the silver disc around their necks with 'Miles Arcanus' engraved on the front. 'And that is what you recruited me to do? Why didn't you tell me?'

'As I've already said, I didn't know how far I could trust you. But you have done a fine job, and I see now you are just the man I need to continue my operations here in the northern provinces.'

'Me? A spy? I would hardly consider myself—'

'And yet look at what you have done! You have proved there is something suspicious going on in the area. Secret meetings have been unearthed, plots uncovered. And all the while you have remained anonymous, your target oblivious to the fact you have been spying on him. You underestimate yourself, my friend.'

Calvus nodded in agreement, seeing that the tribune was right. 'So, what now?'

'Well, we arrest the man in question of course, torture and question him until we find out who he's working with and what the end goal is. Then we execute the lot of them! Not the most glorious work, I know, but necessary nonetheless.'

Calvus studied his boots, thinking of the right words. 'I have a request, sir. The girl, the flame-haired girl, she cannot be harmed. She is precious—'

'Important to you, I know.' Avidius laughed at the dumfounded look on the Briton's face. 'Oh come on, Calvus, did you not suspect I would have someone following you as you followed our target? I know she is important to you, and I can hazard a fair guess as to how. I also know you are originally from Briton, though your Latin is near flawless and leaves no trace of an accent. I also have a fair idea as to why a young Briton would leave his homeland and sign up for the legions in distant Pannonia, rather than just enrolling in a legion on his doorstep. But we shan't go into those details now. You have my word, if we can save the girl, we will.'

Swallowing the remaining spittle in his dry mouth, Calvus said, 'Thank you, sir. So, what's the plan?'

The burnt-out hall of Goridorgis was as silent as a grave. Warriors shifted uncomfortably on the charred remnants of wooden benches, flasks of ale sat on ash-laden tables untouched. The cracking of the hearths flames was the only sound as the King sunk lower on his chair on the raised dais. 'All dead?' he whispered to the messenger, a fearful-looking tribesman who had been given the unenviable task of delivering the message.

'Yes, lord king. They were trapped between two legions. Chief Valao fought in the front rank of his men, leading charge after charge against the Romans. But in the end he fell. The men soon panicked after that, it turned into a rout.' The messenger hung his head in shame.

'But you live. How many others do?' Balomar asked, one small ray of hope left, like the dying embers of a fire.

'A few hundred at best, lord king. All have been taken by the Romans to be sold as slaves. I was set free, and sent here to deliver the news of the defeat.'

'By the Romans?'

'Yes, lord king.'

'Were you told to tell me anything else?'

'Yes, lord king. Surrender now, sue for peace and Rome will give you favourable terms, a promise made by the emperor himself. If you continue to resist, you and your people will be destroyed down to the last child.' There was a gasp of fear, followed by raised voices of angry warriors.

'To the last child?' Fear and sorrow was quickly replaced by rage as Balomar sprang from his chair. His wife Saxa sat sobbing in the seat next to him, distraught at the news of her father's death. 'Have you been ordered to visit any other chieftain's hall? To spread this fear around our cousins and their warriors?' He knew the answer already.

'Yes, lord king. But I came to you first.'

'Good. Adalwin, seize him and hold him prisoner. We may need guidance from the gods on this matter. This messenger can go to them and ask their opinion for us.'

The messenger recoiled in fear, babbling and pleading for his life. Strong arms seized him and he was dragged screaming from the hall. Adalwin approached his king with caution, 'Maybe we should take a walk around the fortress, lord king? Get some air, think about our course of action?' Balomar nodded, feeling the weight of the world on his shoulders.

They walked through the throng of despairing warriors, out into the late summer sun, down the hard mud slope that was the main walkway, past the blacksmith's, baker's, huts and hovels that surrounded the king's hall. Two warriors opened the great wooden gates and let the king and his captain pass through without a word. Balomar kept walking down the road, ignoring Adalwin who had started to veer off to the right to tour the walls. He caught up with his king just as they made it to the woodland at the base of the hill, to the south of the fortress.

Balomar stopped at the trees, perching on a fallen trunk off the side of the road. He looked up upon the capital of his people. Smoke drifted lazily from the glowing embers of the fire that had nearly destroyed his home. 'Once our people lived in nothing but small villages. Each village would be miles apart, and the head of each village would have some sort of quarrel or other with at least a dozen other village heads. And look at us now! We have walls and halls, good armour and swords, bigger tribes, more warriors that are better trained and united under a single leader. What have we done with it?' He kicked the dirt at his feet as he spoke, sending a small dust cloud spiralling into the air.

'Arminius took on Rome with that collection of mud huts and villages. He gave them a bloody nose such as no one has been able to since. Where did it all go wrong for us, eh?'

He looked up at Adalwin, who appeared to have the sense to see the question was rhetorical. Adalwin sat down next to his king, putting a reassuring arm on his shoulder. 'You haven't failed, lord king. Each battle you have fought in you have won, or at least held your own. It is the other chiefs – their small disputes, petty arguments and unwillingness to work together. That is what has cost us.'

'But what of Bandanasp, does he not have the same troubles as us? And yet he wins victory after victory, uniting more men to his cause. I thought my alliance with the Naristae would be a turning point. All I knew of Valao suggested he was a good man, a strong leader. I wouldn't have thought him stupid enough to go stumbling into some trap laid by Rome and her bastard legions! Wotan's arse, I even married his daughter! Much to our mutual dissatisfaction. I've lost more men than I could ever replace, even Aelinia deserted …' He trailed off, suddenly swearing and kicking the dust again. 'Aelinia! Who else could have warned Rome of the Naristae's movements! Fuck her all the way to Hel! May she fall down the roots of Yggdrasil and never climb back up!' All men knew of Yggdrasil, the great tree that held the nine worlds together. 'That messenger! We will give him to the Harii, and have their priests sacrifice him to the old gods.' The king saw Adalwin was taken aback by this, but he paid him no heed.

The Harii stuck to the old ways. Their priests dwelled in old groves deep in the woods, much the same as the priests who worshipped the newer gods. But the Harii still worshipped Isis, Hercules, gods who Balomar thought nothing more than as re-hashed versions of older gods than them. *But they will serve my purpose.* Adalwin looked sternly at his king. 'To have that man killed by those animals could send the wrong message.'

'No, my friend. It will send the right one. We send his soul to the gods, who in turn will tell the tribes peace with Rome is the only option. No,

235

Adalwin, don't argue. We have fought, and we have lost. There is nothing else for it now, I must think of my people – our people.' He nodded with certainty, the path ahead suddenly clear. 'And something else. Someone else must die.' He spat venom as he spoke, thoughts filled with the hooded face of Alexander of Abonoteichos. *I should never have let that man poison my mind.*

XXIII

October AD 171 – Carnuntum

Licina felt another spasm in her belly, but she tried to ignore the pain as she waddled through the corridors of the basilica. The walk from her home to the forum had been harder than it ever had been before. She had got halfway when the spasms grew so strong she thought she may have the baby there and then. A merchant had seen her struggles and taken pity on her, helping her onto the back of a mule-drawn cart, and dropping her off to at the entrance of the basilica itself. She had offered the man coin for his kindness, but he had refused. It had cheered her, to know there still some good people left in the world.

She struggled with the laundry bag. Full of the dyed tunics the clerks wore, it had been a struggle to drag the bag from their quarters into the main building. No one had offered to help her then. Another spasm from deep within her, she lurched forward, biting her tongue to stop the screaming. *Not now baby. I have one more thing to do first. Just one, and then we're free.* She struggled on, her breath coming in deep pants as she heaved in air.

Leaning against a stone arch of the portico in the small rectangular courtyard, she enjoyed the respite from the sun. She stood and sweated, feeling the trickle of it down her face and neck. Her hair she knew would be wild, like a lion's mane. She was just stooping to grab up the top of the bag, which she had tied with a small length of rope, when she felt a hand on her back. 'Domina,' the slave said, as he slipped a small roll of parchment into the folds of her dress. Licina didn't look at the slave, she knew who he was. She waited for him to pass. He glided silently along the cobbles, just as he'd been trained to do.

She scooped up the bag and was just heading for the exit when she heard a shout. 'You there! Stop this instant!' Tribune Scaevola appeared at her back, a triumphant gleam in his eyes. 'Hello there, beautiful. Now, what does a pretty young thing like yourself need with that roll of parchment? What could it possibly contain? And who were you planning on delivering it too?' He showed her his teeth as Licina's face turned from shock to fear in an instant. 'Someone's been spying on me, did you know that? Following me through the streets, peeping through doors, listening in on private conversations. You wouldn't know who that would be, would you?' He leant forward, grabbing her breast and ripping the roll of parchment free from the folds of her dress.

Licina made to reply but found she couldn't. She tried to breathe but sucking in air was more difficult than grabbing smoke. Pressure built in her womb, then with the force of a damn bursting water erupted from between her legs. Hot and discoloured, it poured down her onto the cobbled floor. She screamed, staggered, then her world went dark.

With a spring in his step and a song in his heart, Albinus patrolled the front of the First Century as they stood in formation on the drill field outside the barracks of Carnuntum. It was the nineteenth day of October, and the ancient festival of Armilustrium. Back before Rome was an empire, before the army was made up of professional soldiers, the farmers and peasants who gave up their summers to go and fight for the republic would clean, sharpen, then handover their weapons for safekeeping during the winter months.

It signalled the end of the campaign season, and the soldiers on the drill field were in fine spirits, each congratulating themselves for having survived another year's fighting. Although, of course, the legionaries would not be handing in *their* swords and spears – *they* still gleamed with oil in the sunlight, blades sharp and armour polished to perfection. Each shield had been either repaired or replaced, so each Capricorn adorning the front was whiter than the purest swan, the brass trimmings hard to look at, they reflected so much of the sun's rays.

Satisfied with his men, Albinus stood on the far right of the line and waited for Taurus and the other senior officers to come and inspect them. To his front he could see two bulls being manhandled to a small wooden dais at the front of the legion. They would be sacrificed after the inspection of the troops; priests would check their livers and hearts as their blood was offered to the war god Mars. Albinus had never known the omens to be anything but favourable, and he doubted today would be any different, especially as the Augustus himself would be present.

He had returned from the temporary base north of the river, and had decided to winter at Carnuntum, much to the excitement of the men of the Fourteenth. It was only a few months ago they had been disgraced in the eyes of their emperor and sent west to the Rhine frontier. Now, at summer's end, their reputation was restored as one of the finest fighting legions in the empire.

To make matters even better, news had reached the legion the day before that Balomar, King of the Marcomanni and self-proclaimed High King of Germania had sued for peace. With the Naristae defeated, the Quadi locked into a peace treaty and the Marcomanni effectively surrendering, the war, it seemed, was coming to an end. Just the Iazyges in the east remained a threat, as the smaller tribes continued to throw their weight behind their leader Bandanasp, but the feeling of the men of the Fourteenth was that they could be easily dealt with in the next year's campaigning season.

Albinus smiled at the thought. He couldn't remember the last time he'd felt so relaxed. He was but an hour away from a reunion with Licina. He pictured her in his mind: small, high breasts, those long sweeping legs; hair so bright it made dancing flames look bland even on the darkest of nights; her eyes, emerald green, more dazzling than the sun's reflection off the summer sea. He felt a stir in his groin as he thought of the passion the night would bring – certain comforts he had sorely missed whilst on campaign. He was distracted from his thoughts by a low whistle from Rullus, who held the standard for the First Cohort, just to his left.

Snapping his head round, Albinus saw his centurion and legate as they toured the legion, century by century. They had started at the far left of the line, so the Tenth Cohort had been given the relief of being inspected first.

239

They would now be sharing quiet jokes, farting loudly and being hissed at by their centurions. Albinus wished he was with them.

Before he knew it Legatus Maximianus was standing in front of him, smiling as Albinus saluted. 'Optio Silus, good to see you, lad.' Albinus smiled, but felt a slight annoyance at the term 'lad'; he wasn't a boy anymore, but a man, veteran and officer in the Roman army. He found the term to be slightly derogatory, and wondered if his father would have tolerated it in his younger years. He thought not. 'Sir,' he nodded, standing to rigid attention with his thumbs hooked into his belt.

'You have done exceptionally well this year, Silus,' the legate said. That was another thing Albinus was still uncertain about: being addressed as 'Silus'. It was his last name of course, named after his father, as his father had been named after his. But he still had trouble associating the name with himself. As a child you are called by your first name only, so for his formative years he had been Albinus. No one had addressed him with his father's name, until he had become an officer. It was of course common practice throughout the empire to be addressed by your family name as you grew into manhood, but he wasn't sure the name would ever really be *his*. Some shadows were harder to emerge from than others, it would seem.

'Thank you, sir,' said Albinus, trying to keep the smile from his face. He failed, and felt his cheeks flush red at the praise.

'You know we lost a lot of centurions in the battle with the Naristae. They will need replacing.' Maximianus winked at the gaping Albinus, before moving off without another word.

Albinus continued to stand in stunned silence. *Centurion? Me?* A nudge on his back, Fullo was behind him, his face a beam of happiness. 'Greetings, centurion,' he winked before slapping Albinus again.

There was no more time to ponder his growing status in the legion as trumpets heralded the arrival of the Emperor Marcus Aurelius. Albinus watched as he walked in the midst of praetorians, who all wore matching white tunics, muscled cuirasses and white shields emblazoned with black scorpions. They looked impressive, each man of similar height, marching in unison as they stamped through the drill field up to the raised dais. But Albinus knew they were nothing but show men, not much use in a real fight. They had been called on once to fight in the previous summer, and by all accounts had made a horrible mess of holding their line when the barbarians charged them. 'All bark, no bite,' Taurus had said of them, before making some rather ruder remarks about their sexual preference.

Albinus studied the emperor as he made his way up the stairs, not glancing at the marble likeness of him that awaited him there. Priests in white and red hooded robes stood with heads bowed, long, curved daggers bare in their palms as they stood ready, needing the Augustus to give them the go ahead. Albinus wondered if they were to hear a speech from the man who ruled the world. He realised he'd never heard Aurelius speak, despite being in fairly close proximity to him on a couple of occasions.

As the Augustus paused at the top of the dais, Albinus noted the sooth-sayer, Alexander of Abonoteichos, standing next to the emperor. He hadn't seen him walk up to the podium, either with the priests or the emperor. He thought back to a few years before, not long after he had signed up with the Fourteenth, where he had asked the man to read his future. *What was it he had said? I will crush my demons and lead a prosperous life.* Albinus smiled at the thought of how many people had been given that answer. He still regretted paying a denarius for it.

But there was to be no speech, the Divine Augustus merely nodded for the priests to begin the sacrifice, which they did without ceremony or fuss. Two long sweeps from the curved daggers and dark blood poured onto the timber, the animals hitting the ground with a thump. An anxious wait followed, as the priests leant over the corpses of the bulls, slicing them open to reveal their innards. The priests eventually rose to their feet, robes now more red than white, and smiled and nodded to the emperor. The omens were good it seemed, the gods had accepted the sacrifice.

Albinus smiled as the men roared and cheered, saluting their emperor as he waved and made his way back down the wooden steps, his praetorian's falling in step to escort him back to his temporary headquarters. He hurried off as the men were dismissed, eager to be away and into Carnuntum. His pass of leave already agreed with Taurus and safely tucked into a leather pouch on his belt, he decided he could do without anything he might have in his pack in the fortress, and marched off to find his wife.

241

* * *

The clang of iron-studded boots on stone announced the arrival of Tribune Pompeianus, Calvus and a half century of auxiliaries in the basilica of Carnuntum. They walked with purpose, faces set in scowls; the flats of naked swords cleared all from their path. Through lamplit corridors and cluttered offices full of startled orderlies, they made their way to the rear of the building, and the office of Tribune Scaevola.

Anger filled Calvus, pure violent rage; unhindered and wild it thrashed like an uncoiled viper within him, and he struggled to keep it under control. He thought of the man they were going to arrest, the pleasure he would feel when he was handed over to the torturers for questioning. *Treasonous bastard.* The man's action had put Calvus' friends in the Fourteenth in danger, and he would stop at nothing to see him brought to Roman justice.

Calvus puffed his chest out as two auxiliaries rammed open the wooden doors. He marched through, thunder in his eyes. At least there had been. His expression went from a battle-ready snarl to wide-eyed shock as he saw Licina laying on her back, white dress blood-soaked, face red and puffy, hair wild and dark with sweat as she screamed and snarled with the pains of childbirth. 'Merciful God,' he muttered before clambering to her side.

'Calvus?' Her voice was a whisper as she panted for breath between contractions. 'Help me.' She might have asked what he was doing here, with a guard of armed men. He might have asked how she came to be in labour in the office of a suspected traitor. But there would be a time for such questions. He knelt beside her, clasping her sweaty palm.

'It's going to be okay, Licina. You can do this.' He nodded to her, turned to a small man who knelt between her thighs, his arms crimson red to the elbows. 'Who are you?' he asked with more spite than he intended, the man was clearly helping after all.

'I am Cleitus. Do not fear, friend, I am a doctor.' He said it so calmly, it helped to slow Calvus' thumping heartbeat.

'How is she doing? How long has she been … you know.' He nodded his head in the general direction of Licina's midriff.

'Almost there, friend, almost there. In fact, I can see the head now! One more push for me, my dear, that's it deep breaths. Can you give me one more push? Don't shake your head! You've made it this far, let's finish the job shall we? Now, one, two thr—'

Licina screamed and gripped Calvus' hand so hard he was sure she would crush every bone. He grimaced and roared encouragement at the same time, and before he knew it her grip went slack, and she lay back on the tiled floor and cried.

Silence in the office. Every set of eyes was on Licina and the doctor. Tribune Pompeianus had a dumbstruck Tribune Scaevola by the arms; two auxiliaries had their swords pointed at Scaevola but their eyes on the birth going on before them.

The silence stretched out. Calvus heard nothing but Licina's sobs and the pulsing of his own heart. And then there was noise, beautiful and pure, and it brought tears to Calvus' eyes – a baby's cry, soft and high-pitched. Cleitus picked the bundle up, wrapping the baby in a blood-drenched towel. 'A cloak … can someone give me a clean cloak.' One of the auxiliaries stepped forwards, lifting their cloak from off their shoulders and handing it to the doctor.

With care Cleitus removed the crying baby from the fouled towel, and before folding him into the cloak. Him – the child was a boy. Licina sat up. Calvus hugged her tight as his heart went out to her. Childbirth was about the most dangerous thing a woman could undertake, and she seemed to have breezed through it, and so had the baby. He watched as she took the baby in shaking hands, lips quivering and eyes watering. 'My son,' she stammered, and smiled with the purest joy.

Calvus kissed her on the cheek, his own tears streaming down his white stubble so it glistened like snowdrops. 'Well done, Licina. You did so well. Wait until Albinus meets him!'

Her face dropped at that, concern replacing the happiness. 'He doesn't know, Calvus. He is a father and he doesn't even know.' She wailed; he imagined the shame she must be feeling.

'He will soon love. The legion is back for winter. It won't be too long before Taurus gives him leave and he comes running to see you. Mark my words. Are you okay for the moment? There is something I need to do,

I'm sure Cleitus will stay with you.' The man nodded, moving alongside her as Calvus rose to his feet.

'Is that the girl?' Tribune Pompeianus asked as Calvus moved towards him.

'No. She is the wife of my friend, an optio in the Fourteenth. What the fuck is she doing in here?' This was aimed at a terrified Scaevola, who stood with his arms restrained behind his back.

'She ... she collects the laundry from the officers and clerks. She often passes through here on her way out, to see if there's any more. I ... I found her conspiring with another of the slaves. They passed her a note. It's in my armour, tucked under the left shoulder.' He winced as Calvus tore it free. 'When I challenged her on it, her waters broke and she fainted. And then, well, you saw the rest.'

Calvus stuffed the rolled papyrus into the folds of his tunic. 'Where's the girl?' he spat at the tribune. 'The Briton, red-haired slave. She was pregnant, I swear to god if you have harmed her ...' He let the threat hang in the air, a clenched fist inches from Scaevola's face.

'I haven't, I swear it to the gods! She is at my home. And quite well, I might add.'

'I need to go,' Calvus said, this time to Pompeianus. 'I must know she is safe. Can you arrange for some of your men to take Licina home? And the doctor, if he will stay with her'

'Of course. Take a couple of men with you, just in case. We'll keep this one under close guard.' Calvus turned back to Licina, not listening as Pompeianus listed off the charges that were to be brought against Scaevola.

'I have to go now. Tribune Scaevola has someone very special to me, I must see if they are okay. I have asked for you to be taken home when you are well enough. Cleitus, can you go with her for a while?'

'Of course,' he said. His tone suggested he would be offended to have been asked to leave. Calvus kissed Licina on the cheek, promising to visit her as soon as he could.

He turned from the room, grabbing the two nearest auxiliaries and setting off at a jog through the basilica and out into the open.

Albinus frowned as he left the small apartment he and Licina shared when

244

he was not away with the legion. He looked up at the sun to gauge the time, seeing it was nearly evening. *She must have finished work by now surely?* Licina he knew, had been slightly ashamed when she had first told him of her job washing the dirty linen of the senior officials that worked within the basilica. He had laughed at her embarrassment, pleased she had found work, even if it wasn't particularly interesting. It would help keep her busy when he was away on campaign.

He resolved to walk the main roads between his home and the forum, where the basilica was situated. Maybe he would catch her unaware as she walked home, and he smiled at the thought. He walked in a daze, taking the opportunity to take in sights and smells he was usually kept so far away from. To his right was the baker's Licina was always writing to him about. A red and white leather canopy hung over the front window; a short, fat man inside sweated as he pulled fresh bread from an open oven with a large wooden pole, that ended in a metal shovel. Albinus smiled as he thought how much the pole resembled his own staff of office, and wondered who had copied the idea from whom.

A tavern was on his left now, two drunk men singing old marching songs outside, wooden cups sloshing through the air, dark red wine pouring out onto the street. He recognised the song as one of the Fourteenth's, and whistled the tune as he passed the men. They laughed and cheered, slapping him on the back, offering him wine and a seat at their bench. Albinus refused with a smile. He would have been tempted if it wasn't for the desperation he felt to see his wife after so long. Finally, now he saw the attraction in swapping war stories with fellow soldiers; he had done it so often with men from other cohorts in the legion in the days that followed a major battle. Each man would boast of their prowess and courage in battle, while their friends would grin slyly, shake their heads and wait until the story was over before mocking their exaggerated boasts.

His thoughts turned to his father, as they often did when he was alone. No one had mocked the stories he'd told round night-time fires at the small farming colony he had founded. But, he supposed, no one had need to. There were no lies in his tales, no great boasts or exaggerated truths. He'd always told things straight; it was just one of the many characteristics he possessed that made him the great leader he had been. As usual, Albinus felt insignificant and insecure when he compared himself to his father. He would never be the man he had been: the man who led from the front, would not have to command his men to follow him. The whole legion would have followed Silus into Hades if he'd led them there – each of the five thousand knew and respected him. It saddened Albinus that he would never be that man, never fully emerge from under his father's vast shadow.

A sudden clatter of hobnailed boots grating off the cobbles brought Albinus back from his wandering mind. Men were running down the road towards him – a man in an old brown cloak, bald head and a face full of stubble, looking like he was being chased by two auxiliary soldiers. Albinus followed the lead of the other civilians on the road and parted to one side, like a ship's prow parting the waves the man hurled through the gap, not looking back at the pursuing soldiers.

'Calvus?' muttered Albinus, squinting against the sun's light as the man grew closer. 'Gods, it is you. Calvus, hey, Calvus!' Waving his arms in the air Albinus walked into the now deserted street. He saw Calvus' face go from confusion to delight as he recognised the optio and skidded to a halt.

'Brother! It is so great to see you!' the Briton said through struggled breaths. 'But there is no time to talk! You must go to the basilica now, Licina is there! She is … she has … ahh I don't want to ruin it for you! Run, brother, you will not be disappointed! I must go, but I will find you later! Come, boys, there's no time to waste!' And with that he was gone, back down the street with the two soldiers in his wake.

Albinus stood in a daze. A dozen questions whirled through his mind. Why was Licina still in the basilica? What had she done? And where in the name of the gods was Calvus going with those soldiers? He seemed to be commanding them, but why would a retired legionary be commanding serving auxiliaries?

He shook his head, trying to clear his mind. 'Sounds like you better be going to the basilica, lad.' An old lady, hunched and hooded, gave him a gentle tap on the arm. 'Yes, it would appear you're right.' With a nod to the lady, Albinus turned on his heels and set off towards the forum at a run. He didn't look back.

Licina lay on the stone floor with the babe in her arms. She was exhausted, and starving, but too in love to notice. The babe bunched his little arms up to his chest as he suckled on her breast; he had been unsure at first, but now he gulped eagerly and Licina rejoiced to see it. The feel of it was extraordinary, as if she could feel the life in the liquid as it flowed from her into him. His skin was warm and smooth as silk on her chest. She knew she would remember the first time she had felt the fast beating of his heart for as long as she lived.

Cleitus stood a discreet distance away, having instructed Licina on the correct way to position the baby, giving her some time alone. Licina was grateful, and even more so when the man eased everyone else from the small office. She smiled to herself; giving birth in front of a room full of people had never entered her mind. In fact, she realised she'd had no plan at all, and at least being in a public space meant there had been people around to help her.

Suddenly there was a commotion at the door, and Albinus burst through, pushing the doctor from his path. Licina gasped, as did he, and both stared in shocked silence at one another, the silence stretching out. 'Husband,' she said in as calm a voice she could muster, 'come meet your son.'

'My ... son?' He said the words like a drunk, then staggered like one toward her and slumped to his knees. Licina smelled sweat and leather, and saw the patches under his arms and on the chest of his faded white tunic. 'But ...'

Despite herself, she laughed. 'You are a father, Albinus! I didn't tell you, which was stupid of me. I didn't want you to do anything silly in battle, try to be a hero to get home to me quicker. Does that make sense?' But she could see even as she spoke he wasn't listening. He was starting intently at the bundle wrapped up in the folds of her dress – a small crop of light brown hair, the colour of dry timber or wet sand; a short, stout button nose above a thin-lipped mouth; his skin pale like his father's, long of body and limb. The child took the opportunity to open his eyes for the first time, and Licina heard her husband's intake of breath at the crystal blue gaze that looked up at him.

'Gods, Licina! He looks just like my father.' He still stared in reverence, a single tear drop cascading down his right cheek.

Licina laughed in delight. 'He looks like you, husband! Can you not see? The hair, eyes, nose, mouth, even the shape of his body! It's all you, my love. He's perfect, just like his pater.' A pater familias was the oldest living male in a household. Since Albinus had no living relatives he had become that the moment he became a father. Licina smiled as a rare memory of her own parents flooded her mind: her father scorning her mother for getting Licina to use the term 'pater' when she addressed him. It was an old Greek saying, he said, not used by Romans and certainly not from the people of Gaul. She had persisted anyway, just to provoke a mock angered reaction and some heavy tickling. Her joy turned to sadness as she thought they would never get the chance to meet their grandson, to revel in the joy of unconditional love one felt when they held and smelt the newest member of their family for the first time. She hoped they were watching her now, that they were proud of the woman she had become.

Albinus noticed her tears, and wiped them away with a rough finger. 'I ... I don't even know what to say. It must have been so tough for you, to go through this alone.' His voice quivered.

'Oh, I wasn't alone. Cleitus was here, about thirty orderlies, Calvus and a bunch of soldiers. Oh, and two tribunes, and I think one arrested the other. But more of that later.' She laughed through her tears. 'I have been fine, my love. The pregnancy was tough, but not unbearable. You have been fighting a war! I think you've had it worse than me! I see you've brought home some new scars.' She traced a finger down his arm, mottled with new cuts and rough scar tissue underneath.

'I've been fine. Couple of skirmishes, a cruise to the Rhine and back, nothing major.'

'I always know when you've been lying! Plus, Calvus has been keeping me up to date with what's going on. I hear you're some sort of hero these days?' She tried to keep the concern from her voice; now was not the time for serious conversations about war and death.

'I'm no hero,' he said. 'Just doing my duty.'

'So wading into an army of barbarians with just your wooden staff is doing your duty?'

She saw his frown at the remark, but spoke again before his mood darkened. 'All that matters is that you're home, safe. At least now we can be together as a family, if only for a little while.'

For the first time she allowed herself to think of Scaevola, of the note he had taken from her. *Who was that man who arrested him? How much does Scaevola know about me? About what I have done? Am I safe?* It gave her some small comfort that Calvus was with the mysterious tribune. Surely he would see her safe?

XXIV

November – AD 171, Carnuntum

It was the second time Calvus had stood shivering and coughing on the steps outside the basilica that day. The air was just as damp. A fine drizzle had soaked the city since dawn, black clouds swelled with an endless supply of water blocking out the sun.

Calvus frowned. It was, it seemed, the only face he was capable of pulling in the last few weeks. The days had begun and ended without pause for rest or thought since Tribune Scaevola had been arrested and put to torture. Watching the frumentarii agents at work with their tools had disgusted him. Despite his hatred for Scaevola he had sent the man countless prayers as he'd stood in a dark corner of the cellar of a small farmhouse just outside the city, and watched as the agents made him sing like a bird.

It was all true – everything Pompeianus had suspected. Yes, there was a plot against the emperor. Yes, it involved a number of senators and other high-ranking men within the empire. Yes, part of the plot had been to stir the German tribes into rebellion. And yes, Scaevola was in it up to his neck. He had revealed everything. But the worst part, was the way he had used her – his daughter, Meredith. Flame-haired, high-hipped, long-legged and as beautiful as her mother, he hadn't seen her since she was a small girl, when he had last tucked her into bed before stepping out onto the street and spying a merchant with a bulging purse that chimed a tempting tune – since he had been spotted, committed murder, and fled the country and signed up under the eagles.

Twenty years is a long time to carry that much baggage tucked under your kit and armour. Twenty years he had kept his mouth shut, not even able to tell his tent-mates the story of his shame and pain. But, despite the time and the distance, he had known who she was the moment he clasped eyes on her. The pull on his heart strings left him in no doubt; an image of her mother, the woman that had captivated his heart and given him a reason to live. He thought her safe in Briton, hoped she was happily married and content with her life. To find her here, in Pannonia, slave to a Roman tribune had been harrowing. Stalking her steps the last months had been torture. Seeing her pain, watching her mistreatment, and knowing he could do nothing about it, had caused him heartache like he had never felt before.

He had found her locked in a store room in the kitchen of Scaevola's house when he had forced his way in, using the flat of his sword to dispatch of the two guardsmen who stood sullenly at the front door. The other slaves had been ordered to leave her in there, to forbid her food or water. What sort of monster could give such an order, to condemn another human being that way? What sort of monster could do that to the woman carrying his child?

'He rapes me,' she'd sobbed into the crease of his cloak, 'everyday since he bought me he rapes me.' She had known it was him, known Calvus to be her father. She had recognised him that day in the forum, when Scaevola and his entourage had approached him. 'I have been praying to god you would come for me ever since.'

'God?' he had said.

She hadn't replied, just nodded and bared her left shoulder, showing a small fish tattooed on her collar bone. He had smiled then, reaching into the neck of his tunic and pulling out a small necklace, made from cheap metal. An intertwined X and P were engraved onto a small circular medallion. Each of them laughed to see a sign of the Christ God on the other. Calvus thought they truly felt like a family in that moment, even if they had only just been reunited.

Silence had hung between them like an eagle suspended in the air, judging the angle of its flight as it prepared to swoop down on its prey.

251

'Your mother?' Calvus had finally plucked up the courage to ask. He spoke it in a whisper, all breath with no substance.

Meredith had just shaken her head. He had sobbed like a baby then. He had known within himself that Aife must be dead, or why else would his daughter be here, a slave.

'Men came ...' She tried to talk but a wail of sorrow poured out instead. 'It's okay,' Calvus said, pulling her close. 'You don't need to tell me.' He hadn't known if he was protecting her from telling him or himself for not wanting to hear. Either way, he just couldn't face listening as she spoke of her mother's death.

They had just sat there then, father and daughter in silence, holding each other as the sun bled out in the sky.

Calvus thought of her now as he stood with rain water dripping from the hood of his cloak. Tribune Pompeianus had taken up the office now left vacant by the imprisoned Scaevola, and Calvus had already been there this morning to receive his orders for the day. He was standing on the steps looking out on the forum now, as was the rest of the city, to watch the triumphant Augustus as he paraded with the men of the Fourteenth through the city.

He was still getting used to taking orders again, saluting and standing to attention for hours on end whilst he waited for the tribune to admit him. The familiar pain in the small of his back had begun to flare back up, though it had been much worse when wearing chain mail. He thought it was bad enough with the weight of a rain-sodden cloak and a leather cuirass. Not for the first time he wondered if losing the fingers on his left hand might not have been the worst thing that could have happened to him. He was earning more coin than he had ever done in the legions, and he sure didn't miss cleaning out latrines and building marching camps at the end of a twenty-mile march. He did however, miss his mates. He was looking forward to seeing them parade today.

He shuffled under the pretence of shelter from the stone portico, trying to get some feeling back into his numb feet. The wind blew the rain under the arches to soak those who were huddled beneath, it seemed the gods demanded none be safe from the elements that day. The giant sheets of tarpaulin that masked the great statue of the Augustus were due to be

252

unveiled today, and Calvus could sense the excitement of the crowd as they jostled for position to get the best view. The sheets swayed in the wind even as they sagged with the weight of the rain, almost teasing the crowd who extended necks and climbed onto friends' shoulders to try and get a view over the top. Laughter to his left, and Calvus turned his head to see Licina, accompanied by his daughter.

The sight warmed his heart. There was even a small resemblance; both were tall and slim – well Meredith would be when not with child – flame-coloured hair and dazzling eyes. The old solider noticed the glances they were getting from the men who parted to let them through.

'Father!' Meredith shouted as she spotted him. She skipped along the flagstones and embraced Calvus, who felt the gloom lift from his mind. He pressed his face into her neck, revelling in her scent. It was hard for him to believe he had lasted so many years without her, or how he had borne to leave her in the first place, such was the strength of the love he felt.

He kissed her on the brow, wiping wet hair from her eyes. Looking up he met Licina's eyes, and the two just stared at each other, a silent tension building between them. Calvus had read the contents of the rolled parchment Licina had taken from the slave; it contained details of the legions involved in the war against the marching tribes, their strengths, supplies and winter quarters – all laid bare in neat handwriting. Who had she been planning on giving this too? And why?

It had been common knowledge for some time that the barbarians were getting intelligence on Roman forces from somewhere within the empire. Calvus, like most people, had assumed now that Scaevola had been arrested they had caught the main protagonist behind the rebellion in the northern provinces. Now it seemed, something else was afoot.

Licina met his stare for a few heartbeats before looking away, her face flushed. She carried her babe in her arms, and she swayed and bounced as he began to stir. Faustus, they had named him: Faustus Silus. The boy resembled Albinus so much it had brought back powerful memories of the first time Calvus had seen the boy – Silus proudly parading him round the fortress at Carnuntum.

With a pang of sorrow that hit harder than a ballista bolt, Calvus realised how much he still missed the old man, and how he could do with him at his side now. Licina had been up to something, of that he was sure. But he had been so caught up with tracking Scaevola and his daughter he'd barely had time to notice. But when he thought about it now – his late night visits to her small apartment, her often being flustered and having just returned home at all sorts of strange hours – it all started to make sense.

Not for the first time, he wondered if he should show the document to Pompeianus. He knew what would happen to Licina, had seen it happen to Scaevola. The very thought turned his stomach and brought bile into his mouth, but if she had turned traitor …

'Father!' His daughter's excited squeal brought him back from the depths of his mind. 'Look, here they come!' A rain-drenched golden eagle appeared at the other end of the forum. The aquilifer on horseback, Calvus could see the man smiling and waving to the crowd atop a white gelding as his knees fought to keep the beast at a slow walk.

The crowd roared and whooped, surging forwards even as files of white-shielded praetorians jogged forwards either side of the white horse to keep the road clear. They had their swords sheathed, but each man bore a wooden cudgel, and Calvus knew they wouldn't hesitate to use them if they felt the need arise.

Behind the aquilifer Calvus could make out the First Cohort, hobnailed boots clattering off the wet cobbles as they marched instep eight men abreast. Taurus marched at their front, the red crest of his helmet bobbing up and down as he kept his head to the front and a frown on his face. Calvus knew his old centurion hated formal events such as this. He was a soldier, not a show monkey, and he would be wanting to get around the forum as quickly as possible so he could get back to the fortress, and 'real soldiering' as he had no doubt been telling the men of his century.

Even so his chain mail was freshly oiled, and the running rain water made it gleam silver against the dark clouds. His red beard, dotted with white, had been brushed and it helped to disguise the scars that lay beneath.

Rullus marched behind his centurion, the cohort's standard hefted on his left shoulder. The brass circular discs that he lovingly cared for shimmered like bronze and he smiled and waved to the crowd on both sides.

Then there were the front rankers, Habitus, Fullo and Bucco marching shoulder to shoulder in the centre of the line. Calvus scanned the men to either side, hoping to see either Libo or Longus. He kissed his teeth and sucked air through his mouth when he remembered they had gone to meet their gods, as had too many good men before them.

File after file of smiling legionaries passed them by until Albinus came into sight, walking behind the First Century. His light blue eyes scanned the crowds as he desperately tried to find his wife. He beamed in delight as he saw her frantic waves, laughed as she raised their son above her head. Calvus gave him a nod and a smile, and Albinus saluted him in return. Again, Calvus pondered what he was to do with the roll of parchment. Licina had become a good friend to him in the months since he had been discharged from the army. But Albinus was his brother, a bond forged in blood. There was no way he could betray him, or the ones he loved.

He sighed, shaking his head, retreating further into the crowd until his back hit the stone wall of the basilica. He leant against it, rubbing his temple with the stump of his fingerless left hand. *Christ on the cross, who died to give us life. What am I to do?* His prayer went unanswered, and after a time he opened his eyes and his gaze fell once more to Licina. She was talking to the babe, swinging him in her arms. *She looks so happy.* How could he destroy something as beautiful as the bond between mother and child?

As he stared, a man crept up behind Licina. He wore a dark green cloak, and Calvus could see a brown circular patch stitched onto the back. A writhing snake was depicted on the patch, its leathery skin a medley of yellow and brown and green. He withdrew the hood from his head to reveal a top knot of jet black hair, a tanned face framed by a stubbly beard. His eyes were slits, his hands huge and they grasped Licina by the shoulders.

Calvus daren't move, breathe, as Licina spun round with a gasp. Her face dropped from anger to fear as she looked into the man's eyes and she tried to back away, but all around her was the press of the crowds caught up in the splendour of the parade. The man was shouting, screaming at her in fury but Calvus was too far away to make out the words. Stalking from the shadows, Calvus crept forward, keeping the man's body between him and Licina. He didn't want her to spot him, to make eye contact or yell and distract the man.

Calvus focused on the snake, a memory tugging at the far reaches of his mind. *I know this symbol.* The thought repeated itself continuously until he was shaken by a roar from the crowd. Looking up he saw the Augustus Marcus Aurelius on a golden chariot, a laurel wreath atop his head as he raised his right hand in salute to the cheering masses. His expressionless face did great praise to the masons who carved his likeness into stone statues across the empire; he showed no emotion as he stood draped in purple leafed with gold.

A man was next to him, his face hidden beneath a deep hood. His cloak was green – the same green as the cloak that adorned the man who had hold of Licina. The hooded man turned to the side, to whisper something into the emperor's ear, and Calvus saw the flash of the brown patch on the back of his cloak, the same snake coiled in the middle. Suddenly Calvus had wobbly knees, his breath was shallow and he thought he might vomit. Suddenly all the pieces of the puzzle slotted together, and he didn't like the completed picture.

The man was Alexander of Abonoteichos – the soothsayer who had founded the religion based around the snake god Glycon. This was the man who had told the Fourteenth Legion to hurl two lions into the River Danube in sacrifice. Promised them it would bring them victory. Instead the lions had torn into the shocked soldiers, and men had died before the animals had been brought down.

And Alexander of Abonoteichos, Calvus also knew, was a traitor. And one of his men had hold of Licina, was shaking her violently and hissing in her ear. Again, he thought of the roll of parchment hidden in his room within the fortress, and the details in contained. *Licina, what in God's name have you been doing?*

No time to ponder the thought now, as the man yanked Licina hard to the left, spinning them both round until Calvus got a good look at his face. He knew the man, he realised – from the tavern with Scaevola; he was the other man that had hidden behind the small curtain and whispered treason with the tribune, a forgotten half-memory of seeing the two of them together in the market. With a snarl Calvus leapt forward. Drawing the dagger from within his cloak he hurled himself at the man. Slashing wildly from right to left, he caught the man a glancing blow on the side of his head. Startled, the man let go of Licina and dropped into a fighting crouch, rasping a curved spatha from beneath the folds of his green cloak. Dark blood dripped down his face and stained the small puddles on the flagstones crimson.

Never hesitate. That's what Calvus had been told as a young man on the violent streets of Londinium. He leapt forwards again, his dagger licking out, aiming for the greencloaked man's shoulder. 'Calvus, stop!' Licina's voice distracted him at the last moment. Calvus groaned in anger as his knife missed the target and snagged in the folds of the green cloak.

He tried to wrench it back, but lengths of cloak just came with it. He was pulling the stranger towards him now, so close he could smell the man's foul breath. With a snarl Calvus sent a crashing headbutt that connected with a jaw, smiled through the pain above his eyes at the familiar sound of bone breaking. The man screamed, staggered back and tripped on the folds of his cloak, which was now dragging on the cobbles after being slashed by Calvus' knife.

Men were around them now, white-shielded praetorians with cudgels raised high. They pushed back the crowd and made a circle around Calvus and the stranger. Slowly, the Briton got to his feet and raised his hands above his head. The other man stayed on the floor, hands rubbing furiously at his broken jaw. 'Ahh Calvus, trust it to be you, eh?' Tribune Pompeianus pushed his way through the sphere of shields. He glanced down at the green-cloaked men, then leant in close to Calvus. 'Explain, quickly.'

Calvus gulped, peering at Licina who stood clasping her babe to her chest, his daughter with his arms around her. 'This man,' Calvus stumbled, 'He's one of Alexander's. He's the man I saw in the tavern a few weeks ago, sitting behind the curtain with Scaevola.'

Pompeianus nodded. 'So, you just thought you would attack him? In the middle of a parade, just as the emperor was riding past your position?' He arched an eyebrow, his lips set in a tight grin. 'There's something else to this, isn't there?'

Calvus nodded, slowly. 'I'm sorry sir, but can it wait? Bit of a long story.'

He tried to kick his mind into gear, to think of an alternative other than telling the tribune about Licina.

'Okay. But, when the parade is done, you and I are going to have a little chat,' Pompeianus said, before turning and ordering the two closest praetorians to arrest the green-cloaked man. 'Come with me, Calvus, you deserve to be present for this. After all, it was your hard work that made it possible.

He followed the tribune through the massed crowd. His daughter called out to him, and he turned but said nothing, just gave her a smile and a nod. Licina looked terrified. Calvus paused for a heartbeat and the two shared a look. Then she nodded, and backed away through the crowd. Tears pricked his eyes. Both he and Licina had known what that look meant – knew what she now had to do. His chest felt heavy; guilt weighed down his heart.

They marched behind the last of the guardsmen as the procession came to a stop in front of the giant statue that dominated the forum. Pompeianus grabbed Calvus by the arm and dragged him closer to the front, until he was but two paces away from the Augustus himself.

'Dear Tribune,' the emperor said in a dry voice. 'I trust everything is ready?'

Pompeianus bowed, 'It is, majesty. And may I also introduce one of my agents, Calvus.' With a expression somewhere between horror and awe, Calvus found himself eye to eye with the most powerful man in the world. 'Bow, you idiot,' Pompeianus muttered from the corner of his mouth. Calvus sunk to one knee, eyes fixed on the cobbles.

'Rise, friend.' He did as the dry voice commanded, still keeping his head low, terrified he was going to let out a squeaky fart.

'Calvus here was instrumental in bringing about today's … event.' Pompeianus smirked as he spoke. Calvus saw him look over at Alexander, who stood impassively, his face still hidden beneath his hood.

A hint of a smile showed on the face of the Augustus, but it was quickly wiped away along with the splashes of rain water on his face. 'Then you have my thanks, Calvus. You have the look of a veteran about you. Did you serve in the legions?'

Christ on the fucking cross, is he actually talking to me? 'Yes, majesty,' he said in a croak. He coughed slightly, trying to clear the gravel that had appeared in his throat. 'With the Fourteenth, majesty. I was honourably discharged last year.' He held out his left hand, the fingerless stump laid bare for all to see. Just the thumb and scarred knuckles remained.

'Jupiter Best and Greatest, that is some wound, Calvus.' The emperor stepped towards him, and Calvus felt the shit trying to force itself from his arse as his Augustus put a hand on his shoulder. 'I am very grateful for your service, and on behalf of Rome I will personally see you well rewarded for what you have done.'

Calvus had heard stories of emperors countless times around the cooking fires when on campaign: the mad ones – Tiberius, Caligula, Nero – men who thought themselves gods;, who did as they pleased with whatever and whoever they wanted; Domitian, a man so hated that to mention his name was still met with muttered curses and frowns to this day. But *this* man, who addressed him almost as an equal and stood on the same rain-soaked cobbles as he, was just a man. Rain clustered in the curls of his ash grey hair. His eyes were red-rimmed and great black bags circled them. It was well known Aurelius did not sleep, but to see the fatigue so plainly on his face shocked Calvus. He was the invincible Augustus, best and greatest of all men. But, he supposed, even gods must get tired from time to time.

'Thank you, majesty.' he muttered and bowed again.

'Calvus has also just apprehended another conspirator. Shall I bring him forward, majesty?' Aurelius just nodded, adjusting the hem of his cloak.

Pompeianus sent a runner to bring up the green-cloaked man, then turned to Calvus and whispered, 'Go and stand next to the *honourable* Alexander, would you? Wouldn't want him to do anything stupid now, would we?' He winked at Calvus, who smiled and moved so he was at the shoulder of the soothsayer.

Two praetorians followed him so there was a semicircle of armed men behind the Abonoteichon. Calvus watched as the man lowered his hood and turned to face them. He must have been over seventy, Calvus thought – an old man by anyone's standards. He had shaggy grey hair, which was thinning, and the white top of his scalp was showing through the cracks. His eyes were a mix of green and grey, and looked almost like marble. His lips were thin and when he moved his mouth Calvus saw rotten gums with dark holes teeth had once lived in.

'What in the name of the gods do you think you are doing?' Alexander spoke in a whisper but it was laced with venom, his face set in a snarl. He whirled the cloak from his body to reveal a snake, thicker than his arm, hissing as it rested its head on the soothsayer's hand. Calvus took an involuntary step back; the tanned hide of the snake curled up the arm, wrapped around the soothsayer's neck and draped down his back. It hissed again, two sharp fangs showing at the top of its mouth.

'No need for alarm, friend Alexander. We are bringing up a conspirator who has just been captured. These men are just going to make sure you come to no harm.' Aurelius spoke without emotion, but Calvus could see a mix of glee and anger in his eyes.

He kept his eyes on Alexander as the prisoner was brought forward. He saw with triumph the moment the soothsayer's eyes went from annoyance to fear – the moment he saw the game was up. The prisoner was dumped at the emperor's feet, his arms tied securely behind his back. He moaned in pain and his broken jaw was plain to see from the crooked way his mouth slacked open. He looked up at the emperor, then saw his master standing between armed guards.

Calvus stepped in closer to the soothsayer, until his breath steamed the air on his shaking face. 'I don't know who the fuck you think you are, easterner. Or what you thought today was going to bring. But I do know one thing, *friend*, it ain't gonna end well for you.'

XXV

Licina felt the sweat break onto the skin of her forehead even as she shivered. She had thought Cocconas gone, melted away to the four winds when the Tribune Scaevola had been put under arrest. For him to approach her so brazenly, in daylight in a crowded forum, had shocked her more than she would care to admit.

What was more damning, more shocking, was the look Calvus had given her when he had been led off in the company of the soldiers. *He knows.* She was sure of it now. Calvus knew of her treason and even now could be spilling his knowledge at the feet of the frumentarii, or gods forbid, the emperor himself.

A westerly wind struck her face, catching her tears and sending them spiralling into the sky, where they became just another raindrop. Faustus writhed and screamed in her arms, but she was so lost in her hopelessness that she didn't to notice. *What am I to do?*

Just as she had got everything she desired – Albinus back in Carnuntum, their son born fit and healthy – she had found a way to ruin everything. *Why, why did I do it? Why wasn't I stronger?* Albinus had always been hard on himself for being a coward, for doing nothing to save her when barbarians had forded the Danube and snatched her from him. But, he was far braver than she could ever be. She knew the self-pity was pointless, knew there was nothing she could do to fix it now. A hand on her shoulder, Meredith spoke in her ear. 'Licina? Are you okay? Who was that man, what is going on?'

Licina didn't answer at first, she just continued to stare at nothing, her mind lost in the mistakes of her past. 'Oh, Meredith,' she said after a time, 'I have been a fool. Such a fool.' A single glistening teardrop fell from her eyes, sparkling as it rolled off her cheek and fell silently onto the flagstones. 'Can you come back to my apartment with me? I have something I must do.' She thought she could feel her heart breaking, a great weight in her chest, like a part of her was trying to root her to the ground, compel her to stay.

She forced herself to move quickly through the crowds; Faustus screamed against her chest. It took an age to reach her apartment, and she was relieved when they both clambered in and she could shut the world outside. 'Sit down, Meredith,' Licina said even as she was undoing her cloak and tunic, bearing a breast for Faustus to suckle on.

Closing her eyes and listening to the rhythm of her own heartbeat, she revelled in the feeling of her baby feeding from her. The strength of the love she felt for the boy was never stronger than when she was feeding him; it almost felt as if they were one.

'Are you going to tell me what is going on?' Meredith persisted, her own hands on her swollen belly as she looked at Licina and Faustus with a jealous expression.

Licina hauled in a deep breath, calming her thumping heart. 'I have to leave. And I need you to stay here with Faustus until Albinus gets back.'

'Okay. Where are you going? How long shall I tell Albinus you will be?'

Licina tried to speak but all that came out was a wail. Several sobbing breaths later she finally regained her composure. 'No, Meredith, I need to leave, and I can't come back, ever.'

'But … why?' Meredith had risen to her feet. She now crossed the room and knelt by Licina. Through tear-stained eyes Licina saw the confusion in her friend's face, and didn't even know where or how to begin explaining.

'I can't tell you, there's not enough time. You father … he knows. He'll tell you, and Albinus.' She wrenched the baby from her breast and thrust him into Meredith's arms. Jumping to her feet and grabbing a small leather bag, she rampaged around the small apartment, thrusting things into the satchel.

'But why do you need to leave now? Are you not at least going to say goodbye to Albinus? Or explain to him why you are leaving?'

'I can't! I can't tell him what I've done. I'm too ashamed.' She slumped onto her knees, planting her head on the wooden floorboards. She thought back to her time in the north, to the three spinners and the great tree Yggdrasil that holds the nine worlds together. Was this her fate? Had it already been woven? Well, if it had she resolved to not meet it meekly. She would find justice for herself, bring down the people who were pulling the strings of the treasonous plot she had played a small part in. Her actions had put her husband's life in danger, his whole legion in danger! It wasn't until now she saw how deep she had fallen into the sinister world of whispers and secret rendezvous. Only now could she see how much she hated the person she had become, how much her parents would detest her if they could see her now.

She had to leave, now. There was no way she could stand in front of the man she loved and try to explain the wicked things she had done; impossible to tell him to his face that she had betrayed him again. His face stuck in her mind, then faded to blackness and Julius was there, gazing at her with those love-struck puppy eyes. Then he was gone and Heide was stroking her thigh and winking at her seductively. Funny, how she had managed to affect peoples lives, to be so open and honest with people she hardly knew, and yet still there was so much she had kept hidden from Albinus.

He had no idea who it was that had taken her from their farming colony that winter morning. She had never told him of her exploits across the frozen sea, the bonds she had formed, battles she had fought in. She had always laughed off the scars that dotted her body as nothing but accidents, always thinking it best he didn't know they had been caused by sword and spear. And now, when she needed Albinus more than anyone else, she would skulk off into the wilderness rather than look him in the eye and speak of the despicable things she had done.

Her one small comfort had been seeing Cocconas arrested and dragged off by the praetorians. *May he rot in Hades.* The man had manipulated her, used her and even raped her. She couldn't even begin to describe the relief she'd felt when Faustus had been born with such a strong resemblance to Albinus. If his skin had been darker, his hair jet black, she didn't think she would have allowed the babe to live this long.

Bile rose in her throat at the thought of his lips forced onto hers as

263

they met in a dirty brothel down by the harbour. Had Calvus known even then? Had he been onto her that long? Surely, he would have said something, she thought. Surely, he would have tried to stop her. The thought of the Briton having to tell Albinus what she had done filled her with shame. He would be broken, she knew, distraught and driven by rage and bitterness when he discovered his wife had not only betrayed him, but Rome itself.

Turning under the threshold of the door to the small apartment, she looked back one last time at Meredith, and the small bundle that was her son. 'Look after him, Meredith. Albinus will need you now, to help raise the child whilst he is away with the legion. Make sure he is safe.'

'I will,' said Meredith, tears shining in her eyes. Without another word Licina raised the hood of her cloak and stepped out into the hallway. The last Meredith saw of Licina was her descending the wooden steps, then the door slammed shut.

Albinus stood rigidly to attention as the rain poured down his cloak. The small of his back burned with the pressure of his mail and kit. He longed to adjust the sword on his right hip; he could feel the belt digging into his hip through his armour; it didn't particularly hurt, but it was an annoyance, like an itch you can't find.

He felt the familiar aches and complaints from the soles of his feet; the iron-nailed sandals though practical, were not designed for comfort. To his front he could see the men from his century as they experienced similar problems, each man slightly shuffling and muttering curses as they awaited word from their emperor.

Aurelius was visible through the constant drizzle, standing atop his golden chariot, his purple cloak a beacon of colour on an otherwise grey day. Albinus was too far down the forum to make out what was going on, but there seemed to be some sort of commotion. A man was on his knees in front of the emperor. He wore a dark green cloak and his black hair was tied in a top knot. White-cloaked praetorians flanked the man, whilst more guardsmen moved to surround the soothsayer Alexander.

With a start, Albinus made out Calvus whispering in the Abonoteichon's ear. Alexander tore back the hood from his cloak and pointed angrily at the man on his knees. Albinus noticed both men seemed to be wearing the same cloak. He remembered seeing the soothsayer and his followers in the fortress in Carnuntum and out on campaign when they were part of the emperor's retinue. *This could get interesting.* Taurus was moving down the column towards him, Albinus saluted his centurion as he came closer, tucking his thumbs into his belt.

'What in the name of the gods is going on up there? I'm sure that's Calvus I can see,' he said as he squinted through the rain.

'It is, sir. And the man on the floor is one of Alexander's men if I'm not mistaken. They're both wearing the same cloak, See the brown patch on the back of both?' Taurus grunted as he saw.

'Well, whatever's going on I hope they just get on with it so we can get back to barracks, fucking drenched I am.' Taurus shook rain from his cloak and cursed as it splashed his bare legs. 'Ain't half cold and all!'

Albinus nodded, fighting the urge to let his teeth chatter himself. He wasn't built for winter, he mused. Not enough fat covered his thin limbs, and being taller than the average legionary didn't help, as his tunic sat midway up his thigh rather than just above the knee; he felt the bite of the wind more than anyone else.

'Think the emperor's statue will be revealed shortly. Then I'm assuming we all must hail him, then go get ourselves a warm cup of wine!' Albinus said hopefully, wanting more to get to Licina then back to barracks.

Taurus grunted. 'Well, I'd better get back in position. See you soon, lad.' With a nod he moved off.

Albinus relaxed his posture and took the chance to ease his sword belt into a more comfortable position. There were raised voices up ahead now, more white cloaks appearing and circling the emperor; Alexander was clearly angry, shouting and waving his arms furiously in the air. Well, Albinus thought, at least it looks as though we're going to get some entertainment whilst we stand here and get soaked.

'This is an outrage! I demand to know the meaning of this!' Alexander's voice was as harsh as the icy wind as he shouted in a hoarse voice. He'd whipped back the hood of his cloak to reveal a wet tangle of grey hair that did nothing to hide his growing baldness. His eyes were grey, his skin pale and his Latin hard to distinguish, though Calvus thought that was probably due to the lack of teeth rather than the fact it wasn't his first language.

The Briton moved closer to Alexander, his right hand clasping his bared dagger; he wouldn't take any chances if the old man moved on the emperor. The snake hissed in his direction, and Calvus briefly wondered if his reactions would be quick enough to save him if the snake lunged at him. *Plunge the dagger in its mouth or swipe and take off the head?* He remembered the story he had heard from a preacher at a secret christian gathering he had attended. It had been the snake that had led Eve to eat the apple from the tree – the snake that had caused her to betray her god. Unholy animals they were, full of venom and spite.

'Imperial Majesty, my friend, I implore you to tell me the meaning of this!' He pointed the snake hand at the man kneeling on the floor.

Aurelius just turned to Pompeianus and gestured for him to speak.

'Augustus,' Pompeianus dipped his head, 'I had word some time ago that there was a plot against your life. A band of men, led by a nameless traitor, were planning on overthrowing you and putting their own man on the throne. Me and my agents have been investigating across the length of the empire for the source of the rebellion for nearly a year now.' He dipped his head again, the horsehair crest of his helmet sinking with his head under the weight of the rain water caught within.

'And tell me, Tribune Pompeianus, what did your men find?' Aurelius said, his voice, as always, completely void of emotion.

'We found evidence of corruption here in Pannonia, Majesty. It seemed that the barbarian king Balomar had been enticed into his rebellion from someone within the empire. We believed that the traitor wanted to use the ongoing war as a distraction, to keep your focus on the Germani across the Danube, rather then what was going on within our borders.'

'You have proof?' Aurelius asked.

'Yes, Imperial Majesty. We have a Roman girl – an escaped slave from Balomar's capital. She fled to Vindobona, where she confessed all she knew to the legate there, who passed the girl onto me. We also leaked information regarding our legions' strengths, supply routes and their orders to certain people, to see if the information ended up in the hands of the barbarians.'

'Which people?' Aurelius already knew the answers, of course, this was now just a charade to emphasis his knowledge to Alexander.

'Tribune Scaevola, Imperial Majesty. I had him arrested a few days ago, and he has confessed everything under torture, and given up the names of the men that joined him in his treason.'

'So, Tribune Scaevola was leaking information to Balomar and his armies. And who, dear tribune, was Scaevola taking his orders from?'

Calvus felt Alexander shudder, saw his head roll right to left as he sought an escape.

'Senator Crassus, current Governor of Asia, seems to be one of the main conspirators, Majesty. But it seemed the senator was taking orders from one Alexander of Abonoteichos.'

'Lies!' The soothsayer rasped in his weak voice. 'You have no proof! I have been nothing but a loyal servant to the empire my whole life! By the gods, my daughter is even married to a senator!'

'Ahh yes.' Pompeianus failed to hide a satisfied smirk. 'Senator Rutilianus also appears on the intelligence reports I have received quite frequently. He's even been pouring gold into the legions based in his province, despite it being one of the most peaceful places in the empire. Almost as if he thought a war was coming?'

'Now let us be fair, tribune, how do we know the money was coming from my dear friend Alexander?' Calvus noticed even the emperor had a triumphant gleam in his eye; he appeared to be enjoying the charade.

'The gold, Imperial Majesty, did not carry your likeness, nor that of any of your predecessors.'

'No? Well, that is odd. Tell me, tribune, what did it depict?'

Pompeianus reached within his cloak and produced a small round gold coin. The aureus looked like any other gold coin, Calvus thought, not that he'd ever owned one. The legions were always paid in silver, and he'd need one hundred sestertii to have the same value of one golden aureus. The tribune gave the coin to Aurelius, who flipped it in his hands to see both sides.

'Well, Alexander. This coin is unlike any other I have seen before.' He held it up in his hand, and Calvus could just make out the likeness of a snake stamped onto the side. When the emperor flipped the coin, it revealed the unmistakeable portrait of Alexander. 'Imperator Alexander Augustus Germanicus. How very interesting.' Aurelius flicked the coin toward Alexander.

It hit the cobbles and rolled to a stop at the soothsayer's feet. He disdained to look down upon it. 'What do you have to say for yourself?' the emperor said as he moved towards the man he'd thought a friend. 'Do you deny it?'

Calvus looked into the dark eyes of his emperor, and for the first time thought he saw the hurt the man was going through. Once again he had to remind himself that under the gold and purple there was just flesh and blood, a man like himself with feelings and doubts.

'I deny nothing!' Alexander spat. 'I would have revived the empire to the glory days, elevated Rome to a new golden age. What have you brought, you who shuts yourself away with your philosophy and your stoic way of living. You are no emperor, I see no man fit to lead the greatest empire the world has ever seen. I curse you – you and your line! May history remember you and your dynasty as the plague of Rome! Just as the plague has ravaged your rule! May you never see Rome again. You will spend the rest of your life putting out the fire I have lit across the river. The tribes are awoken, their blood lust rekindled and they will stop at nothing now to bring you down. Your armies will die, your coffers will run dry as you fight to keep hold of the land better men fought to conquer.'

A swarm of enraged praetorians rasped swords from their scabbards as they rounded on Alexander; one spat on his face, another held the point of his weapon to the soothsayer's throat. Aurelius raised a hand, and Pompeianus immediately ordered the guards to lower their weapons.

'Tribune Pompeianus, please place Alexander under arrest, and have him taken to the same place you have Scaevola. I would like to hear what information your men can extract from him. Oh, and him as well.' The emperor gestured to Cocconas, still on his knees with his hands tied behind his back.

Alexander stood still, mouth framed in a snarl. The snake writhed on his arm, baring its fangs and hissing at the guardsmen who surrounded its master. Aurelius stepped off his chariot and walked slowly towards Alexander. Calvus tensed, fingertips brushing the hilt of his knife; his eyes never left the snake. 'You have betrayed my trust,' Aurelius said as he drew near, apparently oblivious to the threat of the snake. 'You will pay for your crimes against your emperors.' Calvus frowned at the term 'emperors'. *Surely there is only one?* 'My dear colleague Verus passed on from this world, shortly after drinking the wine you gifted to me. You remember, in Aquileia? Of course you do. He was a fool, I'll grant you, but an honest one. He didn't deserve the end you gave him.' Aurelius turned and walked away without another word.

Calvus watched as the men were led off. He was suddenly unsure of where he should be, and tried to catch Pompeianus' eye for direction. 'Stay with me, Calvus,' the tribune said when he met the Briton's questioning stare. Calvus moved in alongside his superior and together they followed the emperor as he climbed back upon the chariot and waved to the crowds, who had become muted whilst witnessing the arrest of Alexander.

'Citizens of Rome,' the emperor bellowed in a surprisingly strong voice. 'What you have jut witnessed is the arrest of two traitors – usurpers who would have seen me dead and claimed the purple for themselves.' An angry roar went up for the mob. The relief was palpable for Calvus as he saw the emperor still held the support of the people. 'And I offer you proof of their treachery. Guards, reveal the statue.'

A file of praetorians moved to cut the rope that held the giant sheets of tarpaulin up over the scaffolding that surrounded the statue. Calvus sucked air through his teeth in shock and was joined by the mob and the soldiers and guardsmen as slowly an enormous stone likeness of Alexander was revealed, a coiled snake in his right hand.

The only sound was the wind as it tore through the freed sheets of tarpaulin. 'Tribune,' Aurelius said after a time.

'Majesty?'

'Have it torn down, as soon as you can.' For the first time the emperor's voice quivered.

'Yes, Majesty. I have one commissioned in your likeness, to replace it.'

'No!' Aurelius snapped. 'Build something useful, something the people can use. The gods know they have had a hard time of it in recent years. Let's reward them for their continued loyalty.' Without another word he summoned the chariot's driver, and the man flicked the reins and the horses started off with a snort.

Calvus watched with the others as the emperor disappeared down the cobbled road and turned off at a junction, the praetorians trotting along in his wake. 'Christ on the cross,' he muttered as he rubbed his eyes. After all, wasn't everyday a retired legionary was witness to such events. A tap on the shoulder from Pompeianus woke him from his daze. 'You okay, brother?' He laughed. 'Quite a day, eh?' The two moved off slowly down the cobbles, their route taking them towards the stunned men of the Fourteenth Legion.

'Yes, sir. Unbelievable. I'd never seen an emperor before, feel like we're best mates now!'

The tribune laughed as he strolled. 'Come back to the basilica with me, will you? Once we've seen that our new guests are given suitably comfortable billets, we need to talk about that man I found you fighting with earlier.'

'Sir?' Calvus paused in his stride.

'The man you were fighting with, who is he? And how does he fit in to all of this?'

Calvus explained that he was the man he had seen speaking with Scaevola in the tavern. 'And when I saw him grabbing Licina ...' He tailed off, knowing immediately he had said too much.

'Licina?'

'Err ...' Calvus tried stalling for time, but the tribune gave him none.

'Yes, the basilica, you and I. Then you can tell me everything you've so far not told me.'

They were marching past the first ranks of the Fourteenth now. Calvus nodded sheepishly to his old centurion and his tent-mates in the front rank. They arched their eyebrows at him, clearly confounded as to why Calvus was arresting traitors and in the company of a tribune.

'Calvus!' It was a voice from the rear of the First Century the Briton recognised. Calvus tried not to make eye contact with Albinus; he wasn't ready to see his friend, knowing what he had to do.

'Calvus!' Again the call, and Calvus raised his hand in acknowledgement but didn't turn his head or break stride. *Jesu help me, what am I to do?*

XXVI

November – AD 171, Carnuntum

'Let me go to her first,' he had said. 'There must be an explanation for this. She must have been threatened, manipulated into doing what she did!'

His pleas had gone unanswered, and Calvus had been forced to watch as Tribune Pompeianus ordered a file of auxiliaries to go and arrest Licina. But Calvus was never one to take things lying down. He had been in more tight spots than a slave condemned to the gold mines of Dacia, and he wasn't going to give up now.

He had made his excuses and left the basilica as fast as his ageing legs could carry him. He would not beat the soldiers in a straight race through the streets of Carnuntum, he knew, but if he went off the beaten track he thought he stood a chance.

So now he was rampaging through a small walled courtyard, waving apologetically to a startled woman with wild hair who had been lazing on a bench whilst two ragged children played at her feet. He hurdled the small stone wall on the far side and landed with a splash in a shallow pool. Cursing, he leapt onto dry ground and barraged his way into a small butcher's. The butcher's girl screamed and the man Calvus assumed to be her father raised a wide chopping knife and leapt across a blood-stained counter. Calvus watched the gleaming iron until the edge was a few inches above his head. Years of training and muscle memory kicked in as he thrust up his mutilated left hand, and punched the bottom of the butcher's wrist just as he was about to strike. With a roar of pain and anger the butcher let the blade clatter to the worktop; Calvus didn't break stride and with his right hand sent a crashing blow to the side of the butcher's head. The man slumped to the ground without a sound.

'Sorry, love!' he called to the butcher's girl, 'needs must and all that!' He grinned and pushed his way through rows of hanging carcasses. The stink of rotting flesh and long dead intestines filled his nostrils, and he scrunched his face up in a ball and tried to hold his breath, all the while making a mental note to go elsewhere for his fresh meat.

Through the backdoor and into an empty alleyway, his wet boots slid in something slimy and judging from the smell it wasn't rose water. *Shit! Literally.* He smiled at his own joke and ran through the alley. Darkness crept up on him like a light-footed street urchin and he had to pause to get his bearings. White-clad walls loomed to left and right, an abandoned cart by a rotten old door ahead of him. A rustle came from the cart, then stopped and the silence was absolute. Calvus drew his dagger from his belt, weary of being attacked. It would not be uncommon for gangs of kids to roam the alleys, and even plant obstacles such as old carts in the way to block the path. It was, if he remembered correctly, how Silus had first met Taurus.

Creeping up on the cart, lowering his hood so his hearing was unimpaired, he cast cautious glances to the left and right to check he wasn't followed. His foot made a soft splash in a puddle and he muffled a curse, not wanting to let his would be attacker know how close he was to the cart. With a sudden rush he sprinted round the side and shouted his war cry, knife held point first to his front. A small brown cat hissed in anger, four frightened kittens huddled behind in an old blanket.

Calvus didn't know whether to laugh or apologise, so he did both, gave the cat a quick stroke and carried on his way. Out of the alley and a left at the junction brought him to the cobbled road of Licina's apartment. To his horror he saw the troop of auxiliaries ahead of him. Licina's home couldn't be more than a hundred paces up the street, and he realised he would never get past the soldiers unnoticed. There was only one thing for it now.

Sucking air through his teeth he pushed himself over the flagstones. Giant strides with burning legs propelled him through the throng of slaves

273

and citizens as they went about their business, chatting in surprise and awe about the events earlier that day in the forum. His breath came in rasps and sweat stung his eyes as he caught up with the rear of the small column of auxiliaries. He sped past them on the left, hurdling a stall of fruit and veg and catching his foot on a wooden crate of apples. He stumbled to the ground and hit his knee hard. Ignoring the angered cries of the merchant he picked himself up and carried on, level now with the officer leading the soldiers.

'Calvus, hey Calvus, what the fuck are you doing?' cried the optio leading the arrest party. Calvus ignored the shouts and kept going, the door to Licina's apartment building in sight.

'Column, at the double!'

Calvus cursed at the realisation that the optio was going to try and cut him off hit home. The loud thud of the iron nails on the cobbles grew closer, and Calvus could feel his strength fading with every stride.

But then he was at the door. It opened with a squeak of rusty hinges and he wrenched it back as soon as he was through, slamming it with a crash loud enough to wake Hades in his underworld lair. He searched frantically in the dark corridor for something to bar the door with. With just the light from a small lamp that hung on the wall, he found a thick beam propped against the wall, next to a door for one of the ground floor apartments. He hefted the beam and was just turning to prop it against the door when it thrust open with a burst of light.

Calvus recoiled from the sudden whiteness and used his mutilated hand to shield his eyes. The beam went slack and soldiers charged through the gap. Recovering his senses, he raised the length of timber, gripping the base in his right hand and resting the tip on the stump of his left. The auxiliaries were two abreast in the narrow corridor, thin oval shields with just the shining tops of their helmets showing above. The helmet on the left had a small tuft of dyed horsehair, marking the man out to be the optio. 'C'mon, Calvus,' he said, 'put that down and step aside. We're just following the tribune's orders, you know that.'

'Fuck you!' he bellowed in defiance. Not waiting for the soldiers to take the initiative he surged forwards, the wooden beam licking out and striking the optio on top of his helmet. The man staggered back into his comrades behind him, and Calvus used the space the man had left to swing the timber and send a crunching blow to the shoulder of another soldier. Space to his front now, the two stricken soldiers blocked the pathway of the eager men behind.

Calvus thought about fighting on before quickly retreating up the rickety wooden staircase. He bounced off the walls as he reached the second floor, heart pounding in his chest, blood pumping in his ears. The door to Licina's apartment was in front of him. He could hear the soldiers clambering up the stairs, encouraged by a roar from their optio.

He thudded on the door, waited three frantic heartbeats and thudded again. His hand hit air as the door was thrust open to reveal a terrified Meredith, bearing a dagger in shaking hands. He was too surprised to talk. A hundred questions exploded to the fore of his mind, but he knew they would have to wait. *What in the name of Jesu is she doing here?* His daughter's presence would complicate things, as he would be unwilling to fight and risk endangering her and the baby.

'Licina?' He panted as he stumbled into the room, slamming shut the door and sliding the locking bar in place, not that it would stop the soldiers for long. Scanning the room, his eyes fell on the small straw pallet in the corner. He slumped to his knees and felt the tears well in his eyes, a torrent of guilt and grief engulfed him.

'Where has she gone, Calvus?' Albinus stuttered through chattering teeth; his -immed eyes and cheeks stained with streaks of tears. 'What has she done? What is it she wanted you to tell me?' Calvus saw he held Faustus close to his chest; the babe was fast asleep, sucking furiously on Albinus's finger.

Neither man paid any heed as the door was opened with a bang, and the auxiliaries burst through, swords out and shields held high.

Epilogue

December AD 171 – Carnuntum

It was the Ides of December, and all around the city were people in high spirits as they made preparations for the festival of Saturnalia. The small group made their way through the crowded streets. They all had hoods up against the cold; none spoke. They filed silently through the southern gate and onto a small cobbled road. Following the road to the first junction, they turned left until they were directly to the south of the fortress.

Pulling back his hood, Albinus looked back at the fortress and the giant amphitheatre that stood it its west. Smoke rose from the small cluster of buildings that made up the vici in between the two giant structures. All was quiet, peaceful, but Albinus felt no peace in his heart.

His wife was a traitor, wanted for treason and on the run. Only the gods knew where she had gone after she had abandoned their baby with Meredith. He looked down within the folds of his cloak at the wrapped-up bundle of Faustus and felt such a strong surge of love he wondered how Licina could have borne to leave him.

Meredith herself had given birth to a boy two weeks before, and named the child Marcus Calvus, after the emperor and her father. Calvus himself had been distant with Albinus since the day he had been forced to tell his friend all he knew of Licina and her treasonous behaviour. He had claimed he hadn't known at first it was her he had been following. He had been tracking his daughter and the tribune Scaevola, and somehow along the way had stumbled across Licina in a brothel, whispering in a private room with a man that turned out to be named Cocconas, who was a staunch follower of the traitor Alexander.

Albinus had since discovered through Calvus that this Cocconas was the man who had taken Licina during the raid on their home and delivered her to King Balomar as a gift. He had been the man to first take his wife from him, and it seemed he had done so again.

He had no idea if Licina was still alive, or where she could even be. He longed to see her, to run his hands through her hair and hold her close, tell her everything was going to be okay. He would have run with her, he knew, if she had bothered to ask. He would have done anything for her, even if it meant turning his back on the empire and his brothers in the army.

He scanned the small group now, feeling a wave of guilt at the prospect of ever leaving the men who had come to mean so much to him. Fullo stood at his shoulder, his livid white scars showing beneath that wild crop of blond hair. He gave Albinus a tight smile as their eyes met. Fullo would never abandon him, he knew; even if he said he was marching on Hades himself, he knew his friend would heft his shield and follow.

Habitus looked a little lost, as he had since the day Longus had been cut down in battle. They had made an odd couple, the old Syrian and the young Italian. Always bickering and the first to aim a jibe in the other's direction, Albinus hadn't realised the older man had been so fond of Longus. His hair was now greyer than the dull waters of the Danube, his face haggard and hollow. Taurus had told him he was to finally be awarded his discharge in the new year, but even the long overdue reward had not been enough to cheer him. Albinus wondered if he would sign back up, as Bucco had done. Secretly he hoped he would, but he knew he was being selfish; Habitus had given the best part of thirty years' service to the empire, and if anyone was due to see out their final years in peace, it was him.

Bucco himself was approaching the final of the three years he had signed back up for. Albinus couldn't bear to think of life in the army without him at his side. The man had been one of his father's closest friends and most reliable of men throughout his tenure in the legions, and Bucco had done so much to help Albinus adjust to the rigours of

277

life under the eagle. He knew he would be dead by now if it wasn't for Bucco's advice and friendship.

They approached their destination, a small graveyard just off the road. Mist clung to the stone tombs and Albinus felt a shudder go through his spine. The place seemed to be deserted, which suited him just fine. It was long overdue that they found some time to visit Libo's empty tomb. They had paid a mason good silver to have Longus' name added, and were pleased to have their two friends together.

It felt a lifetime ago that they had lost Libo – a desperate fight in the dark hall of some Germanic chief, all to win back the daughter of another. They had been promised aid from the rival chief on their journey to the north, but his men had lost their courage in the desperate days that followed, as they were hunted through the forests and marshes of Germania. Libo, had died for nothing in the end. *He died because of me. Because of her.* And now she had left him again. He sent a silent prayer to Libo's shade, promised him no one else would die for his selfishness.

'They've done a good job to be fair,' Rullus said as he approached the tombstone. It was as tall as Libo had been, and as thick too – a giant slab of stone protruding from the frost covered grass with a fitting endorsement of the two soldiers and their achievements and valour in battle engraved on the front. 'Just a shame we couldn't bring their bodies back to lie here.' Rullus spoke pragmatically and without emotion, but Albinus could see the hurt in his eyes.

'Aye. But we had no chance of getting Libo's body from that hall, and Longus was burned with his comrades. I'd wager the gods saw that great pyre.' Bucco said, his voice thick.

'I just can't help thinking I could have saved them if I'd been there,' said Calvus, rubbing the stump of his fingerless hand on his tunic.

'Well, you did chop your own fucking fingers off! It's a marvel your name ain't on here with 'em!' They all laughed at Bucco's joke, but it was half-hearted and died off quickly.

'Let's get this over with, shall we?' Habitus said, sitting down on the wet grass and opening a folded cloak and laying it on the ground. The possessions of Libo and Longus were revealed, and the others sat to form a circle around them. It was tradition in the army that when a soldier died in battle, his belongings would be shared out amongst his tent-mates, unless otherwise stated in his will. Neither man had left one, therefore any coin they hadn't squandered on women or wine went into the cohort's funeral fund, which was managed by the standard bearer, Rullus.

'Who gets first pick?' asked Fullo, eyeing up Longus' sword. His had been badly damaged in the final battle they had fought in, and he didn't want to spend all his savings buying a new one. He and Bucco had both spent the previous morning arguing with the legion's quartermaster. Bucco's armour had snapped at the shoulder, the metal plates and straps of the old segmented cuirass damaged beyond repair. The quartermaster had refused to issue them with a replacement sword and armour respectively, saying they would need signed authorisation from their centurion. Taurus was nowhere to be found, so they had left the armoury spitting curses at the balding officer, which probably wouldn't help their cause when they were forced to go back for the kit they would need before spring.

'Albinus does,' said Rullus. 'He holds the highest rank here.'

'No!' Albinus said quickly. 'I will take nothing. Besides, I'm part of a different cohort now, it wouldn't be right.'

'Ha! How could we forget, *centurion.*' Habitus smirked.

Albinus had been officially promoted to lead the Sixth Century of the Tenth Cohort. It was the most junior rank of centurion, and he would still have to refer to every other centurion in the legion as 'sir', but he was immensely proud all the same. More importantly, he knew his father would have been.

'All right, boys,' Fullo said leaning forwards, 'dig in!' With a rush of air the remaining men thrust their hands in to grab the objects they had been eyeing up. Fullo whooped in delight as he snatched up the sword, Calvus doing the same as his good hand grasped the hilt of a knife.

Albinus smiled and rose to his feet; Faustus was stirring and he withdrew the baby from the folds of his cloak. The babe stopped whining as his eyes locked on his father's, and Albinus felt an ache in his chest at the thought of leaving the boy in Carnuntum come spring.

'Meredith will look after the lad,' Calvus said, slapping Albinus on the shoulder. 'You've got no worries there.'

'And you? You'll be here too, right?'

Calvus shook his head. 'I'm going to go east with Habitus, see he gets home and settled all right. Always wanted to see Syria. Might even venture into Asia, check out the taverns.' He smiled sadly at the joke; it had always been Longus' dream to retire to the east and open a tavern, was all the man had talked about some days.

'And that's your only reason for going east? No work for that tribune?'

Calvus shifted uncomfortably. 'Some things I can't really talk about, lad, sorry. But, if I find her, you know—'

'I know,' Albinus said. 'Best I don't know.'

There was a commotion behind them, and two cloaked figures emerged from the mist. 'Well, who've we got here then?'

Taurus smiled to see them, Abas at his shoulder, his skin still golden despite the sun being masked in cloud for weeks.

'Good to see you, brothers,' Abas nodded to them all. 'And how sad to find you here.' The Greek rubbed a hand against the names of Libo and Longus on the tombstone, muttering a quiet prayer. 'They were fine men,' he said, before revealing two skins of wine he had tucked in the folds of his cloak. 'Let's drink to them, shall we?'

The wine was met with a roar of approval. Cups were produced and soon good-natured jokes and laughter lifted the gloom from the day. Albinus stood apart from the rest, rocking Faustus in the crook of his arm. He had lost the love of his life, and it was a wound that would never heal. But he had gained a son, and was now a centurion of the Roman army.

He sent a prayer to Mars, for his son and for the men of his new century. *Keep them safe. Help me to lead them well, to be the man my father was.*

King Balomar had surrendered, the tribes in southern Germania were leaderless and once again split. But the Iazyges to the east were getting stronger by the month, as more men answered the call of their leader, Bandanasp. It seemed to Albinus that as soon as one fight finished another begun.

But he would fight, for his eagle, for Rome. For his son.

HISTORICAL NOTE

The Roman Empire, for all her power and might, never did manage to conquer the tribes that lived in the vast grasslands east of the Rhine and north of the Danube. The Germani people were very different to those who lived in the provinces around the Mediterranean Sea, which Rome had swiftly made her own. They lived by a very different set of rules, had different ideals and spent more time fighting amongst themselves than against Rome. The lands and peoples that surrounded the Mediterranean Sea were more cultured, colonised, and therefore Rome found it much easier to subject them to her laws.

Another point worth noting is the influence the Greeks and the Macedonians would have had over much of the east, long before Rome came to power. Alexander the Great brought half the world to its knees, integrating a Greek way of living on every town his mighty phalanx trudged through. When you take a step back and look at the bigger picture – the world before the Roman Empire – you can see some of the foundations being laid for Rome's conquests long before the legions left Italy.

The Germani people, however, refused to be beaten. They had no literature, no great need for coin or stone buildings; they were nomadic for a long period, moving ever west, out of the great eastern steppe now known as Russia. It was survival of the fittest as far as they were concerned, whether they were fighting Rome or fighting their neighbours, it doesn't appear they were much bothered, as long as they could kill and pillage. These are the people, of course, that would one day go on to become the Saxons and the Vikings, bringing their Norse gods and magic to the shores of post-Roman Britain.

During the early stages of the second century AD, it appears there was a change to the Germanic tribes and their way of life. Rome had ceased to bother to cross the Rhine. The empire had once held some sort of sway as far east as the great river Elbe, though by the time of this novel, those days were long gone. Without the imminent threat of invasion, internal wars within the tribes escalated to a point that some tribes ceased to exist. As described in the story, the Marcomanni, Quadi and the Naristae were the three biggest tribes that bordered the Danube; the Suebi appeared to be the dominant tribe in the north. What had once been villages built of nothing but huts began to form as towns and then fortresses. Chiefs became kings, and these kings became ever powerful. Rome had a problem.

Divide and conquer had always been the rule of empire: keep the tribes fighting amongst themselves, keep their spears facing each other, and not south or west towards the empire. Rome never did manage the 'conquer' part, but they did work hard at keeping them divided. Frumentarii agents would ensure the right bribes fell into the right hands; hundreds of thousands of legionaries and auxiliaries stood guard on the *limes,* ready to repel any attack should that tactic fail. Rebel leaders were replaced with client kings that had been raised in Rome – 'Romanised', as they would have called it – and sent back to their people when the time was right to rule as Rome's puppet.

The Germani though, did break through, around the winter of 167–68 AD. A raid on Pannonia believed to consist of up to six thousand warriors were defeated by local forces. This was just to be the beginning. In the east Germani hordes ripped through Dacia, pillaging their gold mines and nearly making it as far south as Athens. In the west another war band made it to Italian soil, the first time that had happened during the Principate. To say Rome was shocked is an understatement. I have of course, already embroiled these events with my own fiction in the first book of this series, *The Centurion's Son.* It was to be the start of a conflict now known as the Marcomannic War, and would run on for over ten years, till the death of Marcus Aurelius in 180 AD.

Albinus, Licina and co are obviously completely fictitious, as are their stories, but many of the characters in this novel are based on real people. Marcus Valerius Maximianus was very much a real person as is noted as having been in favour of Marcus Aurelius, thanks to his exploits in the wars against the tribes. It is also said that he really did take the head clean off the shoulders of the chief of the Naristae in battle. He did not, however, command the Fourteenth Legion at any point (to my knowledge).

Publius Helvius Pertinax was a senator of Rome who distinguished himself in the Parthian Wars under Verus and once again on the northern frontier. He would one day even rise to become emperor for a very brief time, before he was murdered by his own Praetorian Guard, who then auctioned off the throne to the highest bidder! Sometimes there really is no need for fiction … I will tell this story one day, the story of the war of the five emperors after the murder of Commodus. Watch this space!

The Roman army did begin its transition from the rectangular scutum shield and gladius (short sword) at some point in the latter half of the second century AD, though as to exactly when remains uncertain. I have decided to equip the newly formed First and Second Italica legions with the longer sword (spatha) and oval shield that one day the whole Roman army would use.

There are many fantastic books I could recommend for further reading on Rome and her empire, but to name them all would add ten pages to the book. I shall restrain myself to sharing the few I have found most helpful whilst writing this book: *Marcus Aurelius,* by Frank Mclynn; *The Complete Roman Army, Pax Romana,* both by Adrian Goldsworthy; *Roman Military Equipment,* by M.C. Bishop and J.C.N Coulston; *Handbook to Roman Legionary Fortresses,* by M.C. Bishop. And of course, any primary sources you can get your hands on. Tacitus and Cassius Dio I find to be the most relevant for this time period, but we are so lucky to have plenty of surviving literature from the ancient world.

I have come to love Albinus over the course of the two books I have written, and I hope you have too. There will be one more book in this series: *Shield Of The Rising Sun,* which will be out as soon as I can get it written. Until then, look out for *Oathbreaker*, a stand-alone novel coming in summer 2019.

I would like to end by thanking the fantastic team at Endeavour Media. For as long as I can remember I have immersed myself in stories from the ancient world, and it really is a dream come true to see my own let loose into the public domain. Thank you to my ever-patient and forgiving wife Sarah, who often spends her evenings alone as I try (and often fail) to hit my weekly word target. If it wasn't for Sarah, I never would have had the confidence to write *The Centurion's Son,* and I would certainly not be writing this now.

Lastly, I would like to thank you, the reader. The support I have received in the last year or so has been overwhelming. Writing is often a lonely business, just me sitting in silence, nothing but the tap of my fingers on the keyboard. The odd message I receive, the reviews I read, really helps to push me on.

Until the next time.

Adam Lofthouse, February 2018